The Lollard Oak

'The Lollard Oak is a beautifully crafted, wonderfully insightful elegy to Englishness. Each story is a perfect time capsule, charming, funny, wise and often deeply moving. A must-read for anyone interested in the bones and sinews of our shared history.'

Angus Donald
Author of the bestselling Outlaw Chronicles

'This is an excellent book, beautifully written and profound.'

Jerry Hayes
Barrister, Broadcaster, former MP for Harlow

'When I finished The Lollard Oak, I felt that pang which comes when an enjoyable read ends. It has satisfying villains and plots, and so much historical detail - I didn't know that the Conqueror's body burst when he was buried. How horrible. An enormous achievement.'

Quentin Letts
Journalist, Broadcaster, Novelist, Theatre Critic

The Lollard Oak

The Lollard Oak

by Anthony Thompson

The Lollard Oak

The Lollard Oak

Copyright © 2023 Anthony Thompson. All Rights Reserved.

ISBN 979 8 3290 6498 8

Except for brief quotations in critical publications or reviews, no part of this book may be reproduced in any manner without prior written permission from the author.

This book, including all the passages concerned with current events, is a work of fiction.

Contact: thelollardoak@gmail.com

The cover is a scene from the 11th century Bayeux Tapestry showing the death of King Harold of England at the Battle of Hastings in 1066. (Centre Guillaume le Conquérant, Bayeux, France). The original image is by Myrabella.

'HAROLD REX INTERFECTUS EST' means 'King Harold is killed'.

The Lollard Oak

To David Birt

The Lollard Oak

The Lollard Oak

'It is impossible for an Englishman to open his mouth without making some other Englishman hate or despise him.'

George Bernard Shaw
Irishman

The Lollard Oak

Contents

Chapter One: 2009 1
Chapter Two: 1085 37
Chapter Three: 1381 79
Chapter Four: 1549 113
Chapter Five: 1667 129
Chapter Six: 1839 169
Chapter Seven: 2016 211

About this book 248
Notes 251
Bibliography 270

Appendices:
William the Conqueror and the 'Domesday' survey 272
The Peasants' Revolt of 1381 277
The Lollards 280
The Book of Common Prayer 282
Robert Hooke 284

Acknowledgements 288

Chapter One: 2009

2009 – Dramatis Personae

Freddy Edmundson, Staffordshire farmer
Sally, his wife
Isabella, their daughter

Bill Edmundson, Senior Civil Servant, Dept. of Transport
Caro, his wife

Cuthbert Edmundson, father of Bill and Freddy

Philip, Lord Manolis, Junior Minister, Dept. of Transport

2009

Late April – Kingsgate, near Tamworth

Freddy could not understand why his hands were shaking. It was early in the morning, he was milking his Friesian cows, and he was surrounded by all the familiar noises and smells of his Staffordshire farm. It was, usually, such a calm time of day. So why should his hands be trembling like this? His stomach was tight too. He knew it must be something to do with going to London for lunch with his brother. It had to be. But what? Bill had been charming on the phone – not at all full of himself – and, anyway, it wasn't as if this was the first time Freddy had been to his brother's club for lunch. Freddy was disturbed and puzzled. What was his body trying to tell him? Was it some kind of premonition?

Back in the farm house, Sally was cooking breakfast, and Isabella was getting ready for school. Freddy kissed them both 'good morning' and went upstairs to change. On taking his only suit out of the wardrobe, his heart dropped. He now remembered that the last time he had worn it was at his father's funeral in January, when, as they stood around the grave under flapping umbrellas, the driving rain had soaked his trousers. Bill would notice the absence of a crease immediately; he would have to go down to the utility room and iron them.

Sally had gone to the back door, and was saying 'Good luck' to Isabella. It was a minute or two later that she heard Freddy's despairing cry.

"Oh God, I don't believe it!"

"Freddy, for goodness sake, what's going on?"

She quickly took the bacon and eggs off the stove, and rushed into the utility room, where she found her husband disconsolate at the ironing board.

She held up the suit trousers to inspect the damage. There was a hole where the iron had burnt right through. She gazed up at him, slowly shaking her head. "Alfred Edmundson, can I just say? You are a total idiot. It's a steam iron. And you haven't even used a tea towel. Why on earth didn't you ask me to do it?"

Back in the kitchen, Sally threw the unfortunate trousers into the bin and returned to the stove. Freddy followed her sheepishly, rubbing away at his forehead with his large, rough, farming hands.

"You do realise that now you'll have to wear your corduroys." She turned to look at him. As she did so, her eyes brightened.

Freddy was not amused. "For God's sake, Sal, it's not funny. Bill will think I'm a complete prat turning up at his club in corduroys. What's more my brogues need re-heeling." He sighed. "Oh, bloody hell."

"He'll be sure to keep you away from his smart friends in the bar. Do you know what he'll say?" Sally enjoyed imitating her brother-in-law's haughty, upper-class accent. "He'll say: 'Shall we go straight in?'."

She brought the plates to the kitchen table. "Of course, if he was really posh, he'd pass you off as a marquess or something." But then, becoming suddenly serious, she went on, "Freddy, honestly, I'm very fond of Bill, even if he is a bit pompous, and I know he sounded all charming on the phone, but I have a funny feeling about this lunch. There's something not quite right."

Freddy looked at her steadily. Sal was about to start eating, but she continued talking in a quick, matter of fact manner:

"The thing is it's not like him to invite you to his club unless he was up to something."

Freddy nodded his head, and continued to look at her. She had lovely dimples in her cheeks.

"By the way, when's your train?" she asked.

"9.35."

"Isn't that a bit early?"

"It is, but the next one's not till 11.35, and that would be too late. I'll get a cup of tea at Euston. But, Sal, why did you say 'Good luck' to Isabella? She hasn't got an exam, has she?"

"Heavens above, Freddy! I told you last night she's got an orientation day at the Robert Peel. That's why the Edwinsons picked her up early."

"So, no exam then?"

"Freddy, you must know there aren't exams for a bloody comprehensive."

It was nine o'clock when Freddy, now changed into his corduroys and brown brogues, was climbing into the Land Rover for the fifteen minute drive to Tamworth station. As he did so, Sal threw open an upstairs window, and shouted out that there was a 'cast' sheep in Falcon.

It had been a wet night; the sheep would be heavy. He couldn't ask Sal to deal with it. He would just have to text Bill.

The same time – Notting Hill Gate, London

"Bill, darling, I've been thinking."

Bill sighed. "Yes."

"Oh Bill, stop it. Anyway, I was thinking … when you take the folder out of your briefcase … you must make sure the red 'Secret' stamp is facing towards him."

Bill Edmundson put his coffee down, and pulled the palms of his hands down his face.

"Look, I know you don't like it, sweetheart," Caro continued, "but you have to remember that Toby's your first responsibility, especially when he's away at school and not able to speak up for himself. You must think about Toby, not your brother. Here, have some raspberries with the muesli."

Bill and Caro ate their breakfasts in silence. When he left to go to work, she went to the front door with him.

"For God's sake, Bill, it's not as if Freddy's going to lose out. If he's any sense, he'll bite your hand off. But, whatever you do, don't mention the northern route."

Later that day – The Club

"I'm so sorry, Bill."

William Edmundson was waiting at the top of the steps, smiling dutifully like a vicar, as his younger brother, out of breath, came through the entrance of his club. "That's alright, Freddy. I got your text. Absolutely no problem at all. None at all."

The two brothers could not have been less alike. The older one, a senior civil servant and ex-Goldman Sachs banker, was tall, slim, and perfectly groomed in a bespoke, dark, Savile Row suit and highly polished Lobb shoes. His greying hair was smoothed down, and had a sharp parting. The St James's club was his natural habitat.

The farmer was big and stocky, with a round, friendly, weather-beaten face, and untidy fair hair; in addition to his corduroys and the now muddy brown brogues that needed re-heeling, he was wearing a check viyella shirt and a well-worn tweed jacket.

Bill, who was carrying a slim briefcase, with a metal retaining rod, in one hand, guided his younger brother with the other hand towards the generous staircase that led to the first-floor dining room. "Shall we go straight in? I suppose, what with your sheep problem, you didn't have time to change into a suit."

Freddy knew his brother too well to miss the barb. "Or 'why the hell can't you wear some half-decent clothes to my club?'. But you're quite right. I'll explain in a moment. It's a bit of a story."

The Head Waiter, Jurek, greeted them in turn with a small, dignified bow. "Mr Edmundson, Mr Edmundson, very good to see you. Please, come, I have a table in the corner."

As they took their seats, Bill leaned the briefcase against the leg of his chair.

Freddy recognised it from many years ago. "Isn't that your old music case? Blimey, that brings back memories."

"It is, yes. I found it still in the piano stool after Father died. Very useful."

"You were extraordinary; you played that Beethoven concerto at the end of your last term; I remember you practising in the Morning Room all through the Easter holidays. Why in God's name did you give it up? I never understood that."

"Oh, it's a long story, Freddy. Are you OK with red?" Jurek, anticipating that Bill would have the Montrachet as usual, was hovering with a bottle.

"Yes, of course. I'll drink anything. Anyway, the reason I'm causing you embarrassment is not because I'm being bolshy or whatever; it's just that I tried to press my suit trousers first thing this morning, and made a fearful hash of it."

"You idiot. Why didn't you get Sal to do it?" Bill tasted the Montrachet, and nodded to Jurek.

"That's what she said. And then, just as I was leaving for the station, she called me from the bedroom window to say she'd seen a cast sheep in Falcon?"

"What the dickens is a 'cast' sheep?"

"It's when they roll over onto their back, and can't right themselves. Not that uncommon this time of year. They get very heavy before shearing, especially when there's been rain like last night."

Freddy tried the wine; he knew it was expensive, but couldn't understand why.

He went on, "It's actually quite serious. If they're upside down, the grass ferments in their stomach, the gas can't escape, presses on the lungs, blocks the oesophagus, and they suffocate. I had two die last year. The year before, one of them had her eyes pecked out by the crows while she was still alive."

"Good God. Well, fair enough: you missed your train."

"And got my shoes muddy and trousers wet."

"I hardly noticed."

"Very funny. So, how's life at the Ministry?"

"Actually, we call it the Department of Transport these days. And, since you ask, we do, in fact, have a little excitement. Sir Charles's wife has gone off with her personal trainer. Poor old Charles is a bit dazed; bit like one of your sheep, I suppose."

Freddy narrowed his eyes. "So, does that mean they're going to make you Permanent Secretary? It comes with a knighthood, doesn't it? Not that that will be of any interest to Caro."

"Oh, Freddy, please. Don't start."

"But, Bill, it was you who told me that when you got the letter from the Palace about a CBE, all she said was 'I hope that's not *it*.'"

"Yes, well, we all have our frailties. But going back to the Department, it turns out that Philip and I have pretty much a free hand now."

"Who's Philip?"

"Sorry, Philip Manolis – or 'Lord' Manolis as he prefers. He's Minister of State – the political number two. His boss, the Secretary of State, believes that Gordon Brown has decided to ditch her, so she's lost interest, which means there's no one to stop Philip and me from getting on with things. How do you like the wine?"

"Bit wasted on a Staffordshire farmer, I'm afraid."

"I'm sorry. The club doesn't do Banks's Bitter."

"Ha. Ha. But Bill. Serious question." Freddy leaned forward. "Why am I here?"

Bill shifted uneasily in his chair. He had planned to keep the business end of things till later. "Fraternal affection?"

"Not your style, Bill. Do you remember how you told me that the wardrobe in the green bedroom led to Narnia, and then locked me in it. I'm not sure fraternal affection is quite your thing."

"Oh, for heaven's sake, Freddy."

"No, no, obviously I don't care about that. I just have this feeling that you wouldn't drag me all the way up to London just to be 'fraternally affectionate'."

Bill again tried to make himself more comfortable. "Yes, well, there is something."

"What?"

Two weeks before – Early April – Horseferry Road, London

The Department for Transport on Horseferry Road is a five-minute walk from the Houses of Parliament. Bill Edmundson, back in his office after the Easter break, answered a knock on the door, with an authoritative "Come."

"Ah, Bill, I wonder if I could impose on you for a few moments?"

Bill re-arranged his long limbs so that he could rise up, from behind his desk, tall and lanky in his red braces, to shake hands with his visitor. "Of course, Minister, though I should say I have yet to find your presence any kind of imposition. Do have a pew. Coffee? I have some in this thermos thing."

"Yes, thank you. But, please, especially in these private meetings, do call me Philip."

"So, how can I help you, Philip? You are looking rather well. Been somewhere sunny?"

"Mougins. Up in the hills north of Cannes. Rather a nice hotel in several acres of grounds. Perfect for an Easter break. Used to be Picasso's house. In fact, it's sort of connected with why I wanted to talk to you now."

"How so?"

"Well, on our way down, Simon and I had lunch with Dominique Bussereau and his wife at Le Meurice in Paris. Just got a third star, you know. Amazing …"

"Who paid?"

"Ha! Yes, well. Well, anyway, all Dominique wanted to talk about was how much better their railways are than ours. He explained – at some length – how France thinks strategically whilst the UK is only interested in tactics. It's true, of course, but rather tiresome to have to hear it from a French Government Minister. He was very persuasive. Especially on the economics of the TGV. When he first became Minister of Transport, he was interviewed by Le Figaro, whose reporter had a bee in her bonnet about the TGV being a vanity project and so on. Dominique was embarrassed that he couldn't rebut the criticisms, so he commissioned McKinsey to do a retrospective cost-benefit report on 'le grand projet'. As it happened, he'd received the findings that morning and was in a state of Gallic excitement. Apparently, it's contributing something like 5 billion euros of 'added value' to the French economy each year.

"After lunch we were taken in the ministerial Citroën to Gare de Lyon, and boarded the TGV to Cannes. Dominique made a call to reserve seats for us in a VIP compartment. It was fantastic. Left Paris just after 4; got into Cannes just after 9. Five hours. Five hours! Can you believe it?"

"So, you want to build a TGV from London to Edinburgh …?"

"Manchester, actually. Look, Bill, I'll cut to the chase. I need your support. I've had an email exchange with Gordon Brown and he's very keen. Reading between the lines, it seems he's worked out that most of the constituencies affected are solid Tory, so it has no electoral downside. Of course – although I'm not saying this – what he really likes about the idea is that he thinks it will wrong-foot Cameron and Osborne; they can't be seen to be blocking progress so as to protect a few big landowners. But I don't care about all that; the truth is that, unlike the Commons, in the House of Lords what matters is not the next election, but the good of the country. It's why you guys are so important in our system. What drives me is that we have an opportunity here to do something really big, something absolutely transformational, for Britain."

"I can readily understand your enthusiasm, Minister – sorry, Philip – but I fear that Sir Charles will be very particular about the business case for such a large investment. I do not think that a humble civil servant like myself can have very much say in the matter."

"Oh, yes, très amusant. I'm not so sure that the words 'humble' and 'Bill Edmundson' are natural bedfellows. But the point, Bill, is that Sir Charles will dither. He hates doing anything bigger than mending potholes. He'll set up committees and sub-committees and working parties, and within a few weeks the idea will be buried. Straight into the 'Sir Humphrey' long grass. You are key, Bill."

"Lot of potholes round us in Staffordshire."

"Yes, well, that's the other thing, Bill." He paused. "I will be in charge of deciding the exact route."

For a few moments, neither man spoke. Philip looked straight at Bill, and Bill returned the gaze. They were both calculating the implications of this remark.

"We can work together on this, Bill."

Bill sat back in his black leather office chair. He closed the reading glasses that he had been holding in his right hand and placed them on his desk. He stroked his chin with his left hand. Looking down Horseferry Road he could just glimpse Lambeth Bridge and the brown water of the Thames. He pursed his lips.

From the street, there was a clanging of scaffolding being erected, but, otherwise, the room was silent.

"Is that an offer, Philip?" He paused. "Or a threat?"

"Both."

Kingsgate Manor

The thousand or so acres that made up the Kingsgate estate in Staffordshire, a few miles north of Birmingham, between Tamworth and Lichfield, had been passed down through the Edmundson family since Anglo-Saxon times. It was a family tradition to believe that it was the last remaining piece of land in England to have stayed within the same Anglo-Saxon family since before the Conquest.

When their father, Cuthy, died suddenly the previous November, on his 87th birthday, he left the large Jacobean manor house and extensive garden to his eldest son, Bill, but the Home Farm and most of the woodland went to Freddy, who had been farming it all his adult life.

Few Wills are uncontentious and Cuthy's was no exception. The Edmundson family had, for generations, adhered closely to the principle of primogeniture, and Cuthy had always been a big advocate of the system.

Cuthy had had a little bank of sayings by which he conducted his affairs. 'Only a steward' was one of them; another was 'Father's acorn, son's sapling, grandson's oak'. It was a traditional family belief that only by passing on the inheritance, lock, stock and barrel, to the eldest son could the estate be preserved.

The Will

The family solicitor came down from London to read out the Will, and sat down at the end of the dining room table. There was no forewarning that, whilst Bill got the house, park and gardens, the land would go to Freddy. Caro noticed an involuntary facial twitch, but Bill made no other movement to indicate that he was, indeed, terribly shocked by the news.

After the reading, Bill explained to his brother that he had to get straight back to Whitehall; the Minister needed him urgently. Caro, a well-dressed pillar of ice, remained silent, but she had no doubt who was behind it all. Her good manners fell away the moment she got into the Range Rover for the drive back to London. "That Sally, she's a calculating, working class bitch. Everyone thinks she's so sweet and innocent, but I don't buy that. Never did."

Bill said nothing but Caro kept on. "She's been in there every day, doting on Cuthy. Of course, he changed his Will. We should have seen it coming, Bill. Can we contest it?"

"And never speak to Freddy again? No. Absolutely not."

"You can afford to buy the land off him, Bill. He needs the money."

"He won't sell, Caro."

"We'll find a way."

Sally and Freddy

Cuthy did like Sally; he'd always liked her – ever since she was a little girl. But she was not behind the change in the Will. Caro was wrong about that.

Sally's father, Edwin, had had a small engineering business in the village doing bits and bobs mainly for local farmers; he was in and out of the estate all the time, especially during harvest. Whenever machinery broke down, the call went out for Edwin. He was almost illiterate but could fix anything. His invoice would be a scrappy note – lower and upper case letters mixed up – scribbled on a torn, oil-stained piece of cardboard from a cornflakes packet. But, despite the apparent slackness, everything was itemised, never did he over-charge or under-charge, and it was the same very reasonable rate, regardless of the day of the week or the time of day or night. He was a good and skilful worker, and an honest and respected man. His daughter was just the same.

From a young age, if it was school holidays, Sally would come out with her father in her blue boiler suit, with a black French beret atop her short blonde hair. An uncomplicated, happy, blue-eyed girl who, by the age of thirteen, could take an engine apart and put it back together again.

Sally and Freddy couldn't remember a time when they hadn't known each other. He took over the running of the Home Farm after finishing at Cirencester and within a couple of months – it was late August in 1988 – it happened.

What happened was as natural as a leaf falling to the ground. One hot evening something on the baling machine had sheared off at the top of a field called 'Falcon', that rose up on the western side of the estate. Freddy, tired and sunburnt, walked back to the house to call Sally's Dad; he was tied up with another job, so Sally came out instead in the battered old Land Rover. They met up in Falcon. Having looked at the problem, she realised she didn't have the welding equipment she needed to fix it; she could be back in 20 minutes.

Freddy shook his head. "No, don't worry. We're way ahead on the baling; it can wait till morning. But come and have a look at this." Behind the baler there was the corner of what seemed to be an unusually large stone sticking out of the soil. "I think the baler must have caught on this."

"Oh, absolutely. You must have set the plough deeper than usual. You'll have to get rid of it. Here, I'll give you a hand."

They knelt down either side of the stone. As they scraped the soil away with their hands, they chatted about the rumour, racing round the village, that the vicar was having an affair with one of the flower ladies. And then, as they tried to get their hands under the stone on either side, they bumped heads. Freddy apologised profusely.

"Here, let me kiss it better." He kissed her forehead gallantly and laughed.

"No, no, it was my fault." She kissed his forehead in return. But she didn't laugh. Instead, she put out her hand, covered in soil, and pressed it gently against his red cheek. Their eyes met. They got the stone out, carried it together to the hedge row, and dumped it there.

"I've got some beer in the Land Rover. I thought you must be thirsty."

"Oh God, I could murder a beer. You are an absolute angel."

They sat together on a bale of straw in the middle of a field, in the middle of England, drinking cans of Banks's Bitter on a warm August evening. As they did so, the red evening sun hovered over the great oak tree below in the next field, and, beyond that, above the three spires of Lichfield Cathedral in the far distance.

She patted his leg affectionately. He put his arm round her shoulders. The kiss on the lips that followed was a little tentative to start with, but soon each of them realised that the other was not holding back.

When they disengaged, Freddy found that Sally had tears pouring freely down both cheeks.

"Sal, what on earth's the matter?"

"We mustn't do that."

"Why not?"

"Because." Sally would not elaborate. She was sobbing. "I must go."

"Oh, for heaven's sake, what's going on, Sal?"

"You know what's going on."

"No, I do not. All I know is that …"

Freddy stopped. He couldn't say what he wanted to say. A few moments ago he was at ease; now his head was spinning. They sat in silence.

"Well. What is it you know, Freddy?"

When Freddy opened his mouth to reply he didn't know what words would come out. It was the strangest feeling. It was his voice that spoke, but it was as if there was someone else, who was not Freddy, speaking through him. The speech was deliberate:

"What I know is that I've just kissed the girl that I've always loved more than I've loved anyone. Ever."

He'd said it. He couldn't take it back.

"You can't say that."

"Why?"

"'Cos I don't want to get hurt."

"I don't understand what's going on, Sal. Why should I hurt you?"

"Oh, for God's sake! You know we can't have a serious relationship, Freddy, and I'm not going to have a casual relationship with you."

"Who said anything about a casual relationship? I'd marry you tomorrow and be the happiest man in England if I thought you'd have me."

Sally had stopped crying. She looked at the great ball of fire above the cathedral far away. There was nothing hesitant about the sun.

"Do you mean that?"

"Yes." Freddy looked straight at her without moving.

Sally's face melted into laughter: "Of course I'd have you."

Sally had assumed that Freddy's family would be up in arms at him marrying a village girl; she assumed that everyone in the village would be against her marrying into the 'big house' and putting on airs; she assumed it just couldn't happen. Their backgrounds were so different. He had gone to Shrewsbury – a Public School – whilst she had learnt not very much at the local comprehensive. He spoke with this incredibly posh, cut-glass accent whilst she was Staffordshire through and through. Love affairs like this only happened in Mills and Boon books, not real life.

But the glacier that is the English class system was on the move in the 1980s. In the event, no one objected, partly because it would have been 'bad form', partly because Sally was a 'good sort', but, most of all, because it was obvious that they loved each other.

They were married the following Spring. It was as simple as that.

Cuthy

Cuthy's wife, Emma, had died of cancer in the 1970s. Bill had just gone to Winchester and Freddy was at a boarding school in Worcestershire. Of the two, Bill was the more affected; he had prodigious talent as a pianist, and Emma, herself a good musician, had, from his earliest years, been his teacher. Cuthy's response had been to retreat into his bank of axioms. He was determined to 'keep his eye on the ball' and 'not let the side down'. If, as happened from time to time, it was ever suggested to him that, perhaps, the Manor was a little big for him now, he would simply say that he had to 'keep the show on the road'. In truth, he loved the old place too much.

Following their marriage, Freddy and Sal moved into The Old Forge at the end of the drive, where most of the farm buildings were now located. Cuthy would walk down there, along the horse chestnut lined drive, for Sunday lunch. Then the occasional weekday dinner became an everyday occurrence and, without anyone saying anything, Cuthy had become part of their close family.

Cuthy was not an unkind man, but he was unimaginative. He had been born adequately wealthy and, with the help of a good solicitor and an honest stockbroker, had managed to hold onto it. He had made his Will many years ago, leaving the estate in its entirety to the elder son, Bill. Freddy's farm tenancy rights would be protected, and he would get a share of the investment portfolio, but that was it. Everyone understood that this was how things were done. He never thought of re-visiting his Will, in as much as he thought about such things at all, which was, it must be said, very little.

But then there was a small occurrence that disturbed the old man's ease. Freddy's daughter, Isabella, was like her mother. A chip off the old block. One Sunday, after lunch, he was about to walk back up the drive when the eleven year old Isabella insisted on accompanying him to the Manor. Bertie, the terrier, needed a walk as well. It was late September and the conkers were everywhere. As they went, Isabella ran this way and that, with Bertie jumping around her. She picked up some conkers and brought them back to Cuthy; grandfather and grand-daughter admired the beautiful fresh, reddy-brown colours.

"What would you like to do when you grow up, young lady?" asked the old man.

"Oh, I'm going to farm here when Mummy and Daddy die," she said without a care, running off to find more half-opened horse chestnuts.

Later that evening, Cuthy, reflecting on what she had said, was struck by the realisation that it wouldn't be that simple. If the land didn't belong to Freddy, he wouldn't be able to pass it on to Isabella. He tried to watch television – the Antiques Roadshow, his favourite programme – but it irritated him. In bed he couldn't sleep; whichever way he turned, he was uncomfortable and agitated. Eventually, when he did sleep, he dreamt of a conker fight. His 'Conqueror' of 86 – an eighty sixer – was hit and shattered. It couldn't last forever.

The next day he called the solicitor to clarify what would happen to the Home Farm. The problem was that the tenancy under which

Freddy rented the farm from his father had been signed in 1985, and the law about the succession of farm tenancies had changed a year earlier. If only they had settled things 12 months earlier – as the solicitor rather undiplomatically reminded Cuthy he had advised him to do – then Freddy's tenancy rights could have been passed on to his children and grandchildren. That was not now possible.

Cuthy felt awful. He had always believed in primogeniture, but this was wrong. Bill had made a lot of money during his time at Goldman Sachs; now he had a secure senior job in Whitehall with a fabulous pension to look forward to. And, for goodness sake, he was not the slightest bit interested in farming, and knew nothing about it. Cuthy had a duty to look after his younger son and family. They, especially dear Sally, did so much to look after him without ever asking for anything in return.

Within a few days he had changed his Will. Bill would have the house and gardens; Freddy the land. Cuthy knew he must tell Bill, but he put it off. He was frightened of Caro.

Caro

Bill's CBE was Caro's worst nightmare. He had peaked too early. A few years earlier, when Bill was still a banker, they'd given the Conservative Party half a million pounds. What did they get for it? A lunch in Parliament with Norman Fowler.

It was then that she realised she had to get him out of Goldman's, while there was still time to get to the top of the Civil Service. Such a move was the best bet if he was to get a knighthood or peerage. And now they'd gone and fobbed him off with a CBE. After he got that letter, she went upstairs and cried.

With Caro, it all went back a long way. As a little girl, she and her brother, Jeremy, noted the conspiratorial looks between the other mothers when their unknowing parent committed the faux pas of saying 'toilet' and 'pardon'. But there was one particular incident at a village fête which was like a deep scratch on the polished surface of her memory. It was soon after they had moved into the house, which her father had unexpectedly inherited from a cousin. A diminutive, chain-smoking lady in a tweed suit approached. She had an accent that would have made Royalty sound common.

"How absolutely splendid that you are moving into Astley Hall. Now, do tell me, have you got any land?"

"Oh, yes. We've got forty acres around the house, thank you very much," replied her innocent father.

"Ah. No land." The small lady puffed on her cigarette, smiled through the smoke, blinked several times, and turned to the mole man who was standing close by.

"Now Paul, you are just the chap I was hoping to see. You must come and pay us a visit with your strychnine worms. Do tell me, what is it you charge?"

Caro's parents could not bring themselves to acknowledge the slights, snubs and insults. But Caro and her brother saw them all. Jeremy's response was to grow his hair long and become a Marxist. Caro's was to plot revenge. In due course, Bill Edmundson would become the means.

They had met at a college ball towards the end of their first year at Oxford. They walked hand-in-hand around Christ Church Meadow with the dawn mist on the Cherwell. He was a lost soul; he had been allowed to give up reading Music, in favour of PPE, but his heart wasn't in it; he simply didn't know what else to do.

As far as Caro was concerned, he was clever, diligent, good looking, and tall. She could provide the backbone. It was not long before they both wanted the same things; she saw to that. She had checked him out in bed, and that was all fine.

They delayed getting married. It was better to have the big party when you're in your early 30s; you can ask more influential guests than when you are younger. Inviting Herbie, the then CEO of Goldman's, worked particularly well. For a boy from Brooklyn, staying as a special guest at an old country house was the real deal. Much classier than the five-star hotels he was accustomed to. He wanted to be invited back. Bill became a senior partner rather younger than was usual.

Within a few years they had had, as planned, two children: Emmy and then Toby.

Philip

Lord Manolis has his detractors, but no one has ever accused him of being stupid or idle.

On his first morning in Mougins, he sat in the early April sunshine on a sun-lounger by the hotel pool, with his mobile phone, and talked to the chief executive of the engineering consultants, Ove Arup, back in London.

No, a high-speed train from London to Manchester was not a new idea – it had been doing the rounds for years, decades even. Yes, they had done the scoping work and, yes, it was detailed. No, it would have to be a new line – the existing tracks and stations could not be adapted to take a high-speed train. Yes, it would cost a lot more than the tunnel, and no, the private sector was not interested. Yes, he could email the relevant maps and papers.

The man from Ove Arup laughed heartily when he heard about McKinsey's report for Dominique Bussereau.

"Why are you laughing?"

"Can you imagine McKinsey writing anything that might embarrass a government? They're not stupid those guys. Most of their work comes from Government. We consultants have to be good at 'handling', Philip."

"Okay, I get it, but since you mention 'handling', how do you think I should 'handle' this?"

"Look, if you're really serious, you have to do two things. First, sort out your Department. You know how good Sir Humph … , sorry, Sir Charles, is at laying down smoke. He will have a field day with this. Second, this could be electoral dynamite. You must get the opposition on board; if you don't, Cameron and Osborne will eat you alive in any election campaign."

A day or two later they had a table booked for lunch at La Colombe d'Or in St Paul de Vence, north of Nice. The restaurant is famous for the priceless works of art adorning its walls; that is how Matisse, Chagall, Picasso and many others had paid for their lunches. It's a place where you expect to see familiar faces from the worlds of film, television and politics, but Philip was certainly not expecting to find himself and Simon walking into the restaurant at the same time as the Shadow Chancellor of the Exchequer and his wife.

It was George Osborne who suggested they share a table; the Maître d' did not know who they all were but, with many years of dealing with celebrities, he picked up the unmistakeable little signals and trusted his instincts. He organised a table for four on the terrace with its glorious views. He was correct in his calculation that the unfortunate Japanese couple, who had taken the trouble to book this particular place months ago, would be too polite to complain.

George was making good use of the Parliamentary Easter recess, and had, like Philip, travelled down on the TGV. George was also familiar with Le Meurice – his grandfather's favourite hotel. The courses came and went, four bottles of expensive Burgundy were emptied, and by the time they were all agreeing upon the excellence of the home-made grappa, it was the settled policy of both major political parties that the UK should have a high-speed train between London and Manchester. However, Philip, when composing his email to Gordon the following day, thought it wise not to mention the lunch with Osborne.

Lord M now turned his attention to the Civil Service. What the Ove Arup partner had said only confirmed what he had learnt during his time at 'Education': you couldn't get something like this through without Civil Service backing. But getting that wasn't going to be straightforward. The Department for Transport had always been packed with people who believed in the principle of incremental change: by 1954 the UK had only eight miles of motorway. Just after becoming a junior minister, he'd been invited for dinner with Sir Charles, the Permanent Secretary, who talked on and on about the philosophy of Karl Popper and the virtues of 'Piecemeal Engineering'. Sir Charles would block the scheme. Of that, he was certain.

On the other hand, recently, Sir Charles had lost his spark. There was a rumour circulating about marital difficulties. It was helpful. Most years at least one Oxbridge college was in need of a new 'Master'; obviously Sir Charles would have had his eye on Balliol, but that was unlikely to come up for some time. It shouldn't be too difficult to sort out a suitable alternative.

His replacement at the Department had to be Bill Edmundson. He had had a glittering career at Goldman Sachs where he was the brains behind some of the biggest infrastructure projects across the planet. This new train-set was right up his street. Everyone at 'Transport' deferred to Bill; he was the obvious successor to Sir Charles, and it shouldn't be too difficult to slot him in as Permanent Secretary.

Unfortunately, there was a problem, and it wasn't a small one: Kingsgate. When he looked at Ove Arup's optimum route, he realised that it went clean through Bill's Staffordshire estate. He was a clever man; he would find a way to block it, just as, for different reasons, would Sir Charles.

Fortunately, there was a solution. He would have to speak to Bill.

Early April – Horseferry Road, London (continued)

"Look, Bill, if anything I am about to say gets out, I shall deny it, and – please excuse the cliché – I shall have your guts for garters."

Bill nodded.

"The thing is, by chance, I met up with George Osborne in the south of France and we had lunch. To cut a long story short, he's even keener on this idea than I am. Obviously, it suits him personally because of his constituency, but actually he's also a bit obsessed with our failure as a country to think long-term. It was curious; he was saying in English almost exactly the same things I'd heard Dominique say in French just a few days before.

"The point is, Bill, this is going to happen. It's 'an idea whose time has come', as Victor Hugo, I think it was, said. If it doesn't happen now, it will happen in five, ten, or fifteen years' time. You get my drift."

"Pray continue."

"So, for now, it's not a question of whether or not there will be a new line: there will be. Period. The issue is this: does the route pass north of Tamworth, or south? Ove Arup have already done a great deal of scoping work, and it seems they prefer the southern route."

Philip did not have to spell out the implications of this remark. Bill was silent. This was indeed a threat. He thought of how his father, Cuthy, had paid so much to have all the electricity cables buried on the estate so as to preserve its sense of timelessness. And now this.

What, Bill wondered, would the offer be?

"Naturally, as a potentially interested party, Bill, you could not be involved in any decisions on the route."

"Of course not."

"But I could be. Or, to be absolutely blunt: I will be. I will chair that committee, and I will appoint its members. Do you follow me, Bill?"

Philip interpreted the almost imperceptible incline that Bill gave to his head as a 'yes'.

"Excellent, because it seems to me that there's something to be said for a northern route."

Bill was more a bridge player, but he had played poker at his club from time to time. He knew a bit about arranging the facial muscles so as to eliminate all expression. He did this now.

Philip continued: "And then there's All Souls."

"All Souls? What might a distinguished Oxford college have to do with a high-speed railway line?"

"They will need a new Warden in the not too distant future."
"Ah."
"Obviously, Sir Charles would have preferred Balliol, but that won't be coming up for several years, and, by then, they'll probably have to have a woman. I can't see him turning down All Souls."
"Has he been offered it?"
"Er, no. Sir Charles is not quite, so to say, in the loop yet."
"Are the Fellows going to offer it?"
"I think I know enough about how the higher education budget works to help them make a sensible choice. As they say, there's no creature on this planet more feral than an Oxbridge don in pursuit of a research grant."
"It would seem that you have been giving all this quite a bit of thought, Philip."
"I have, Bill. I have."

The Old Forge

Like his brother, Freddy did not show his feelings when the Will was read out. Unlike his brother, he was thrilled.

It would make an incredible difference. It wasn't just that he would be able to pass the farm on to Isabella; it was that he could get the capital he desperately needed to farm profitably. Farming was now very 'capital-intensive', as the man from the NFU was always saying.

Cuthy had loved the idea of farming – on his old passport under 'Occupation' he had put 'Gentleman Farmer' – but he was a dilettante. From time to time, Freddy had tried to get him to spend money that was badly needed, but Cuthy would look at Freddy's proposal and say: "Too many noughts." Eventually he would then stump up something to keep Freddy quiet, but it was never enough.

Freddy needed a seven-figure sum to repair the buildings and get the right machinery, but, just now, with most of the banks all but bankrupt themselves, there was little chance of a loan.

A housebuilding company had come to him recently about Well Meadow; this was the field beyond Falcon, where the land fell down on the west side towards the village. The other side of Well Meadow was the road. It wasn't Green Belt and the housebuilders were confident that they could get planning permission for a development. It was a lovely, quiet village. Very desirable. He knew a farmer who had sold a similar ten-acre plot for over a million pounds.

He walked back with Sally along the drive, the horse chestnut trees now bare, to The Old Forge. Sally put her arm round his middle and squeezed him tight.

She said: "Well Meadow." It was all she needed to say; it was what they were both thinking.

"I know. Incredible, isn't it?"

"I bet Caro thinks I'm the one who's been scheming behind their backs. Mind you, she's right that I wanted to. And I would have, if you hadn't stopped me."

Freddy was mulling something over. "I had a word with the solicitor after Bill and Caro left. Apparently, Dad only changed the Will last month."

They walked on. It was Sally who broke the silence. "Do you know what? I think it might have something to do with Isabella. Do you remember when she walked back up to the Manor with Grandpa after lunch? Apparently, Grandpa asked her what she wanted to do when she grew up, and she said she was going to farm the Home Farm. She told me about it after. She admitted to feeling guilty about it, because she doesn't actually want to farm. She said she thought that if he believed she wanted to farm here one day, it would make him leave the land to you. Can you believe what goes on inside that little head of hers?"

"Well, well, well. Seems like we've got a very clever little girl."

"Your genes or mine?"

"I think we both know the answer to that, Sal." They stopped and kissed. Sally was breathless when they broke off. "The school run's not for a couple of hours. Come on."

Bill and Caro

Bill and Caro were having a gin and tonic before dinner in their Notting Hill house. It was the evening after his conversation with Philip at the Department.

"So basically, darling, the deal is this. I steer the Department towards believing that the future prosperity of the country is entirely dependent on getting a few business people from Manchester to London a bit quicker. In return he makes sure the route goes nowhere near Kingsgate. Oh, and small detail: I become Permanent Secretary, and get a 'K'."

Caro got up and came over to sit down on the sofa close to her soon-to-be-knighted husband. She patted his leg. "Well done, darling. But can you trust him, 'Sir William'?"

"I don't think I have to, 'Lady Edmundson'. The power is pretty evenly balanced."

Bill explained the significance of the north and south routes around Tamworth.

"But how badly would we be affected by a south route?"

"Yes, well, you're right to ask. When Philip first confided in me what he was up to, I have to admit I was completely pole-axed. It was only when I saw the exact route Ove Arup were proposing that I started to relax. It's actually a very intelligent proposal, and I can see that in all sorts of ways it makes perfect sense. But the important thing is it would be behind the ridge. You know there's that big field – it's called 'Falcon' – that runs over the hill. The one with the views over to the west, towards Lichfield. The line would run in a sweeping semi-circle through the land further south, and come out below Falcon and on through that next field, 'Well Meadow', the one which Freddy is going to sell off for housing. So, basically, the southern route would be terrible for Freddy – it completely buggers up any chance of selling land for housing. Who would want to buy a dream house in the countryside with trains going past your window at 220 miles an hour?"

"So, are you saying that, if the worst came to the worst, the southern route wouldn't actually affect the Manor that much?"

"I am. Awful for Freddy but it wouldn't make any difference to us. Of course, Philip, bless him, doesn't realise that. He's been looking at maps that don't show the topography of the land. He can't see there's a large ridge running between the Manor and the southern route. Anyway, it's all academic. Philip will ensure it's the northern route. Apart from anything else, he and Simon don't get invited for country house weekends all that much."

The prospect of a knighthood worked as a strong aphrodisiac for both Bill and Caro. Over dinner they behaved like silly teenagers. They had an early night. After their amorous exertions, Bill fell into a deep sleep, but Caro remained wide awake. Good old Bill hadn't 'peaked' too early after all.

She couldn't sleep. Although she did think about how she could now avenge the humiliations of her childhood, and of how her silly brother, Jeremy, would hate her being called 'Lady Edmundson', the real cause for her insomnia came from another source. As she lay there in the darkness, it had dawned on her that an opportunity to buy the land back off Freddy had just fallen into their laps. They could have both the knighthood and the land. Grand slam. All they had to do was play the cards in the right order.

Bill must tell Freddy about the new railway line without mentioning the northern route; in any event, since that was an unspoken understanding between Bill and Philip, it would be inappropriate for Bill to reveal it. All Bill had to do was show Freddy the Ove Arup maps with the recommended southern route ploughing straight through Well Meadow. The penny would drop. In an instant Freddy would see that the land was 'blighted', he wasn't going to be able to sell it for housing, and he wouldn't get the capital he needed for the farm.

Then Bill could strike.

Bill's twenty years at Goldman Sachs had been lucrative. He could easily afford the several million that would be needed to pay his brother top-whack for the land. Freddy could continue as a secured tenant, but would have the funds to sort out the farm. Bill would be his saviour. But Bill and Caro would have the land. She would need to stiffen Bill up a bit, but it looked pretty watertight.

She put the plan to Bill the next morning over breakfast, explaining that he had to do it "for Toby's sake." This, of course, was the killer argument.

"Toby's always wanted to farm the estate when the tenancy expires on Freddy's death. This is your chance to do what's right for Toby."

"Really? Are you sure Toby wants to farm? I had no idea Toby was minded that way."

"Oh, Bill. You men, you don't notice anything."

Caro was going out on a limb here. Bill, of course, was completely right: Toby had no interest in farming whatsoever. She would have to drive back to Kingsgate after lunch via Toby's Prep School in Oxford which he'd only just gone back to yesterday. They could go to that patisserie in Summertown, and she would brief him on what to say to his father when the subject came up. Toby, with a place at Eton in the bag, was no fool.

Late April – Lunch (continued)

"Now look Freddy, if it were ever to get out that I had told you what I am about to tell you, I would be unceremoniously sacked. I could even be prosecuted."

"Well, why do you want to tell me then?"

"Because it affects you. Directly. A lot. And my loyalty to my brother is stronger than my loyalty to Her Majesty's Government."

"Crikey. What the heck's going on? Are you working for MI6?"

"Freddy, please, keep your voice down. And, no, I'm not working for MI6."

Bill told his startled brother about the new high-speed railway line. When Bill got the Ove Arup papers out of his old music case,

Freddy could see the Crown logo printed on the 'Department for Transport' folder, together with the word 'SECRET' stamped in red letters.

Bill passed the papers across the table with an explanation that, obviously, he couldn't let Freddy keep them.

Freddy looked at the map, with, right there, a large double track railway line cutting clean across all the familiar irregular field shapes and names.

"The thing is, Freddy, the Conservative Party is backing this as well; George Osborne has told me himself that he's putting it in the Party's Manifesto for the election next year. It's not going to be fought over politically by any of the main parties. It really will happen."

Freddy could not believe what he was looking at. His stomach was turning over and over.

"Oh, shit," was all he could say as he tried to take in the enormity of what was in front of him.

Bill watched his brother writhe in pain and felt awful. He recalled how Caro had said to him that morning: "I know you don't like it, but your first responsibility is to your son, not your brother."

A soon-to-be Permanent Secretary with 20 years at Goldman Sachs could have no difficulty in persuading a Staffordshire farmer that his proposal was extraordinarily generous. It was, quite simply, to buy the land – with something like a million pound uplift for the possibility of planning permission on Well Meadow – and give Freddy a sitting tenancy at standard rates.

He went on to explain that, this way, Freddy would have all the reserves he needed to upgrade the farm in every imaginable way. (And, as he spoke, he reminded himself, as Caro had pointed out, that he was not cheating Freddy in any shape or form; it was all above board and strictly by the book. Freddy would not lose out.) But they would have to do it quickly. Once the proposal for the new line was made public – or leaked out – the independent valuers would have to take out that million pound uplift.

"I can afford it, Freddy. Daddy would have wanted me to do this for you. Can we shake hands on it?"

Freddy pushed the roast guinea fowl around his plate. He felt backed into a corner. He could not be less hungry. Bill drank some of the Montrachet and studied his brother's face.

Eventually Freddy said: "So, now it's me who's like a sheep on its back."

"What?"

"I'm like that sheep of mine this morning, aren't I? I'm stuck with my legs in the air with no choice but to accept your offer."

"Oh, come now, Freddy. It's not in the least like that. But I do think my offer is good."

"Yes, well, it probably is. But I'm not going to accept it."

Bill was kicking himself. He had tried to reel the fish in too quickly. He pretended all was well.

"Look, Freddy, you need time to think it over. You must talk it through with Sally and so on."

"No, Bill, you're not hearing me. Daddy gave me that land, and I'm keeping it."

"But, Freddy, you'd be mad to turn down my offer. You know you need the money and I can help you."

"Then just give me the money, or lend it to me or something, if you love me so much."

"Well, I won't do that."

"Why not?"

"Because Daddy was wrong to break up an estate that has been kept together for a thousand years. He had no right." Bill could feel the fish slipping away; how could he have been so stupid as to force the issue?

"Well, that's what he did, Bill; railway line or no railway line, I'm keeping it. To me there's more value in that land, in that soil, than you can possibly imagine."

Neither brother wanted a desert or coffee, and the lunch, now dominated by an angry silence, was soon over. The parting was polite.

Freddy walked back to Euston. As he went, he saw well-heeled, self-satisfied businessmen and women rushing from one important meeting to another; these were the types who would be travelling across his land at 200 bloody miles an hour. Bastards. How he hated them. There was nothing he could do. He felt sick, sick, sick.

The Return Journey

Freddy was booked on the 17.27 Liverpool train that stopped at Tamworth, but he got to Euston an hour early. He needed a drink to steady himself, and went into the 'Irish Pub'.

He knew he was being an idiot, but he had really meant it when he had said that stuff about there being more value in the land than his brother could imagine. He was not going to let it go. Come what may. His brother might be smooth as silk, but, underneath all that charm and elegance, he was just an old-fashioned bully, who was used to getting his way, and Caro was the same. Come to think of it, it was probably her idea.

Then he thought of Sally. She was more practical than he was. They normally saw eye to eye on things, but now he started to feel that this time she would be beyond upset with him. She hadn't grown up with money; she would want the security of Bill's millions. They could pass it on to the children; that's what she would say. She would mean it.

As his mind overflowed with these thoughts, Freddy had had a second pint, and then a third, and then a fourth. He missed his train and was drunk. He looked at his phone. A dozen text messages and missed calls – all from Sally. He was angry and ashamed; his whole world, which just this morning had seemed so perfect, had been blown apart. He couldn't bring himself to reply. He couldn't even bring himself to look at the texts. He knew what they would say.

And then he fell asleep on the train. When he woke, it had passed Tamworth, where the Land Rover was parked. He had to take a taxi home from Stafford. It was nearly 11 p.m. when he walked into the kitchen. Isabella was still up, and spoke first.

"Dad, you are well and truly in the doghouse."

"Freddy, you cannot do that to me." Sally was incandescent. He'd never seen her more angry. "How could you? I have this incredible news and you cut me."

"What news? If you must know, I've also got some incredible news. And it's incredibly, fucking, catastrophic."

"Do not use that language in front your daughter."

"Oh, for goodness sake, Mum. What's happened, Dad?"

Freddy stood by the kitchen door, trembling. He had been dreading this moment for the last six or seven hours. He told them what had happened and how he had recklessly rejected his brother's offer.

But, as he spoke, Sal's face relaxed into a warm, forgiving smile. She was just like that little girl in a boiler suit and beret all those years ago. Good God, how he loved her! How could he have been such a prick? Isabella started to giggle.

Sally said: "Alfred Edmundson, I am so totally proud of you. I love it that you told that brother of yours to fuck off … sorry, I didn't say that … I know what the land means to you, you idiot. And you should bloody well know me by now. I've never wanted money, and I've always been happy … especially with you."

She came over and nestled her body tight against his and squeezed his bottom with both her hands. Isabella covered her eyes. "Oh, Mum, stop it, that's disgusting."

Sally looked up at her adored husband. "Anyway, you misery-guts, my news is *much* more interesting than yours."

Falcon

She had been walking Bertie in the morning. They were making their way along the hedgerow that separates Falcon from Well Meadow when she noticed Bertie sniffing around the large stone they had moved together all those years ago. She thought about how it was that that little event had brought them together; perhaps, without that stone, nothing would have happened. Life could be like that.

She went back to the farm, rounded up the farmhand, and took the tractor and trailer to pick up the stone, and bring it back to the farmhouse. She wanted to do something sentimental with it to celebrate their wonderfully happy marriage. She washed all the mud off, and discovered it was covered in carvings. It looked very old. She took a photo, scanned it into the computer, and emailed it to the Lichfield Museum, asking if anyone there could shed any light on what it might be.

Within minutes the museum curator was on the phone. Could he come out? He had forwarded Sally's email on to an expert he knew at the British Museum in London, who said it was lines from an Anglo-Saxon poem and was probably from the 11th century. Since it was near Tamworth, the ancient capital of the Anglo-Saxon Kingdom of Mercia, it might be an important find.

By lunchtime the curator had arrived with a metal detector and a knapsack full of tools and things. He thought it possible there might be some artefacts in the area where the stone had been found originally. They walked up to Falcon. Remembering that summer's evening long ago, she recalled how the big oak tree at the bottom of Well Meadow, the one that's always been called 'The Lollard Oak', lined up with the far-away spires of Lichfield Cathedral. This made it easy to locate the previous position of the stone. Immediately there was a signal on the detector.

Isabella had been listening quietly. She opened the kitchen drawer and took something out. She turned it this way and that in her delicate fingers.

Sally went on: "So, Freddy, my sweet, darling, pissed-as-a-rat husband …"

Isabella handed the small, metal-looking thing to her father. "Look at this workmanship, Dad." It was much heavier than he expected. A couple of inches long, an inch wide and an inch high, it was a deep golden colour, and covered in intricate snake-like decorations made of tiny beads that wove in and out.

"Is it gold?"

"Yup," said Sally.

"What is it?"

"It's a 'sword-hilt pommel' – it would have been on top of the handle of a sword."

"How old is it?"

"About one thousand, four hundred years."

"Good God. Was there anything else?"

"Yup. This is the only thing I took. I wanted to have something to show you."

"What else is there?"

"Sit down."

They had unearthed dozens of mud-caked items in very little time. The curator had brought a large plastic bottle of water and a toothbrush in his knapsack. Sally dribbled the water while he gently brushed. After they had cleaned a few pieces the curator, who had a new iPhone, photographed them and emailed the photos to Marilyn, the British Museum expert. She called straightaway to say they must stop digging. She would call again. When she did, it was to inform them that she and a colleague were leaving now, and would get to Kingsgate by five o'clock. She instructed them to speak to no one; this was not a request: it was a legal requirement. She informed them that the police would be arriving within the hour to secure the site, and that they should not leave it unattended in the meantime.

"You're making this up."

"I am not. I rang you again and again. You wouldn't answer. I must have sent you a dozen text messages. I suppose you didn't open a single one. I cannot tell you how angry I've been with you, Freddy."

She paused to take a deep breath and went on: "Anyway. So the lovely Marilyn from the BM plus her rather dishy Dutch sidekick, Jan Mark, who's doing a doctorate at Oxford, have been here until only an hour ago. She said a lot more work will have to be done to excavate the entire site, but, even with what they've seen today, it's the largest hoard of Anglo-Saxon gold[1] ever found anywhere in England. The quality is 'extraordinary', she said."

"Sal, this is not funny. If this is some kind of joke, I am really not in the mood."

"I swear to you, Freddy, this is God's own truth. Every single word of it. She said it will be designated 'Treasure Trove', which means it belongs to the Crown, but – and this is the best bit - there will be a reward."

"How much?"

"Equal to the market value of the find. And guess what. The finder – that's me – gets 50%, and the owner – that's you – gets the other 50%."

"Did she say what the market value might be?"

"At first she was cagey. She said she didn't want to get our hopes up. But I kept pushing and, eventually, she said that, from what she'd already seen, she'd be surprised if it was below three million."

"Three million! Jesus Christ! Three million!" Freddy was shaking his head. "My God, Sal, you realise what that means?"

"Of course, I do. But now you've told me about your lunch with Bill, there's a cherry on the cake. They stayed for dinner and she said it's going to be the biggest thing she's ever had to deal with in her career. Apparently, the law gives her power to protect the land from looting or damage in these circumstances. There's a cop up there now. She regards the whole area as a major archaeological site, and says it'll take years to investigate it properly. Tomorrow she's going to slap a ban on building work anywhere in the vicinity. For example, if we'd been planning to put up wind turbines, we should forget it, though we might get compensation. So, no buildings, no roads, bridges, railway lines, nothing. All the way down to the main road. Nothing will be allowed."

"Railway lines? Not allowed?"

"That's exactly what she said. That's *exactly* what she said."

The Lollard Oak

Chapter Two: 1085

1085 – Dramatis Personae

Edmund William Edmundson, also known as 'Brother William', and, later, as 'Father William'
Alfred Edmundson, his brother
Cuthbert Edmundson, their father
Emma, their mother

Richard, half-brother of Emma
Isabella, daughter of Richard, and mother of …
Isabella, born April 1066, the author of three letters to her son
Edwin, son of Adam – see below

Edwin, Estate Blacksmith
Adam, his son

Aethelwig, Abbot of Evesham Abbey
Wulfstan, Bishop of Worcester
Stigand, Archbishop of Canterbury and Bishop of Winchester

Walter de Lacy, a Norman Baron
William, Duke of Normandy, King of England

1085

4th September 1144 – Isabella's first letter from Evesham Abbey

My dear son Edwin,

Please forgive me for burdening you with the woes of an old woman, but I am finding what is left of my life so very difficult. There is no one left who can remember Uncle Edmund – or 'Father William' as they called him here. When he was alive, I was respected as his niece. Now I am an ancient, contemptible nuisance. The new generation of nuns are not interested in what we went through; they think my mind has gone, and gossip about me openly.

But there is something more important than my lost pride to distress me. It's an entry from Edmund's diary. I can't find it. It was on a separate piece of parchment. It should have been in the library with the rest of Uncle Edmund's diary, but it's just not there, and I don't understand why. I fear a conspiracy.

It was about Uncle Edmund's encounter with King William in Gloucester late at night on Christmas Eve in 1085. He showed it to me in 1110. That was when I came here after your dear father's death. I shivered reading it: it's the only record of what the king said when they were alone together. That was 30 years ago, but it still haunts me. The thought that it may have been lost for ever is unbearable.

I am sending you now the rest of his diary. It's all I can do. Please read it to the children. They must know what happened. We must not forget.

Your loving mother,
Isabella

10th April 1060 – Edmund's diary

Maman has given me this book for me to record my experiences and thoughts whilst I spend time with her family in Normandy. The two of us crossed the sea from Pevensey to Fécamp yesterday and arrived here this evening. And what a reception we got! Her family had not seen her for eighteen years since she left for England with my grandfather back in 1042. He was King Edward's steward[1].

They have all been so kind and welcoming. They are very pleased that, although I have an English father, I look and dress like a Norman. Maman was careful about that before we left, even in the way she cut my hair! They say my French is 'parfait'; I overheard Maman's uncle say it was 'incroyable' that I could speak with such a Normandy accent. And they were delighted that I enjoyed the pork with apple sauce that had been specially prepared for our arrival. Maman has to go back in two weeks but I'm staying here for six months; it will be a happy time.

I hope no one but me will ever read this. It is embarrassing, but I have fallen in love. I was sitting next to my cousin, Isabella, at dinner. Her father, Richard, is Maman's half-brother. She is also 15 and very, very beautiful. She has dark brown eyes which absolutely shine. She laughed at my 'English jokes'. It was as if I had known her always.

4th September 1060 – Edmund's diary

Today is my 16th birthday. We have been picking apples all day and I'm exhausted. The apples go into the stone cider press and they say that, by this time next week, it will be strong cider. Uncle Richard has promised to give me a barrel to take home as a present for maman when I travel back at the end of the month. I can't wait to see her face.

Everyone calls me 'Guillaume' which is French for my middle name, William. Maman always wanted me to be called after her

The Lollard Oak

grandfather, but the English can't pronounce 'Guillaume'. It is not very comfortable being both Norman and English. They all want me to be 'Norman', but the longer I've been here the more I feel 'English'.

The thing I most hate are the discussions about politics. Not long ago there was a feast to which a family called de Lacy were invited. Walter de Lacy serves in the household of William FitzOsbern, whose father was Duke William's steward. Everyone was talking about what would happen in England when King Edward dies. Uncle Richard – to be polite – asked me, as 'the only Englishman' there, what I thought. I said that my father had told me that you can only become King of England if the Witan[2] chooses you and that he was sure that, when the time comes, the Witan would choose Harold Godwinson. I even explained that, according to my father, it is Edgar the Aetheling who is descended directly from the great King Alfred, who was the rightful heir, but that Harold is now so powerful, no one will go against him. I also mentioned that, according to Father, the Witan would never appoint a king who could not speak English. I probably shouldn't have said that.

"But, Guillaume, what is this 'Witan'?", asked my uncle.

As I was talking, I noticed how Walter de Lacy[3] was going red in the face. I got flustered and mumbled something about 'important men'. Suddenly, this de Lacy man was in a fury; he said that Duke William would 'teach the English a lesson they would never forget'. His language was actually much worse than I can write down. Isabella, sitting next to me, whispered in my ear:

"En fait il vient d'une famille paysanne ... he is only, how you say, a peasant."

She re-assured me that they all think he is a horrible, vulgar man who thinks he is more important than he really is. I should not to take any notice. I tried not to be shaken, but I was.

I saw the Duke once. It was last June. He came to Falaise to see his mother. He rode into town at the head of over a hundred horsemen. I have never seen so many horses. What a sight it was!

The Lollard Oak

The Duke is a huge man, and quite scary, even from a distance. The stories about him are hair-raising. His father was never married to his mother, and he gets into a fury if anyone mentions it. Once, after a siege where the soldiers had shouted 'bastard' at him from the battlements, he had all their arms and legs cut off, and left them in a field as live carrion for foxes. The crows pecked out their eyes while they were still alive.

I cannot wish for such a man to be our King.

22nd June 1063 – Edmund's diary

Tomorrow Isabella arrives. She is going to stay until Christmas. My knees are jelly at the thought of seeing her again. My brother, Alfred, who is only a year younger than me, teases me about my 'love'; even Father and Maman smirk rather than tell him off. I hate him.

23rd June 1063 – Edmund's diary

There are no words in either French or English to describe how beautiful Isabella is. I am like a clod of heavy English clay beside this spring meadow of Norman wild flowers. I knew that, in the three years since I was in Normandy, the girl I knew then would have become a woman, but nothing could have prepared me for this. She caught me admiring her breasts; I think she straightened to make them more prominent. The red ribbons in her hair matched her red and white checked dress, but it was seeing her eyes again that set my heart pounding.

I took her on a tour of the house. She wanted to know everything about our family. I explained how Tamworth was the royal seat of Mercia, and that generations of Edmundsons had been stewards to Mercian kings. In those days we had a large house beside the west gate of Tamworth, known as King's Gate, and so, when we built this house on our landholding, we kept the name. In Father's room she picked up a gold, sword hilt pommel – she knew what it was – and examined it.

"Mon Dieu, look at this workmanship. You Anglo-Saxons are so skilled. We have nothing as beautiful as this."

I couldn't help showing off to Isabella. Father had instructed me never to tell anyone about the chest, but now, with Isabella turning the heavy pommel this way and that in her delicate fingers, I couldn't resist saying that it was just one of many gold artifacts that King Wulfhere had given to one of our ancestors. I opened up the chest. Her lovely dark eyes widened and she put her little hand to her mouth.

I also wanted to show her how much land we have – 18 hides[4] in all – so I took her to the top of Falcon where there is a view over to the west. I pointed out the tower of the church in a small town called Lichfield in the distance. She took my hand and laughed: "You are a very handsome man now, Edmund." I was so embarrassed by this that I failed to return the compliment. Sometimes I hate myself.

Tonight we had the village dance. Everyone was excited to see the Norman beauty. My goodness, can she dance! Alfred, who had been enjoying more than his share of the strong Normandy cider that Isabella had brought with her, was playing the fool dancing along with her. I knew it was funny, but I couldn't laugh.

30th July 1063 – Edmund's diary

The evening was beautiful and warm, and everyone was out. I walked up Falcon to see the sun set.

They must have heard me at exactly the same time as each other. They both turned round quickly and, just as quickly, let go of one another's hand. They knew I had seen and I knew that they would not have turned round like that, or let go of each other's hand in that way, had it been meaningless. Each of us knew what each of us was thinking, and we all knew it was impossible to speak. And so, not a word was said as we walked back to the house together.

The Lollard Oak

It had been a lovely day until then. As we made our silent way home, I remembered the village dance and the thrill on her face as she danced with Alfred. The thought that she *likes* me but she *loves* him has settled, like an uninvited and unwelcome guest, in my mind, and I cannot be rid of it.

10th April 1064 (7 months later) – Edmund's diary

Abbot Aethelwig greeted me across the table with a cautious smile. "So, please, sit down, young man, and tell me what you're running away from."

I didn't know what to say; I hadn't expected that question. I told him I felt I had a calling from God. His countenance darkened, becoming more grimace than smile. For a minute or so, he was silent; then, very suddenly, he got up, came round to my side of the table, and sat down in the chair next to mine. Looking me straight in the eye, he went on: "You see, Edmund, I'm not being hard or anything – and I can assure you that any son of your father's is dear to me – but we all, well, nearly all, come here to the Abbey here at Evesham because we are running away from something. I think you're running away from something and you have to tell me what it is. If you won't, I can't accept you."

As his eyes held me fast, mine were filling up. I felt a tear find its way down my cheek. I told him about Alfred and Isabella. I explained how Alfred, knowing my feelings for her, was refusing to marry her because he felt he would be doing wrong by me. I had to find a way to give them the freedom to marry, because I knew that that was what they should do.

The abbot put his hand on my shoulder. "You are your father's son".

There was a long silence – he continued to look at me in an intense but not unkindly manner – before he asked abruptly: "What else?"

I told him I had a terrible but sure foreboding that there would be war between England and Normandy following King Edward's death. I could not fight against my mother's country. Nor could I fight against my father's. Nor could I not fight. Perhaps, if I became a monk, I might be able to do some good.

The old abbot, having folded his fingers together, rested his chin on them.

"That is interesting. Bishop Wulfstan and I are also worried."

Another silence.

"And what about God? Where does He come into all this?"

"Perhaps God has sent me these dilemmas because the only possible solution is to draw near to Him."

The Abbot leant back and laughed, with a deep, guttural laugh. "Very good. I like that. I can assure you, young Edmund, the only possible solution to all our dilemmas is to draw near to Him. Do you speak French?"

"Yes," I said.

"How well?"

"Perfectly."

"I see."

That was it. I am to stay here overnight; he will give me his decision in the morning.

1st January 1066 (20 months later) – Edmund's diary

The reason Abbot Aethelwig has allowed me to come home for a whole month is because of Edwin. The Abbot had been admiring the carving on the large wooden cross I hang around my neck, and wanted to know more about it. I didn't tell him the whole story – Edwin had asked me not to – but I did tell him about Edwin's remarkable talents. So I returned here for Christmas and the New Year with silver from the Abbey for Edwin to turn into a cross for the high altar.

No one will read this until after I have died so I think I can tell the whole story here. What happened was this. After my first visit to Evesham, I went back to Kingsgate to settle my affairs, such as they were, before becoming a postulant monk, and taking the name 'Brother William'.

One morning I took Dash, one of Father's cob horses, to the forge to be re-shod by Adam, Edwin's son. It was a warm spring day and, outside the forge, Edwin was carving some lettering on a large stone. The old man looked up at me, his lined face covered in stone dust. "Adam's such a fine blacksmith now, I have to learn a new trade," he said with a wry smile.

I read his precisely carved lettering:

> 'The weary cannot control fate
> Nor do bitter thoughts settle things.'

"Ah, 'The Wanderer'," I said. There must have been an edge of surprise in my voice, for Edwin replied:

"Do you think it's only you rich ones who love poetry?" The old man rose stiffly to his feet and put his arm around my shoulders. "When you work with your hands, you have time to think. And I think that, in thousand years from now, people will read this, and they will think that mankind has not changed so very much."

I stayed to watch Adam re-shoe Dash. We were born on the same day so he is more brother to me than estate worker. He does the work that his father and grandfather – and, probably, many generations before that – have done, and with no less skill. As he went about his business, we chatted. He was not keen on monks and monasteries: they had too much money, too much land, too much wine. Their life wasn't safe either. Had I heard about the monk, who, returning with the rents from a monastery estate, had been set upon by robbers and left for dead? Edwin had been listening. He came in and said, gently wagging his right index finger towards me: "I have an idea for you."

His idea was this carved wooden cross with its silver hook and chain. I had forgotten the conversation until, a few weeks later, when I was finally leaving for Evesham, he came to the house, and gave it to me. He hung it round my neck like a trophy. Everyone examined and admired it – it is carved in the old Anglo-Saxon way with birds and animals intertwined: a beautiful piece of craftsmanship.

Edwin then took me to one side where nobody could see. He turned the cross over, and had me take the shorter stem in my right hand, then, with me holding the longer stem in the fingers of my left hand, he told me to press down with my left thumb on the centre of the cross. There was a gentle click. A hidden lever had released the longer wooden stem in my left hand; this slipped away to reveal a steel blade inside and, at the same time, the hook holding the chain fell away. The shining blade was decorated with the same design as its wooden casing, but its point and edges were sharp. In my hand was a dagger.

"So, you see, 'Brother William', if the cross cannot protect you, this will. Do not to show it to anyone. It is our secret."

I clicked the scabbard shut – when it was closed you couldn't tell it came apart – and re-attached the hook; he shook my hand firmly and I left to become a monk.

That was 18 months ago. My month back here is finished, and tomorrow I will return to Evesham with the Abbot's silver, now transformed into a decorated cross. Like my little dagger, it is a masterpiece.

Isabella sat next to me at dinner last night; we spoke in French, although her English is now good. She admitted she had no idea I was ever thinking of becoming a monk; she had always expected to marry me rather than Alfred. Her baby is due in April and, just after midnight, she said to me with those lovely, dark, shining eyes: "This is going to be the happiest year of my life. You must come back for the christening, Edmund." Like all my family, she refuses to call me 'Brother William'.

28th April 1066 (4 months later) – Edmund's diary

I have just read the previous entry in this diary. Those were the last words Isabella would say to me. She died yesterday, a few hours after the baby was born. Adam came here this morning with the news. Alfred is heart-broken. Although nothing had ever been said, Adam understood how much I loved her. The baby – it is a girl – is well.

Why does an almighty God let such a thing happen? Why? We all went outside last night to gaze at the comet[5] in the sky. Some monks say it is the star of Bethlehem; others say it is the harbinger of a catastrophe. I think it is neither. I think the universe is cold and meaningless.

Oh, Isabella.

30th April 1066 – Edmund's diary

The christening was today. Isabella's last words were a request that her daughter also be called Isabella. Maman has taken charge of everything. A girl from the village is feeding the almost unbearably sweet, little baby.

When I arrived Alfred greeted me with the words: "Where's your fucking God now?" Immediately he apologised, threw his arms around me, and wept. I ask the same question.

30th July 1066 (3 months later) – Edmund's diary

I have come to Worcester with Abbot Aethelwig to see Bishop Wulfstan. The abbot told the other monks that the Bishop wanted to learn more about Normandy. On the way, he confided that that was only part of the story.

The bishop, the abbot and myself are all unusually tall. It sounds silly, but I can't shake off the feeling that I am here because of my height rather than my knowledge of Normandy.

Despite the physical similarity, Wulfstan and Aethelwig are very different in character. Aethelwig could have been a soldier; he is forceful, decisive and exudes energy even when he is quiet. He is formidably intelligent and never speaks more than is necessary. Some monks are frightened of him but I have found that, as long as you are truthful, he is kind. He walks quickly with his bald head jutting forward; he always gives the sense that there is some matter of great importance at stake and no time to lose; his cassock flows out behind him, barely able to keep up.

Wulfstan, on the other hand, is the embodiment of calm and charm. On greeting us, he made me feel that the privilege of meeting was for him, rather than me. I mentioned this to a Cathedral canon I was sitting next to at lunch; he laughed saying:

"Yes, it's a great trick, isn't it; he does that to everyone."

I watched him in conversations with small groups and noticed how he takes trouble to make sure that no one is left out; he turns slightly towards one person, then slightly towards another; when listening he inclines his head a little and raises his eyebrows to show that, not only is he listening, but that what has just been said is of unusual interest. In an odd way, he reminds me of Edwin: they are both craftsmen.

After lunch we went to the Bishop's private study. Immediately Wulfstan leaned forward across his desk and asked me to tell him what I knew about the Normans and Duke William. I told him about Walter de Lacy at dinner, and how it seemed that the Normans really did believe that the Duke would be the rightful King of England. And I told him the stories I had heard of the Duke's reaction against anyone who was disrespectful of his mother, and of the impressive display when he rode into Falaise with his cavalcade of horsemen.

The Bishop widened his eyes at the mention of horses. "How many horses were in that cavalcade do you suppose?"

"About a hundred, your Grace?"

"As many as King Harold has in his entire army." He took a deep breath. "Brother William, unlike Father Aethelwig here, I do not know your father, but I do know that the Edmundson family is much respected in Mercia. I can also see for myself that you are both intelligent and sensible, two qualities that seldom go together."

"Thank you, your Grace."

"What is more, Father Aethelwig tells me you can be trusted. So, can I trust you not to repeat anything you hear me or Father Aethelwig say?"

"You can, your Grace."

"Good. In a moment I will explain why you are here, but first I must tell you a little about what we have been doing in recent months. As you know King Edward died last January and Harold Godwinson was crowned King the next day. At the time, several members of the Witan, including myself, were concerned about the legitimacy of a coronation that did not abide by the usual procedures, especially when the whole matter remained open to not unreasonable challenge by several contenders. By contenders I mean not only Edgar the Aetheling, but also Duke William in Normandy and King Harald Hardrada of Denmark."

"It was agreed that Ealdred, the Archbishop of York, and myself, assisted by Abbot Aethelwig, should meet separately and quietly to talk through these concerns."

"When we first met, we agreed we needed to understand better what the threats from Normandy and Denmark might be. We sent monks to both places to learn as much as possible about the intentions of Duke William and Harald Hardrada. We quickly learnt what is now common knowledge: that both men will launch invasions. The king is making preparations to defend England and we hope he will prevail. But, as bishops, we cannot assume he will. Although we cannot do it publicly, we have to prepare for his defeat. We have to try not to be ambushed by events. Do you follow me?"

"I think so."

"In the near future we may have to respond to unpredictable situations. To make this possible, we have – or, I should say, Father Aethelwig has – set up a system for getting messages around the kingdom very quickly. It is good for exchanging information, but not so good when it comes to sharing thoughts. We cannot get together easily to discuss, and argue, and think things through. Doing everything by written message is not satisfactory. Also, it's dangerous." He paused and smiled, "Especially in these times, no one wants to leave their thoughts in writing."

"So, Father Aethelwig is suggesting a different approach. He suggests we have someone who can travel between us all, and whom we can completely trust to represent our views. He has recommended you. He says you have the necessary qualities to do this work. Not least, so I understand, you are a good horseman."

I thought about how Father and Alfred are training the local fyrd[6] in Tamworth every day, how they are preparing to risk their lives in battle, whilst all the time I kneel in the Abbey praying. The other monks at Evesham seem to have an uncomplicated belief in the power of prayer; they are confident that it really can move mountains. I don't have faith like that. Especially after Isabella's death. At that moment, all I felt was relief that the Bishop was giving me something to do.

Tuesday 17th October 1066 – Edmund's diary

In the Abbey this evening we waited and waited for Compline to begin. Eventually Aethelwig strode in, went up to the altar plinth, bowed, and turned to us. He announced in his brisk, unemotional way, that he had just received news from the south coast. On Saturday, the English army had been defeated in battle. King Harold was dead. Many English soldiers had fallen.

There was an audible intake of breath, and a faint sob. I was not the only one to have relations who were there.

The Abbot recited Psalm 46:

> 'God is our refuge and strength, a very present help in trouble.

The Lollard Oak

> Therefore will not we fear, though the earth be removed, and though the mountains be carried into the midst of the sea;
> Though the waters thereof roar and be troubled, though the mountains shake with the swelling thereof …'

I prayed harder than I have ever prayed before. I pleaded with God that Father and Alfred might have been spared. But I feared the worst. The Abbot stood at the doorway as we filed out. He spoke briefly to each of us. To me he said: "Brother William, I also have prayed for your father and brother. Your duty now is to be strong. You will come with me to Worcester tomorrow. We leave after Lauds. Expect to be away for more than a week."

His large hand clasped my shoulder tightly. Dear God, please let them be alive and unharmed.

Wednesday 18th October 1066 – Edmund's diary

We arrived at the Bishop's Palace at 10 o'clock this morning; the bishop was expecting us. He and the abbot talked for several hours; I was the only other person in attendance.

It was mostly about Edgar the Aetheling. Wulfstan was in favour of making him king.

"We have to start by being honest with ourselves, Aethelwig. The Witan allowed itself to be bullied by Harold last January. It seemed an obvious choice but we didn't have time to think it through. Too many important considerations were passed over. Firstly, we knew that Duke William had good reason to believe that he should be the king: King Edward had promised him the throne years ago. Secondly, Earl Harold, as far as we can gather, had – only last year – said he would support the Duke's claim and said it to the Duke himself. Thirdly, even last January, we knew the Duke would not let it rest: we knew he would fight for it. And, lastly, we knew – we knew, Aethelwig – that Duke William is an exceptional commander, and that when he fights, he fights to win. And, on top of all that, we knew that it was Edgar, not Harold or William, who had the strongest claim.

"Dear God, Aethelwig, if ever there was a time to hasten slowly, that was it. But what did we do? We let Harold rush us into making him king. It was sheer weakness on our part. Are we to do the same now with Duke William?

"This time we should be guided by what is right. Edgar is the only living descendant of the royal house of Cerdic and think what that line of kings has done for England. They may not all have been 'Alfreds', but, Aethelwig, we now have a prosperous country. So Edgar must be our starting point. He should have been crowned king last January; that's what we should do now."

Aethelwig did not agree.

"This is madness, Wulfstan. Think: the boy is an immature fourteen year old who has been pampered by his Hungarian mother and sisters. His first language is still Hungarian. It cannot possibly work. To make him king will do nothing but ensure war with Duke William. For what? In the end the Duke will prevail and what will we have achieved? Nothing. Yes, I know there will be powerful support for Edgar but it's foolish."

And so the argument went on. At the end the Bishop looked at me.

"Brother William. Take all this to the Archbishop Ealdred in York. He knows well enough that Aethelwig and I are accustomed to not seeing eye to eye, but he needs to hear it all."

I will set out for York tomorrow. I've done it before and should get there on Sunday. A messenger is coming with me and there are arrangements for changing horses, and for food and lodging, along the way. They suggested I spend tomorrow night at Tamworth; it would be a comfort to my mother. I see Ealdred on Monday, the 23rd, and be back here on Saturday, the 28th.

Not knowing about Father and Alfred is an unceasing torment.

The Lollard Oak

Tuesday 24th October 1066 – Edmund's diary (Doncaster)

Yesterday was the second time I had met Ealdred; he is a well fed, friendly man.

"Ah ha, my pillar of Worcestershire!" At our previous meeting he had referred to the bishop, the abbot and myself as 'The three pillars of Worcestershire' because of our height. "These are bad times. We are still shaken from the battles with the Danes at Fulford[7] and Stamford Bridge[8] and now this. Come. Sit down. Tell me what Wulfstan and Aethelwig are thinking."

I gave him an account of the argument I had heard last Wednesday in Worcester. He sat and listened without saying anything. When I had finished, he sniffed, got up, and walked up and down the room.

"When we don't know what to do, Brother William, it's best to do nothing. Wulfstan is right about hastening slowly. The Witan will not want to be seen to be abandoning the House of Cerdic; they don't want to be called 'traitors', but then Aethelwig is right to be doubtful about Edgar. The thing is: have we got the stomach for a fight when there is so much to lose? Are we willing to put our lives and wealth at risk for the sake of an Anglo-Saxon king who isn't really an Anglo-Saxon, and may well not be much of a king?"

"On the other hand, if we do go against Edgar, would the Duke be any better? He might be worse. Or, perhaps he just wants to extract money from us and go away, like Cnut[9] in 1016. After all, at bottom, he's a Viking. The truth is we just don't know."

"I suppose I could simply refuse to crown either Edgar or William. Neither would want to be crowned by Stigand, and it would take months for the Pope to replace us. That might buy time. The Duke wouldn't like it." He stopped walking up and down, and laughed:

"He might cut off my head in a rage. Then they would have to make me a saint."

"Whichever way you look at it, Brother William, this is a damnable mess. What does Stigand think? Do you know? Does anyone know? For all his unscrupulous behaviour, he is Archbishop of Canterbury and we can't leave him out. You must tell your fellow pillars not to forget Stigand. He may be excommunicated, but it's never a good idea to underestimate Stigand."

Thursday 26th October 1066 – Edmund's diary

I got to Kingsgate at dusk on my return from York. As our horses approached the house, Maman came running down the lane towards us, shouting: "Ils vont bien! Ils vont bien! Ils vont bien". Tears were streaming down her face. My prayers had been answered. It had taken them ten days to get back, but they had arrived yesterday, uninjured.

Father and Alfred were in a different mood to Maman. They had seen dreadful things. The Tamworth fyrd had fought well, so there was no shame, but there were a dozen familiar names who will not be returning home. Suddenly, and for the first time, it all felt real. They had had to spend the day visiting households nearby. "I'm not sure it wasn't worse than the fighting itself," said Father.

The battle was near a town called Hastings in Sussex. It lasted all day. Neither of them actually saw the death of the King, but there was no doubting it. And not just the king, but his two brothers as well. Father is insistent that the English should have won; he believed that the defeat was caused by a single, reckless error by some ill-trained English soldiers on the right flank. The Norman cavalry on that side had pretended to retreat – it was well-known trick – and some of the English, believing they had won the day, charged down the hill after them. Father and other thanes screamed at them to stop, but it was too late. The shield wall, which had held all day, was broken; the Norman cavalry turned and there was a rout. The slaughter was terrible. Father told me all this. Alfred was silent. He has seen things that I haven't seen. There is a gulf between us now.

The Lollard Oak

I am too tired to write more. I feel haunted by Alfred's silence. I try to imagine what it was like for him, but my mind recoils.

Sunday 29th October 1066 – Edmund's diary

When I finished telling Wulfstan and Aethelwig about my visit to Ealdred, Aethelwig was furious. He banged the table with his fist: "It's all 'on the one hand this', and 'on the other hand that'. It won't do."

The Bishop leaned across the table and gently patted the Abbot's fist: "Father Aethelwig, calm down, don't be so harsh. We are all confused; the whole country is confused. None of us wants to find ourselves on the losing side, and Ealdred is in the eye of the storm because it will be him, not Stigand, who has to anoint ..."

Aethelwig interrupted: "There is only one question before the country now."

"And what is that?", asked the patient Wulfstan.

"Can the result of the battle be reversed? That's the question. If it can be, then, yes, perhaps we should play for time. But if it can't, we have to do whatever gives us the most influence over the Duke."

"Many good people, including, I expect, the Witan, will say 'yes, it can be reversed'."

"It doesn't matter how 'good' they are, Wulfstan. What matters is: are they 'wise'? Anyway, come on Wulfstan, what do *you* say?"

Aethelwig then stared at the flagstones rather than at the bishop. The bishop turned to me and said:

"Brother William, you know as much as we do and, unlike us, you have actually seen the Duke. What do you feel about this?"

Aethelwig looked up at me with an expression as if to say: 'I would also like to know what you think.'

I had been thinking about it. Of course, I had. Apart from anything else, as I rode along, mile after mile, day after day, I needed things to think about other than what might have happened to my father and brother. And, as I thought about it, I always came up

The Lollard Oak

against the same problem which I now articulated: "Who would lead an army against the Duke?"

They both laughed.

"You see, Wulfstan. Well, Brother William, the answer is 'no one'. There is no one."

The bishop responded: "There are the Earls Edwin and Morcar but, yes, you are right: there is no one adequate. And, without a leader, we cannot challenge the Duke."

"And if we can't challenge him, we must submit. And there's an end of it."

They were both quiet as they took in the implications of this. Aethelwig eventually asked:

"What about Stigand?"

"What? As a leader against the Duke? Are you mad?"

"No, no, of course not," Aethelwig said. "I was moving on. The point is: Ealdred is right; we cannot ignore Stigand. We all assume that Stigand will not crown the next king, regardless of who it is, for the simple reason that no one wants to be crowned by an excommunicated Archbishop of Canterbury. It's exactly as it was for you when you refused to be consecrated by him: you didn't want the validity of your consecration to be open to challenge. But, just because of all that, we must not forget the even more simple truth that no one in England will go against Stigand. Ealdred is right: Stigand is the key."

"Stigand does what's good for Stigand."

"Ho, ho. So, the gentle bishop has a sharp side. Yes, he is, as Ealdred says, 'unscrupulous', but he never fails to weave a magic spell around anyone who might be useful to him. I think Duke William could be useful to him. Did you hear that the Duke was flying a papal banner at the battle? In any event he obviously has Pope Alexander's support. If I was Stigand, I would want to make friends with William so that he can help lift the excommunication. There's no advantage for Stigand with Edgar as king."

"You must go and see Stigand, Aethelwig. He doesn't like me because of that consecration business, but he respects you."

Tuesday, All Hallows Eve 1066 – Edmund's diary

Tomorrow, I leave for Winchester. The abbot is not sure where Stigand is, but calculates he is most likely to be there. He is Bishop of Winchester as well as of Canterbury, this 'plurality' being the cause of his excommunication. A messenger is also going to Canterbury.

Monday, 6th November 1066 – Edmund's diary

I have a room at the Archbishop's Palace in Winchester and, at the suggestion of His Grace – he said I wouldn't be disappointed – I went out at dawn this morning, and walked across the water meadows to St Catherine's Hill, a mile or more south of the city. At the top there are circular trenches, the remains of a pre-historic fort; beech trees grow there now. It was a chilly morning and the sky was deep blue. I watched the sun rise over the golden downland to the east and south. Behind me the city was swathed in mist. I could see, half-submerged, the bell towers of churches, the palace, and the Old Minster.

I was entranced. As the sun climbed imperceptibly in the sky, I sat on one of the ridges of the old fort and ruminated. This is the England my father and brother were fighting for. Men and women looked out from this same spot a thousand years ago. No, more, much more. Long before the Romans. What long-forgotten disputes enraged them then? A thousand years from now, another 'me' will sit in this same place and see the same sun and the same fields. What thoughts will he have? Will all this loveliness still be stained with anger and fear?

The Archbishop was right: I wasn't disappointed.

He has agreed to see Aethelwig. A messenger has been sent with a proposal to meet in Oxford next Saturday. He must think I might

The Lollard Oak

be useful: he has asked me to stay here and treats me like a friend. He wanted to know about my family. He is especially interested in my mother's relations and that I speak perfect French. He knows that at some point he will meet Duke William, and I have a feeling that I shall be the interpreter.

Saturday, 11th November 1066 – Edmund's diary

It was curious to see Abbot Aethelwig with Archbishop Stigand. The abbot is not a diplomat; normally he likes to get to the point without any flummery, and hates it when others fail to be as straightforward as he is. But suddenly, yesterday, he was on best behaviour: it was all "Your Grace this" and "Your Grace that".

But he read his man well. He explained to the excommunicated Archbishop how Duke William, as king, would influence the papacy. He suggested that the Duke, being a man of action, would respond well to decisive leadership on the part of 'your Grace'. Although the Duke sees himself as pursuing a 'just cause', he is a pious man, and will be gratified to receive 'your Grace's' confirmation that, in the eyes of God, it is, indeed, 'just'. And then once William has come to trust 'your Grace', he will, as Cnut had done so successfully only 50 years ago, leave the governance of England to such as the Archbishop.

I watched Stigand throughout this performance; he was soft clay in Aethelwig's hands.

Saturday, 25th November 1066 – Edmund's diary

Although his position as an abbot does not give Aethelwig any formal authority beyond Evesham, it is plain that everyone defers to him. He arrived here in Oxford two weeks ago with messengers and scribes; he was intent on taking charge and, after their meeting, the Archbishop was content to give the energetic abbot a free hand.

The Lollard Oak 1085

Messengers were sent in all directions; their messages bore the Archbishop's seal but were dictated by Aethelwig. They went to Duke William and to all of the Witan. Within a week Stigand and Aethelwig could send to William the assurances he wanted. Yesterday we heard from Edgar and the earls Edwin and Morcar that they too have agreed to submit.

This morning I walked with the abbot along the River Cherwell down to where it meets the River Thames. I think he just needed to put words onto all the thoughts that are crowding his mind. This is what he told me.

As soon as he heard the news of the defeat at Hastings, and the death, not only of Harold but also of Harold's two brothers, he knew it was an irreversible event. He commended me for seeing that too. Without a leader capable of uniting the country and matching William's military skill, there was no means of defeating the Duke.

He did not think Harold would have been a good king – he too was a 'bastard' but at least he was 'our bastard'. His first worry was that many English thanes would not accept William as their king; many of them were vain, ignorant and stupid hotheads who would be incapable of seeing that trying to remove William was a fool's errand. There is nothing more pointless than fighting a battle you cannot win, but there is something in the English temperament that rebels against such a self-evident truth.

But his main worry was what would happen following resistance to William's rule. It would fail, but failure was not the problem. William would then respond in a disproportionate way. William believes, profoundly, that his cause is just, and such a belief can make even a kind man cruel. But William is not a kind man. He will not stop at putting an English rebellion down; he will crush it, and then treat its leaders, and the English as a whole, savagely.

So how would this end? With, he asserted, the dispossession of land, the loss of rights and laws, the subjugation of the English people, the end of Anglo-Saxon England, and, with that, the

The Lollard Oak 1085

destruction of our culture of literature and art. We had to find another way.

I listened, but, in truth, he was talking to himself. There is, he went on, a side to William's character that we can use to our advantage. The Duke is loyal to those who are loyal to him; he is pious – he makes his confession to a monk at least once a week; he is faithful to his wife; he is loved by his soldiers; he does not ask them to do things he won't do himself; he is intelligent. If we accept him, he will accept us.

The best course of action for the English now is to swallow our pride, and submit graciously to his sovereignty. The Duke will not wage war on an enemy that wishes to be a friend. In one stroke he will be disarmed. If he wants to take wealth from us then he must want us first to be wealthy, and, to be wealthy, we must be able to go about our business in peace.

By this means the old order can be restored and we can salvage something from this disaster. This was the least worst road to go down. All others lead to ruin.

On Monday we make the short journey to Wallingford[10] with Archbishop Stigand and his train where we will meet the Duke face to face. I am to translate.

Monday, 27th November 1066 – Edmund's diary

We were with Duke William for over an hour. He really is a giant of a man, taller even than me and much broader. He towered over the Archbishop. Stigand assumed his most charming manner; he was friendly and flattering to the mighty Norman, as only he can be. As I translated I did my best to make his words, in French, sound yet more gracious.

It didn't work. Not once did the Duke smile in response. It was very disconcerting. Stigand, already small in comparison with the Duke, looked weak and insignificant.

As I did my translations, first one way, then the other, I was distracted by the sight of Walter de Lacy standing behind the Duke next to the Duke's brother, the Bishop of Bayeux, who was dressed in chain mail. de Lacy, also in armour, stared at me unflinchingly; I assume he recognised me, but he said nothing. My mind went back to that dinner in Falaise and how Isabella had whispered in my ear: "We all think he is a horrible man." But I could not let the thought of Isabella distract me.

It was agreed that there would be a further submission at Berkhamsted in a week's time, when Edgar, accompanied by other bishops and the earls, will attend.

William told Stigand to remain with him until that meeting, but that we – all the rest of us – were to leave. Stigand opened his mouth momentarily, as if he were about to refuse the instruction, but, on seeing – as we all did – the Duke move his right hand onto the hilt of his sword, he remained silent.

On our journey back to Oxford, Aethelwig did not speak. Before retiring, with a serious demeanour, he asked me what I thought of the day's events. I told him of my discomfort that not one of the Normans had smiled. He replied: "Yes. I have underestimated how difficult this is going to be."

23rd June 1067 (7 months later) – From Cuthbert to Edmund

My dear son Edmund,

I am writing with some terrible news. Early this morning we found Edwin and his servant boy murdered behind the hedge along the lane that leads to the house. Their throats had been cut. Adam is inconsolable. When he saw his father's body in the lamplight he let out a howl such as I have never heard from a human being; his grief is unbearable to witness. I need not tell you what an irreplaceable loss this is to me, Maman and Alfred. He was family. The servant boy I only knew by sight; Maman is with his parents now.

I feel it is my fault. Yesterday afternoon we got news that the King's men would be here any day; they have found out I was at Hastings. We were worried beyond measure. There are stories of confiscation and exile; the least punishment is to have to buy one's own land and be left all but destitute. The King has taken possession of all land and can do with it as he wills.

Edwin came to the house yesterday evening; he had heard that they were searching houses and, on our behalf, was worried about Wulthere's chest. He suggested that he and the boy take it in the cart, and bury it far from the house, deep under the plough. It was obviously a sensible thing to do; I could hardly refuse. They then came with Dash, the cob, and cart and the big stone – the one with carved writing from outside the forge; he was going to bury it on top of the chest to give protection against a chance discovery. As they rushed off, I asked where they were going; he shouted back that he had a good place in mind. Then they were gone. It was dark when we went out to search for them; several hours later we found them behind the hedge.

We had heard stories of outlaws roaming the countryside but there had been nothing here. The bastards took Dash and the cart and the chest, even that worthless stone, and left just the bodies behind. The loss of the treasure is great of course – it breaks my heart to think that the amazing workmanship of our ancestors will be melted down and never seen again – but that is as nothing compared to the loss of Edwin and that poor boy.

Please come; we need you here.

Your loving father,

Cuthbert

30th July 1067 (A month later) – From Aethelwig to Cuthbert

Cuthbert,

I have come to an agreement with the Earl of Hereford, William FitzOsbern. You are not to be exiled, you are to be allowed to buy back up to 2 of your 18 hides of land, and you can keep the house and other buildings without cost. With this letter there is a sealed copy of the agreement.

All I can ask is that you believe me when I say that I have done *everything* in my power to help you. What we are up against is the King's unwavering conviction that all the thanes who fought at Hastings were committing treason against their rightful king, and that the law must be applied. I put your case to the Earl as clearly and forcibly as I could. Were the Earl free to judge for himself, I think the outcome might have been more favourable, but he is, even with this agreement, stepping outside the instructions given to him by King William, and, he says, he cannot go further. I am satisfied that this is, indeed, the truth.

I had hoped it would be helpful that Emma's family is known to Walter de Lacy, but de Lacy is a deeply unpleasant man, and so this has counted for less than it ought to have. The main thing in your favour has been Brother William's work as an interpreter; the Earl needs your son's services, and with our Norman masters that is the only thing which counts, albeit not so very much.

I know this will come as a blow on top of your other troubles and I am sorry.

Yours, in friendship,
Father Aethelwig

23rd December 1085 (18 years later) – Edmund's diary

Because I speak French, Abbot Walter recommended me for a position as a 'Royal Confessor'. I didn't want it, but he insisted – it confers status on the Abbey – and my vows require me to obey. It means that I can be called upon to take the King or Queen's confession, and that I am now to be called 'Father William'.

It was not information that I could withhold from my family when I visited Kingsgate in August. It was bad enough telling them

The Lollard Oak

myself, but it would have been far worse had they heard about it from someone else. The vicious row which ensued was predictable.

The break-down in relations with Alfred that occurred after the events of 1075 had, I thought, healed over, but, as I feared it would, this set him off once more. He accused me, again, of conniving with thieves and murderers, of hating my own people, and of living comfortably whilst the ordinary English starved. He mocked how a confession with King William would go, imitating the King's deep voice:

"I feel so very bad about having that Anglo-Saxon serf torn limb from limb. What penance must I do?"

"Alfred, you know it's not like that."

"Yes, and what is it 'like' exactly? Will he tell you how difficult it was for him to decide whether to tear him limb from limb, or just stuff a red hot poker up his arse for failing to bow low enough? And what will you do to save his fucking everlasting soul? How about a dozen 'Hail Mary's'? That should fix it. It's disgusting. After what that bastard has done to your own brother, how can you want to make that vile creature feel better? And don't tell me there's any other reason for doing these bleeding confessions."

I had no answer.

He went on: "I'll tell you what you can do, 'Father bloody William'. If you're going to be all alone with the bastard, doing his confession, you've got a chance to kill him. If you had any loyalty to your family and your people, you'd hide a dagger under that habit of yours and slice his throat open. At least every single Norman from then on would know how much we hate them. Why don't you do that?"

"Why don't you do that?". "Why don't you do that?". Alfred's words will not leave me alone.

Tomorrow I shall be at the Royal Palace in Gloucester. The French monk is ill and I have been summoned; I find that Alfred's question has, without my volition, been turned in my mind from 'why don't you do that?' into 'why *did* he do that?'.

I must explain everything. I will start with my last diary entry, nearly 20 years ago. It was the day of Archbishop Stigand's submission at Wallingford. That entry finishes with Father Aethelwig saying, presciently: "I have underestimated how difficult this is going to be." When he was dying eleven years later – eight years ago now – I sat beside his bed and he spoke about those times.

"I am not proud of what I did. I was too sure of myself. I convinced myself that with a little cunning we could manage William and mould him into a kind of Cnut. I thought I had the measure of Duke William. I believed he had two reasons for invading England and neither of them needed him to spend time here."

"The first reason was that 'he had to': there would have been too much loss of face if he hadn't. The second reason was 'he wanted to be a king, not just a duke'."

"So, I assumed that, with his hands full defending those unsettled borders with France and Brittany, he wouldn't want to get sucked into the affairs of England. He didn't speak the language; why would England be of interest to him? Much better just to copy Cnut, hand the country over to a few trusted earls, take the taxes, and let it run itself. It seemed obvious."

"How wrong I was. There is something in the character of the French and Normans that we Anglo-Saxons do not understand. They actually like to control others; we don't; not so much anyway. That is what I saw at Wallingford. When the Duke ordered Stigand not to leave with us, we all saw how his hand went to his sword hilt just as Stigand was about to protest. I realised then that I had a wrong picture of William in my mind. But it was too late."

"On all sides I had been too much respected: Wulfstan, Ealdred, Stigand; I could persuade them Jesus was a gentile. I had no difficulty in persuading myself that anyone who disagreed with me must be wrong. I despised all those who wanted to resist the Normans: I was wise and they were insular, narrow-minded fools." Aethelwig looked up at me from his bed. "It's not how things have turned out, is it, Brother William?"

He died shortly afterwards.

To my shame I treated Alfred with that same haughty contempt; I was in thrall to Aethelwig. Now, more than I can say, I regret our bitter arguments; I regret not seeing that Alfred's uncalculating honesty had more intelligence to it than all my learning. Alfred saw a William who, by force and terror, ruled a country he did not love: that was all the information he needed to be able to judge him evil. I wish the rest of us could have had that simple clarity. Instead, led by the bishops and archbishops, we were supine. We let a gang of thieves and murderers take our beloved land without a real fight. Yes, we might well have lost, but we would have been an inspiration to those who came after.

I am told that land once owned by 5,000 Anglo-Saxon thanes – most of the land in England – is now the property of just 190 Norman knights. Has there ever been a greater theft of land by one people from another in the history of the world? I doubt it.

I had been disturbed by William's treatment of Stigand at Wallingford, but I was not horrified by it. Somehow, by a trick of mind, I couldn't see things as they were. The confiscation of the thanes' estates, the extortion, such as Father had to endure in buying back his own land, the slavery of thousands of Englishmen forced to build castles for the Normans, so that their subjugation could be made permanent: it was all either divine justice, or a Job-like test sent from God.

Alfred and I saw the same thing. Whilst he was outraged, I was walking around our Abbey cloisters contemplating the theology of it.

It was only in February 1070 that the fog in my head cleared suddenly away. That was when the first refugees from the north dragged themselves wretchedly into Evesham. By April there were over a thousand, and the Abbey itself was made into a home for them. Aethelwig did not hold back; he did everything possible to provide shelter, sustenance and care. They arrived in a steady trickle: cold, wet, exhausted, and starving. Many died soon after their arrival, some, cruelly, from filling their starving stomachs with food which they were unable to digest, but mostly because they were too weak to live. And these were the survivors.

What we saw was bad enough, but, for them, it was the horrors they carried in their minds – and could not escape – that really tormented them. There was screaming and moaning at night. We kept a watch and gave what comfort we could. The stories made sleep difficult for us too. Husbands, wives, children murdered; whole villages razed to the ground; men put to the sword; women raped; all the livestock slaughtered. We later learnt that tens of thousands of plough oxen had been killed for no purpose other than to ensure that there could be no recovery. This was how King William was 'controlling' his people.

It was at this time that I stopped translating for the Earl of Hereford. Alfred took over from me; with Father having lost nearly everything, it provided an income. When the Earl died in 1071 it was only natural that his son, Roger de Breteuil, who was only 15 at the time, should want Alfred to continue. This worried me, but only a little at first. I had seen Roger grow up. I knew he had none of his father's qualities; he was consumed with his own self-importance, no one dared to deny him, and he was without restraint in everything, especially drink. I knew that Alfred, whose French was as fluent as mine, had been adopted as a drinking companion – there was never a time when Alfred was capable of turning down the offer of a glass or tankard. So, when, in 1075, I heard of Roger's ambition to unseat the King, and of his promise, in return for support, to restore to Alfred all our land, I brushed it aside. Why take seriously the vomit-laden nonsense of a drunken nineteen year old?

I then discovered from Alfred that he and Roger had exchanged 'vows': Alfred was clutching at the tiniest of straws in the hope of recovering our land, but he was also adamant that he had to honour his promise to support the young Earl. The rebellion, which included the Earls of East Anglia and of Northumberland, was insane in its conception and hopeless in its execution. I was in despair that my impulsive brother could have such a misplaced sense of honour, but he was blind to all reason.

Yes, I know, to use the word 'blind' is unfortunate. I pleaded with Alfred to abandon his involvement with 'The Revolt of the Three Earls', or, as we all called it at the time, 'The Revolt of the Three Fools'. But, when I discovered that Alfred had been taken prisoner at Bridgnorth by Walter de Lacy, my despair turned to abject fear. If only it had been Bishop Wulfstan, who was also there preventing that rag bag army from crossing the Severn. Father Aethelwig did intercede on Alfred's behalf with the king but it was no use. The king reminded the abbot that, in earlier days, rebellious subjects would have had their arms and their legs cut off, and left to die. He waved Aethelwig away, commenting that the traitor should be grateful it was nothing more drastic than blinding with a red hot iron.

Maman's hair had been dark, almost black, until then. It turned white overnight. Both of them, Mother and Father, were all but paralysed by it. The extraordinary thing was how young Isabella responded. She was only nine but, from one day to the next, she became an adult. She nursed Alfred so lovingly, changed the bandages on his eyes, and was constantly by his side. She still is. And then there was dear, loyal Adam; we were so lucky to have had Adam.

I suppose Alfred needed to have someone to point his rage at, but I wish it had been someone other than me. I look at poor, blinded Alfred, angry and hating, his life in ruins, and I can hardly remember the brother who used to dance so badly, and make us laugh so much. His is the story of England.

We have all seen and suffered too much. No Englishman or woman left living has escaped. There will be no restitution. Not in my lifetime. The Normans, seeing themselves in possession of all the land and wealth of England, cannot but regard themselves as superior to the Anglo-Saxons. We English, having lost everything, call these unwelcome visitors 'scum' and 'bastard' in feeble retaliation. And, in the dark hours of the night, we lie helplessly awake, aware of an over-

The Lollard Oak

riding, all-powerful, black Satanic presence across our land. We look up in loathing; they look down with contempt.

Tomorrow morning, before I leave for Gloucester, I shall send this diary by messenger to Adam for safe-keeping. I have Edwin's cross around my neck; my course is set. It will be my end as well as his. There is nothing left to say.

14th October 1144 – 2nd Letter from Isabella to Edwin

My dear son Edwin,

Thank you for sending news that the diary arrived safely, and for your kind, if inaccurate, remark about me being 'still like that nine year old girl'. If only!

But I am most relieved to write that, at last, I have found the missing parchment. A young novice had taken it to line a cabinet drawer in her cell; I don't think she can read. Her poor little eyes would have popped out of her head if she could. Edmund wrote it on these separate sheets of parchment after he had sent the rest of the diary to Adam at the forge; it was too dangerous to send it to us at Kingsgate. As you will see, it is astonishing.

Your loving mother,
Isabella

26th December 1085 – Edmund's diary

Despite being a monk, and despite having a letter sealed by the Abbot, I was searched first on my arrival in Gloucester on Christmas Eve, and then again in the ante-room next to the King's chamber. For the first time in my life, I was doing something brave. I felt proud and terrified in equal measure. One of the soldiers, as he patted me, took hold of Edwin's cross, admiring its workmanship and unusual weight.

The head steward who accompanied me was eager to talk. They were worried about the King; for several days he had neither eaten nor left his chamber. He was not sure if he had slept either. Also, he had spoken very little, and, according to the steward, when he did speak, it was difficult to understand, other than that it was about his wife, Queen Matilda, who died two years ago.

They were all hoping that 'the monk from Evesham' might be able to help. As I entered the chamber I tried to keep my mind fixed on a single, narrow track. My purpose was to kill the King; I was not to be diverted. I took the short stem of Edwin's cross in my right hand and turned it over.

In the centre of the large chamber, which had more than a dozen torches around the walls, was a long, wide and heavily built oak table, almost black, and highly polished. It was positioned so as to divide the room with the King on the other side from me. In my preparations I had never considered this possible arrangement of furniture. I could feel my resolution wavering. There was no way of reaching him without going all the way around the table and, to do that, I would give him warning.

An equal surprise was the sight of the King himself. I had forgotten just what a big man he was. Yet how different now to the warrior who had intimidated us at Wallingford! Now his hair was white: then it had been fair; now his skin was cracked like parched mud: then it had been smooth. But it was his sunken, red, and watery eyes that really shocked me. Could this be the man they used to call 'the terror of the earth'?

He beckoned me over.

"Father William, Matilda wants you to look at this." His voice was the same deep voice I remembered from twenty years' ago. I approached the table and, as I did so, he turned a very large illuminated book round so that it faced me the right way up. The illuminations were dazzling, of a quality and sophistication I had never seen before.

"Matilda made the Bishop of Durham bring it with him when he came here earlier this week. It comes from the monastery at Lindisfarne[11]. She wanted me to see it," he continued.

Has he lost his mind, I wondered. "But your Queen died two years ago."

"Yes, indeed, she did, but she comes back to me every day now. You probably think I'm mad but I am not. I tell you she comes to me. I see her just as clearly as I am seeing you now, Father William. She wanted me to see this and she wants you to see it too."

"Why does she want us to see it?", I asked.

"For the same reason that she wants us to see this."

On his right there was some folded cloth lying on the table. He picked it up and carefully unfolded it. It was an embroidered bishop's cope. He lay its full length – about five feet – across that end of the table. The needlework was breathtaking in design and intricacy and colour.

"Opus Angli …", there was a tremor in his voice, "… canum[12]. 'The work of the English'." It seemed that he was on the verge of crying. I remained quiet.

"Can you say why she wants us to see these things?" I asked again.

King William drew up a chair and sat down; with a wave of his hand, he indicated that I should do likewise on my side of the table. I did.

"Matilda – I swear to you – came here, here, in this very chamber, to tell me I am not long for this world. She begged me to examine my sins, especially my 'English' sins. I must repent before it is too late. I said I didn't know where to start. She wouldn't answer me. She just recited an Anglo-Saxon poem called 'The Wanderer'. As she did so, a tear fell down her cheek. I didn't know why – I don't know the language. She said the only thing I had to know was that the English can write poetry of such beauty that it is unnatural not to cry. She then told me that the Bishop of Durham would bring these Gospels from Lindisfarne, and the Bishop of Lincoln this cope.

"So now, Brother William, I see in front of me 'the work of the English'. How did I not see it before?

"I came, we all came, on our high horses, despising the English. We were going to stamp out their insolent resistance. We were the masters and they, you, our slaves. I could do what I liked. And I did. All the while I did not notice that the English have a government like no other, that everything in every shire, in every hundred, is organised so that people can live orderly lives. I did not notice that you have laws that come from your soil, like an old elm tree, 'the law of the land' you call it. We came and took all the land, but the law survived. And now I have before me these Gospels and this cope – this Opus Anglicanum."

He stared across the table at me, his reddened eyes wide open. They were like eyes that had looked into the jaws of hell itself, and can never be the same again. It reminded me of that look on Alfred's face after the battle at Hastings.

"How could we, Father William, coming from so slight a place as Normandy – a place, in comparison to England, with no culture, no poetry, no stories, no history, no law, no settled government, a place where the laws are made from steel, not respect for one another as here? How could we come and imagine ourselves even your equals, let alone your masters? How could we? And how could I then ravage this country so mercilessly? And steal from you all your land and wealth? What is my reward? Sleepless nights and your undying hatred.

"There is something I should tell you about myself, Brother William. I became Duke of Normandy when I was seven. There was chaos there for the first twelve years of my reign. A few brave men, close friends of my father's, protected me. One of them, my steward, Osbern, would sleep near me in my chamber every night. And then, when I was 13 an assassin crept in, cut his throat clean through, and left. Why did he spare me? I don't know. I pretended to be asleep and that is what I told everyone afterwards. But it's not true; I was awake. I saw, in the faint light, everything; I heard the slice of the knife and the gush of the blood."

He paused and shifted in his chair. "I may look, now, like a mighty king but, inside, I am still that little boy. I was a little boy who believed he was about to have his throat sliced open. I am still stuck in that moment of time."

We sat together in silence for a long time.

"I am a practical man, Father William. I have these regrets – and I do have them, truly I do – but what good is it? It might make me feel better but it does nothing to put right what I have done wrong. What can I do? That is the question I have been asking myself. And Matilda."

"I am so overwhelmed with the guilt of it all that I cannot think clearly. Today Matilda has given me instructions. She tells me there is no simple way to make restitution. I cannot give the land back; my fellow Normans will not allow it and, anyway, who would I give it to?"

"Her instruction is to make a complete survey of England, of every landholding in every shire and hundred. I am to make a record of who owns it now, and who owned it in 1066. She reminded me that only in England does the organisation exist to make such work possible. It is a survey that will last forever. My repentance will be to make an everlasting record of my shame."

"But Matilda says it will be more than that. She says it will be like a piece of grit in the oyster shell of England; it will always be there, reminding the English of how great their loss has been; it will never cease to irritate them, generation after generation, and it will irritate them into a struggle to reclaim their country and their land. That is to be my restitution. It is not everything but it is something. And, as Matilda says, I can do it without the sin of pride because no one will ever believe I did it other than to exert more control, and exact more tax."

The King closed his red and watery eyes. Within a few moments he had fallen asleep in his chair.

My stomach tightened into a knot. Silently I extracted my long legs from the chair. And silently I made my way around the table. I had turned Edwin's cross around and could feel, but not hear, the gentle click as the long stem and chain came away. The light of the

The Lollard Oak

torches reflected off the steel, and I held the smooth blade next to the grizzled skin around his throat.

What stopped me avenging Alfred and England? Was it fear? I would have to kill myself, or be tortured and mutilated. Was it forgiveness? Our Lord taught that with repentance comes forgiveness. Was it that I persuaded myself to believe his 'grit in the oyster' idea? It might be far-fetched but it was not quite nonsensical. Or was it, simply, that it would do no good?

I slipped out of the King's chamber and went to the room reserved for me at the Palace.

The next day – yesterday – was Christmas. I wanted to return to Evesham as soon as possible but, before I left, the steward came to me in a state of excitement. He thanked me for coming more than was required by simple politeness. What had I had said to the King? The change in the King was miraculous; he was eating and cheerful. I shrugged my shoulders and said that I had done nothing but listen.

He handed me a note bearing the King's seal. Inside were these words: "Father William, Thank you for sparing me. Merci."

18th October 1144 – 3rd Letter from Isabella to Edwin

My dear son Edwin,

You must have read the missing diary entry now. What do you think? Was King William really awake? Did Edmund really mean to assassinate the King? Was the King going mad? Or did he really see his dead wife and receive her 'instructions'? I just find it difficult to believe that this most cruel of men genuinely repented. As for the bizarre idea, that what they now call 'The Domesday Book' will inspire the English to get their country back, that is just the sentimental nonsense of an old, mad man, is it not? I am glad Edmund stayed his hand.

Something strange happened the first time I read this entry – Uncle Edmund showed it to me when I came here in 1110. Your father, Adam, had died the previous year and I wanted to be near

The Lollard Oak

Edmund, the only person left who had known Alfred, Grandpa, Grand-maman, and Adam.

Adam and I married in 1095, five years after my poor father, Alfred, died. Adam had always been a second father to me, and so it never occurred to me that I could love him 'as a man'; for his part, he thought it impossible for him, a blacksmith, to marry me, a 'lady'; that is how he saw me, even though we had lost almost all our land and wealth.

When you arrived soon after, it felt like the horrors were behind us. But then I started to have this horrible nightmare. In it, a baby was in my arms which had two heads on one body. One head was ugly like a demon and was sucking me dry of milk. The other head was angelic, but couldn't get at my breast and was starving to death; it had lost the strength to cry and just whimpered faintly.

I would wake screaming and Adam would put his arms around me. Once he suggested that, in the dream, I was England and that, I – England – was being sucked dry by the Norman demon, while the English people suffered. I said that didn't make sense because my mother was Norman and my father was half-Norman? He said: "No, no. You are English. Anyone who loves England is English." It's true, I do feel English.

This nightmare went on for years. Every night when I said my prayers I would plead with God not to let me have it. But then, when I came here, and read that final diary entry, it stopped and never came back.

In my long life I have noticed that very few things are completely good or completely bad, but I don't think this rule applies to the Conquest. The bad that followed on from that day in October 1066 was total. Something imperfect but, to us, of immeasurable value – our Anglo-Saxon world – was lost forever, and replaced by something very inferior.

Worse, it changed us Anglo-Saxons into a sullen and angry race. We look up at our masters, the Normans, and are consumed with loathing for their arrogance, their undeserved wealth, and the

The Lollard Oak

unparalled theft of our land. And we have to endure the Normans looking down on us with contempt. They imitate our English accents and laugh, as if their French language and Norman ways were superior.

It's not that we were an equal society before, but there was a commonality between the thanes and the ordinary people; we belonged to one another; we needed each other; there was a shared bond, a language, history, culture; we were one people. What price can you put on that? Today all that has gone; there are two peoples, speaking two languages, living separate lives. The Normans wealthy with a wealth stolen from the English; the English, poor, condemned to servitude, and without hope of equality.

And where is there an end of it? Is it not sad how habits of mind harden as they pass from generation to generation? It is almost eighty years now since the Conquest, but I recall that poem 'The Wanderer' which Queen Matilda recited to the King William, and of how:

> 'The weary cannot control fate
> Nor do bitter thoughts settle things.'

The unrelenting truth is that the 'bitter thoughts' are still with us. Nothing is 'settled'.

I look out from my cell here in Evesham and see, in the far distance, the sun setting behind the Malvern hills. I am reminded of my Uncle Edmund on that hill outside Winchester watching the sun rise. Like him, I imagine another 'me', a thousand years from now, watching the same sun go down behind the same hills, and ask myself: 'What kind of England will she see?'

Your loving mother,

Isabella

Chapter Three: 1381

'When Adam delved and Eve span,
Who was then the gentleman?'

John Bull
Lollard preacher

1381 – Dramatis Personae

Cuthbert Edmundson, Gentleman of Tamworth
Emma Edmundson, his wife, sister of Edith de Lacy
William Edmundson, their son, aged 20
Alfred Edmundson, their son, aged 19
Isabella Edmundson, their daughter, aged 16

Roger de Lacy, Baron of Weobley, owner of Ludlow Castle
Edith de Lacy, his wife, sister of Emma Edmundson
Osric, Steward to the de Lacys

Bishop John Gilbert, Bishop of Hereford
Raphael, his Chaplain

Edwin, Blacksmith to the Edmundson estate
Adam, son of Edwin

John, an itinerant Lollard preacher

1381

Monday, 15th July 1381, St. Swithun's Day[1]
Roger de Lacy (Ludlow Castle) – *translated from the French*

It makes my blood boil. For three hundred years the de Lacys have kept the Marcher lands secure from the Welsh, and what have we got for our pains? 'Baron of Weobley'! 'Baron of Weobley'! Last year, I noticed how my cousin – the Earl of bloody Lincoln – sniggered when the herald announced my arrival: 'Roger de Lacy, Baron of Weobley'.

It was in 1345, when I was 16, and my father had put down the Welsh, that King Edward promised to make him 'Earl of Ludlow'[2]. At last, our family would be the equal of the greatest in the land. But then there was Crécy[3] and the war in France, and the plague, and it never happened.

I want it for myself, of course I do, but I also want it for my father. I wish I could say I want it for my son. Edith reminds me not to set my heart on earthly things. She's probably right, dear thing, but, by God, is it not galling to own half of Shropshire and Herefordshire – Osric, my steward, says it's 250,000 acres in all – and to have the title 'Baron of Weobley' pull derision down upon my head?

In any case, this is my chance. The planets are aligned. My father's error was not to cultivate influence at court. Now, with the assassinations of Sudbury and Hales, and Courtenay as the new Archbishop I have the perfect opportunity. With all the turmoil of recent weeks the King will not go against Courtenay, and, Courtenay, with a little prodding, will, I am sure, arrange things for me. When he was at Hereford, he enjoyed his visits here; Osric recalls how he once finished off 64 squabs[4] at dinner. And the man who can prod Courtenay is John Gilbert[5], our new Bishop. They were friends at

The Lollard Oak — 1381

Oxford. Although I don't much care for him, Gilbert is just the man to press my case.

The next few days are vital. Bishop Gilbert is coming to Ludlow on a 'visitation'. I have to get what they call the 'procuration' right. Osric has been informed by the Bishop's chaplain that no nuns are accompanying the Bishop. I was a bit slow on the uptake when I heard this; Osric had to explain. The chaplain was simply asking that we 'procure' the services of a suitable servant girl to bring wine to the Bishop in his chamber late at night. Then there's the business with the Lollards. It seems that the Bishop has an especially virulent hatred of Wycliffe and his followers, who are called Lollards; I don't know much about it but, I am assured, it was their heretical teachings which caused the great insurrection in London. Anyway, if it smooths the way to have a couple of Lollard heads on a pikes outside Broad Gate when the Bishop arrives, so be it. And then there's the money. I fear that this chaplain will not give Osric an easy time.

With all five boys gone, I shouldn't care about securing the line, and yet I do. Edith doesn't. She still weeps for the boys. Not openly, but sometimes I hear the muffled sound. I have no such luxury. My job is to secure the line. Edith's two nephews, William and Alfred, are coming. I will look at them and make up my mind. I hope one of them will come up to scratch. The elder one – William – is at Oxford: that'll go down well with the Bishop. He'll have to change his name to 'de Lacy' though.

Edith de Lacy (Ludlow Castle)

I know I'm not alone – there are so many mothers who lost their children during La Mortalité des Enfants[6]. It's nearly 20 years now, but still it weighs upon me. They would be five fine young men now. Five! Roger's family were so pleased. How our worldly wealth is scorned!

It should be a joy that my nephews, Emma's boys, William and Alfred, are to come here with, so I understand, young Isabella. But it will just make me yet more miserable. The Friar says he will give me a sleep potion called 'dwale'. But what I most want is to sleep, and not wake up.

Emma Edmundson (Kingsgate Manor)

Early today, it being St. Swithun's Day, we inspected the saplings. It's a family ritual. Every year, on Shrove Tuesday, we each plant an oak sapling in a place of our choosing – as long as it doesn't interfere with the crops – and then, on St. Swithun's Day we go round together to see how they are doing. It's always Isabella's trees that do best.

On Friday they all leave for Ludlow. Although they will be back within the week, it is impossible not to worry. Cuthbert dismisses my fears telling me what I already know: that the rioting was mostly in London and the leaders have not been spared. But it doesn't work.

I am also worried about Edith. It will be difficult for her to see my children when she has lost all of hers. Her letters are very upsetting. The priest says that, because Hugh, the youngest, wasn't baptised, he will stay in Purgatory forever, unless they pay for a monk to pray every day for his soul. She says Roger calls it 'the cost of heaven'. Cuthbert calls it 'blackmail'.

Friday, 19th July 1381

Cuthbert Edmundson (Kingsgate Manor)

I know, I know, I know. There is Norman blood in the Edmundson family going back to before the Conquest, and I know it is not sensible to feel miserable about William giving up our name. Anyway, William – or 'Guillaume', as he likes to be called since his stay in Falaise last year – already has a Norman name. In fact, there have been 'William Edmundsons' since the reign of Edward the Confessor. Nevertheless, if Roger does make William his heir, the price will be to change his surname to 'de Lacy'. And, yes, it makes me sad. So. There we are.

Of course, the inheritance would be stupendous. It will make William the greatest in our family line, going back to King Offa. But then, as an Anglo-Saxon, I cannot but feel there's justice in it. All that land was stolen at the time of the conquest so, although it's a long time ago, it's only right that it should come back to us.

It would have been madness not to delay the visit. Who knows what might have happened, had they travelled during the rebellion? We certainly could not have sent William on his own to Ludlow with just Edwin as his servant. Edwin's hearing and eyesight have got a lot worse recently; his son, Adam, does most of the work at the forge now. William is too much the Oxford scholar for these troublesome times. It's better that his brother, Alfred, and Adam go with them.

William is very tall now, a bit lanky. Alfred could not be more different. In fact, he is very much like Adam: stocky and barrel-chested. Alfred may be gentry, but it's not difficult to imagine him as a blacksmith like Adam. Adam is built like an ox, just as his father was. Last Sunday, I saw him hit the target – again and again – at 300 yards. Alfred is good too.

They leave today but, with the harvest almost upon us, I have said they cannot be away for more than five days. That gives them just two nights at Ludlow, but it will be enough. Roger will make up his mind on the spot. He's like that.

I can't say I'm happy about Isabella going. At first, Emma – backed up by William, but not Alfred – would not hear of it. But the girl is a lioness. As in every argument between mother and daughter, there's only ever one winner. Before they left, I decided to give her what we call 'Edwin's Cross'. It's nothing to do with our Edwin; it must have been made by another Edwin, long ago, and is now a family treasure. It's a clever thing: a beautifully carved wooden cross that clicks open to reveal a hidden blade, and so becomes a little dagger. It will protect her one way or another.

Bishop John Gilbert (The Bishop's Palace, Hereford) – *translated from the French*

Today we travel on a visitation to Leominster Priory. Tomorrow, we go to Ludlow. There we stay in the Castle with Roger de Lacy and his wife, Edith. Although the Lollard-inspired rioting has now been put down, I have been instructed by the new Archbishop to reduce the number of clergy and servants to accompany me on visitations. It is not possible to include nuns. Not even Adelaide.

I have a new Chaplain, Raphael. He is small, deferential and, thank God, speaks French[7]. The new Dean, John Harold[8], doesn't. One cannot say it these days, but I do abhor this recent trend for appointing English-speaking priests. I know we are now all supposed to treat Anglo-Saxons as 'equals', what with the plague diminishing the population, but I maintain, in my old-fashioned way, that it is wrong for appointments to be made on anything other than merit. Anyway, no one understands their Latin.

But, Raphael: yes, well. It seems that the aristocracy rather like Raphael: he has some learning and a certain mannered, obsequious charm. They only become aware of his animal cunning, which is unshackled by any moral sense, when it is too late. Raising money is a necessary evil, but, since it must be done, it is better done by someone less fastidious than myself.

We need to re-build St. Lawrence's[9] – the Church at Ludlow – in the modern style, and it will be expensive. Raphael says that donations from the common people are 'helpful', but only in as much as they provoke the rich into displaying their wealth. At Ludlow, Raphael has only one target: de Lacy. "The woollier the sheep, the bigger the fleece," is his maxim.

He goes about this 'fleecing' business in a very thorough and orderly way. I have been given two tasks for the Ludlow visitation. The first is to comfort Edith. Raphael has learnt that her youngest son died unbaptised during 'La Mortalité des Enfants'. Therefore, I must to explain to her why it is necessary both to increase the number of priests dedicated to praying for his soul, and also to provide the right kind of church for them to pray in. The cost, I must re-assure her, will not be great, when set against the prize of her son's immortal soul.

My second task concerns Roger. As is common knowledge, Roger wants to be an Earl. This makes him, in Raphael's words, 'low hanging fruit'. With the appointment of Courtenay – my old friend from Oxford – as Archbishop, Raphael persuades me that it is within my gift to get the powers-that-be to right this wrong. So, I must put it to de Lacy that, were he to cover the cost of rebuilding St. Lawrence's it would 'redound to his advantage'.

Of course, it's all appallingly vulgar but, as I say, necessary. Anyway, the food will be plentiful and good. A pity about Adelaide.

Isabella Edmundson (The Swan Inn, Bridgnorth)

It's strange but my very first thought was how Mother would say she had been right. But, then, very quickly, my bruised pride gave way to terror.

This is what happened. The five of us – William and Edwin at the front, Alfred and Adam at the back, with me in between – had been travelling without incident for two hours. With no shade it was hot. First, we went along the old Roman Road to a place called Weston, where we stopped to rest the horses. We then turned south.

It happened beyond Albrighton, at a place called Burnhill Green, according to William. I was some way behind William and Edwin when we first saw them: four men with four large mastiffs. It was obvious they did not mean us well. We kept going, pretending not to be watching, but they kept shadowing us at a distance.

Then, suddenly, there were shouts. "Go! Go! Go!" – the orders of masters to their dogs. The huge mastiffs were running straight at us, baying and barking. I had once seen such a dog pull down a horse twice its size. That had been terrifying; this was much more so.

But what happened next, I will never forget. I turned in my saddle to see both Alfred and Adam, in what seemed like a single movement, pull their longbows from their saddle-holders, leap to the ground, take an arrow from their quivers, and – with the dogs baying and charging towards us not 50 yards away – draw their bows. Adam shouted: "Take the right". His arrow flew first, followed, only a second or two later, by Alfred's. It was a thrilling sight: both arrows went straight, and sank, like ploughs carving through clay, into the skulls of the two leading dogs. The silence was instantaneous. The two great beasts lay sprawling, whilst the other two dogs veered away, turned, and ran back to their masters, whimpering. When I looked, both Alfred and Adam had another arrow drawn. But the four men and their surviving dogs were running away. They were not going to trouble us anymore.

I dismounted and rushed over to my brother and the blacksmith. Alfred was as shaken as I was, but – I could tell – was also bursting with pride that, in a moment of such danger, he had kept his nerve. I kissed Adam as well and, in doing so, held his left arm: it was solid like an iron post. He was embarrassed by my girlish admiration.

We were so glad to reach Bridgnorth, set on a high cliff above the River Severn. It has been a hot, hot day. The ostler took the horses and poured buckets of water over their steaming backs. Inside, without asking us, the innkeeper came with a flagon of ale and some cups. We told him about our adventure with the dogs. He nodded knowingly.

"That would be the Legge brothers, that would. Bone-headed bastards with their dogs. You did us all a favour there, you did."

As he spoke, there was shouting in the street. Adam rushed out. We followed to see Adam charge at a young ruffian who, with his friends, had been throwing stones at a small, deformed, red-haired man who was cowering on the ground. Adam went at the ruffian with such fury that they both fell to the ground. Adam was on top. Seeing his strength, the others, instead of coming to the aid of their companion, backed off.

The Lollard Oak   1381

Adam pulled the stone-thrower to his feet, holding his arm high up behind his back. "If you come near again, I'll break every bone in your body." He yanked the arm even higher and the ruffian yelped like a wounded dog. He then let the wretch go, who ran off with the rest of them. Meanwhile, Edwin had got the small man to his feet – he had blood pouring from a gash on his forehead – and took him into The Swan.

The dogs scared me, but this was exciting. Now, twice in one day, I have seen how strong and fearless Adam is. He would never let me know it, but I can feel he is pleased that I think well of him. I do. Very much. I think he's wonderful.

William Edmundson (The Swan Inn, Bridgnorth)

The time I spent in Falaise last year means that my French is perfect. It may be too perfect. The English Normans speak French with an odd English accent, and it can cause awkwardness if one answers them with a proper Normandy accent. I must be careful about this with my uncle Roger.

I understand that Bishop Gilbert will be there. He, of course, is Norman too, and so the three of us will be able to speak French together at dinner. I have been rehearsing the questions I will ask him about 'transubstantiation' and 'consubstantiation'; there are a lot of arguments about this important matter at Oxford.

Father was correct about Alfred and Adam joining us, but wrong in allowing Isabella to come as well. I thought it best that my brother and Adam ride with the pack horses at the rear; this meant that they were well-placed to defend us when we were attacked by the dogs. It was frightening, but I stayed calm.

The innkeeper is over-familiar, but I decided not to tell him who I am. I shall return to Bridgnorth as the heir to Roger de Lacy – that is certainly what Father expects – and it will be amusing to see the change in his demeanour.

The Lollard Oak   1381

Although it is now evening, it is still very warm. I had just retired to the bed-chamber when I was disturbed by rowdiness in the street. I looked out to see a horribly deformed little man being attacked. Adam, to his credit, had put the young perpetrators to flight. The little man has a cut to his forehead. But how very ugly he is! He stoops, has a thin nose, a sharp chin and a large forehead. His long, curly red hair hangs neglected over his face, uncut and lank. I know I shouldn't think it, but he is a disgusting sight. Edwin has taken him inside. He is a kind man, Edwin.

Alfred Edmundson (The Swan Inn, Bridgnorth)

The odd little man is called John. I have used most of my savings to pay the innkeeper to look after him when we leave tomorrow. He will need a few days to recover. Apart from the deep cut to his head, he is horribly bruised all over. It turns out that he is a Lollard preacher; he has a harsh, rasping voice.

He was in London during the rioting, and is on his way back to Wenlock Priory where, he says, the Prior will give him refuge. He has no family.

I thought he would want to rest, but, as soon as Edwin had finished bandaging him, he started to talk as if he was preaching from a pulpit. At first, he was subdued: there were just the four of us around him — William had gone upstairs — and the innkeeper. All people are equal in the eyes of God; everyone should be able to read the Bible in English; they would then see for themselves what Jesus had taught; it would open their eyes; a great light would shine into the souls of men; the world would be a place of love.

He got to his feet and became more animated. "Things cannot go right in England," he shouted out, "and never will, until goods are held in common and there are no more villeins and gentlefolk, but that we are all one and the same."

People came into the inn, curious to find out what all the noise was about. John, now standing on a bench, was unstoppable. "In

The Lollard Oak 1381

what way are those whom we call lords greater masters than ourselves? How have they deserved it? Why do they hold us in bondage? It is against the will of God. If we all spring from a single father and mother, Adam and Eve, how can some claim that they are lords more than us? They are clad in velvet lined with ermine, while we go dressed in coarse cloth."

The inn was soon crowded. He spoke of how the Church and our rulers fear nothing more than that the ordinary people should discover for themselves what the Bible really says. He might have been mad in his manner but there was sense in what he said. Some laughed at him, but more were quiet and thoughtful.

Not everyone agreed with him. A red-faced merchant was having none of it. What about all the killings in London? How could it work if we were all equal? Do we want to be ruled by people of learning, or by a mob? Yet, for every question, he had an answer. Yes, the rioters did get drunk and they did do bad things, but we are all fallen creatures from the time of Adam: did that make a just cause unjust?

"As for people of learning, are they not the most corrupt of all? Does not their learning descend like a great curtain between them and knowledge of their corruption? Do they not use their learning to extend their power and wealth, rather than to do God's will? Did Jesus not say that, 'except ye become as little children, ye shall not enter into the kingdom of heaven.' Did he not say that 'Whosoever therefore shall humble himself as this little child, the same is greatest in the kingdom of heaven'? The men of learning imagine themselves wise, but is there any wisdom other than the wisdom of humility?"

I glanced at Isabella and Edwin and Adam. They were nodding in agreement.

He hardly drew breath. "And what humility do we find among our Norman rulers? Are not all our laws made by people with French names? And is it not the purpose of those laws to oppress those with English names? And is not all the land taken from people with English names by people with French names? How can that be right? Whose country is this? Is it England or is it France? No, I say to you, things cannot go right in England, and never will, until we are all equal. That is what the Bible says, and that is God's holy law."

Suddenly William was beside me. He had come down from the bed-chamber, and pushed through the crowd. He whispered urgently. He had heard enough. We must get Isabella, Edwin and Adam away from this man. It was dangerous to be near him. The man was a heretic and a traitor, and, quite possibly, a murderer. He might have been with those who killed Archbishop Sudbury.

We left but I didn't mention my payment to the innkeeper.

Edwin (The Swan Inn, Bridgnorth)

Riding at the front I couldn't hear or see what had happened with those dogs. I had gone on another twenty or thirty yards before William caught up with me, and made me turn back. Those two boys had done well. Isabella dismounted and threw her arms round her brother. Then she did the same to Adam, and he went bright red. She's a fine girl.

This poor man, John, is in a bad way. As well as the cut to his forehead, he was kicked and punched all over his body by those ruffians. He said to me that, being so ugly, and having such very red hair, he frightens people and they get angry; he added that they would feel ashamed of what they had done later. He explained that, at the end of a hot day, people are bound to be bad-tempered.

What an unusual man he is! He was more worried about his attackers than himself. While I bandaged his head, he looked at me. Although he is ugly, his eyes are beautiful. Blue, they are. Light blue. He asked about my hearing and my eyesight: how did he know? He touched my ears. And then my eyes. His fingers are long and beautifully shaped. And gentle. Like a woman's. No, not like a woman's. More like a child's. Very soft. Like a child's, they were. I didn't expect his hands to be soft like that.

The Lollard Oak   1381

Saturday, 20th July 1381

Bishop John Gilbert (Ludlow Castle) – *translated from the French*

As we approached Broad Gate I saw heads on pikes on either side of the entrance. I have heard that, in London, trials have been suspended and summary justice authorised. I did not believe this to be the case here. Have these wretches been given the chance to defend themselves? I doubt it.

We were greeted by Roger and Edith in the Inner Bailey, and, without ceremony, I asked whether the men whose heads I had just seen had received a fair trial. I could tell from Roger's discomfort that, as I suspected, nothing of the sort had happened. They were Lollards, and that, for Roger, was enough.

Much as I deplore Lollardy, we must give them an opportunity to repent. This requires time and patience, and, if necessary, torture. St Augustine teaches that, whilst, sometimes, to save a man's soul, we must torture him, in doing so, we must refrain from enjoying it. That is surely right.

Anyway, I made my point, dropped the matter, and smiled graciously. We have business to conduct over the next day or so, and what's done is done.

On the stairway, outside my chamber, I encountered a young lady. She is de Lacy's niece. Her long, fair hair flows down, and over, her young, but not small, breasts; she has intelligent blue eyes and full lips. Her chamber is immediately above mine. Might it be divine intervention that Adelaide could not come?

Roger de Lacy (Ludlow Castle) – *translated from the French*

I had forgotten what a pompous prelate he is! What insolence! Does he not understand that I own not just this castle, but seven others, and, for what it's worth, 250,000 acres? Who does he think he is? How dare he insult me like that? How dare he?

I think it better that I do not sit next to 'His Grace' at table this evening.

At least he's brought only twenty or so priests and servants with him this time. And no nuns. We're used to 80 or more coming with the bishop on his 'visitations', and they all have to be fed and looked after. Worse, we have to pretend to be honoured by their presence. Anyway, I want an earldom, and he wants money, so we just have to make the best of it.

Osric tells me that the Bishop is insisting that his Chaplain must have one of the two other chambers near the Great Hall. Osric had planned to use those chambers – with their views across to Wales – for the nephews and niece. He suggests that the best solution would be to move the two nephews to the Portcullis Tower, where they can share the accommodation with their servants. In that way the Bishop's wishes can be met. After our unfortunate start, I fear I cannot afford not to indulge 'His Grace'.

I must find out exactly why the Lollards are heretics. It is something to do with 'transubstantiation'. I wonder if my nephew, William, the one who is studying at Oxford, can explain it to me.

William Edmundson (Ludlow Castle)

Could I really be Lord of all this when my uncle dies? I can feel everyone watching me, asking themselves: 'Does he measure up?' I am watching myself, asking the same question.

Uncle Roger's Steward, Osric, met us at the outer gate where the ostlers took our horses, and servants carried our belongings from the pack horses to our chambers. We crossed the large Outer Bailey, over the moat, through the Portcullis Tower, and into the Inner Bailey. It makes Tamworth Castle appear very small.

Aunt Edith came out. She looks old; you would not believe she is only forty five, a year older than Mother. According to Mother, she

The Lollard Oak   1381

never got over the death of her five children. Having told us how much we had grown, she was apologetic about our chambers: the Bishop and his retinue were causing complications. Isabella is in the chamber near the Great Hall, but Alfred and I must share rooms with Edwin and Adam in the Portcullis Tower. We change into our finery for dinner. Tomorrow Holy Mass is at nine, and then we go to Bromfield for the Sunday archery[10].

Isabella Edmundson (Ludlow Castle)

Aunt Edith came up the stone stairs with me all the way to my chamber.

We passed two men on the stairs. One was large, and dressed in a fine, embroidered cloak; the other was small, in a simple cassock. Aunt Edith introduced me to His Grace, the Bishop of Hereford, and his Chaplain. They are staying in the rooms beneath mine. The Bishop took my hand and kissed it; he called me 'my dear child' and was very charming; the Chaplain smiled in that priestly way: more with his face than his eyes.

It is a magnificent room with a window facing the west. Aunt Edith pointed out the grey lines on the horizon: they are the mountains of Wales. The Welsh are violent and rapacious; for many centuries, it has been the duty of the de Lacy family to serve their King and Country by keeping this border safe. The warm evening sun – it has been another hot day – lit up the miles of countryside beneath us in a green and golden glow.

Then suddenly she hugged me; there were tears in her eyes. How I looked like my mother at sixteen! That was such a happy time. We sat on the bed, and she told me stories about growing up with mother. She sighed, saying it was like being with her sister all over again.

At dinner, I was on Uncle Roger's left, with the Bishop on my left. I had never eaten roast squabs before: they were delicious. The Bishop kept passing me more, showing me how to get the meat off the tiny birds, and which sauce – there were so many on the table – to have with them. He insisted that I get my father to build a 'colombier' at Kingsgate; one needs several hundred holes for the nesting pigeons to produce a good number of the little birds, which must be taken before they can fly, so that the meat is soft. There's not much I don't know about pigeons now. I drank too much wine; he kept filling my cup.

Alfred Edmundson (Ludlow Castle)

That dinner was awful.

I was on the end of the table next to Aunt Edith. She was on my left. She is tired all the time. Her eyes are sunken. She must sleep badly.

Looking down the long tables below, I saw Adam with Edwin. They were talking to some of the Bishop's retinue. He must have been telling them the story of the dogs; I saw him pretend to pull a bow and then slump onto the table; then he pointed up at me. I gave him a little wave and made as if to slump as well. They were having a much better time than us on the high table.

But that wasn't why I was miserable. First, there was the business with William and the Bishop.

My brother was sitting on the other side of Aunt Edith and next to Uncle Roger. For some reason, our uncle, who, I am sure, is not interested in religious matters, wanted to know what William had learnt about 'transubstantiation' at university.

William had put on what we call his 'Oxford face' – his eyes narrow, and his nose rises a little, as if it has detected a disagreeable smell. He explained to Uncle Roger that, when the priest consecrates the bread and wine, a miracle occurs, which transforms the bread and wine into the actual body and blood of Jesus. The bread and wine did not appear, to human eyes, to have changed, but they had. He quoted someone called Thomas Aquinas, who said, as I best recall, that: 'The presence of Christ's true body and blood cannot be detected by the senses or by reason, but by faith alone, which rests upon Divine authority.'

I should have kept my mouth shut, but I couldn't stop myself saying:

"But what if the bread is just bread, and the wine is just wine?"

There was silence around the high table. At the tables below the servants continued to chatter. The Bishop fixed me with his eye:

"Are you saying, young man, that, when Our Lord and Saviour broke the bread and said to his disciples: 'This is my body', that he was lying? And are you saying that those who witnessed how He made the blind to see, and the deaf to hear, were liars too? Are you saying that such a man was not honest? Is that just nonsense, young man?"

"No, of course, not. I am sorry. I should not have spoken as I spoke." I said.

"Nor thought as you thought. As Our Lord said: 'There shall be more joy in Heaven over one sinner that repenteth, than over ninety and nine just persons who need no repentance.' But remember this, young man: 'faith' and 'authority' are the cornerstones of our civilisation. Take those away, and we are no better than the beasts of the field. 'Faith' and 'authority'. Am I not right, Roger?"

"Oh, yes, yes, absolutely. 'Faith' and 'authority'. Very important."

At this, the Bishop turned away with a smile that was more menace than smile, and stretched out to pick up a platter of squabs. I could tell William was furious with me. Uncle Roger looked straight at me, and, without allowing any expression to alter his face, he winked.

And then there was Isa. I always call her 'Isa'.

She was sitting between Uncle Roger and the Bishop. She was drinking too much and behaving without dignity. The Bishop, sitting next to her, insufferably pleased with himself, plied her with delicacies and wine. Normally, she is quick as a fox to spot a dubious

The Lollard Oak   1381

character a mile off, but there she was laughing and giggling at his every comment. I hated it.

Before I forget, I should mention something which happened earlier. On our way from Bridgnorth we came over the Clee Hills and, all at once, saw Ludlow lying far away in the Teme Valley. It was just possible to pick out the towers on the Castle. It was wonderful to see England – a patchwork of light green fields and dark green woods under a cloudless, blue sky – so spread out before us. We stopped and gazed. After a little while, it occurred to me how sad it was that, with his poor eyesight, Edwin would not be able to enjoy this view. I rode over to him so that at least he wouldn't feel left out.

"What a sight that is!" he said, as I came up.

"But Edwin, I thought your eyes were not good."

"Why are you shouting at me?"

It seems that both his sight and his hearing have come back. How can that be? It's like a miracle.

Sunday, 21st July 1381 (8th Sunday after Trinity)

Roger de Lacy (Bromfield Heath) – *translated from the French*

That was easy. I had assumed that William, being the elder one, and at Oxford, would be the obvious heir, but it won't work. There is a type of man – they are usually men – who is clever and decent, but whose judgement is so reliably bad, that one only has to ask them what course to follow, to be certain that, by doing the opposite, one will have made a good decision. I know he's young, but I judge William to be just such a fellow.

As for Alfred: I like him. He's his own man. Last night he spoke his mind about transubstantiation, but then, when he saw what a wasps' nest he had trodden on with the Bishop, had the good sense to back down quickly. He did it well. At the same time, I could see he was not intimidated by 'His Grace'.

Strong, too. I watched him with the archers here today. Not a 300-yard-man, like that servant of his, and nowhere near our

Boraston giant, who was shooting at over 400 yards, but he was well clear of 250 yards. That's not usual for a gentleman.

They all leave tomorrow morning. I will get the lawyer in.

William Edmundson (Bromfield Heath)

I am *so* angry. The ignorant *fool*! Or did he do it deliberately, to ruin my future? Either way, I could feel that, after Alfred's stupid remark at dinner, Uncle Roger was cooler with me – less inclined to talk.

Immediately following Mass, the Bishop invited me to his chamber near the Great Hall. It is below Isabella's room. He warned me about the dangerous ground my brother had been treading on. Doubting transubstantiation is no ordinary heresy: it is the heresy that opened the gates to the recent insurrection.

He explained it like this. John Wycliffe – whom I have seen in the street in Oxford – is the main culprit. He originated the heresy, and his Lollard followers have spread it. Questioning transubstantiation may sound innocent, but it is not. Either God became man, or He did not. If He became man, then He must be present in the consecrated bread and the wine. If He did not, we have no Christianity. That is how important it is.

The Bishop commended me for quoting Thomas Aquinas on 'faith' and 'authority'. It is easy to see why 'faith' is necessary, but it is no less important to recognise that we live in a line of 'authority', stretching back through the Popes to St. Peter, and from St. Peter to Christ – to God – himself. Break that line, and everything else goes: the authority of the Church, the King, the State; everything.

Last month, he continued, we had a glimpse of what can happen when divine authority is brought into question. 'Authority' has planted our land thick with trees; if we cut them down, how can anyone stand against the winds that then will blow? Our civilisation is a fragile vessel. Break it, and Satan runs loose. Chaos, destruction, burning, looting, murder.

I rode the short distance from the castle to Bromfield with Raphael, the Bishop's kindly chaplain. We discussed the question of translating the Bible into English, another of Wycliffe's projects, and readily agreed that it is not for nothing that it takes years to train a priest. The word of God cannot come to the ordinary Christian other than through those in authority.

It is another hot day. I am afraid that Alfred demeans himself – and our family – by taking part in these events. When I inherit, I will not allow it.

Edith de Lacy (Bromfield Heath)

This is the first time I have come to the Sunday archery. At dinner last night, my nephew, Alfred, asked me to come and watch him; I promised I would, although it doesn't interest me. In fact, I hate it. Seeing all these fine young men, who have come here from so many villages nearby, I could not stop wondering – as is my way – how my boys would have done. But I had promised.

Near me, on a small cob, I recognised one of Cuthbert's servants, who came with Emma's children yesterday. He was cheering a burly young man who was with Alfred. I asked if it was his son. It was; he is a good archer, and I said so. He was very pleased.

I then found myself telling this man – Edwin – about my sons. He knew what had happened and was respectful. I suspect, however, that he was thinking that such tragedies are not uncommon.

He told me how he had lost his wife and daughter in childbirth a few years ago. He went on to relate a conversation he had had with a friar returning from a pilgrimage to Jerusalem. The friar had described to him a fruit they have in the Holy Land called a 'sabra'; it has the sharpest of thorns on the outside, but, inside, is sweet.

"This friar, my Lady, asked me to think of my loss as being like the prickly skin of this fruit. He told me that, if only I could get past my pain, I would discover, and be surprised by, the sweetness of the love within. And it was true, my Lady, I think now, not of my loss, but of my love for her, and her love for me. It truly is sweet, just as the friar foretold."

We were quiet for a little while, before he said: "It is not my place to advise you, my Lady, and I hope you will forgive me for telling you my story."

"No, no", I replied, "I am grateful to you."

And, in truth, I was. To re-assure him I laid my hand on his. Just for a moment. It was hard and leathery but, in it, I saw a whole lifetime of honest work. Looking at this unwashed servant, with his weather-beaten face, dressed in coarse cloth, I could not but be intrigued by the subtle way he had given advice. So rough on the outside; so gentle within. Like the sabra fruit of which he spoke.

I think I shall sleep tonight. Osric informs me that the Bishop would like to speak to me alone. Why would he want to do that?

Monday, 22nd July 1381 (Mary Magdalene)

Alfred (Ludlow Castle)

I could not sleep tonight. It was past midnight and so hot here in the tower.

But that was not the only thing to trouble me. On the ride back from Bromfield, I asked Adam about his time with the Bishop's servants in the Great Hall at dinner yesterday evening. He didn't answer. For a moment I wondered if his hearing had gone, just as his father's had returned. He talked about the Boraston giant. Did he really not hear my question? Or was there something offensive in my asking it? I was puzzled.

"Why won't you speak of last night in the Great Hall, Adam?"

Again, he didn't answer. I could see he was uncomfortable. At last, he told me how the Bishop's servants used the nickname, 'The Archangel', when referring to their master. He had asked them why they called him that. One of the servants, with his hand cupped over

The Lollard Oak 1381

his mouth, had said with a conspiratorial snigger: "Because, good Sir, when a young lady is visited by the Archangel ... you know what I mean, sir?"

I dared not mention this to William. He had had a long and earnest conversation with the Bishop yesterday morning and is in awe of him. He would dismiss this story as the kind of insolent, vulgar gossip you should expect of peasants. Anyway, at the moment, he can hardly bring himself to acknowledge my existence.

Yes, well, probably, it is just insolent, vulgar gossip.

But what if it isn't? I was pursued by the memory of last night in the Great Hall, of the way the Bishop had been making her laugh, of how he had been filling her cup ...

It was so hot. I went down to the Inner Bailey to be in the open air. Soon my restlessness had me climbing the stone steps to Isabella's chamber. I noticed, as I passed it, that the door to the Chaplain's chamber on the lower floor was not closed. I thought nothing of it until, on the next floor up, I saw that the door to the Bishop's chamber was also open. In the gloom, I picked out the shape of Raphael, his Chaplain, sitting on the stairs that led to Isabella.

Suddenly my heart was thumping.

"You shouldn't be here," said the little man, putting on his most unhurried, contemptuous voice.

"I wish to see my sister," I said.

"You can't," he said flatly; "His Grace is praying with her."

I may not be as strong as Adam, let alone the Boraston giant, but I can pull a long bow and fly an arrow more than 250 yards: picking up the repulsive Raphael, and removing him from the staircase, was the work of a moment.

Isabella (Ludlow Castle)

I had this vivid dream. I picked up Alfred's long bow at the meeting at Bromfield, and fixed an arrow in the string. Everyone was watching. Adam came up behind me and very gently held my left

The Lollard Oak 1381

hand on the bow, and my right hand on the arrow. He did not himself exert any force, but just his touch was enough to give me the strength to pull the bow. The arrow flew. It flew up, up and up, further than any other arrow, further even than that of the giant from Boraston. Everyone cheered; I passed the bow back to Alfred and took Adam in my arms to kiss him. But, just then, the Bishop came up; he pushed Adam aside, offering me a cup of wine with the words: "My dear child."

"My dear child." What is happening? I don't understand. Again, "My dear child". What was this? It was not a dream.

He was telling me that I was a child of God, that I had been chosen to do God's work, that he must remove my night-tunic, just as he had removed his, so that we could worship God as God intended. He kept repeating, "My dear child". His large, powerful hands were holding me down.

"You fat, ugly pig. Get off me!" Edwin's wooden cross lay on the table next to my bed. I could just wriggle my right hand free to take it. I pressed the back of Edwin's cross. Thank God! The scabbard fell away. I was holding the blade next to his neck, and screamed at the Bishop: "If you put that into me, I'll put this into you."

I would have too, but, as I said it, the door was flung open. Oh God! No! Not that horrible chaplain as well.

"Isa!" It was Alfred!

The Bishop had rolled off my bed. He put on his night tunic and, with Alfred standing silently by the door, he left, pretending all the while that, if there had been any untoward behaviour, it was certainly nothing to do with him.

Apart from the day that Jack, my terrier, died, I can't remember when I last cried. But now, in Alfred's arms, I gave way. I have never cried like that before: I shook and sobbed with my whole body. Alfred, dear thing, held me without saying a word.

A little later, sitting on the bed, I held his hand tightly: "Alfred, please, do not tell anyone. Not Mother, not Father, especially not

The Lollard Oak   1381

William. But not Adam or Edwin either. No-one. Will you promise me?"

At first, he didn't understand. "We have to stop this bastard."

"No, it will be my word against his. He will destroy me. And our family too. You don't understand how powerful he is." I felt the same burning rage, but, more clearly than him, I could see my weakness. This was no time for courage.

We gathered up my clothes and belongings, and, walking barefoot so as to make no noise on the stairs, we went to Alfred's chamber in the Portcullis Tower. I failed to sleep in his bed, and he failed to sleep on a rush mat on the floor.

William was insistent on the importance of a formal parting. But Alfred, supported by Adam and Edwin, who instinctively sensed that something was terribly wrong, argued that, with thunderstorms on the way, we needed to get to Bridgnorth as soon as possible. Osric the Steward was in no doubt that we would regret any delay; he promised to explain the urgency to His Lord and Ladyship.

Bishop Gilbert (Ludlow Castle) – *translated from the French*

It seemed, at first, a familiar story: a member of the gentler sex, who, I have observed, can be of any age, develops a passion for a priest, which leads to inappropriate behaviour. It is disagreeable but, as a man of the cloth, with a certain – how can I put it? – 'presence', it is something I have had to learn to live with.

But this case is different. It has transpired that it is nothing less than a deliberate trap, planned and executed by her brother, who thought he saw an opportunity to exploit his sister's fine looks. I must move quickly. If I don't, I could be falsely accused. There could be damage to my reputation; it could even, in due course, hurt my prospects of an appointment to York or Canterbury.

I met Roger early this morning to apprise him of the situation, namely that, under the cover of darkness, his wife's nephew and niece had attempted a foul plot against me. Their purpose? To extract

The Lollard Oak   1381

money. As we all know – but are too polite to say – the Anglo-Saxons continue to harbour this childish resentment towards those of us with Norman ancestry. It is pathetic, but, more, it is sad. Given his relationship with them, through his wife, I have decided, on this occasion, not to pursue it further, but, naturally, I must have an assurance that the connection between this wretched Edmundson family and the de Lacys is now at an end.

It was helpful that Raphael was quick to discover that they had all fled, without any of the normal courtesies, at first light. To Roger, this proved their guilt.

Roger de Lacy (Ludlow Castle) – translated from the French

I don't believe the old goat for one second. But, especially with Emma's children gone, I cannot investigate the matter. And, even if I could, how am I to go against a bishop?

And then there's his vile little Chaplain, Raphael, who says he witnessed everything. It is a hateful, hateful business. Is it any wonder we suffer these insurrections?

Oh God, I cannot say anything to my dear Edith. She loved having them – especially that pretty Isabella. It is the first time I have seen her happy since the boys died.

Edwin (on the road from Ludlow to Bridgnorth)

Thinking back, my first sense that something special had happened was on Saturday morning at the Swan in Bridgnorth. I was woken early by bird-song. I haven't been woken by bird-song for years, but now, these last three mornings, it has been such a racket.

It was also last Saturday that I looked out from the Clee Hills over towards Ludlow and could see everything.

I don't know what to make of it. You will laugh at me, but I think it is a miracle. I don't mean 'miracle' in the sense of 'a wonderful thing' – although it is – but no, I mean that it is, literally, a miracle. I remind myself that I'm a blacksmith – a very good blacksmith, if you will forgive me for saying – but, at the end of the day, nothing more than a blacksmith. I know how to work iron, or shoe a horse, but nothing else, and certainly I am very ignorant when it comes to religion, or anything that requires a fine mind, and the kind of learning that such as William have. I know that a miracle could not happen to me. And yet still I cannot explain it.

There was that funny little crippled man, with the red hair and blue eyes, and the gash on his forehead. It was horrible how he was treated. To be honest, I agreed with what he was saying about us all being equal in the eyes of God. It was strange how he knew about my sight and hearing, and touched me like that.

I don't know what's up, but, while I'm riding along feeling happy, the others are at sixes and sevens. True, it's hot and muggy – I'm sure we'll have a thunderstorm before the day is out – but that's not it. William is riding up ahead and not speaking to his brother, and Alfred and Isabella are at the rear, exchanging whispers every now and then, as if there's some dreadful secret.

Adam and I are in the middle with the pack horses, but even Adam's not himself. Yesterday at Bromfield I noticed – I wouldn't have seen it last week – how he was looking at young Isabella. Is he mad? Surely he knows that he cannot have feelings like that for a lady?

Another hour and we'll be in Bridgnorth. We can't get there soon enough, if you ask me.

William (The Swan Inn, Bridgnorth)

We felt the first spots of rain about a mile short of the West Gate. It was almost a relief. It had been building up through the day. By the time we reached the gate we were completely drenched by the downpour. Thunder was crashing all around us, and the sky, almost black, was lit up by massive bolts of lightning. But we hardly noticed all that.

The Lollard Oak   1381

I was in the lead, and so was the first to see it. Stuck onto a pike, outside the gate, was a battered and horrifying head. From the red hair and the great cut across the forehead, we knew at once whose it was.

We sat together on our horses in the rain and the dark, in the thunder and lightning, and were speechless and numb.

I heard Isabella say: "My God!", and Edwin say: "Yes."

He had got off his little cob, and knelt down in the mud in front of that ghastly pike.

Alfred (The Swan Inn, Bridgnorth)

The innkeeper took me aside and returned the money I had given him to look after John. He told me what had happened.

After we left on Saturday morning, the constable and his men arrived at the inn, demanding that he hand John over. After the scenes of the previous evening, the innkeeper had anticipated some such thing, and so he had hidden the Lollard in the attic. But it was no good. They searched everywhere. It was not long before they found him, and dragged him off. They didn't have to be rough; he put up no resistance, and went with them like a lamb. The constable was a relative of the innkeeper's wife, otherwise he would have been arrested too.

First, John was tortured in the castle; everyone knew that. Then, later the same day, he was hanged, drawn and quartered in St Leonard's Close. They jammed his head onto a pike, took it to the West Gate. They threw his other remains off the cliff into the river valley.

The innkeeper was looking at me intently. "I can tell you are a good man," he said. "I know little about our Christian religion, but I do know that, when Our Lord was crucified, with the two robbers on either side of him, one of them said of Jesus, 'this man hath done nothing amiss'. I saw John being hanged, and those words were in my mind. They still are."

Tuesday, 23rd July 1381

Isabella (Kingsgate Manor)

In the end, you could say, nothing actually 'happened', but I still feel shocked. I can speak to Alfred about it, but I must hold my tongue with the others.

I would like to imagine it won't change me, but I fear it will. For instance, last night, at The Swan, I went to bed fully dressed: I was thinking I should make it as difficult as possible for any unwanted visitor.

My room overlooked the High Street, and my bed was by the window. I was awoken early by creaking floorboards; I raised myself up in bed to peer out into the street. Edwin was leaving the inn.

What was he doing?

I decided I must follow him. I crept barefoot down the stairs, putting my shoes on in the street. Although there was still only a little light I saw him turn into Whitburn Street, which led to the West Gate.

I stayed at a distance from him but could see that he was carrying a sack. When I realised what he was up to, I went back to the inn, making sure he didn't see me.

I was not surprised that, soon after, Edwin was agitating for us to leave quickly because there might be another storm later. What he had done was dangerous. He knew it, and he knew we had to get away from Bridgnorth as soon as possible. At first, Alfred was not being co-operative. I told him to trust me: we must not delay.

We returned home by way of a village called Wolverhampton, so as to avoid any possible contact with the Legge brothers.

Wednesday, 24th July 1381

Edwin (Kingsgate Manor)

The way she hurried the others into packing their things made me wonder whether Isabella knew. I cannot ask her, in case she doesn't.

The heat of the past few days has gone; today is grey, and there is thin rain. Adam has brought a spade to help me with the burial; I think it was fair to tell him. Obviously, we could not go to the churchyard. We were not sure what might be best, so we came up to the top of Falcon from where you can see the new cathedral spires. Adam suggested we take a line from here to the Cathedral, and then go to the edge of the Edmundson land at the bottom of Well Meadow in front of us.

I was lowering my sack of hessian cloth, which contained John's head, into the little grave that Adam had dug, when, to our astonishment, Isabella appeared, walking down from Falcon. She was carrying a book and a small plant-pot.

Yes, she did know. She came up, opened the book, and read:

> "Man that is born of a woman hath but a short time to live, and is full of misery. He cometh up, and is cut down, like a flower; he fleeth as it were a shadow, and never continueth in one stay. In the midst of life we are in death: of whom may we seek for succour, but of thee, O Lord, who for our sins art justly displeased?
>
> Forasmuch as it hath pleased Almighty God of his great mercy to take unto himself the soul of our dear brother, John, here departed, we therefore commit his body to the ground; earth to earth, ashes to ashes, dust to dust; in sure and certain hope of the resurrection to eternal life through our Lord Jesus Christ; who shall change the body of our low estate that it may be like unto his glorious body, according to the mighty working, whereby he is able to subdue all things to himself."[11]

We all said: "Amen." We stood there in silence, with the rain coming down gently upon us, and upon the newly dug earth. Isabella handed me the pot she was holding.

"It's an oak sapling. I thought you might like to mark the spot."

Thursday, 25th July 1381 (St. James the Apostle)
Emma Edmundson (Kingsgate Manor)

This morning a letter arrived from Edith. Nearly everyone was in turmoil. Roger had said to her on Sunday evening that he 'liked the Edmundson boy' and was going to get the lawyers in, but then, on Monday morning, he had changed his mind. It was all off. He was in a foul mood. The Bishop and all his retinue had returned to Hereford: they had been expected to stay for a week. On Sunday evening, the Bishop had sent Edith a message proposing to meet her: on Monday he was gone.

It was all very odd. But she, Edith, was not troubled. She couldn't explain why but, since their visit, she felt light and calm and happy. She had slept well.

I showed the letter to Cuthbert and the children. Cuthbert was intrigued, but William fell back into his fury with Alfred.

"I hope you feel pleased with yourself now, you moronic farmer. What have you done to our family? All because you couldn't resist sounding your stupid, moronic mouth off."

Alfred just stood there and let William push him. Thank goodness he didn't respond because, although he's a year or so younger, he's much stronger than William. Isabella was beside herself, screaming at William:

"Stop it! Just stop it! It's not Alfred's fault."

But Alfred insisted it was his fault. "I am sorry, William, it was entirely my fault. You are right to be angry."

The Lollard Oak   1381

50 years later: St. Swithun's Day – July 1431
Isabella Edmundson (Kingsgate Manor)

It is fifty years since we planted this tree in Well Meadow, the one we now call 'The Lollard Oak'. Adam and I have maintained the old family tradition of rising at dawn and going round the new oaks on St. Swithun's Day. We have ended up here as usual. It is mid-morning and, already, hot. We have some ale and cups, so we can sit here on the ground in the shade of the Lollard oak, and refresh ourselves.

At the time, that week in 1381 seemed like a disaster. I was raped – well almost – by a bishop. My brother William's hopes of inheriting the vast de Lacy estates were dashed. His relations with Alfred, never easy, were – for a time – all but broken, and Alfred had to stay silent about the real reason that William did not inherit.

(Many years later, just before she died, Aunt Edith told me that it was Alfred, not William, who was to be Uncle Roger's heir. I never told William. Nor Alfred. I actually felt sorry for William on hearing this.)

There was much else that went wrong. Roger de Lacy did not get the earldom he so wanted. The money Bishop Gilbert needed to rebuild St. Lawrence's, a project that was to be his legacy, was not forthcoming. But, looming above it all, was the wicked murder – for that is what it was – of John the Lollard, in Bridgnorth.

What a cataclysmic few days! It was just a month after the Great Revolt. That went wrong too. And yet, looking back now, I'm not so sure. It is as if, peeping out of the dull earth, there are green shoots.

Do you recall how Edwin recovered his hearing and his sight? I never thought of him as a religious man but, to his dying day, he said it was a miracle.

You might say that nothing good could come from that repugnant Bishop and his loathsome, little Chaplain, Raphael. And yet, was it not the memory of that horrible experience, high up in Ludlow Castle, which brought me back to the words of John the Lollard? He said: '… we are all equal in God's eyes'. Those words grew inside me. Like this oak tree. They have kept on growing. First, I realised that, in the eyes of God, the Bishop, for all his learning and

The Lollard Oak   1381

wealth and fine clothes, was no more important than me. Then it struck me that if, in the eyes of God, I was the equal of a bishop, did it not follow that Adam was the equal of me? And, continuing down this highway, if that was so, why should not our liking for one another become something more than liking? It did. And no wife has been more loved or happier.

Another green shoot – a lot more than a shoot now – is this tree here, which gives us shade, and provides a place for me to have these thoughts. It stands here quietly, a tribute to that good man and everything he believed in. God willing, it will stand here for many more centuries. It is now full of acorns, like the one that I planted.

Thinking of the Lollards, did you know that the Pope excommunicated John Wycliffe thirty years after his death? They then exhumed his body from the churchyard in Lutterworth and threw his bones into the stream there. And all because, like Alfred, who protected me from the debauched Bishop, Wycliffe wondered whether the wine might, in fact, just be wine, and the bread, bread. At the same time, he had this outlandish idea that, to be a good Christian, it was necessary to be familiar with what it says in the Bible. The authorities were terrified of him. See what a storm he brought down upon his head for daring to question authority.

Questioning authority: that was always the difference between William and Alfred. There is a story from the time of the Great Rebellion – as that insurrection in 1381 is now called – about the burning of the rent and tax records, together with the university archives, in Cambridge. A woman called Margery Starr danced around that bonfire crying "Away with the learning of clerks! Away with it!". We are supposed to disapprove of such peasant ignorance but, in my Anglo-Saxon heart, I'm with that lady.

But the most curious of all the green shoots must surely be my god-daughter, Edwina. At Christmas in 1381, I received a letter from Aunt Edith. Although she had thought it impossible, she was pregnant. She wanted me to be a godmother, and for the child to be called Edwin, or, if it was a girl, Edwina,

When I recall that summer of 1381, I wonder whether it was for better or worse. Good things have a way of emerging out of bad. I remember how a nun, from Norwich, wrote at the time: "All shall be well, and all shall be well, and all manner of thing shall be well."[12] Can this really be true? Is it not a fact that God allows bad things to happen to good people? That was John's fate. But now I look at this oak tree and feel that, perhaps, in fact, he didn't die.

Chapter Four: 1549

'We do earnestly repent, and are heartily sorry for these our misdoings; the remembrance of them is grievous unto us; the burden of them is intolerable.'

The Book of Common Prayer

1549 – Dramatis Personae

Cuthbert Edmundson, Gentleman of Tamworth
Emma Edmundson, his wife
William Edmundson, their son
Alfred Edmundson, his brother, an Actor

Edwin, Blacksmith to the Edmundson estate
Adam, son of Edwin
Isabella, daughter of Edwin

A Young Playwright

John, late Prior of Wenlock Priory

1549

The George Inn, Southwark – 1595

"Alfredo! Here!"

Clasping his precious beer, Alfred threaded his careful way through the crowded inn to the corner where the young playwright had settled. The old actor was a familiar presence in this south London hostelry.

"So, Alfredo: what do you think?"

"Not so quick, young man. Cannot an aged thesp have a little time to wet his throat?" Alfred Edmundson finished half his tankard, put it down, sat back, and stared hard at his youthful companion. "Very well, but, first, you tell me why my opinion is of interest to you. You heard the applause at the end. You saw grown men wiping their eyes. Isn't that enough? How were the takings?"

"Yes, yes, I know, and yes, the takings have been very good. But I was watching you come off stage. You seemed pre-occupied. You feel it's still not quite right; is that not so?"

Alfred took up his tankard and drank from it, looking steadily at the young man. His face lit up.

"Ha! So, you think you can find the mind in the face …"

The playwright laughed, nodded his head, and got out his notebook. "Very good. I like that. I'll use it one day[1]."

"No, if you must know, at that moment, I wasn't even thinking about the play. I was thinking about why the Friar[2] had to have an Irish accent. And it brought back a memory."

Alfred picked up the tankard, but before drinking, he put it down again, and went on: "It's lonely at the end for the Friar, you know. He was the one trying to do good, and he was the one who caused the tragedy. He's completely shamed and humiliated. It's very sad."

Alfred shook his head. "You know that passage in the General Confession about being 'heartily sorry for these our misdoings …'."

"You mean 'the remembrance of them is grievous unto us, the burden of them is intolerable …'"

"Yes, that's it. You see the Friar will never be free of that 'remembrance' and that 'burden'. And it's sad."

"Alfredo, what's up with you? You've been at this game too long for all this. You're as hard bitten as they come. You do your job and you get paid. When did Alfred Edmundson last leave a theatre without the correct coinage in his purse?"

The old actor smiled, and they clinked their tankards together across the dark oak table.

"So, come on, Alfredo, tell me: why does Friar Lawrence have to have an Irish accent?"

"Ah, yes. The accent." Alfred paused for a moment. "You know when the young ones are trying too hard, I say to them: 'Just take someone you know. Bring to mind how they walk and talk, then put your trust in God.' You see when I was boy, we had this lovely old priest, John Bayly[3], or Father John as we called him; he would come to Kingsgate – secretly – to say the Mass. My mother lived in terror that we would all burn in hell unless we received the sacraments in the traditional way. She absolutely believed it."

"And this John Bayly was Irish?"

"Indeed, he was. You know how small people sometimes have an especially powerful personality. He was like that. Curly red hair and piercing light blue eyes. Very unassuming, he was. Didn't so much walk as shuffle. From the moment I read that soliloquy in the second act, you know:

> 'Within the infant rind of this small flower
> Poison hath residence and medicine power …'[4]

… I saw again the red head of Father John bobbing and shuffling to and fro among the herbs and shrubs at Kingsgate. He had been

The Lollard Oak

Prior of Wenlock Priory in Shropshire. It was dissolved in 1540. Absolute disaster for him, that."

Alfred broke off to drink some more.

"Father John always made an effort to be cheerful, but there was a sadness about him – the Irish, they season their good cheer with a twist of melancholy, do they not? He was so like Friar Lawrence. I don't have to act the part; I just remember Father John. He was well-known in gentry circles – well-liked. He went from house to house in Shropshire, and Staffordshire, administering the Holy Eucharist to true believers. Dangerous work, it was."

"Still is." The playwright shook his head. "But it's not really about belief, is it? Yes, they fight over this and that doctrine, but isn't it really a tussle over power? King Henry and the Pope were in an arm wrestle over who had ultimate authority."

"Ha! You young ones scoff at religion. You think it's all hocus pocus. It has to be about something else! But you're missing something. My mother taught me that each time the priest says the right Latin words in the right order up at the altar, a miracle occurs: the bread is turned into the *actual* body of Christ[5], and the wine becomes the *actual* blood of Christ. Beside that truth, for her, everything else was very unimportant."

"But you must admit that it was convenient for the Catholic church that you should all believe this 'hocus pocus'? As long as the priest was performing a miracle, you couldn't do without him, could you? The priest gave you bread and wine with one hand, and snaffled your purse with the other. Come on: one way or another, it's about power, Alfredo."

"You may be right, but it's not the reason I stopped believing in the old ways."

"What was?"

"Oh, something happened."

"Is that the memory which came back?"

"Yes."

"Go on, tell me, Alfredo. I love a story."

Alfred's story – A week in June, 1549

The time was the beginning of June in 1549, that is forty six years before Alfred's conversation with the young playwright. Two years earlier, the old, fat King had died, but the break with Rome had continued under his son, Edward VI, who was still a boy.

The place was Kingsgate Manor, a family estate near Tamworth, in Staffordshire. The people were the Edmundson family – Cuthbert and Emma, together with their sons, William, sixteen, and Alfred, eleven.

William was tall with dark hair, solemn and serious. His private, unspoken ambition was to be a bishop, but, sharing, as he did, his mother's fervent belief in Roman Catholicism, he was fully aware that he must wait patiently until the day when England reverts to the 'one true faith'. That it would, he was sure.

Alfred was fair, and somewhat short for his age. Unlike his elder brother, he found Latin and, indeed, any bookwork, a struggle. Instead, he watched. Later, he would say that this watching was what made him an actor. From a young age he would entertain the servants with imitations of his father, mother and brother, and, even better, of the servants themselves. He combined this God-given ability with a trusting – believing – nature; if you told him something, however outlandish, he believed you. Everyone loved him for this quality, but his strangely credulous nature did make him an easy target. It was a frailty his otherwise earnest brother could not resist exploiting.

Alfred's best friend was Adam. Adam was the son of the estate blacksmith, Edwin. Edwin lived at the forge where he had sole care of his son and his little daughter, Isabella, at whose birth his wife had died. The forge was to be found half a mile down the chestnut tree-lined drive, opposite the lychgate to the churchyard sheltered by yew trees. Alfred and Adam were the same age; they had grown up together, and they did everything together. This included riding Alfred's little cob-horse, Dash, down the lanes and across the fields;

The Lollard Oak

they were getting a little big now, but Dash didn't mind carrying the two of them.

It was a time when religion was, literally, a burning matter. The question of the legality of Henry's marriage to Catherine of Aragon, upon which the future peace of the realm was said to depend, was known as 'The King's Great Matter'. And it was an unintended consequence of this 'Great Matter' that England had become Protestant.

A liturgy, entirely in English, had been coming for some time but Thomas Cranmer, the Archbishop, was now forcing upon all the parishes of the land the revolutionary new English 'Book of Common Prayer'. This was also a 'matter' on which the country was deeply divided, as, often, were individual families. Mercifully, the divisions in the Edmundson household were, mostly, good-natured. But they were there.

Cuthbert had taken the trouble to read the new 'Book of Common Prayer', and was frustrated that neither Emma nor William would deign to do the same. As head of the household, it was his duty to guide them.

"I challenge you," he said over dinner, "to read the Prayer of Humble Access – 'We do not presume to come to this thy table, trusting in our own righteousness …' and fail to be moved by it. This is more than a new adornment to our national life; it speaks to our deepest thoughts and strongest feelings."

But Emma was not moved. She found it impossible to discard the old beliefs as if they were no more than worn-out clothes. William was even more frustrated with his father than his father was with him. "Can you not see that the Catholic Latin liturgy is the glue which attaches England to the continent? It is what holds our European civilisation together. To abandon it is like the severing of a limb: painful, damaging, and unnecessary."

And what did Alfred think? The question was a courtesy. It was assumed that Alfred did not think about such things.

"Did Jesus speak to his disciples in Latin or English?", he asked. There was something disconcerting about Alfred; did he say this kind of thing because he was stupid, or because he was clever, or because he was cleverly acting stupid?

Father John, the late Prior of Wenlock Priory, had been coming to the family's large and rambling manor house for several years now. He did so discreetly, and they protected him. During these visits, Emma and William would receive the holy sacraments of bread and wine during services held in the dining hall; he would use the Latin liturgy, and observe the true doctrine of the Roman Catholic church.

It was Sunday, 2nd June, the Sunday before Whitsuntide. William was helping his mother prepare the dining-table as an altar, arranging in their correct positions all the 'Eucharistic elements': the candles, the chalice, the ciborium, the paten and much else in anticipation of the imminent arrival of Father John. Alfred was watching.

On a side-table there were the 'cruets', two small glass decanters ready to receive the wine and water. A bottle of wine and a jug of water stood close by. It was a warm summer's day and Alfred was thirsty. He took a cup from the sideboard and went to fill it with water from the jug. William rushed across the room, pretending to be furious, and grabbing both the cup and the jug from his hands.

"Don't you realise what you are doing? This wine and the water are the blood of Jesus Christ. Don't you understand the Holy Eucharist? Drink this and you are taking the Lord's name in vain; it is a blasphemy, and 'whoever blasphemes against the Holy Spirit can never have forgiveness, but is guilty of an eternal sin.'[6] You will burn in Hell for all eternity, you stupid, stupid boy."

Alfred stood there, his mouth half open, in a state of shock. He could feel the tears welling up in his eyes. He ran from the room, across the hall, and out of the front door. And he kept on running until he arrived at his special sanctuary – Dash's stable box. He leant his head against the little horse's warm flank, and wept.

In the dining hall, Emma was genuinely furious.

"That was not funny, William. You must not do that; you know how hard Alfred takes these things. I am so cross with you."

She was on her way out to find her younger son when, just at that moment, there was the distinctive clip-clop of Father John, coming down the metalled drive. She had to greet him and, in doing so, forgot to comfort little Alfred.

For Alfred, things got worse. Much worse. The following day, Monday, Dash lost a shoe as he trotted down the drive to pick up Adam at the forge, opposite the little church. Edwin was out on a call, but would be back within the hour. Adam was sure his father could fix the shoe on his return, so Alfred, needing to clean out the stable, and with Adam promising to look after Dash, walked back to Kingsgate.

The awful news came a little later. Edwin, breathless, had run all the way up to the house; Adam and Isabella, following him at a distance, were now half-hiding behind a chestnut tree. Dash was dead.

Adam had not tied Dash to the halter rail properly. He had gone inside the forge for a few minutes and, in that time, the little horse had pulled himself free, made straight for the churchyard, and began to munch on the poisonous yew trees[7] there.

Isabella had been the first to see what had happened, but, by the time she got there, it was too late. Within the hour, the poor animal had died.

The whole family, and all the servants, were now outside the big house, discovering what had happened. There was no-one who was not fond of Dash. They looked at Alfred, expecting him to cry; they knew he was inclined that way and, if ever there was a reason to cry, this was it. But he didn't. Quite the opposite. He stood there silent and expressionless. Both Emma and Cuthbert attempted to give him a hug, but he swung his shoulders round to push their sympathy away.

On Tuesday morning, Adam came up the drive with Dash's bridle and saddle. It was awkward. Neither of them knew what to say.

The Lollard Oak   1549

Adam put the tackle down in the main hall, and Alfred, without explanation, took him into the dining-hall. Emma went to the closed door but could not hear what was said. When they came out, Adam looked perplexed, whilst Alfred said nothing, and would not respond to her gentle overtures. When she talked about it with Cuthbert that evening, her husband tried to reassure her.

"He's shocked. There's nothing to be done. We can't bring Dash back, but we do need to get another cob; we need it for the cart. But, of course, it won't be Dash."

Emma sighed. "Poor Alfred. I just wish he'd say something. The silence is awful. He hasn't said a single word since he heard the news yesterday afternoon. Apart from anything else, it's not fair on Adam."

Wednesday passed, and still Alfred was tearless and silent. It was the same on Thursday and Friday. Not a word. On Saturday morning, at the breakfast table, William decided to take things into his own hands.

"Look here, Alfred." It was not a good start. "We all understand how sad you are about Dash, and we all understand how you're feeling jolly angry, but you've got to pull yourself together and get over it."

Alfred got up, and, with his breakfast uneaten, left the room.

That evening Emma watched from an upper window as Alfred walked out of the garden and into the fields. She decided to follow him. Her anxiety had begun to overwhelm her. Perhaps, he was planning ... Alfred made his way from the house over to the west; he went up an incline into a field called Falcon, where the recently-scythed hay lay in neat, curving rows. At the top, there was a view of Lichfield Cathedral in the distance. The sun was a great red ball, hanging in the darkening blue sky above the three spires.

Alfred had sat down; Emma, still some distance behind, called out to ask if she might come and sit next to him. He didn't move, so she did. They sat there together, between the rows of hay, for some time, mother and son, without speaking.

They were not alone. In the air, scented with newly-cut grass, a million tiny insects created a faint buzz, and, amongst the earthy stubble, the occasional beetle and a thousand restless ants went about their business. Emma watched an ant struggle valiantly as it bore the heavy burden of a blade of dry grass, many times its own size, on its long journey home.

Eventually, she broke the silence.

"Tomorrow is Whitsun and the Church is introducing the new liturgy[8], and I've decided to go. I don't agree with it, but I think it's best to have an open mind. Anyway I'm going, and I'm going to pray for three things. I'm going to pray for Dash. I'm going to pray for you. And I'm going to pray for Adam."

She fell silent again before, after a few minutes, saying, softly:

"Will you come with me?"

Alfred, not immediately, but soon enough, nodded his head.

It was only Alfred and his mother who, hand in hand, under a blue sky, walked down the drive that morning, through the avenue of blossoming horse-chestnut trees, and to the little church. They arrived just as the service was about to start, were given some papers held together by string on which the new liturgy was printed, and sat at the back. There was a welcome coolness inside the Saxon church with its re-assuring damp and fusty smell; the old oak benches wobbled noisily on the yet older flagstones.

Alfred had not spoken, but he was attentive. Whilst it was strange to hear the prayers in English, it was completely extraordinary to understand them. The priest was intoning:

> "Ye that do truly and earnestly repent you of your sins, and are in love and charity with your neighbours, and intend to lead a new life, following the commandments of God, and walking from henceforth in his holy ways: Draw near with faith, and take this holy Sacrament to your comfort; and make your humble confession to Almighty God, meekly kneeling upon your knees."

Alfred and his mother both knelt. Together with the priest, and those in the congregation who could read, they said aloud the unfamiliar words of the new liturgy:

> "Almighty God, Father of our Lord Jesus Christ, Maker of all things, Judge of all men: We acknowledge and bewail our manifold sins and wickedness, Which we from time to time most grievously have committed, By thought, word, and deed, Against thy Divine Majesty, Provoking most justly thy wrath and indignation against us. We do earnestly repent, And are heartily sorry for these our misdoings; The remembrance of them is grievous unto us; The burden of them is intolerable. Have mercy upon us, Have mercy upon us, most merciful Father; For thy Son our Lord Jesus Christ's sake, Forgive us all that is past; And grant that we may ever hereafter Serve and please thee In newness of life, To the honour and glory of thy Name; Through Jesus Christ our Lord. Amen."

The priest then stood up and faced the congregation, and, whilst making the sign of the cross, forgave them their sins:

> "Almighty God, our heavenly Father, who of his great mercy hath promised forgiveness of sins to all them that with hearty repentance and true faith turn unto him; Have mercy upon you; pardon and deliver you from all your sins; confirm and strengthen you in all goodness; and bring you to everlasting life; through Jesus Christ our Lord. Amen."

A little later, Emma felt Alfred rest his head softly against her shoulder. Once more he was her dear little boy. Then she noticed that, almost imperceptibly, he was crying.

"Mother," he said, as they walked back up the drive, "is it true that other people feel that way about what they have done?"

"What do you mean?" asked Emma, who, such was her joy on hearing his treasured, unbroken voice again, was hardly able to speak herself.

"Do other people feel that remembering what they have done wrong is an 'intolerable burden'? I mean, actually, 'intolerable'? Do other people feel that?"

"Yes, my dear, we have all done things that make us feel like that. All of us."

"But, Mother, I have done something much more terrible than anyone has ever done."

"Oh Alfred, why do you say that, my darling?"

"I've sent my best friend to burn in hell. For eternity."

At this, the tears returned, re-doubled.

Mother and son did not go back to the house. Instead, they walked together across the fields, until they came to the big tree in Well Meadow that has always been called 'The Lollard Oak', and sat down in its shade.

In gasps, the story of what had happened in the dining-hall with Adam came tumbling out. He had been so angry with Adam; all he wanted was revenge. He was determined that Adam should be punished for letting Dash eat the poisonous yew. He had found the communion wine, poured some into a cup, and told Adam he had to drink it. He didn't tell Adam why.

But, no sooner had Adam drunk it than Alfred was engulfed by guilt. How could he have done such a thing? To his best friend? To his only friend? Adam had not intended to harm Dash; Adam was just as fond of the little horse as he was. But it was done. He couldn't take it back. Adam would burn in hell for eternity. He thought of how he had picked up a piece of blackened wood from the fire, only to discover, too late, that it was still burning, and that was but a small part of the agony to which he had condemned his friend. For eternity. How could he do such a thing? How *could* he? It was beyond forgiveness.

The Lollard Oak   1549

It was neither quick nor easy to persuade Alfred that what his older brother, William, had said in jest was a nonsense. Fortunately, Father John came during that week. The red-haired Irishman with his pale blue eyes, sat the eleven-year-old down and spoke in his gentle, Irish way about these things.

"Do you know what, young man? Our Lord and Saviour was always breaking the stupid rules the High Priests and all those dressed-up types were making such a fuss about. He didn't give a fig about all that nonsense. And nor should you. And I'll tell you another thing – just between you and me – the longer I've been a priest, the more I think that, perhaps, the bread and wine are just bread and wine. How dreadful is that? And as for this burning in hell: I don't believe it. They made it up to frighten us into being good. But what, I ask, is good about frightening other people? That's not the Jesus I know."

Before the summer was out, a new little cob was found and purchased, and Alfred and Adam resumed their happy, carefree escapades.

Back at The George Inn, Southwark – 1595

"Now, that was, indeed, a magnificent memory. But more, my dear old Alfredo, it was an interesting one. I have some questions. But first, another beer?"

The young playwright was soon back with the beer.

"Now, my first question is: did your brother William ever become a bishop?"

Alfred leant back and laughed. "Yes, I know he doesn't come out of it so well, does he? But, that Sunday – it was the 9th of June 1549 – when he heard from our mother what had been going on, and realised how stupid he'd been, he came and asked me to forgive him."

"The boy had a heart."

"Oh, yes, he may have been a bit pompous and pleased with himself, but, even then, at least he knew he was a bit pompous and pleased with himself."

"Earlier, you said that, until all this happened, you believed what the Catholics believe, that at the Communion Service a miracle occurs and the bread and wine really are the *actual* body and blood of Christ. Have I got that right?"

"You have."

"And then 'something awful happened', that changed your mind. So, what exactly was the 'awful' thing? Was it the horse dying, or was it forcing Adam to drink the wine?"

"No, no, no. You don't understand. Yes, of course, it was awful about Dash, and yes it was awful thinking that I had sent Adam to burn in hell, but, do you know what, the really awful thing was realising what a horrible, horrible person I was. Before all this to-do, I thought of myself as being quite a decent little boy. Everyone liked me. Then, suddenly, I discovered that, underneath, there was this evil that I couldn't control. It still scares me."

"But what made you change your mind about the bread and the wine and the miracle?"

"It was Mother. She said that the words of Cranmer in the new prayer book had performed a much greater miracle than anything to do with bread and wine. It was a sign from God, she said."

"Because when you heard those words '… we do earnestly repent, and are heartily sorry for these our misdoings; the remembrance of them is grievous unto us; the burden of them is intolerable …' something flipped over inside you."

"Exactly. It was like a miracle. I had been in a dark dungeon of my own horribleness; those words unlocked the door and I walked out into sunlight. I thought I had done something uniquely terrible but, on hearing that prayer, I realised I wasn't unique. I was bad, yes, but I was not alone in being bad. That feeling of 'not being alone', of connection, is the most wonderful feeling a person can have."

At this, the young playwright leant back, and nodded his head thoughtfully.

"It's why I write, Alfredo. I agree with your mother. Words do have a miraculous power to set us free. When I was born, there was no Latin Mass, except, I suppose, in country houses like yours; every day we heard and read and spoke the words of the Book of Common Prayer. Even today, I can recite much of it off by heart. We are so fortunate to have that rock-like foundation to our language. Whatever little way I have with words, I owe more to those lovely prayers than all the other writings I know. They run through me like my blood. But enough of that. You still haven't told me: did your brother William become a bishop?"

"Good heavens, no. He's now inherited Kingsgate and is quite the country squire. To be fair to him, he did not enclose a single acre[9]. Not one. Yet, it's true, he gave up his Catholicism and went into the church for a time. The locals used to say of him that his sermons were long and incomprehensible, but that he was kind. He even took it upon himself to teach Adam and Isabella the scriptures. And then …"

Alfred began to laugh.

"And then what, Alfredo?"

"And then." Alfred wiped a tear from his cheek. "And then it turned out that the lessons with Isabella were not confined to the holy scriptures. So, he made an honest woman of her. Five children, they've had."

Chapter Five: 1667

'When the Norman conquered our forefathers, he took our England ground from them, and made them his servants. God hath made you an instrument to cast out that conqueror, and recover our land and liberties out of that Norman hand.'

Gerrard Winstanley: 'The Law of Freedom in a Platform'
A pamphlet addressed to Oliver Cromwell in 1652

Dramatis Personae

William Edmundson, Owner of the Kingsgate Estate
Alfred Edmundson, William's younger brother
Sarah Edmundson (née Lockyer), Alfred's wife
'Little Cuthy' Edmundson, Alfred and Sarah's son
Emma Edmundson, Mother of William and Alfred; widow of Cuthbert; friend of Edith de Lacy

Edwin, Blacksmith to the Kingsgate Estate
Isabella, his wife
Adam, their son

Fitzwilliam de Bourgh, Kentish Landowner
Anne de Bourgh (née de Lacy), his wife; niece of Edith and sister of Roger de Lacy
Catherine de Bourgh, their daughter; goddaughter of William Edmundson

Edith de Lacy, Aunt of Anne and Roger; friend of Emma Edmundson
Roger de Lacy, Brother of Anne de Bourgh; nephew of Edith

Dr Christopher Wren[1], Surveyor for Royal Works
Robert Hooke[2], Curator of Experiments at the Royal Society

Peter Giffard, Gentleman
John Giffard, his son, Constable of Staffordshire

1667

Day one (Monday 27th June): The evening
Dr. Wren to his sister, Susan[3],

... in which he explains why he does not want to go to Lichfield.

My dear Susan,

Robert and I have stopped for the night at a village called Milton Keynes, which is half way to Lichfield. Not being in London makes me fretful. A decision on the new St Paul's is imminent and the birds of prey are circling. With me gone, they will try to persuade the King to re-build the cathedral in the 'Gothic' manner. It is not mere vanity that I argue for something modern; this is an opportunity to say to the world that England is the equal of all, and it will not come again. But I need time to get the designs right. Robert can then make a model which, I have no doubt, will enthral those who see it, and win the heart of the King.

But, for the present, I must submit to the Royal whim. Amidst all the woes besetting our nation, first the plague[4], then the fire[5], and now this calamity in the Medway[6], the King is distracted by his 'promise to Lichfield'[7]! His 'promise to Lichfield', ye Gods! Who cares about blasted Lichfield? But if I do not go there 'to advise', I lose the King's favour, and, thereby, the chance to resurrect St Paul's in a manner which will be the pride of our nation for generations to come.

We shall be away for five days in all. The advantage – not a small one – is that the two of us can talk without interruption.

As for the cathedral at Lichfield, it is to be repaired, not re-built. It was besieged – for the third time in as many years – by the

The Lollard Oak 1667

Parliamentary forces in '46, and, during that siege, some vile Parliamentarian pointed the artillery at the central spire of the cathedral. It crashed down through the roof and wrecked a good part of the ancient building. It is Robert they need more than me, but few see past his unfortunate appearance and excitable manner, and no one gives him the recognition his capabilities deserve.

Tomorrow, for two nights, we stay with gentry farmers situated between Tamworth and Lichfield. I fear it will be like Dorset! Very dull, with no conversation beyond crops and cattle. And, good God, what will they will make of Robert!

Emma Edmundson to Edith de Lacy

... in which she tells her old friend about the arrival of the de Bourgh[8] family.

Dearest Edith,

I was expecting to send you an account of the arrival of your niece and her rich husband that was full of excitement. But it has not turned out so well.

You know how I have this habit of noticing every detail. It was on this account that Cuthbert's friend, Peter Giffard used to call me 'the constable'. Once he and Cuthbert had a wager about it – Cuthbert could never resist a wager. It was after a party at Chillington; we were the last to leave, and, as we did so, Peter asked me to recall the colour of the dresses of all the ladies who had been there. It was not difficult, but what an odd thing to ask of me! As I completed my recollection, there was much laughter, and Cuthbert had to pay Peter a guinea. (Did you know John, Peter's son, is now the actual Constable of Staffordshire?)

Despite my advanced age, this habit will not leave me alone. When the de Bourgh carriage drew up this afternoon, Fitz stepped out of the carriage first. He is very small, isn't he? Catherine, followed next – very beautiful – and then, after a curious wait, came Anne. As

The Lollard Oak

she emerged, I noticed her put up the collar on her blouse, and I could not help but wonder why.

I suppose you, being a de Lacy, are accustomed to a carriage and six, but none of us had seen such a sight before. What beautiful black horses! All of them shiny and groomed! The arrival drew a gasp from the servants, who had lined up in the sunshine behind William, Alfred, Sarah and myself. To swell our numbers, Edwin and his wife, Isabella and their son, Adam, had come up from the forge. Alfred was annoyed because 'Little Cuthy' – we still call him that although he's now bigger than his grandfather, my Cuthbert, ever was – had not returned from shooting crows in the woods.

But, as I say, I can't help noticing things. When Anne and I kissed, first on one cheek, and then the other, I took the opportunity to glance downward and saw, on both sides of her delicate neck, brown and black marks. It reminded me of marks I once saw on a woman in the village many years ago: she had been strangled to death by her drunken husband.

I did not tell William. I fear, however, that William would not be surprised; he never liked de Bourgh. Although they both fought for the King, William cannot recall seeing him at an actual battle.

This visit will be difficult for William. It is the first time that Catherine, his goddaughter, has come from their Kent home to Kingsgate, and he has not seen Anne since before Naseby[9] in '45. I don't think his feelings for her have changed.

Like Anne, we all assumed he must have been killed at Naseby. It was a Jewish family, searching for gold and silver on the battlefield, who found him. They carried him, barely alive, to their home in Leicester, and nursed him back to health. It took a year before he recovered his memory, and during that time the Jews, not knowing who he was, and fearing for his safety and theirs, kept him secretly. On his return here, it was too late: Anne had married de Bourgh.

At the time your nephew, Roger, tried to persuade her not to marry 'the midget', but she was, as he put it, 'unreachable'. Fitz was transfixed by Anne's beauty and, once William was out of the way, he behaved as if she was his by divine right. Poor Anne, she was only 18. Now she is 40. But not a whit less lovely!

We all suffered in the war[10] but none more than William. The burning down of the old house by Prince Rupert's[11] men, for no reason other than that Cuthbert and Alfred were in the Parliamentary garrison at Lichfield, was heartbreaking for everyone, but for William it was especially sharp. Being a Royalist, he felt not only responsible for it[12] but also insulted that his position had been no protection. Then there was the disfigurement at Naseby, and the King's defeat. Despite all of that, it was, I am sure, the loss of Anne that caused him the greatest pain. But, like Alfred, he keeps himself to himself.

I did urge him to find another, but he was adamant that no woman would want to wake up to his 'horrifying face'. Of course, he doesn't understand that a mark of physical courage is irresistible to our sex. I think he decided that if he couldn't have Anne, he would have no one.

On their arrival William was civility itself – he takes his old school motto, 'Manners Makyth Man'[12], seriously. Unfortunately, our guest did not acquire a reciprocal capability at Eton. Rather, he looked at our new house, of which we are all very proud, without comment. I could see William thinking, 'Catherine is my goddaughter, so I must make the best of it'.

Soon Little Cuthy returned to the house with two dead crows, red in the face, and wiping the sweat from his brow. We were still in the front hall. Alfred was on the point of scolding him for his absence, but Sarah whispered in his ear, and he introduced their son to our guests gracefully.

On greeting Catherine, Little Cuthy turned an even brighter red! There was no mistaking it, and I shivered a little to see a young man take to a lovely girl. But Catherine looked away: Was he too young for her? Or she too grand for him? My heart ached for the boy!

He has turned out well. Back in '49 I was anxious when Alfred returned from London with Sarah as his new bride. It was too soon after the execution of her brother[13], the Leveller, outside St Paul's. I

The Lollard Oak

feared things would go awry. But I was mistaken: she has been the best of mothers and wives.

When I saw the young man blush, the years rolled away and I remembered when William was first introduced to Anne long ago. But I fancy that Catherine is more like her father.

Tomorrow, we have yet more guests. From London. An 'architect' called Dr. Wren, together with his assistant, a Mr. Hooke. They have been sent to advise on the repairs to the cathedral, and we are required, by Royal Warrant of all things, to be hospitable. I fear they will be very dull.

How are you surviving the hot weather? I don't like it; it irritates my throat and makes me hoarse. When the de Bourghs stepped down from their carriage, Isabella, the wife of Edwin, our blacksmith, fainted. She is sturdy, not at all the sort of person one would expect to succumb to the heat.

William's diary

... in which he writes of Fitzwilliam de Bourgh's haughty manner, the arrival of the gentlemen from London, and a large gift.

Yes, it was lovely to see Anne again and pleasing to discover that I have a beautiful godchild, but the pain was sharper than I had expected. I remind myself not to dwell on what might have been.

But why did she marry Fitz? Of all people? She is slight physically but that belies a fiercely independent character. We talked about him once. We thought that wealth ought to give a man self-confidence, whereas, with Fitz, it seemed to sap it. He interpreted friendliness in others as a calculation to get something out of him, but yet was drawn to surround himself with exactly the sort who were, indeed, making just such calculations.

Why did she marry him? The question claws at my mind. His insecurity now hides behind a mask of superiority and contempt. Kingsgate may not be a stately home like his, but it is a large, handsome, well-proportioned country house. Could he not say something agreeable?

Following their arrival, Sarah took Anne and Catherine up to their rooms, chatting away. Mother followed quietly, but it was obvious how pleased she was to see Anne once more; she would have loved Anne to be her daughter-in-law.

It fell to me to show our rich guest around the new house. I had imagined this circumstance in anticipation of his coming, but what a fool I was to think it could have been anything but galling! The worst of it was his silence. His only effort at courtesy was to compliment me on the new furniture, following my comment that we had lost everything in the fire. We agreed that the war had been a bad thing. I asked him if Rosings had suffered in any way. He said it hadn't. I took him out into the knot garden at the side. We stared out at the fields beyond.

All of a sudden, he declared that he would take a walk to see the cathedral. I was surprised that he could know that there was a view of the cathedral from the top of Falcon, and I politely praised his acute sense of direction. He muttered something about a map and strode off. It is a great relief to know that he will go to Tamworth Castle tomorrow to call upon his cousin, John Ferrers.

Tomorrow also brings our visitors from London. The letter from the Royal Household asking for accommodation says they are coming to 'advise on the repairs to the cathedral'; but what advice is there to be given? The work is progressing well and I cannot believe that an 'architect' has more knowledge than the Lichfield masons. No, the timing is suspicious. We finally finished the re-building of Kingsgate only last month, and it must be that they have come to inspect. It is not an unreasonable thing to do, but it unsettles me.

I only learnt about the gift after my father's death. Prince Rupert gave it to him not long after Naseby, and it was so extraordinarily generous – some £30,000[14] – that he feared a catch, and so decided to keep it a secret, even from his family.

I say 'Prince Rupert gave it to him' but, to be precise, it came with two conditions. The first was that the money was to be spent only on the re-building of Kingsgate. The second was that Father should not enquire into the source of these funds. After his death, within weeks of the Restoration, when I discovered the enormity of my inheritance, I asked the lawyer whether our benefactor was Prince Rupert. He replied: "That is not for me to say, nor for you to ask."

But it must have been the prince. Firstly, had I not cut off his assailant's hand at Newark[15], he would surely have been killed; the next day he thanked me, saying that, by my quick sword, I had won his everlasting gratitude. And then at Naseby, although I remember nothing of the battle, I am told that I distinguished myself. But what persuades me most is that, during the campaign of '45, he admitted to me how much he regretted the burning down of Kingsgate. It happened after the second siege of Lichfield in '43, when he tunnelled under the wall. He said he felt responsible for Kingsgate because, if he had not returned to Oxford[16] so soon after Parliamentary forces had surrendered, leaving the soldiery behind under the command of weak and incompetent officers, it would not have happened. It was known that Father and Alfred were defending Lichfield for Parliament, so Kingsgate was an easy target for burning[17]. That I was a Royalist cavalry officer counted for nothing.

Soon after, when I was stationed at the Royal Court in Oxford, I tried to find out who was responsible for this barbaric act. The wall of silence convinced me that it must have been someone important and, most likely, the prince himself. No doubt, on discovering that I was the heir to a house which his soldiers had burnt down, he wished to make amends. But, of course, at the same time, he would not have wanted me to know about his role in it.

We shall have a strange mix under our roof this time tomorrow. I hope nothing goes wrong.

Day Two (Tuesday 28th June): The evening
Dr. Wren to Susan,

... in which he writes of his conversation with Robert Hooke, a curious dinner, and the sight of Lichfield Cathedral at sunset.

My dear Susan,

Through this long, hot day in our somewhat down-at-heel Government carriage, the conversation with Robert has been dominated by domes. I do wonder if Robert actually sleeps at all[18]. Last night he took my sketches for the new cathedral, and now they are covered with his scrawly handwriting. His great obsession is the softness of the London clay. This morning, without so much as a 'Good Day', he greeted me with: "Firstly, Christopher, it's about the weight, and, secondly, its distribution. But it can be done. It can be done."

In the carriage he drew out of his pocket a fob watch on a long silver chain. He proceeded to show me that, holding the slack chain at either end, it naturally forms a curve which distributes the weight of the chain evenly between the links.

I questioned this: "Surely the higher links at either end carry the weight of the rest of the chain and, therefore, the greater force is on those links rather than the lower ones?"

"But what of the lateral force that is pulling the chain apart?" he countered. "That is the greater, the lower the link. You are the superior mathematician, Christopher, but my instinct is better. And it tells me that the shape of this chain[19] ...", he held it up again, "when inverted, gives us the means to disperse the forces in an arch in the most even way possible. And the more equal the distribution of forces, the less stone we will need, and so the less weight."

Later we had another demonstration of his 'instinct'. We were only a few miles short of Kingsgate Manor, our destination, when we were driven off the road and into the ditch by a carriage and six coming very fast from behind us. The carriage had a single, but

The Lollard Oak

obviously wealthy, occupant, and, as Robert wryly observed, the arrogance of his wealth had been distributed evenly down to his driver. We found that two spokes had been broken. To the amusement of our coachmen – and me – we then discovered that Robert's trunk was full of instruments and tools; he refused all offers of help and, despite the heat, set about effecting a most elegant repair in very little time.

The house is spacious and Jacobean in style. The previous half-timbered construction was burnt down during the war by Royalists and it has been re-built in brick; the windows are high and of good proportions using the local sandstone. The work has been done well, but goodness knows how Mr. Edmundson has paid for it – they are minor gentry, comfortable but not rich. Mr. Edmundson was for the King, but his brother (who also lives here with his wife and son) and his late father were for Parliament: hence the destruction.

We are not the only guests. The great de Bourgh family is here! Mr. Edmundson is a godfather to their daughter, Catherine, and the three have come to visit. You might think that it did not require much instinctive intelligence to calculate the identity of the owner of that carriage and six, but Robert, gloriously unworldly as ever, did not. He was about to relate the story of our recent upset, when I, seeing no advantage in having an awkward relationship with the greatest landowner in the realm, quickly restrained him.

Fitz de Bourgh condescended to remember our father[20] from Oxford in the '40s. You may recall that he was one of the young 'gentlemen' with booming voices who, we surmised, had acquired the habit of shouting because their houses were so big. Father referred to them as the 'Eton mob'. Their families had money which the King needed, and so, despite the times, they had licence to be drunk and rowdy.

Mr. Edmundson is unusually tall and has a terribly disfigured face. At Naseby he received a wound that has left a huge diagonal scar across his left cheek, down one side of his mouth and through to his chin. But he has other oddities. Although plainly an intelligent

The Lollard Oak 1667

man, he treated Robert and me as if we were government inspectors. Soon after our arrival we were invited to examine the foundations of his newly built house; he had had a large hole dug at the side for this purpose. Then, before supper, we were taken on a tour of the attic to see the roof trusses. No, I did not bore him with the details of my invention for the Sheldon Theatre[21]. Instead, Robert took an excessive interest in the joints that had been used. It was hot, and I wanted my supper!

When, at last, we did sit down in the dining hall there was a curious drama involving Mr. de Bourgh and a maid. The meal began with a broth – Mr. Edmundson has a theory that hot liquid is more refreshing in warm weather than something cooler. A maid, aged, I suppose, about 50 was serving. Mr de Bourgh was sitting opposite me, and speaking to Sarah Edmundson on his right, when the maid came with a bowl to his left-hand side. She then spilt this steaming broth directly into his lap. I saw it all, and it was not just a drop, but the entire bowl. He screamed and, indeed, it must have been painful. On rising from his seat, he turned to face the maid. We all looked up at them, expecting fury from Fitz and contrition from the maid. But they just stared at each other. Then he rushed from the room. Meanwhile the maid left quietly by another door, and, so far as I could tell, was unflustered. No one knew what to say, although I think I caught a momentary smile pass across the table between William's brother, Alfred, and his wife, Sarah.

Anne de Bourgh soon followed her husband out of the room, and was, in turn, followed by their daughter, Catherine. Then Emma, the elderly Mrs. Edmundson, left but in the other direction towards the kitchens, presumably to inform the errant maid that her period of service was now over. Finally, our host, William, amid profuse apologies, made his exit, leaving Robert and myself in the company of the younger brother, Alfred, his wife, Sarah, and their son Cuthy.

In no time Robert and Cuthy at the other end of the table were talking about muskets. Robert, with a characteristic indifference to etiquette, asked to see the young man's weapon. He was soon taking

The Lollard Oak 1667

everything apart to expose and explain the mechanisms, and, in due course, the little experiment he devised to show how gunpowder works resulted in a cloud of smoke enveloping both him and Cuthy.

I was not uplifted at the prospect of having to converse with a stolid Staffordshire farmer and his wife at my end of the table. However, as it turned out, I can recall less interesting exchanges at high tables in London and Oxford. I do not have time now to do justice to what was said, but I can say that it left a definite impression.

Tomorrow, we visit the cathedral which is only a few miles from here. Before sundown, William took us to a field where, at the top of a rise, there is a clear view of the two remaining spires. It was a wonderful scene. In the foreground, at the bottom of the slope, stood a magnificent oak tree they call 'The Lollard Oak', and, exactly behind it, in the far distance, the wounded cathedral. Beyond, the red sun hovered over the remaining spires in a pale blue sky with faint, streaky pink clouds. It was still warm and the entire landscape was bathed in a green and golden glow.

As we stood there William told us how his mother, Emma, had witnessed the fall of the central spire from that spot in '46. Robert is now eager to question her as to what, exactly, she saw and heard. Goodness knows what's on his mind.

Emma to Edith,

… in which she discloses information about Fitzwilliam de Bourgh.

Dearest Edith,

The great heat of the day has been surpassed by a most extraordinary evening.

Dinner began with a broth because of William's contrarian idea that, on a hot day, a hot drink cools one better than a cold one. With so many guests we needed our blacksmith's wife, Isabella, and his son, Adam, to help, and Isabella was serving the broth in the dining hall. When she came to Fitz – who had just returned from his visit to John Ferrers at the castle in Tamworth – she simply poured the entire bowl into his lap. Just like that. He was on my right, and was speaking to Sarah on his right, and therefore looking the other way when it happened. I saw it all. It was deliberate.

Fitz got up like a hare from cover and, not unreasonably, was on the point of shouting at Isabella, but then said nothing and fled from the room. Anne followed, but not as hastily as one might expect of a wife. She appeared angry rather than worried.

I left the table too and followed Isabella through to the Servants' Hall. She was there alone, staring out of the window at the old stables. I said in as kindly a tone as I could muster – after all I have known her for her entire life – "Please come to my room, Isabella".

I went up to my bedroom, which is situated at the corner of the house. One window overlooks the front drive, and the other the new knot garden. I stood at the latter and waited. Soon there was a quiet knock.

"Isabella, I saw it all." She looked at me in silence.

She just stood there, forlorn. Oh Edith, I have not been a stranger to sadness in my long life, but this was as great as any I have ever seen. I sat down on the long stool at the end of my bed.

"Come here, my dear."

She did, and I put an arm around her. Soon her whole body was heaving as she sobbed. It was sometime before she spoke in such a way that I could understand what she was saying.

"I cannot tell you … I cannot tell anyone … Ever."

But, little by little, the story came out. She had married Edwin back in '38 and they had tried to have children. At first, she assumed it was her fault, but when she spoke to other girls, she realised that Edwin was – she hated to say it – 'lacking in manliness'. Then came the devastating events of April '43. I had left with the other servants to go to Tamworth just in time, but Edwin and Isabella were at the forge when the King's men arrived. When they realised what the soldiers had come to do, they ran up to the house and tried to put out the flames. The soldiers laughed at them. The commanding officer, a very small man, ordered Edwin to be taken back to the forge under guard. He then forced Isabella into the old stables.

"Is that why you fainted yesterday?"

She cried more but, on calming down a little, she said, spitting out the words: "I cannot forget him."

"I told Edwin that nothing had happened. I lay with him soon after, and then, when I discovered I was expecting a child, I pretended it was his. He mustn't know. He could not love Adam more if he really were his own son. I so wish I hadn't poured that broth over Mr de Bourgh; now Edwin will hear of it and wonder why I did it. How stupid of me!"

Between tears, she added: "It's not the sort of thing I normally do." At this we both laughed half-heartedly, and I assured her that I would take things in hand so that Edwin would not have reason to be suspicious.

We sat talking of that day 24 years ago. How is it possible that Isabella could suffer this torment in silence for so many years without me knowing? I do not feel well about myself that this has happened. But then for Anne – of all people – to go and marry the man who had burnt down our house and raped Isabella! Of course, it is impossible that Anne knew, but, still, it is so upsetting.

I washed her face, and then spoke, as I had promised, to the servants and to Adam.

But, Edith dear, is it not a most curious thing? I mean Adam's parentage. I now know that Adam is the son of one of the richest men in England. I cannot quite fathom it. It is difficult not to look upon him differently.

I must go to bed, although I have little hope of sleep, especially with this cough. Oh dear, William is at the door.

The Lollard Oak 1667

William's diary,

… in which he reflects on why he became a Royalist, and on his liking for Mr. Hooke.

What on earth must Dr. Wren and Mr. Hooke think of us! Not only did we lose Fitz, Anne and Catherine from the dining table, but then my mother went off in pursuit of Isabella. Soon after I felt compelled to go and enquire after Fitz, leaving our two 'inspectors' with just Alfred, Sarah and Little Cuthy.

I went to the de Bourgh rooms and Anne came to the door. She pretended that, although Fitz had decided to retire, all was well. The tremble in her lower lip told another story. She looked so frail that I wanted to take her in my arms! I apologised for the behaviour of my staff, and returned to the dining hall.

There I found our London guests fully occupied in conversation, so I made my excuses again. I walked up and down in the knot garden. I thought about how Fitz will expect me to dismiss Isabella from our service; goodness knows, what she did was bad and, from that perspective, there can be no alternative. But does that mean I must dismiss Edwin as well and make the family homeless? I have not the smallest doubt that that is what Fitz would do in such circumstances, and he would do it without a moment's thought. Further, if I fail to act in this way, it will confirm my inferior status.

These thoughts took me back 25 years to the onset of the fighting. Until then, my sympathies had been, like my father's and brother's, with the Parliamentary cause. And yet I joined the King. Looking back, I now see how dishonest I was with myself. I knew all the arguments and so I could persuade myself either way. I chose to believe that the country needed stability, that to take up arms against the King was treason, that it was a step into the unknown, that it was an unnecessary risk, that it would lead the country into the abyss, and so on. The arguments may have had force but they were not related to why I joined the King. All I was thinking about was Anne.

The Lollard Oak 1667

Like most of the old Norman names, the de Lacys were unequivocally for the King, and similarly convinced of his divine right to be the monarch. It was inconceivable that her family would have tolerated her marriage to a man who had fought against the monarchy. I enlisted for the King so that I might be acceptable to her. In the event I lost first my face, and then her. In return I have this damnable scar which, though I tell no one, never leaves me free from pain.

At first, as I walked, absorbed in my own ruminations, I did not hear the voices coming from the casement window above. But then, on stopping and listening, I heard Mother's rather husky voice, in earnest conversation with Isabella, but I could not detect what was being said. When the speaking stopped, I realised Isabella had left. I would go and ask Mother what she thought I should do.

She did not equivocate.

"You cannot dismiss her."

"Why not? Is it not my duty to do so? Surely?"

"No. It is your duty not to do so."

"How come, Mother?"

"I cannot say … you must trust me."

"What has Isabella said, Mother? I demand that you tell me."

"I cannot say, and I will not say, William, and there's an end of it."

So, I pondered, am I to go against my mother, whom I love? Or do I risk causing offence to a very rich man, whom I heartily dislike?

On returning to the dining hall, I was gratified to discover that the conversation had not flagged. It was still light outside, and so I proposed to take our guests to the top of Falcon to see the cathedral as the sun sets. I walked with Mr. Hooke across the fields whilst Dr Wren came behind with Alfred and Sarah – I do hope that Alfred has not let slip his involvement with the Levellers.

Mr. Hooke is a lively man of unusually wide interests, but I cannot say that I have ever met someone whose features gave one less hope. His back is bent and his face ill-shaped. Like mine, one might say, yet his is so by nature, whilst mine is so by war. Whatever: I feel an affinity with the man; he will have endured much rejection on account of his unhappy appearance.

He was interested to learn that in'"46 'other had heard the bombardment and seen the spire topple and fall. He is eager to know more.

Despite all that has happened I find myself retiring to bed with a light heart. I do not think that Dr Wren and Mr. Hooke disapprove of the re-building work. They have completed their commission and are now enjoying their time with us. I wish that our other guests were similarly disposed.

Day Three (Wednesday 29th June): Morning

Dr. Wren to Susan,

… in which he tells her about a dream.

My dear Susan,

Last night I had a most vivid dream. This is how it went.

Robert and I were two small figures standing together in the balustraded gallery beneath the dome of my new building. It soared high above us. Far below was the crossing of the nave and the two transepts. We were facing east towards the altar but could not see it.

The cathedral seemed empty but then we heard steps: first a man walking from the north transept towards the centre of the crossing, then, another coming in the opposite direction from the south transept.

It was the first man who spoke. The voice, full of easy charm, echoed in the vast space. It was immediately recognizable as that of the late King Charles. He said:

"My Lord Protector. I thank you for coming. I have a question I wish to put to you. It is this. Not long after my execution, and before the Battle of Dunbar, you wrote to the General Assembly of the Church of Scotland,

pleading with them and saying: 'I beseech you, in the bowels of Christ, think it possible that you may be mistaken'."

"I did." The deep voice was equally clear, and equally recognizable as that of Oliver Cromwell.

"Now, when I heard that you had made this plea – which, I thought a good one, but which, of course, was ignored – I determined that, in due course, I should put the very same question to you, Mr. Cromwell. So, I ask you now, Mr. Cromwell: 'Can <u>you</u> think it possible that <u>you</u> may be mistaken?'"

At this Mr. Cromwell laughed. "I fancy that you are not really asking me a question, Your Highness. I think what you are saying is that this is a question that we should all ask of ourselves before asking it of others."

"Precisely, my Lord Protector. We should, shouldn't we? But we didn't, did we? Neither of us."

"No, we didn't."

"With terrible consequences."

"Yes."

The two men put their arms around each other's shoulders, and walked towards to the altar, and from our sight.

On waking, it was wonderfully clear what the re-building of St Paul's means to me. It is more than the mere reconstruction of a church. It is to be an inspirational symbol. Great as the undertaking will be in itself, it will also stand for something greater: the healing of a nation[22]. You, dear Susan, will understand what I mean.

It then seemed to me my dream was a continuation of the conversation I had had at supper last night. So I must now tell you about that too.

After Mr. de Bourgh made his dramatic exit, and old Mrs. Edmundson, who I had been speaking to at the head of the table on my right, departed, I turned to speak with Alfred who was on my left. Alfred is not unlike the estate manager who worked for our grandfather in Wiltshire: short, built like an ox, and incapable of small talk. His wife, Sarah, who was opposite us, and who had also lost her interlocutor – de Bourgh – gave me more hope. Searching for something to say, I lighted upon the green ribbon in her hair.

"Is your ribbon what I imagine it to be, madam?"

She laughed, and I noticed that she is a most attractive woman. Her hair is fair, and her eyes are blue and bright. "Ah, Dr. Wren, that is what Mr. de Bourgh asked me?"

"And dare I ask what your answer might be without ending up with hot broth in my lap?"

"It is, indeed, a dangerous question."

"But, please, tell me."

"My brother was Robert Lockyer, Dr. Wren. On the day of his execution by firing squad outside St Paul's Cathedral, I swore that I would wear the green ribbon of the Levellers in his honour, every day, for the rest of my life. He faced his end without even a bandage over his eyes. He was the best of the best, Dr. Wren."

I could feel a moral strength in her restraint. She continued: "A stranger in the crowd put his arm around me, and thus it was that, as I lost a brother, I gained a husband."

Alfred smiled a sheepish smile. There was no point in hiding my royalist sympathies, but I was glad that Robert, whose views are more passionate than mine, was so engrossed in weaponry.

Her words took me back to the time when Leveller arguments were heard across the land. She had certainly not forgotten them. "All freeborn Englishmen have a birthright, Dr Wren, which we inherited from our Anglo-Saxon predecessors, and it is wrong that we should be deprived of it[23]. I believe that the poorest man in England has a right to choose his own government[24]."

I countered as a royalist. "But is it not closer to the truth to say that the greatest part of the people possess, not a birthright, but a brutal ignorance, and that what you Levellers call 'freedom' is nothing more than an opening of the floodgates to licentious liberty[24]?"

And so it went, as it used to all those years ago, back and forth. She claimed it was tyranny for an Englishman to have to live under laws which he had had no hand in framing. I asked whether she would be content to be subject to laws made by a blacksmith. She contended that the blacksmith at Kingsgate had as good a judgement as the highest in the land to tell a fair law from an unfair one. I asked how that could be, and she answered: "Because our blacksmith is one of us; he is an Anglo-Saxon not a Norman. He is my equal; he is your equal."

"Unlike Mr. de Bourgh?", I asked with my eyebrows raised.

"Since you ask, I will venture to say that our guest does not think of us, or even of you, Dr Wren, as his equal. That is not the Norman way. And we all know how he came by his great estates and wealth. Tell me, Dr. Wren, which Englishman can entirely forget that when the Norman duke conquered England, he disposed of all our English ground to his friends as he pleased, and made the conquered English his servants? And are not all the kings, from that time until now, successors of that conquest? And have not all the laws of property been designed to confirm that conquest? Dr. Wren, we believed that God made our Lord Protector Cromwell the instrument to recover our lands and liberties from out of that Norman hand[26], but he didn't. He broke faith with the English people. And he murdered my brother.

"But we cannot live our lives with bitter feelings, Dr Wren, that will settle nothing. You will think that I am just a simple country girl, and that I am not your equal. And perhaps you are right, but also perhaps you are wrong. I hated Cromwell – as, I presume, you did – but there was something he said that follows me around from those days to this, and it will not leave me alone. He said to the Church of Scotland over a dispute: 'I beseech you, in the bowels of Christ, think it possible that you may be mistaken[27]'. I now feel that, on both sides, we were all too sure that we were right and that everyone else was wrong. We listened only to our own side. I think Cromwell, in the end, understood that."

So that is the conversation which left an impression on me strong enough to fill my dreams. As for Alfred, my view of him has also changed. As we walked across the fields yesterday evening to see the cathedral under the setting sun, I mentioned my seed-drill[28] for sowing corn more evenly and without waste. On our return, he came to me with a proposal. He will plant half a field with my invention and half in the traditional way. A record will be kept of all that is done, and then a comparison can be made between the times and costs of planting, and the subsequent yields. It could have been Robert speaking!

And so to Lichfield and this blasted cathedral.

Emma to Edith

… in which she tells of some shocking news.

Dearest Edith,

Something has happened. I am all a-tremble. I shall write down each thing in turn.

I woke early. What Isabella had told me yesterday evening was still flying round my head, like a bird trapped in a house. I was shaken by the thought that the monster who had burnt down our house and raped Isabella should now be our guest. It was not possible that Anne could have known what her husband had done, but should I tell her now? How could I tell her? Who else can I tell? I was in confusion about the right thing to do.

As I stood staring out of the window that overlooks the drive, consumed by these thoughts, the front door opened. It was de Bourgh! I cannot bring myself to call him Fitz anymore. He walked across the gravel to the left, and towards the stable yard. He soon returned with a halter which I recognised as belonging to Dash, our little cob horse. He went past the front door. I crossed the room to the other window, and saw him go up to the left of the knot garden and into Falcon.

I dressed and went downstairs. In the dining room I found the funny little man, Mr. Hooke, busy with some drawings. He rose hurriedly when I entered, saying that he was most eager to talk to me.

Speaking very quickly, he explained that William had taken them to see the cathedral in the sunset yesterday evening, and had mentioned that I was there when the central spire toppled down during the third siege. Could I describe to him what I seen and heard?

It is more than 20 years now, but I told him what I could. At first, I saw the spire start to collapse in silence. Then, after quite a long time – 15 or 20 seconds, I suppose – I heard the dull thud of cannon fire, a sound I was all too familiar with. Within a minute the spire had wobbled, first one way, then the other, and fallen. It was no more.

Mr. Hooke seemed to be delighted with this account. He even complimented me on my observational skill. Following this, in a hurry and with excitement, he showed me his plan for measuring 'the speed of sound'. On his next visit he would like to erect a flagpole of equal height to The Lollard Oak and measure various angles with a special instrument; by this means he can calculate the exact distance from the top of Falcon to the cathedral. He plans to bring a cannon to Falcon and, with the aid of a telescope placed under one of the spires, measure the time difference between the firing of the cannon and arrival of its sound.

I think I understand this, but I do not understand what purpose is served by knowing the speed of sound. However, I do like Mr. Hooke: he has enthusiasm, a much-neglected virtue. He left soon after for Lichfield with Dr. Wren.

When the young people came down, I learnt that Little Cuthy had agreed to ride with Catherine around the estate. Cuthy is smitten, poor boy. Of course, he has no inkling as to how very small our estate is compared with what Catherine is accustomed to at Rosings, but I said nothing.

Unlike Little Cuthy, Catherine is not an experienced rider, and so, when, back in my room, I watched as Adam brought Dash, around for Catherine, it made perfect sense. Dash would be ideal for her. At the same time, he had a large bay for Little Cuthy. Bearing in mind what I now knew, I was curious to see how things would go between Adam, her half-brother, and Catherine, his half-sister. Might some primitive sense of recognition be engendered by this encounter? I did not have to wait for an answer.

"What kind of a horse is this? How dare you insult me? Get me a proper horse like Cuthy's."

Not a muscle moved in Adam's face as he replied: "I think this is a good horse for you, my lady."

But Catherine was not to be crossed, and so Adam acceded to her ill-mannered demand. He returned in a few minutes with another large bay. I saw Little Cuthy say something to Adam, at which Adam nodded. Clearly, they were both worried that something might go wrong.

The three of them were just off the drive, when Catherine's bay bolted. The boys chased, but could not catch it. Catherine held on, screaming in terror – everyone could hear her back in the house. The runaway horse galloped all the way up Falcon, and then down into Well Meadow. It continued all the way to the Lollard Oak, a mile or more from the house.

Dear God, I could not wish what greeted her there on the devil himself. Her father was hanging from a branch of the tree; Dash's halter was a noose around his neck, and he was dead.

I have been with Anne all day and what I have learnt is truly astounding. I will tell you all, but must have some rest now; I have a bad sore throat.

William's diary,

... in which he describes the aftermath.

John Giffard, the Constable for Staffordshire, has just left; we were at Naseby together. He was quick to complete his investigation and his statement to the County Coroner will record that it was 'Death by Misadventure'. There will be no mention of suicide.

The Lollard Oak   1667

The body is in the church. It will be taken to Rosings tomorrow. Anne and Catherine will also leave, and Sarah and Mother will go with them.

It was Little Cuthy who climbed the tree, untied the halter, and lowered the body to the ground, where Adam took it in his arms. Adam stayed with Catherine beside the body, whilst Little Cuthy galloped back to the house and came straight to me. I went to find Alfred and Sarah, told them the news, and asked them to go to Catherine immediately. I sent Little Cuthy to the forge to tell Edwin to go and stay by the dead man. Only then did I go to Anne's room.

It was as if she knew what had happened. She just nodded her head, and said only: "As long as Sarah is with her." Her eyes remained dry. Mother came rushing past me – she had just heard the news from Sarah – and took Anne in her arms.

I left them, and went to write a letter to the Constable, sealed it, and gave it to Little Cuthy, who had returned from the forge, and who then rode immediately to the Giffards at Chillington – a journey of an hour or so.

I had a sense that things might go badly between mother and daughter, and I was not mistaken. It was Adam and Sarah who brought Catherine back to the house, leaving Alfred and Edwin to guard Fitz's body by the oak tree. Catherine was on Dash, with Adam holding her from behind. Anne went out to greet her daughter, but Catherine slid off the little cob, and, before running straight past her mother into the house, shrieked: "It's your fault; you killed him; you killed Father." Sarah followed her in, and has stayed with her all day. She tells me how the poor girl has been clinging to her like a small child or animal, weeping inconsolably. Every now and then a ghostly howling spreads through the house, and the rest of us, unable to help, just listen.

Mother, in like manner, has been with Anne. They went to Mother's room; I could hear them talking from the garden below. I do not know what passed between them, but not once did I hear tears. Mother was coughing a lot; I must get Doctor Andrewes.

The Lollard Oak   1667

It was mid-afternoon when John Giffard arrived. He was accompanied by an assistant, Tom, who I remembered as one of the sergeants, who had served with us in the war. John examined the body, spoke to everyone, and completed the formalities in his brisk, military way. Afterwards he took me aside into the knot garden.

"I was at Eton with him. Like Anne's brother, Roger. I'm afraid I didn't much care for him. Got his way a bit too often." We walked on in silence. John continued: "He treated anyone from a family with less than 50,000 acres as below the salt. That included me." I could see that, even after all these years, it still rankled. "Bit of a nerve. Unlike the de Bourghs, we fought at Hastings."

I could not but add: "So did we."

John laughed: "Oh, very good. On the losing side."

"Indeed."

Then, having solemnly agreed that we should not speak ill of the dead, John looked out across the fields, and mused: "I was never quite sure what he actually did during the war."

"You are not alone in that, John," was my equally uncharitable response.

"In my experience as Constable, it is not helpful to have a husband or parent who has committed suicide. I would like to make things easier for Anne and Catherine."

"What do you have in mind?" I asked.

"I can call it 'Death by Misadventure'. Tom will back me up."

I had no objection. Having stayed on to speak to our London guests on their return from the Cathedral, he returned to Chillington.

The servants took food and drink to the ladies upstairs, and I joined Alfred and Little Cuthy, and Christopher and Robert – as I now must call them – for dinner. I had no appetite and, after a while, I made my excuses and came up to write this.

As I sit here now, late at night, in my candle-lit bed chamber, there are some strangenesses that puzzle me.

Why did the horse bolt and go straight to The Lollard Oak where her father was hanging? At dinner we wondered whether the horse was following some profound instinct. Perhaps animals have an intelligence 'which passeth all human understanding' as it says in the prayer book.

And then Little Cuthy tells me that, at the tree, Catherine threw herself into Adam's arms. He said they looked so alike in their shock: it was almost as if they were brother and sister.

And then there was Fitz himself. Why did he suddenly go up to Falcon yesterday just after he had arrived? He seemed to know the place.

Someone is tapping at the door. Is it Mother? It doesn't sound like her tap.

Day Four (Thursday 30th June): The evening

Dr. Wren to Susan,

... in which he reflects on various mistakes.

My dear Susan,

Our visit to the cathedral yesterday was a waste of time. The local masons are well able to manage without our 'advice'. I suspect they regarded the assumption that they were thought to need it as an insult.

But all that has been over-shadowed by a dreadful tragedy. Fitzwilliam de Bourgh has died. On our return, Kingsgate was a house in shock. A Mr. Giffard, the Constable of Staffordshire, was there to greet us. He asked whether we had seen Mr. de Bourgh this morning. We hadn't. There was something about a 'riding accident'. Robert, whose imagination always runs ahead, wondered whether it was suicide. I found myself recalling how I expected our visit here to be 'very dull'!

And then, at dinner this evening, there was another extraordinary thing. William had left the table, pleading a lack of appetite, which left just the four of us; the ladies were consoling, or being consoled, elsewhere. We wanted to talk about something other than the death

The Lollard Oak 1667

of England's greatest landowner, so Robert took it upon himself to tell Alfred and Cuthy about our visit to Lichfield and the building problems created by the collapse of the central spire. In doing so, his royalist affiliation led him to become excessively agitated about the fact that the 'vile' Parliamentary artillery had 'deliberately' fired a cannonball at the spire.

At this, Alfred, who, up to that point, had not spoken at all, interrupted and said, whilst looking at his plate: "It wasn't 'deliberate'."

We turned in his direction.

"It wasn't deliberate," he repeated, still looking down. We were silent, not quite knowing what to make his comment.

He raised his head and stared at us defiantly: "It was a mistake."

"Were you there?", I asked.

"I fired it."

"Father, you never told us", said Cuthy, clearly shaken by this information.

The whole incredible story then came out.

It was in '46; 21 years ago. Alfred and his father, Cuthbert, were with the Parliamentary forces under Captain Brereton laying siege to Lichfield which had been occupied by the Royalists since '43 – that was when Prince Rupert laid the explosives in the tunnel under the wall. The siege had been in progress for several months and the soldiers were bored. One day father and son were watching the crows fly noisily around the spires of the old cathedral, when, as a whimsical wager, Cuthbert offered Alfred a guinea if he could kill a crow with a cannonball.

"And you won the wager." Robert had a calculating look on his face.

"How do you know?", asked Alfred.

"I didn't. It's just that the whole thing is so ridiculously impossible, it cannot be otherwise. So," he went on, "after somewhat disturbing the peace of this unfortunate bird, you won your bet, and ten pounds of cast iron continued on its way into the side of the spire at exactly the right point to cause it to collapse."

"I didn't mean to. It was a mistake. We told Captain Brereton there was a sniper up there. We never spoke of it again." Alfred just said: "I am so sorry. I feel so ashamed." A single tear made its way down his leathery cheek.

After some moments, in which we considered the consequences of this bet, born of boredom, Robert and I started to cry too – with laughter. And the more we thought about it, the more we laughed. Soon, both Alfred and Cuthy joined in. When, eventually, we calmed down, and wiped the tears away, there was a gentleman's agreement to keep it secret. Which, I suppose, I have now broken!

There was no such merriment this morning. We went in a convoy. In front there was the de Bourgh carriage – the one that drove us off the road two days ago – with Anne, Catherine, Emma and Sarah inside. This was followed by a second carriage provided by William Edmundson containing the coffin of Fitzwilliam de Bourgh. Then Robert and me in our shabby old government contraption.

Robert explained why he was interested in what old Mrs. Edmundson had seen. He has a plan to measure the speed of sound. But his mercurial mind then slipped on to another topic. The events of yesterday, he said, had set him thinking once more about 'gravity'. He is 'captivated by the mystery of it'. Imagine, he said, a Lichfield Cathedral set in space, far beyond our planet Earth. There, a heavy block of red sandstone, such as we had seen lying on the floor of the cathedral yesterday, would have been propelled by the cannonball away from the spire into the distance and disappeared entirely. Similarly, he pointed out, without this strange force, 'the de Bourgh man' would not have died after throwing himself off the branch of that oak tree, but, rather, he would have floated in the air beside it.

He showed me a calculation he had been working on at night. It was a messy equation on a torn scrap of paper, and it stated that the force of gravity between any two objects is equal to the product of the masses of the two objects, multiplied by the reciprocal of the square of the distance between them. He is now intent on sending these scribbles to Isaac in Cambridge. There can be no question but that Isaac is a better mathematician than Robert or myself, but I still fear that, in this, he is making a mistake. Isaac is as closed as Robert is open. He is a large planetary body with a gravitational field that sucks everything into it; nothing ever re-emerges other than as a 'Newtonian' construct. If Robert writes this letter, Isaac will take it, digest it, and then regurgitate it as his own, and everyone will talk of 'Newton's Law of Gravity'[29]. That is his way. But Robert won't listen; he is adamant that Isaac would never be so underhand.

As we travelled, I wondered to myself whether one day, they will all talk of 'Wren's Great Dome', despite my relying on Robert to work it all out. And then I thought: Will both Isaac and I be celebrated by future generations, whilst dear, kind Robert – surely one of the most inventive scientists who has ever lived – lies forgotten by history? Such things happen.

Emma to Edith

… in which she reveals all.

Dear Edith,

In my previous letter I said that what your niece told me yesterday was 'truly astounding'. The carriage has stopped for the night at a village called Milton Keynes and so I have a chance to tell you all.

Anne hated Fitz. Only a few days ago when they were preparing to leave Rosings for Kingsgate, he had – as I suspected – all but strangled her. It was not for the first time. The immediate cause for the assault was that, with Rosings being in Kent, they had had to take measures to protect the house from a possible attack by marauding Dutch sailors, and Anne had inadvertently said: "We must be sure not to have another house burnt down."

"What do you mean by 'another'?", was Fitz's furious response.

"I don't know," said Anne in confusion. "Haven't there been other houses destroyed by the Dutch?"

"No, there have not! You mean to insult me, and I will not have it." He then took her by the throat and, had her screams not attracted servants to the room, she believes he would have killed her.

I asked Anne why this innocent remark of hers could provoke such rage.

"Because it was Fitz who ordered Kingsgate to be burnt down."

"No!" I put my hand to my mouth and affected to be surprised by this information. I could not tell her that I already knew – not yet anyway. However, that she knew what Fitz had done only inflamed my revulsion at her decision to marry this man. "I don't understand, Anne. When did you find this out? How *could* you have agreed to marry him?"

"Please, let me sit down. I will tell you everything". And so, we sat together on the long stool, just as last night with Isabella.

"It was after Naseby in '45. Before that, I had expected to marry William; I knew your family was not rich, and so I planned to persuade my father to give me a dowry that would be enough de Lacy money to enable Cuthbert to re-build Kingsgate after the war. But that idea fell apart after Naseby. When, finally, I had to accept that William was dead, I asked my brother, Roger, to help me but he wouldn't. He was sure that Father would not allow de Lacy wealth to be used on behalf of a Parliamentary family. We were not even formally engaged. It was out of the question.

"All this time Fitz was pressing me to marry him, and, apart from Roger, all my de Lacy relatives wanted it. But I wouldn't, even though I had long given up hope that William might, somehow, have survived.

"And then something happened. Roger had friends from Eton who were in a drinking club at Oxford. Whilst drunk, de Bourgh had confided to another member that he had burnt to the ground the house of 'that peasant family', the Edmundsons. Roger knew that de

Bourgh was jealous of William, and suspected that he had destroyed Kingsgate out of sheer spite.

"Oh, Emma, you think of me as this dear, sweet thing. But you couldn't be more mistaken. I'm a de Lacy. We didn't come by all our land and wealth by being sweet. Although I was only eighteen, I came up with a plan. Roger helped me with it, but it was my plan. And it was not nice. I was going to take revenge on de Bourgh for what he had done to the family of the man I loved.

"I employed a lawyer to deal with everything, and he negotiated an agreement with de Bourgh. I would marry him, but only on the condition that he gave me, outright, a large sum. It was to be sufficient for the re-building of Kingsgate – although Fitz would never discover this. That is how I would make Fitz recompense William's family.

"I married de Bourgh so that I could take £30,000 – a huge amount but very affordable by so rich a man – and pass it on to your family. The only condition was that its source would remain secret. Emma, I saw an opportunity to make the man responsible for the destruction of your house pay for its re-construction, and I took it.

"For twenty-one years I have kept this to myself. I can do that sort of thing. I know I don't look hard, but I am. Very hard. I never told anyone about it. Roger knows, obviously, and the lawyer, but no one else, except, now, you.

"I especially didn't want Cuthbert, or any of the Edmundsons, to know. I didn't want them to feel indebted to me; although I loved William more than I could love anyone, before or since, I was not betrothed to him. I just wanted his family to have a fine new house. There was even the danger that they might refuse my money out of pride, or that the information might leak out and filter back to Fitz. Also, I knew that, if it was given anonymously, they would assume it must be Prince Rupert. The lawyer had told me that secret arrangements are normal with royal gifts, because they do not want others to hope for similar generosity."

"You see, Emma, it was the least I could do for the family of the man I loved. I cannot believe that any woman has been more heartbroken than I was when the news came that William was alive. By then, I was married and pregnant with Catherine."

As she told me this story, she would break off and look out of the window. I allowed her time to think her own thoughts.

"I am such a much more complicated person than anyone realises, Emma. I love violently and I hate violently, and I can't tell which is which. I can't distinguish between my love for William and my hatred for Fitz. Being cruel to him, condemning him to a loveless marriage, and taking his money from behind his back, to give to the family of the man I really loved, was all part of loving William. The rest of the world imagined that Fitz was the bully. What a mistake that was! It was me who treated him ruthlessly, and there was nothing he could do about it. And I kept it up, year after year.

"When he objected to my demanding that William be a godfather to Catherine, I simply told him that if he didn't agree I would tell everyone that he had burnt Kingsgate down. Despite his wealth – or maybe because of it – he was always insecure. Any threat to his reputation as a 'good fellow' was more than he could bear.

"But then when I said I wanted Catherine to meet her godfather, and that I would bring her here, he insisted on coming too. They say that criminals need to re-visit the site of their crime. I think that some demon made it impossible for him to stay away.

"But he did not bargain for that maid. When I saw her faint on our arrival, I had an uncanny sense that she had seen Fitz before. I felt sure that it was seeing him again, rather than the heat, which caused her to collapse. And then that incident with the broth put the matter beyond doubt. I will never forget how she looked at him.

"In our bedroom, I asked him: 'Did you rape her, Fitz?'. My hatred for him exploded. I followed him round the room. 'You disgust me, you vile, pathetic, weak, cowardly little midget of a man, you raped her, didn't you?'

"He knew I knew the answer. He didn't say a word. His humiliation was complete and, I have to admit, I wanted to break him. He sat in the chair by the window all night and I don't think he slept at all. He always snores in his sleep and, whenever I woke – which was often – he was not snoring. And then, at first light, he was not there.

"Catherine is right. I did kill him. For twenty years I humiliated him. It's extraordinary to have that power over someone."

Anne spoke for hours. There was much for her to say and much for me to take in. I resisted the temptation to tell her about my conversation with Isabella. I can't. For Edwin and Adam's sake. And yet I cannot but marvel at the fact that Catherine and our blacksmith's son, Adam, should have the same father, and should have been together when he was found.

Today Sarah and I have come with them in the carriage. Catherine has attached herself to Sarah like a wounded animal. It was a compelling sight. Catherine, rich, aristocratic, proud, and, as Sarah would put it, 'Norman', is mourning the loss of her father. And Sarah, kind, modest, and stubbornly Anglo-Saxon, is, with her green ribbon, still mourning the loss of her brother. They are irreconcilable opposites; Catherine is everything Sarah hates. Sarah is everything Catherine despises. Yet, there they were united and together, in their comforting and their being comforted.

Last night I went to tell William about Anne and the money. But, on coming out of my room, I saw Anne in her night-gown tapping on his door at the far end of the corridor. I presume she wanted to tell him everything herself, so I shall keep out of it.

Edith, my dearest, it is probably very vulgar of me, an old woman, to have this thought, but do you suppose that, last night, with William and Anne together again, that …? Oh heavens, I don't know how to put it.

The Lollard Oak

William's diary,

... in which a wound is healed.

It was not Mother. It was Anne. We said little then, and there is little to say now.

When we lay on the bed together, she traced the index finger of her right hand along my scar. Then she knelt beside me, bent down, and kissed it, repeatedly, along its length. I cannot adequately describe the softness of her lips; all I know is that, from that moment, there has been no pain. No pain at all.

Later, I looked down at her, her head resting on the pillow, and her eyes shining in the candlelight. She looked back at me in silence; only her eyes spoke.

I asked: "Do you mean that?"

She answered: "You know I do."

April 1668

William's diary,

... in which he discloses some news that the perspicacious reader will have anticipated.

Anne's latest letter comes with the information that the nurse says the boy is unusually tall for a new-born baby! She had already told me that she had not had intimate relations with Fitz for many years, and that therefore the identity of the father of the child she was carrying was not in doubt. Whilst, of course, I believed her, yet still I feel a glow of satisfaction with this news of the child's 'unusual' height.

Anne tells me he would have been called 'Emma', had he been a girl. She goes on to say how her de Bourgh relatives are gratified that she has named the boy 'William' in memory of 'Fitzwilliam'. In response to these compliments, she says: "Yes, isn't it wonderful that he can bear his father's name!".

For now, young Catherine de Bourgh, through no fault of hers, stands between us and happiness. Anne could not come to live here: that would be a cruel denial of what her daughter has gone through. For me to move there would be similarly unkind.

Anne's brother, Roger, an excellent man, is staying for a few days. Yesterday he said something which perplexes me. We were standing at the top of Falcon, looking out at Lichfield Cathedral and its restored central spire, when he turned to look down on our house in the valley below. He mused on how pleasing it was to see de Bourgh money put to good use for once. I explained that it was Prince Rupert who had funded the re-building. He put his arm around me and said, "Yes, of course".

Emma to Edith

… in which she admits that she is not well.

Dearest Edith,

I am not well. But you know that, so I won't go on about it. When Doctor Andrewes was here this morning, I felt more sorry for him than I do for myself. For months I have known that the growth in my throat will do for me. I fear the pain, but not the death which will release me from it. But poor, Dr Andrewes, he believes it is his duty to conceal from me what I already know. He was tying his hands in knots, drawing breath, and making odd faces. I took hold of his hands and said: "Dr Andrewes, please, it's alright, I know I am dying. We all die."

My only worry is William and Alfred. They don't talk easily to one another and their relationship is fragile. I had a glimpse of this not long after the doctor had left. His departure coincided with the arrival of a cannon. William had arranged with John Ferrers at the

The Lollard Oak

castle for the loan of a cannon, and today it came on a huge wagon drawn by two equally huge shire horses. I watched it all from my bedroom window.

In a way, it's because of me. When that funny Mr Hooke was here last July, he took an unusual interest in the fact that I had witnessed the fall of the cathedral spire during the war. It inspired him to want to replicate what happened in reverse, and we have been exchanging letters on the subject. His idea, if you remember, is to have the cannon fired from the top of Falcon with him observing the smoke it emits from the cathedral spire. He proposes to measure the time between that and the hearing of the explosive 'boom'. Together with some measurements involving the Lollard Oak, which he calls 'triangulation' – he has been using similar means to survey the city of London following the Great Fire – he believes that he will be able to measure the speed of sound. He says this has never been done before, and that it is an 'important experiment'. I'm not sure why, but never mind.

With me not being well, William has taken charge of the arrangements.

The horses drew the wagon and cannon past the corner of the house where my bedroom is, along the side of the knot garden, and out into Falcon. I had a perfect view. As the procession was half way up Falcon, and, it must be said, making a mess of the crops growing there, Alfred suddenly appeared. Usually, he is not one to make a fuss, but today he could not contain his fury. I immediately understood why. I should have realised the potential problem. And so should William.

Dr Wren had sent Alfred drawings for a piece of machinery for seeding. Edwin had constructed it and, last month, Alfred drew out lines to mark where he had used the new machine and where he had seeded using traditional methods. He had promised Dr Wren to keep an exact record of what was done, so as to understand what benefit there was to be gained by the use of this new method. Now, 'without so much as a by-your-leave', as Alfred put it, William had taken two horses and a large wagon straight through Alfred's carefully constructed experiment. William marched back to the house, away from his brother's onslaught, but he was closely followed by Alfred. Soon, downstairs in the hall, they were shouting at each other.

"Well, it's not your land!" I heard William say.

"It's as much mine as yours!" retorted Alfred.

"That is simply not true!"

"You just sit here owning everything and doing nothing. It's disgusting."

I made my way down to pacify them. Sarah was already there for the same purpose, but soon we realised we were only spectators. I asked her to walk with me.

We went slowly across the field and up past Mr Ferrers' bewildered men, who had come with the cannon from Tamworth. At the top, looking across to the three spires, I felt an urge to go into Well Meadow, and be, for one last time, under the Lollard Oak. Sarah took me down the incline, and, as we went, I told her what Doctor Andrewes thinks, and that, now it is upon me, I am not frightened to die.

She listened, all the time holding my arm in case I stumbled, except, of course, it was also so that she could touch me. It was comforting when, from time to time, her grip would gently tighten.

The great oak tree is noticeably bigger than it was when I first came here in 1618. However, as soon as we reached it, I realised how foolish I was to have walked so far. I felt panic when I considered the impossibility of climbing back up the slope. Sarah folded her shawl so that I would have something to sit on, and returned to the house assuring me that all would be well.

Naturally, after she left, I looked up at the branch from which de Bourgh had hanged himself last July, and thought about him. Was he bad or weak? I suppose both. Was he the perpetrator or the victim? Again, quite possibly both. As I tried to imagine his state of mind, I realised how he had come to the conclusion that he could not live with either his past or his present. He then did what was necessary, and did it quickly. It was, I suppose, in its way, almost noble.

I then considered about how things had turned out, and it gave me a little shiver. On the one hand, it was his unacknowledged actual son, Adam, who was there to take him in his arms at the last; on the other hand, it will be his supposed son, William, who stands to inherit all the de Bourgh land. On top of that, when I recall seeing how Anne entered William's bed chamber late at night nine months ago, I am certain that the supposed son is, in fact, an Edmundson, and my grandson.

What muddles and heartaches we make for ourselves by imagining that one man has more worth than another! I was there by myself under the Lollard Oak for more than an hour … except it isn't quite true that I was by myself … I can't explain it but I now think that I may never have been less alone.

Eventually, Sarah returned not only with William, Alfred and Little Cuthy, but also with Edwin, Isabella and Adam. Everyone wanted to be with me! They – well, Edwin – had quickly constructed a kind of bed, like a litter, to put me on and carry me back.

Not only had the awful row subsided, but William and Alfred seemed to be on the best of terms as they discussed, and agreed, how best to lift and take care of me. And so it was that, for a little while, we were all together, under the benign shade of our beloved tree, from whose many thousands of twigs and branches were bursting, the first green leaves of spring.

Chapter Six: 1839

'Our Queen reigns over two nations between whom there is no intercourse and no sympathy, who are formed by a different breeding, are fed by a different food, are ordered by different manners, and are not governed by the same laws.'

'Sybil or The Two Nations' by Benjamin Disraeli (1845)

1839 – Dramatis Personae

Cuthbert Edmundson, Owner of the Kingsgate Estate
Emma, his wife
William, their elder son
Alfred, their younger son
Isabella, their daughter

Edwin, Blacksmith to the Kingsgate Estate
Sally, his wife
Adam, their son

Sir Robert Peel, Leader of the Conservative Party
Julia, Lady Peel, his wife

Edward de Lacy, Oxford friend of William's

Feargus O'Connor, MP and leading Chartist
Zephaniah Williams, John Frost and William Jones, organisers of the Newport Chartist Uprising

Sir Nicholas Tindal, Lord Chief Justice
Mr Kelly, Counsel

Captain Hawkesworth, Captain of HMS The York

John from Dilwyn in Herefordshire, Blacksmith and Convict
Archibald Mosman, Australian Entrepreneur
Richard Hill, Cricket reporter for 'The Sydney Morning Herald'

1839

Sunday, 14th July 1839

William Edmundson, the eldest son of Cuthbert and Emma Edmundson, of Kingsgate Manor near Tamworth in Staffordshire, had recently left Oxford University with a First Class degree in Greats. He was now 22 years old, and due to inherit the 1,000 acres or more of good agricultural land, but he had no interest in farming. He wanted to go into politics.

It was, therefore, his good fortune that, on Wednesdays, his mother played whist with Julia Peel, the wife of Sir Robert Peel[1], a former Prime Minister and the current leader of the Conservative Party. The Peels lived at Drayton Manor on the other side of Tamworth, and William had been invited for lunch there today.

The invitation did not extend to William's Oxford friend, Edward de Lacy, who had been staying at Kingsgate since the end of Trinity Term, but this was not a difficulty. The de Lacy family estate in Yorkshire was an uncomfortable distance from Oxford, and so Edward had become a frequent visitor to Kingsgate, where he was treated as family.

William's main concern was that he did not have a suitable horse on which to ride to Drayton. He did not hunt, but there were occasions when one needed a good hunter. In his imagination he saw himself arriving at the gates of Drayton like the Emperor Tamburlaine who, as they say, 'rode in triumph through Persepolis'[2]. He could hardly do that on Dash, the cob.

He had left it late, but, yesterday, Edwin, the local blacksmith, who knew about horses, took him to the horse dealer in Lichfield. A charming Frenchman from Falaise in Normandy was selling a beautiful, pure black 'trotter' of 16 hands. William spoke excellent French, and enjoyed the opportunity to display this capability in front

The Lollard Oak 1839

the Staffordshire farmers and tradespeople, who were there to buy or sell.

Edwin, whose French was non-existent, did not realise that a price was being agreed, nor that it was twice what he would have offered. He had, however, noticed something about one of the hind legs, which was 'not right'.

And so it was that when Edwin did discover about the price, he had no doubt as to what was going on. The man from Falaise was hardly fluent in English, but he readily understood that being called 'a cheating Froggy bastard' was not meant as a compliment. Very soon, the horse was not for sale.

And so it was that, much to the amusement of William's younger brother, Alfred, he had to make do with Dash.

After lunch they walked down to the lake, where the duck were paddling about. Like William, Sir Robert had been at The House[3]; he had also, like William, left Oxford with a First in Greats.

Sir Robert did not disguise the fact that this gentle walk was also by way of an interview for a position on his staff. These days politicians were supposed to be experts on any number of subjects, and so it would be helpful to have someone like William, who could – to use the latest idiom – 'do research'. Chartism[4] was a case in point. There had been a petition to Parliament during the summer, with over a million signatures, demanding universal suffrage. What did William think about Chartism?

William was quick to relate how his fellow undergraduates at Oxford had referred to the movement as 'government of the mob, by the mob, for the mob'[5], adding that 'Julius Caesar' and 'William the Conqueror' were supposedly among the signatories. Sir Robert did not intend to be haughty but, being a seasoned politician, he had heard these points before. He was not sure that it was sensible to dismiss the chartists so readily.

He was watching the ducks. "You see how peacefully these ducks float about. Not one of them can imagine what will happen come winter time. Suddenly there will be dogs and guns, and their contented world will be blown apart. I fear it could be the same for England. There are deep divisions in our nation which make me uneasy. We might be like the duck, Mr Edmundson: we can't see the shock that's coming."

When they walked back through the park, Sir Robert explained how William could assist the Party in Westminster; it would be a first step on the ladder.

On leaving, Lady Peel accompanied William to the entrance hall.

"Now William, I want to tell you something. You have made a good impression on Robert. I know how he intimidates everyone but, you know, he doesn't really mean to; he's just a fearful cold fish. But don't be put off. Underneath, he is a very good man."

At the bottom of the steps, a stable boy was holding Dash's reins. "Have a lovely ride home in the evening sun, and you can tell your mother from me that it has been a most successful visit. I do love Emma so. Ah, how nice to see a young man on an English cob! Now, you see that is just the sort of thing Sir Robert likes! All the young men like to show off on great big hunters these days! Ghastly!"

William wanted to approach Kingsgate from the west, which meant continuing on the road to Lichfield, taking the lane on the right at the bottom of the hill, and then turning into Well Meadow at The Lollard Oak. He trotted up from there to the top of Falcon, where, behind him, there was the view out to the west with the three spires of Lichfield Cathedral silhouetted against the evening sun. In front of him, to the north-east, he looked down across the fields towards his home nestling in a dip in the landscape. One day, all of this would be his.

***

At Kingsgate, Alfred had spent the hot Sunday afternoon down at the forge helping Edwin and his son, Adam, fix the old threshing machine in preparation for the harvest. Both Alfred and Adam had turned twenty one a few weeks ago.

The Lollard Oak   1839

In the manor house, Isabella, sixteen years old and the youngest of the three Edmundson children, was playing the Broadwood grand in the drawing room. Edward de Lacy was there too, examining the loose sheet music which lay on top of the piano.

Cuthbert and Emma were outside on the terrace in their somewhat dilapidated rattan chairs, reading. At least Emma was reading. Cuthbert's head had drooped, his eyelids had closed, and his book was lying unread on his lap.

"Isn't that William?"

Cuthbert opened his eyes. "Ah, yes, Isabella plays beautifully, doesn't she?"

"Oh, for goodness sake, Cuthbert! I said: 'Isn't that William?'. Look. Up there. On Falcon."

"Ah, yes, of course. Yes, I rather think it might be. But she does play beautifully."

"Cuthbert, you were fast asleep. It's not good to be so besotted with the girl. Yes, she is good, but then so is Edward. He sings rather well."

The evening was warm as they listened to the tenor voice, accompanied by Isabella, sing:

> 'Twas there that Annie Laurie
> Gave me her promise true.'

"Of course, I'm not sure I don't prefer a man to have a bass voice," Emma mused.

Cuthbert said: "Yes, it's definitely William."

***

Everyone was pleased for William. Even Alfred gave him a hearty slap on the back as they went in for dinner. Cuthbert was positively triumphant as he sat down at the end of the table. "So, tomorrow's St Swithun's Day!"

He turned to Edward. "Edward, we have this tradition of walking around our little estate together on St Swithun's Day. We end up under a large tree called The Lollard Oak, have a picnic, and drink our blacksmith's cider."

Edward appeared discomfited by this information.

"Father," intervened William, "Edward and I have been invited to go fishing at Chillington for a few days. Edward was at Eton with Peter."

"How nice. Lovely trout pool there."

"We're expected there for lunch tomorrow."

"But tomorrow's St Swithun's Day."

"I'm sorry, Father. I completely forgot."

"Well, you just send them a message saying you can't come till Tuesday," said Alfred.

"No, I won't do that." William did not take kindly to receiving orders from a younger brother.

"Why the bloody hell not? Are the Giffards more important than your own family?"

"Alfred, is it not possible for you understand that, whilst it may be acceptable to swear at the forge, it is not acceptable here?"

"William," said Alfred, drawling in imitation of his brother's manner, "is it not possible for you to understand that you are an inconsiderate, pompous ass?"

"Stop it! Both of you." Isabella adored her very different brothers, and couldn't bear it when they fell out.

Emma was quick to put things right. "Edward and William, you must go to Chillington tomorrow. You will have a wonderful time. We are just going to have to struggle along without you."

Cuthbert's thoughts had turned to the impending harvest.

"Going to be a good crop, wouldn't you say Alfred? Of course, it all depends on price. Now, look here, William, if you're going into politics, I want you make it your business to keep the Corn Laws. There are some very foolish and, frankly, unpatriotic types who would destroy our nation's farming for the sake of a few pence off the price of wheat. You must have talked to Sir Robert about it. What does he think, William? He's on our side, is he not? Must be."

"We spoke about the Chartists, Father, but not the Corn Laws."

"Chartists! Goodness knows what that's all about?"

"Oh Father, even I know that the Chartists …".

"Alfred! No politics at dinner, please." Emma smelled danger.

"But, Mother, it was …"

Emma had turned to their guest: "Now, Edward, do tell me, who is your favourite modern composer? Have you heard any pieces by the Jewish man, Felix Mendelssohn? They are supposed to be exceptional. What do they say about him at Oxford? Oh, I do so wish we could have a good English composer. Lots of poets, but no composers."

The next day: Monday, 15th July 1839 – St Swithun's Day

The blacksmith, Edwin Edwinson, his wife, Sally, and their son, Adam, were not the social equals of the Edmundsons. But neither were they servants. Edwin paid rent for the forge at the end of the drive, and there had always been warm relations between the two families. Adam and Alfred were born within days of each other. They played together as children, just as their respective fathers had before them.

It was normal, therefore, that the Edwinsons should accompany the Edmundsons on their annual St Swithun's Day walk. Edwin left the cider for the kitchen staff to take to the Lollard Oak later, along with the food. Soon after ten o'clock they all set off in the warm sunshine, albeit without William and Edward. Emma led the way with Sally, talking about cheese making. Then came Cuthbert and Edwin discussing crop rotation. Finally, there were the three younger ones, Alfred, Isabella and Adam, throwing a cricket ball around, and, to diminish the heartache of no longer being children, they played tag, as in years gone by.

The Lollard Oak   1839

It was nearly two o'clock when they all arrived at the old oak tree. The day was hot and sultry – Edwin predicted a thunderstorm later – and Cuthbert was mightily relieved to see that a servant had thought to bring one of the rattan chairs for him to sit on.

But the chair was rickety and not in good enough condition to take all of Cuthbert's weight. Exhausted by the long walk, he fell into it clumsily. Both he and the chair collapsed into an untidy heap on the hard ground. Edwin helped him back to his feet but he was grazed, bruised and dizzy.

Emma was alarmed. She became suddenly aware of how she had been pushing away the uncomfortable observation that Cuthbert was increasingly absent minded and muddled. She looked at him now, dishevelled and shaken, with his straw hat awry, and, in that moment, she saw, for the first time, an old man. It frightened her. She had to get him back to the house, nearly a mile away, as soon as possible. She was helped in this by Edwin and Sally, leaving Alfred, Isabella and Adam with all the food and cider.

The two young men were alike in that they were both strong and well-built, but Adam was taller and his hair was black, whilst Alfred was fair. His sister was also fair, but delicate. And, as befitted an intelligent and sensitive sixteen-year-old girl, she had brought a collection of verse by Wordsworth and Coleridge, called 'Lyrical Ballads'.

The three of them ate and drank, gossiped and teased, and were as happy and carefree as three young people ought to be with plentiful food and drink under a great oak tree on a warm summer's day. Alfred and Adam drank more of Edwin's cider than they needed to. This led Alfred to fall asleep against the old tree, and Adam to sit entranced as Isabella read from her book.

Isabella saw Adam as an enterprise: he was too clever to be a blacksmith; she wanted to make something of him. For his part, Adam looked at her in wonder. It was a privilege to be able to stare at her beautiful, fine-boned face, to be entranced by her big, round, sincere, light blue eyes that exuded an intense intelligence, and, not least, to hear the music of her voice.

A sympathetic witness to this scene would have had no difficulty in noting the uncomplicated fondness they had for one another. As the afternoon wore on, they themselves had the same palpable sense that this was a precious time. It fell to Alfred to suggest that, once the harvest was out of the way at the end of August, they should all do something, go somewhere, together. Just the three of them.

Isabella knew exactly what she wanted. "Oh, we must go to Tintern Abbey and find the place where Wordsworth wrote this poem."

***

The thunderstorm came suddenly. A few warning drops of rain and then the downpour. They ran for the house, leaving everything but the poetry behind. By the time they reached the rose garden, they were drenched, and then, from the safety of the drawing room, they watched the sky light up and the thunder crack.

Next day the scene under the Lollard Oak was pitiful: a large branch of the tree, planted late in the 14th century, had been struck by the lightning, and come crashing down upon the abandoned picnic.

Six weeks later: Tuesday, 27th August 1839

It took the cob, Dash, two hours to pull the cart from Kingsgate to Birmingham on Monday. Edwin left the three of them at The Bull in Price Street and made his way home. They were up at seven o'clock the next morning, in good time for the Hereford stagecoach which left Digbeth at eight.

The three soon found their coach. On top, at the back, there were two benches, facing one another, each with seating for two people.

The Lollard Oak 1839

They grabbed these quickly; it would be so much more fun to be out in the open air on a sunny day.

The coachman was walking up and down with his passenger manifest. He bellowed in a high, nasal voice that identified him as, unmistakably, from Birmingham: "Mr O'Connor! Where's Mr. O'Connor? Has anyone seen Mr. O'Connor?"

"Now that, I fancy, could be myself, Mr Coachman. I am bound for Hereford, if you please." This voice was, equally unmistakably, Irish, and it came from a big man with generous side-whiskers.

With his case secured in the box on the centre of the roof, Mr O'Connor, in a fine top hat and polished riding boots, squashed himself into the bench next to Adam at the back, facing the direction of travel. Alfred and Isabella found themselves opposite two giants.

Mr O'Connor was old enough to be their father, and so felt a responsibility to put the others at their ease. "Feargus – spelt F, E, A, R, G, U, S – is the name, and an excellent morning to you all." He shook hands first with Alfred who was sitting opposite him; Alfred then introduced the others.

"So, Adam, you are a blacksmith, I fancy," he said on letting go of Adam's enormous hand.

Adam shook his head in amazement at the stranger, as if to say, 'How could you possibly know that?'

"Look at those hands of yours! What else could you be? Now, as for Alfred here, he is not a blacksmith, but neither is he a dandy: I will take him for a gentleman farmer."

"Oh, but what about me?", intervenes Isabella, holding out her hands for inspection. "Am I a blacksmith?"

"Oh, yes, definitely a blacksmith, my lady," says the Irishman. "I shall call you 'An *Harmonious* Blacksmith'."

"Now, I must admit, that is quite clever. I do, indeed, play the piano." Adam again looked bemused. Isabella leant forward placing her slender fingers on Adam's knee, and explained: "There's a piece by the composer, Handel, called 'The Harmonious Blacksmith'. It was written about you, Adam," she said patting his cheek affectionately. She turned back to Feargus, "Adam has a wonderful baritone voice, Mr O'Connor. Very harmonious."

The coach moved off. Feargus wanted to know what would be taking these fine young people to the City of Hereford on such a beautiful day. No, they were only staying in Hereford overnight; they were going on to Monmouth tomorrow, and then Tintern.

"Then I must give you some bad news: I, too, am on my way to Monmouth. But what takes you to Tintern?"

Isabella took command. "Let me tell him." With plenty of time to fill, there was no reason not to relate the story in full. She warmed to the task. Not only did she tell of the picnic under the old oak tree, but also of how it came about – how William went to Chillington, of the stand-off between William and Alfred, and of William returning from lunch with Sir Robert Peel, a bit too full of himself.

"Sir Robert Peel?". The man from Ireland was intrigued. "Well, well, well."

"Why do you say that?" asked Alfred.

"Oh, I know Sir Robert."

"How?"

"Of course, it would be wrong to say I *know* him. I don't think anyone *knows* Sir Robert. You know what they say: they say he's like an iceberg with a slight thaw on the surface[6]."

"But how do you know him?" Alfred persisted.

"Well, since you ask, I was, in fact, myself a member of Parliament not so very long ago. From '32 to '35 to be precise. Until they got rid of me."

"Oh, no! It must be awful to lose an election," said Isabella.

"Oh, no, no, no. I didn't lose an election. I was voted back in '35 by the electors. But then the Parliamentary officials disqualified me."

"But why? How can they do that?"

"Because I didn't own enough property, my dear."

"What!" They all made the same exclamation simultaneously.

As soon as Isabella had completed her tale, they wanted to know more about this Feargus. He was happy to oblige.

"I was the Member for Cork. I believe in self-government for Ireland. We Irish are different; we should be governing ourselves. That's what I think, and that's what took me into Parliament. But when I got there, I found that it's not just Ireland that doesn't have self-government but the whole bally country. It's easier for us Irish to see what's wrong, and now I would like to wake the English up. Things can never go right in England, nor Ireland, nor Scotland and Wales, for that matter, until there's some equality. Just as it says in the Bible. Just now the rich make the laws for the rich, and the rich make the laws for the poor, and the poor can go hang. And often they do."

"But are things really that bad?", asked Alfred. "My father says our system of government is better than anywhere else."

"It may, indeed, be so. But let me put it like this. If a man with one leg broken gets himself to the doctor, and asks that his leg be put in a splint, does the doctor say he cannot do that because there might be a man with two broken legs? No, we must make things better where we can."

"But," Alfred was not convinced, "what would you actually change?"

"A great amount, Alfred, but politics is not for everyone. I don't want us to be getting to Worcester and have Isabella and Adam say to you, 'Oh Alfred, why did you have to ask him that question? He wouldn't stop!'".

Isabella was agitated. "How do you know we're not interested in politics, Mr O'Connor? We might be very interested for all you know."

"Very well, my lady, I will start by telling you about two of the things I want to change. Did you know that at election time there is a good deal of bribery and intimidation?"

Alfred was quick to acknowledge that in some places it was not good.

"No, no, no, it's more than 'not good', Alfred. Small fortunes are given out at election time. I have seen it with my own eyes. Goodness

The Lollard Oak   1839

knows what goes on in private. Worse, I once saw a man who voted 'the wrong way' surrounded by men twice his size, and you don't want to know what happened next. I can tell you: all this goes on at election time throughout 'our green and pleasant land', as the poet, William Blake, puts it. So, you see, one of the most simple things for which I'm campaigning is secret voting. We must have a system that stops one person knowing how another has voted. In one fell swoop we can stop the shenanigans.

"And next I would ask you to consider the unequal constituency sizes. Here's an example. In Tamworth, with a population of 8,000, we find our friend, Sir Robert, as one of the two MPs. But then next door there is Birmingham with 200,000 people, but also just two MPs. What this means is that the richer man in Tamworth has twenty five times more influence over the laws, which we all must live under, than the poorer man in Birmingham. That kind of thing is repeated across the country. And it's not right. The size of each constituency should be equal. Well, at least roughly. So, there are my first two changes. What do you think of that?"

The others were listening intently. "But that's only two things," said Alfred. "I agree those two things ought to be put right, but I can't see that there's anything else much wrong. I have heard that the Chartists want 'democracy'. They say that everyone – even people who can't read or write or have no property – should be able to vote. It's complete madness! Can you imagine the kind of senseless laws we would end up with if the least educated ended up with the most power? No one's property would be safe, and, in no time, there would be civil war. You must admit that that's a really stupid idea."

***

They had been travelling for nearly an hour, and Adam had not said a word. He now shifted his large frame on the bench.

"I don't think that's right, Alfred." Adam was, usually, as quiet as he was big, but now he went on, "Working people are no more

The Lollard Oak 1839

against property than you gentry; it's just that we'd like more of a chance to get some for ourselves. Father and I can earn good money in the smithy and, if I'm honest, we wouldn't half mind having a place of our own in the village."

"Oh no, Adam!" Isabella covered her mouth with her hand in shock. "Your family's been at the forge from the beginning of time. You're part of Kingsgate. I couldn't bear it if you weren't there."

"Well, I don't think anything's going to happen very soon, Isabella. I was just saying that, underneath our dirty clothes and dirty hands, working people are just the same as gentry. We want the same as you."

"But you can't seriously mean that everyone should have the vote, Adam." Alfred was flummoxed.

"Why not? I may not have your brother's learning, but nor have you, Alfred. And, although it hurts me to compliment you, I would say there's more common sense in your little finger than in William's whole body. Anyroad, that's what my father, Edwin, says. Now Father can neither read nor write, but, as my mother, Sal, always says, he can tell at a hundred yards with a blindfold on if a man's to be trusted or not [7].

"My father says of William, Mr O'Connor ..."

"Feargus, Adam, please. Always Feargus."

"Well, Feargus, my father says that William reads too much and watches too little. I mean take that horse he nearly bought off the smoothy bastard from France last month. He was so busy showing off his French, he didn't notice that the Froggy was keeping him away from that rear leg until after they'd shaken hands. Then your brother was too embarrassed to go back on his word. That's what Father saw. He told us everything. It was then that Father told the Froggy to 'sod off back to France', or summat like that. Your brother didn't like that one bit. It was only when he actually saw the leg, that he realised he was being diddled. Father told us that, the moment he set eyes on him, he could see the Froggy was a slimy cheat. But poor old William, for all his fancy Oxford education, was like a lamb to the slaughter. That's what Father said."

"You see, Mr O'Connor, sorry, Feargus, you have to trust someone, and I trust my father. He's a man who doesn't say much, but he sees everything. And I know what he would say if he was sitting here. He says that learning both gives and takes away; it gives knowledge, but, as fast as it does, it robs a man of his good sense. The more a man spends time with his books, the less he spends time with his fellow man. Yes, we may need men of knowledge to build our bridges, and cure our illnesses, but does that knowledge make a man wise? Often, those with the most knowledge are the biggest fools. They are proud. They think because they're right about one thing, they must be right about everything. This is what my father says. He tells me that the only wisdom is the wisdom of knowing how little you know. I think there's a good deal of truth in that. So, if you ask me, I would say that any system that keeps people like my father from voting is a bad system. That's what I would say."

At this, Isabella and Alfred starting clapping. "Where the bloody hell did all that come from?", asked Alfred. Adam was as surprised as the others and turned bright red. The blacksmith had never thought to say anything philosophical like that before, but he felt he had spoken well enough.

***

At Worcester there was lunch in a tavern while the horses were changed. After eating, Feargus took Adam, an arm around his shoulder, for a stroll across the Close to the Cathedral's West End and a view of the river beyond.

"What do you suppose they're talking about?" wondered Isabella. Alfred was equally puzzled.

"What were you two conspirators up to?" Isabella asked once they were back on the coach. She hated mysteries.

"I think Adam may be able to help me," said Feargus.

The Lollard Oak   1839

"Are you really a Chartist?", Alfred was impressed. Chartists were dangerous revolutionaries who would no more hesitate to destroy the nation than they would dither over a pint of beer. And yet, here was this Feargus, a big, warm-hearted bear of a man, not at all as Alfred had imagined a Chartist.

From Worcester to Hereford, they talked only of Chartism. Feargus explained the petition that had been rejected by Parliament that summer.

"When we complain that such and such a law is bad, and such and such a law is unjust, we have missed the target. That is the symptom, not the disease. Imagine how things would be if Napoleon had prevailed. We would now be living under his French laws. Would we be arguing about whether they were good laws or bad laws? No, of course not! We would be up in arms about them not being our laws. But when we look at Parliament today, do we see our Parliament? No, we see a Parliament that belongs to just a small part of the nation, that's making laws for all of the nation. So, is it any wonder, we live in fear of insurrection and riot? To make our country better, we must give all men a say."

"And women," said Isabella. On saying it, she saw that her brother was about to respond frivolously, so she added: "Well, answer me this, Alfred, who would you most trust to make a good decision? Mother or Father?" Alfred stayed quiet.

An hour short of Hereford, the coachman stopped. They were at the top of Fromes Hill where the land drops sharply away to the west. It was clear, sunny, and still. They looked out below them. There, in every direction, a vast view stretched out of patchwork fields, folds in the land, hills, valleys, woodland, and, here and there, little wisps of smoke, rising vertically and silently from rural homes. The scene continued out to the Welsh mountains on the misty horizon. Isabella noticed that Adam was wiping away a tear; she went up beside him, put her hand around his waist, and gave him a gentle hug.

The Lollard Oak 1839

During the long journey to Monmouth the three of them had come under the spell of Feargus O'Connor, and, by the time they arrived at the ancient town, there was little they did not know about Chartism. Feargus was going to speak at the Chartist rally on Sunday. 50,000 people were expected.

One of the things they learnt was how badly the movement was split.

There were those, like Feargus, who believed in 'moral force' to achieve their ends. He had organised what he called 'monster rallies'[8] throughout the country, the purpose of which was to persuade Parliament that, with such enormous support for their cause, it would be best, as in 1832[9], to pre-empt trouble and, bit by bit, give way.

But there were also those who were convinced that peaceful action was a dead-end. The rich and powerful would never relinquish their hold on government without a fight. In the end, it would come down to 'physical force' and there was no point in pretending otherwise.

"We are wanting the same thing but, oh my goodness, we have such different ideas about how to go about it. To be honest with you, I am worried about South Wales. I know the leaders; they are a headstrong lot; I would be lying if I told you I had any control over them. I don't know for sure what they're up to, and I don't know I could stop it if I did, but I do fear it will go terribly wrong and, if it does, it will ruin our movement. I hold to the view that no political change is worth the shedding of a single drop of human blood, but down there, in the valleys, there's many who disagree."

On the way to Worcester, listening to Adam, Feargus had had an idea. What if there was someone working for the Chartists in south Wales, who he could trust completely to be his eyes and ears? He had heard rumours that they were actually arming themselves with pikes and suchlike; they might welcome an extra blacksmith. His Brummie accent might also be useful to them. Feargus could pay him to inform on what was brewing, and they would never know. It was worth a try.

Friday, 30th August 1839

There were a number of signs to help them find the spot where Wordsworth was supposed to have composed his 'lines'. Unfortunately, the same signs did not help it to be, as Wordsworth had found it, a place of 'deep seclusion'. There were those who had come to the Wye Valley to admire the scenery, had nothing else to do, and were bored. Others, like Isabella, were dismayed not to be alone with the ghost of Wordsworth. And then there was the curate, who felt a calling to perform an act of public service, by means of selflessly reciting the long poem out aloud, with exquisite feeling, and from memory. This, at least, provided a source of merriment to balance the disappointment: by the time they had returned to Monmouth, Alfred, borrowing Isabella's copy of the poem, had mastered the pious manner and unctuous voice of the hapless cleric to the tearful delight of the others.

Saturday, 31st August 1839

Monmouth was beginning to fill up with Chartists in readiness for the great event that, tomorrow, would take place on the fields to the east of the River Wye.

Feargus, taking care to avoid them being seen together, had given Adam instructions on who to speak to and what services to offer. Thus, it was that Mr Zephaniah Williams, one of the most prominent of the organisers, met Adam and quickly took him under his wing. Later he introduced the blacksmith from Birmingham to Mr John Frost and Mr William Jones. Apart from manufacturing pikes, they needed someone to travel between them, and to Birmingham and beyond. Adam, a true working man, but with enough money from his father to be self-sufficient, was manna from heaven.

And so it was that Adam, together with Alfred and Isabella, were to be found on the platform on Sunday, looking out on a great sea of humanity. They sat behind Mr Williams. He turned round to say that he had been to rallies before, and thought this was closer to 100,000 than the 50,000 they had expected.

Just before the proceedings began, there was a disturbance behind the stage. Mr Williams got up, saying, "It's that bloody Feargus again, throwing his weight around."

They could hear Feargus shouting, "I'm sorry but it's not worth a single drop of blood! Not a single drop!".

Mr Williams was shouting back, "You're a spent force, Feargus. A broken reed. We don't need Irish armchair Chartists here."

Isabella whispered to Adam: "Are you sure you want to get mixed up with this, Adam? I have an uncomfortable feeling."

Adam whispered back: "I've promised; I can't go back on my word."

It was noticeable how much less enthusiastic the crowd was at the end of Feargus' speech, with his calls for restraint, and to not expect too much, too soon. After the speeches came the Welsh hymns. These finished with a hundred thousand voices, many taking the bass and tenor lines, singing 'Ar Hyd y Nos'[10]. If Adam did have any doubts, the thrilling enormity of the sound had swept them all away.

There was only a short time before Mr Williams had to depart, taking Adam with him. It was too hasty. Isabella, caught up in the excitement, had thrown her arms around Adam's neck, kissed him full on the lips, and given him her copy of 'Lyrical Ballads' as a keepsake. He went bright red, and then, suddenly, he was gone.

Alfred and Isabella carried with them a letter from Adam to Edwin and Sally. He explained why he must stay in South Wales, expressed his devotion to 'the most loving parents who have walked this earth', and promised to write regularly.

Monday, 4th November 1839

The information that Adam relayed to Feargus was to no avail as far as the rising in South Wales was concerned. The preparations went ahead unabated, and the date was set for Monday 4th November.

The plan was as follows. They would muster on the Sunday and then descend on Newport from three separate directions under cover of darkness. John Frost would lead the contingent from the west; Zephaniah Williams, along with Adam, would come from the north west, and William Jones would bring his small army from Pontypool in the north.

The authorities would have no time to respond. The thousands upon thousands of men (and many women) were armed with the pikes made with Adam's twelve inch 'stay nails'[11], and by nightfall on Monday, Newport would be a Chartist stronghold. They would prevent all the mail from southern Ireland and South Wales from leaving the town, and the failure of these letters to arrive at their destinations would be the signal for uprisings across the country in the big towns and cities from Birmingham to Leeds.

Parliament would, at last, be forced to listen. Democracy was close at hand.

***

Perhaps it was the weather. That is what Frost, Williams and Jones said in their prison cells. The torrential downpour on the Sunday night had put all but the most ardent Chartists off. In the end, the cover of darkness became, less a means of surprising the authorities, and more an opportunity for many rebels, who were less committed to the cause, to get home, dry out, and warm up. In the event, fewer than half of those following Frost and Williams were still there at first light, whilst the thousands with Jones at Pontypool did not arrive at all.

Adam could see from the very beginning – and had told Feargus as much – that the whole organisation was in disarray. Worse, for Adam, he found himself caught in an impossible dilemma. If he was to help Feargus, he had to be trusted by Frost, Williams and Jones, and to be trusted by these fiery Welshmen, he had to make the pikes. But what would his pikes be used for other than the shedding of blood? Everything was wrong and upside down. Isabella had been right when she said she had an uncomfortable feeling about it. But it really was too late to turn back now.

And then, suddenly, at first light, Adam found himself at the front of the great crowd outside the Westgate Hotel, in the centre of Newport. That was when the soldiers opened fire.

After the first volley, there was an eerie silence; the shouting and yelling stopped in an instant; everyone was shocked, including the militia themselves. Adam saw men close by, men that he had marched with all night, fall. Some of them were dead. Was this really happening? Or was it a dream? He had never imagined anything like this.

In later years Adam would always describe what happened next in the same way, and it was what he said at his trial. He had had no choice. If he hadn't charged, the soldier, who was re-loading, would have fired again and, in all likelihood, another Chartist demonstrator would have died. He never claimed he was brave, but nor did he admit to being reckless. No, it was simply that he had had to do what he did.

And he was equally clear that he did not mean to kill the soldier. Yes, he did mean to punch him – and he did – but the purpose was to stop him firing again and killing another Chartist. How could Adam have anticipated that, in falling over, the soldier would hit his head on the cast-iron boot-pull which was set into the pavement by the hotel's front door?

Two and a half months later – Friday, 17th January 1840

Sir Robert was hosting a shooting party at Drayton over the weekend; William was not be needed until next week, and was free to return to Kingsgate. He arrived late in the afternoon to find the house in a state of unbearable tension.

The Lollard Oak   1839

It was common knowledge that the verdict and sentence had been yesterday, but everyone had a different opinion as to how long it would take Alfred to make the journey from Monmouth to give them the news.

Edwin and Sally sat by the open fire in the main hall, their ears alert to any sound that might be that of a horse on the drive. No one knew what to say and, mostly, no one said anything.

It was dark when Alfred did arrive. They all – family and servants – rushed to the front door.

It could not have been worse.

"It's High Treason. He is to be hung, drawn and quartered."

For the rest of his life, William would never forgive himself for saying in response to this news: "It's 'hanged', not 'hung'."

"I must go to him now. I must go to him now." Sally's voice grew louder with repetition. "I must go to him now." She, alone, was not in tears. "I must go to him now." She was almost shrieking. "Edwin, you must take me to Monmouth now. I must be with him. He must not be alone. He must not be alone. Can we take the pony and trap? The pony and trap. Please."

It was Emma who held her as the floodgates opened, and the terrible sobbing began. Edwin stood there, quiet, helpless, broken.

After a few minutes Emma spoke through her tears. "William, you and I will go to Drayton first thing in the morning. We will speak to Sir Robert. Sally, Edwin, we will stop this. I promise you; we will stop this. We will find a way."

Saturday, 18th January 1840

They arrived in the pony and trap at the gates of Drayton Manor at 8 o'clock the next morning. Soldiers were everywhere. What was going on? An officer from the Life Guards trotted up to them to inform them that they could not enter and must turn around immediately. William explained who he was. The officer asked them to wait. He would send a junior officer to the house to clarify the position.

As they waited, William asked who was staying at Drayton that warranted the heightened security. "I cannot say, sir," came the military reply.

Julia was waiting for them in the entrance hall. "Emma, my dear. I know why you're here. We had the news from Monmouth late last night. Robert and William are now huddled away in the library talking about it. He knows about your blacksmith. Well, he's a constituent, isn't he."

With William standing beside her, Emma was confused. "Why do you say 'William'? I don't understand."

"Oh, heavens, I'm so sorry. It's William Melbourne. The Prime Minister. Not you, William," she said, squeezing his arm. "He's come here to shoot all our beautiful duck, and now this. Glory be! Look, I think Robert will see you – as a friend – but I'm not sure about the Prime Minister. What you must remember is that they cannot interfere with the administration of justice. I know Robert is very particular about that; it would damage your cause if you were to suggest it."

"What can we say?"

"Oh dear, I'm not sure. I know they're worried about demonstrations breaking out all over the country. I heard Robert say, 'We can't afford any more Peterloos[12].' I think that's what's uppermost in their minds. You could help them to understand that people like Adam are loyal to Her Majesty. It's Her Majesty who, alone, can change the sentences. I shouldn't say this but – they have to tread carefully with the judges – they were both absolutely horrified by both the verdicts and the sentences. When the soldier came to tell us of your arrival just now, the Prime Minister gave me this transcript of the Lord Chief Justice's sentence which came with the messenger last night. I don't know if you can bear to read it. Come into the drawing room where it's warm and sit yourselves down. You're both exhausted."

William took the papers. "No, let me read it here. Please, mother, you go." As Emma accompanied Julia into the drawing room, William took a deep breath.

THE CROWN COURT AT MONMOUTH
16th JANUARY 1840
SENTENCE[13]
LORD CHIEF JUSTICE TINDAL

Adam Edwinson
Blacksmith of Kingsgate
in the County of Staffordshire

"After the most anxious and careful investigation of the case, before a jury of great intelligence and almost unexampled patience, you stand at the bar of this court to receive the last sentence of the law for the commission of a crime which, beyond all others, is the most pernicious in example, and the most injurious in its consequences, to the peace and happiness of human society - the crime of High Treason against your Sovereign. You can have no just ground of complaint that your case has not met with the most full consideration, both from the jury and from the court. But as the jury has pronounced you guilty of the crime with which you have been charged, I should be wanting in justice to them if I did not openly declare, that the verdicts which they have found meet with the entire concurrence of my learned brethren and myself.

In the case of all ordinary breaches of the law, the mischief of the offence does, for the most part, terminate with the immediate injury sustained by the individual against whom it is levelled. The man who plunders the property, or lifts his hand against the life of his neighbour, does by his guilty act inflict, in that particular instance, and to that extent, a loss or injury on the sufferer or his surviving friends. But they who, by armed numbers, or by violence, or terror, endeavour to put down established institutions, and to introduce in their stead a new order of things, open wide the flood-gates of rapine and bloodshed, destroy all security of property and life, and do their utmost to involve a whole nation in anarchy and ruin.

It has been proved, in your case, that, one, you did murder a soldier who was, at the time, acting on behalf of Her Majesty the Queen to preserve the peace of the realm, and that, two, you did over a number of weeks construct instruments of war with the purpose that they be used to kill, maim, injure, and intimidate the servants of Her Majesty the Queen in their lawful duties. However, it is not required of me to impose sentences for these two grievous crimes for the practical reason that they are overridden by a third, yet more grievous. It has been proved, in this court, that you combined with others to lead from the hills, at the dead hour of night, into the town of Newport many thousands of men, armed, in many instances, with weapons of a dangerous description, in order that they might take possession of the town, and supersede the lawful authority of the Queen, as a preliminary step to a more general insurrection throughout the kingdom. It is owing to the interposition of Providence alone that your wicked designs were frustrated. Your followers arrived by day-light, and after firing upon the civil power, and upon the Queen's troops, are, by the firmness of the magistrates, and the cool and determined bravery of a small body of soldiers, defeated and dispersed. What would have been the fate of the peaceful and unoffending inhabitants of that town, if success had attended your rebellious designs, it is impossible to say. The invasion of a foreign foe would, in all probability, have been less destructive to property and life.

It is for the crime of High Treason, committed under these circumstances, that you are now called upon yourselves to answer; and by the penalty which you are about to suffer, you hold out a warning to all your fellow-subjects, that the law of your country is strong enough to repress and to punish all attempts to alter the established order of things by insurrection and armed force; and that those who are found guilty of such treasonable attempts must expiate their crime by an ignominious death.

I therefore most earnestly exhort you to employ the little time that remains to you in preparing for the great change that awaits you, by sincere penitence and by fervent prayer. For although we do not fail to forward to the proper quarter that recommendation which the jury have intrusted to us, we cannot hold out to you any hope of mercy on this side of the grave.

And now, nothing more remains than the duty imposed upon the court - to all of us a most painful duty - to declare the last sentence of the law, which is that you, Adam Edwinson, blacksmith of Kingsgate in the County of Staffordshire, be taken hence to the place from whence you came, and be thence drawn on a hurdle to the place of execution, and that you be there hanged by the neck until you are dead, and that afterwards your head shall be severed from your body, and your body, divided into four quarters, shall be disposed of as Her Majesty shall think fit, and may Almighty God have mercy upon your soul."

Following the Sentence, the Court was informed that the execution was to take place in Monmouth on Saturday February the First in the year of Our Lord Eighteen Hundred and Forty at eight o'clock in the morning.

***

The Lollard Oak 1839

When we find someone in the most extreme of circumstances, we imagine, or, rather, try to imagine, what they are going through, and, in doing so, we experience a small portion of their suffering. But we are also aware, as we go out into that howling, icy storm, that we can, within an instant, and at any time, retreat into the warmth and safe shelter of our own lives. And, when we do so, our greatest pain is merely the distressing knowledge that, for them, such a retreat is not available, and the tempest will not subside.

The right words are a flimsy, outer garment that protect us only a little from the torrential downpour of grief, and we go to Shakespeare for such words. Thus, at this unendurable time, we are drawn to compare the circumstances of Edwin and Sally, of Cuthbert, Emma, William, Alfred and Isabella, and, most of all, of Adam, with King Lear, who, wishing he was dead, says:

> '… I am bound
> Upon a wheel of fire, that mine own tears
> Do scald like molten lead.'[14]

Monday, 20th January 1840

Mr Kelly, the counsel for the defence, came, unexpectedly, to Kingsgate Manor on the following Monday. The upset and rage of this kindly, decent lawyer were not equal to that of the two families that had gathered in the drawing room, but his sense of guilt was very great. It had been his task to show the jury that Adam's crime was not one of High Treason, and he had failed.

Others in the room were also nursing a sharp, if irrational, guilt: Cuthbert felt that, had he not fallen carelessly into that chair under the Lollard Oak, the children would not have drunk too much; William cursed himself for going to Chillington; Alfred regretted suggesting they 'do something, go somewhere, together'; and poor, inconsolable Isabella now hated that silly, sentimental poem. Each saw only their particular part in a sequence of events that had led to catastrophe.

But Mr Kelly's burden was not irrational. The room was silent as he spoke.

He could have called Feargus O'Connor and Alfred as witnesses – Isabella was too young – but he had not done so. They had both offered to come to Adam's defence, and it was reasonable to suppose that their testimony might have made a difference. He owed it to the families to explain why he had not taken this apparently obvious course.

The charge of 'High Treason' depended for its success on the prosecution being able to prove that the events in question were not limited in their scope to Newport, but were, in fact, intended to be the first link in a chain that would lead to a national uprising. As counsel for the defence, it was, overwhelmingly, his task to show that there was insufficient evidence to believe that such a link existed.

The prosecution contended that the rebels, knowing how the mail from South Wales and the south of Ireland to the rest of the country passes through Newport, were planning to stop it, so that, when it failed to arrive elsewhere, the Chartists in those places would, by this failure, be informed that the Newport rebels had succeeded. This was, therefore, according to the prosecution, a signal for a simultaneous insurrection in all these other places, with the purpose of overwhelming the resources of the state. That was the reason, the only reason, that the crime could be regarded as 'treasonable'.

Mr Kelly had sought to argue that the riot outside the Westgate Hotel was caused only by a desire to obtain the release of Chartists, who were being held prisoner there. Not only was the so-called 'plan' concerning the mail not implemented, but also, in as much as it existed at all, it was very obviously a wild, fanciful and impractical idea, that none of the accused set store by.

Mr Kelly then asked the silent room to imagine what would have happened had Mr O'Connor testified on behalf of Adam. The prosecution would have used that testimony as cast iron proof that

Adam was, indeed, linked to the Chartist movement nationally. And, since Mr O'Connor was the nearest thing the Chartists had to a national leader, it would be impossible to deny it. In short, far from helping Adam, it would have sealed his fate. Mr Kelly could not do it.

As for not calling Alfred: that had been Adam's decision, and his alone. He was resolute that Alfred must be kept away. Alfred had attended the rally in Monmouth, and Adam feared that, were Alfred to testify, it could lead to his prosecution. He remained insistent to the end that he 'could not endanger his friend's life to save his own'[15].

Three weeks later: Monday, 10th February 1840

HMS The York – Spithead, Portsmouth

My Dearest Mother and Father,

Can you believe it? It was Her Majesty the Queen herself – herself! – who commuted our sentences to transportation[16]. And now I hear that, today, she marries the German Prince, Albert! I do wish them well! But, even more than that, much more, I wish you both well. The love and affection you have sent to me these last weeks and days has been a bright light in the darkness. I know I have been rash, but I still hold that, if I am guilty of anything, it is of loving my country too much. In that, you are my accessories, for it is from you that I gained that great affection and too great enthusiasm.

In the prison cell in Monmouth where we parted with such sorrow, I awaited my fate with what little courage I could muster. I am not ashamed of how I bore myself in those days. If I have some fortitude, it is also from you, and I thank you for it.

It was at one o'clock in the morning when the guards came in to tell us of Her Majesty's decision. Seven hours later and I would have been hanging by a rope. They took us to a ship near Chepstow, and now we have arrived here in Portsmouth. In a few days I will be taken to Australia.

The Lollard Oak 1839

The others are going to Van Dieman's land, but I am going to Sydney. I am lucky. They say that the conditions are good in Sydney. The town is growing quickly and will soon be as big as any English town, and, best of all, they are in urgent need of blacksmiths. If I get a good record I will be released after seven years. They no longer give prisoners land, but I know I can work hard and get on.

Please tell Isabella that I have held on to the book of poetry she gave me. I like the poem called 'The Rime of the Ancient Mariner' very much. I am going to learn it all off by heart on my way to Australia. It's long but, if that curate we met at Tintern can do it, so can I. Please, remind her about that. It'll make her laugh.

But do not tell her that, in my trial, they used the book against me. It was by my bed in my lodgings, and the lawyer said that it proved that I was not really a blacksmith, but an educated man who knew what he was doing. He even suggested that, because Wordsworth had written in favour of the French Revolution[17], I too must be involved in a plot to overthrow the government and kill the Queen. It was nonsense, every word of it. But I mustn't get angry. It doesn't do any good.

I will write as soon as I get to Sydney. You must write to me to tell me how things go at Kingsgate.

I am sorry but I weep as I write that word 'Kingsgate'. The word itself releases a flood inside me. It is so difficult. I try to be brave. When I fell over as a little child, you would tell me to be brave. I try to remember to do that now but sometimes I cannot. I tell myself that I must make the best of this bad job. I will do that. I promise.

Your loving son,
Adam

Five months later: Wednesday, 15th July 1840 – St Swithun's Day

The Forge, Neutral Bay, New South Wales, Australia

Dear Isabella,

You won't read this until October or November, but I wanted to write to you on this particular day. I know you and Alfred will be sad. How I wish an angel could take this directly to you now! You would then know that I am well, and not unhappy, except that I do miss both you and your idiot brother. (We always used to call each other 'idiots', so it is said with affection for the idiot!)

You will have heard from Mother and Father that I arrived here a month ago. I feared the journey very much. I was told that men had been known to commit murder, so that they might be executed, rather than endure the conditions. But for me it was very different. Firstly, I was the only convict on board; they are sending them all to Van Dieman's Land now. Next, the sailors and passengers knew about me being a 'Newport Rebel', and regarded me more as a hero than a criminal. But, most strangely of all, after we had set sail, I received an instruction to attend Captain Hawkesworth in his cabin.

"So, this is the man with friends in high places!" That is what he said. Me? Friends in high places? I could only assume he had mixed me up with someone else. He then handed me a letter he had received. It was from Lady Peel, Drayton Manor, Tamworth! I have never met her, but she said she knew me well. She said I was of excellent character, and that I came from a good, hard-working, patriotic family. She then asked Captain Hawkesworth, as a favour to her and her husband, to ensure that I was treated well on the long voyage, and that he should expect to be well-rewarded for doing so. The captain then showed me an envelope with the same handwriting on it, addressed to Sir George Gipps, Governor of New South Wales. He had been instructed to deliver it, in person, on behalf of Lady

The Lollard Oak 1839

Peel. I have written to her, but my guess is that it is your mother I should really thank.

I thought it would take me the whole voyage to learn 'The Rime of the Ancient Mariner'. But, in the comfort of my own little cabin, I set to and, within a month, I could recite it without a mistake. Then, as we crossed into the Southern Ocean, there were actual, real live albatrosses flying about us! One morning I was standing next to Captain Hawkesworth looking at these enormous birds, and could not resist saying:

> 'At length did cross an Albatross,
> Thorough the fog it came;
> As if it had been a Christian soul,
> We hailed it in God's name.'

The captain looked at me as if he had seen a ghost. "But Adam, you are a blacksmith! How come you know Coleridge?"

I answered him by reciting more. The next day I was summoned to his cabin to be told that he wanted me to give a performance to the ship's company! I practised for a week. I had special voices for the wedding guest and the mariner, and made it as dramatic as I could. And do you know? They all sat in silence listening to me, a convict. A hundred eyes fixed upon me, right to the end.

After that Captain Hawkesworth lent me some of his books and we talked about them for hours. Don't tell Alfred, but he said I have the brains of an Oxford man. 'Pride and Prejudice' was our favourite. The story is good, but it also has a sharp point. I suppose it's obvious that she gives Norman names to the 'proud' people, like Darcy and Catherine de Bourgh, whilst the Bennett family are very Anglo-Saxon, but it made me think a lot about the divisions in England. For a few weeks I felt like a scholar.

Here in Sydney, I am a blacksmith again. I have to take the boat across the bay once a week to register, but, apart from that, they let me come and go.

The Lollard Oak   1839

Sydney is a great natural harbour with fine trees all around. It is winter now but feels like an English summer. We are on the north shore; the main town is on the south. I work for a blacksmith called John and live above his forge. John comes from Dilwyn in Herefordshire. He is an odd character. He has red hair and light blue eyes, and he looks at you with a great intensity. But the main thing about him is he cannot stop himself from talking. He knows his fault but says it is a disease he cannot control. But he is kind. Very kind. He treats me as his equal, gives me more food than he has himself – "you are young, and I am old," he says – and pays me wages, even though he doesn't have to.

Everyone laughs at him. They cheat him, but he does nothing about it. The only exception is a Mr Mosman[18] who owns a lot of land further along.

John's story is makes me shiver. In 1795, he was caught stealing a sheep. In those days, it was enough for transportation. What happened was he went out one night with his younger brother, who took a sheep from a field belonging to the local squire. He asked John to take the rope holding the animal, saying he would be back in a moment. When his brother was gone, the local squire and his men came with lanterns and arrested John. At his trial he wouldn't say what had actually happened because he didn't want to get his brother into trouble. After he was transported, his father died and the younger brother took the forge that John was going to inherit. John just says: "It is God's will". In 1802, his seven years were up, and he was given 30 acres here in Neutral Bay[19], but the land is rocky and hilly, and not good for anything.

I would like it if you could send me a book or two to this address. I love the poetry you gave me – I have it here on my little table – but I would like to know what else you think I should be reading.

Before I go, I must tell you about the terrier puppy that John has. His name is Bertie. He was born on 10th February, the day that Her Majesty married Prince Albert. He loves to play with a bone; he

The Lollard Oak 1839

crouches down near it, pretending it is his prey, jumping this way and that, and then suddenly leaps upon his quarry. But he is a bit barky.
Adam

Four years later: Monday, 15th July 1844 – St Swithun's Day

The Forge, Neutral Bay, New South Wales, Australia

Dear Isabella,

Today is the 5th anniversary of our afternoon under the Lollard Oak and I always write to you today.

Thank you for the latest books. I am reading 'Ivanhoe' by Walter Scott, which is both very exciting and very interesting. I wish I could talk to you about it. I have quite a library now. John says I can put book shelves up in the living room, as the floor of my bedroom has piles of books everywhere. Also – can you believe it? – he has bought a piano, so I can learn to play. It's no Broadwood Grand, but we've had it tuned and it's serviceable enough. Then there was another surprise! When Mr Mosman heard that John was getting a piano, he came the very next day with the music of 'The Harmonious Blacksmith'. Do you remember, on the coach leaving Birmingham, how you patted my cheek, and said to me, "It was written for you, Adam" and that I had a "wonderful baritone voice"? The piece is difficult but, give me a month, and I will be playing 'The Air' well enough.

John is not well. He runs out of breath all the time, and gets sweaty even when the weather is cool. I am worried. I love John. Last night I dreamt we were having the picnic under the Lollard Oak at Kingsgate, and John was there as well. He was standing, leaning against the trunk of the tree, very relaxed, and singing that Welsh hymn – 'All through the night' – which we heard in Monmouth. When I woke up, there was a muddle in my mind between John and the tree. One moment the John was the tree, the next the tree was John. Oh dear, I can't explain, but, somehow, I feel so strongly that the red-headed man here in Australia and the tree there in England are connected. You probably think I'm going mad!

Since he has been ill, people have been coming to ask after him, even those who were not good to him before. I have to do all the work, and, although I work quickly, there's more than I can manage. Mr Mosman says I should take on extra help. There's enough money to pay for a helper, but, as a convict, I am not allowed to do anything, and poor John is not up to it.

Yesterday, after church, I took Bertie to Kurraba Point, where the land goes gently into the water. I read my book and watched him play with his bone. I was wondering how he knows to do that, and thought how he must have inherited it. Somewhere, deep inside him, there is a wild dog with the ancient instincts of a wolf.

As I read in 'Ivanhoe' about how bitter the Anglo-Saxons still felt about losing their land to the Normans more than a hundred years after 1066, I wondered whether I was not like Bertie.

Although it's written by a Scotsman, I think he understands us English better than we understand ourselves. Then there was Mr O'Connor, the Irishman, who could see that most of the English are no more able to govern themselves than the Irish. And what about those thousands of Welshmen at Newport!

Here, in Australia, you get a glimpse of what kind of country England might have been without the Normans. Yes, there is 'high' and 'low', but it's not like England. Here, we all rub along more or less as equals. Take Mr Mosman. Whenever he sees me, he slaps me on the back, and calls me 'mate'[20]. Can you imagine a great landowner in England behaving like that? As for John, he has no notion whatever of 'high' or 'low'.

Here, in Australia, I look back at my homeland and feel sad. I see an England divided between a Norman ruling class – together with all those who have stepped into Norman shoes – and all the rest, be they Scottish, or Irish, or Welsh or English. It's a division that has seeped into our bones.

The Lollard Oak 1839

So, as I say, reading Ivanhoe makes me feel like Bertie. In the same way that he can't escape being a wolf, I can't escape being an Anglo-Saxon. We still carry our loss down through the generations, deep inside, without realising it's there. I think back to when I charged at that soldier in Newport. What I now see was not me charging at him, but an Anglo-Saxon charging at a Norman. I was carrying the rage of centuries within me. It wasn't voluntary. I was flinging myself at the poor man, just as Bertie jumps on a bone.

Perhaps I shouldn't say these things; I know how you all get on with that de Lacy fellow. Perhaps you will say I'm writing nonsense, but it's what I feel, and you're the only person I can say these things to.

Speaking of 'charging', when Spring comes, in October, I am going to learn cricket. Mr Mosman thinks I could be a good bowler and wants me for his team: he says a big man like me charging up to bowl will terrify the batsman.

Adam

Two and a half years later: Sunday, 1st November 1846

The Forge, Neutral Bay, New South Wales, Australia

Dear Isabella,

I am writing today because on 1st February next year, which is about the time you will get this letter, I will be a free man.

That is when I inherit the property that John has left me in his will. Mr Mosman is the executor and has apprised me of my good fortune: I am the sole beneficiary of all his possessions. I am not such a fool as to imagine I will be wealthy – thirty acres of stony ground in Neutral Bay[21] could never make a man rich – but it seems that John was careful with his affairs, and so there is a good amount in the bank account. Also, there is the forge, the business that goes with it, and the house.

The Lollard Oak 1839

And so, what I want to tell you is that, when you read this, I will be a man of means! I will even be eligible to vote!

My dear Isabella, just seven years ago, I was sitting in a dark cell in Monmouth gaol at the dead of night waiting for the dawn, when I would be taken and 'drawn on a hurdle to the place of execution, and there hanged by the neck until I was dead …'. Mr Frost and Mr Williams were in the cells on either side. That night I heard the noise of grown men crying. I do know what fear is.

What I am about to say does not fill me with that kind of dread, but I am reminded of it because I have to summon up a great deal of courage to write this. I suppose you have already guessed what is coming. Isabella, a life in Australia would not have the grandeur of your life in England, but you would be comfortable, and want for nothing, especially love. For, my dearest Isabella, I have always loved you, I always will love you, and I love you with the strongest love a man can have for a woman.

Yes, life here would be different. For one thing it is warm. Think of an England without either the shivering, or the putting on of airs. They say the population of Sydney is now 50,000 people; that is bigger than many an English city, and on the south shore there are a lot of shops. There is even talk of an opera house. On Sunday mornings I take the ferry across to go to St James's Church where I sing in the choir; in the afternoon, in summer, I come back and play cricket for Mr Mosman's team not far from here. It is a good life!

I am writing this on my bended knee. Will you come here, Isabella? Will you marry me?

Yours,
Adam

The same day: Sunday, 1st November 1846

Kingsgate Manor, Tamworth, Staffordshire

My dear Adam,

The most wonderful thing has happened. I am writing to you very quickly for I want you to know as soon as the great distance between us allows!

I am to marry Edward de Lacy! Yes, really! I am so very happy and I know that you will be happy for me too! He has been coming here for years and I always thought it was because of William, but then he started coming when William was in London. Mother, who, as you know, notices everything, says that she has been expecting it for years!

I must tell you exactly what happened. Sir Robert had invited William, Edward and Alfred to shoot duck at Drayton yesterday, and I went too. I know my station at these events: I stand behind the gun and say, 'Jolly good shot!' when they hit a bird, and 'You definitely pricked it!' when they miss. I was with Edward on the far side of the lake among the trees, away from the other guns, when he got a bird that fell into the lake just by the bank. There were no dogs for picking up, so I went to get it.

I suppose it was not very ladylike but no one could see. But, oh dear, can you imagine my embarrassment when, first, I slipped on the mud, and, then, in trying to regain my balance, I went head over heels into the lake? As it was happening I meant to be brave and not utter a sound, but the water was very cold, and I couldn't stop a squeaky noise coming out. Edward put his gun down immediately, and rushed headlong into the lake to save me. Within a few seconds he had lifted me out and was carrying me in his arms back to the bank. Can I tell you a dreadful secret? I was hoping he would bend over and kiss me! It was just like being in a novel. So romantic!

Alfred, who had heard the commotion, had come running through the wood, and saw Edward coming out of the lake with his prize. How he laughed to see us!

But then, when Edward shouted at him to go away because he had 'something to say' to me, Alfred meekly obeyed! It now transpires that I am the only one in the family that hadn't the faintest idea that Edward was deeply in love with me, but, at that moment, even I was not so stupid as to fail to understand what was coming next. Anyway, what with all the excitement – and after all I do like him – it seemed fearfully bad manners for me not to be deeply in love too. So, when he said, still carrying me, with both of us completely wet through, and me holding the dead duck, "Will you marry me, Isabella?", I replied, "Of course, I'll marry you, Edward, but please put me down!"

And that was that! Isn't it wonderful! Of course, it means moving to Yorkshire where the de Lacy's have thousands of acres, so I suppose I won't be living in total poverty. He's promised to buy me a brand new Broadwood!

Anyway, I just wanted to dash something off and get it to you as soon as possible. According to my calculations you will receive this letter in three months' time at the beginning of February: isn't that when your sentence ends? In my imagination you are reading it just before you go off to play for Mr Mosman in the warm, bright sunshine. I would love to see you bowl your fast balls. Cricket is now very much the thing here as well, especially with the gentry; I don't understand it, but I think it to be a real gentleman's game.

With love from,
Isabella

The Lollard Oak 1839

Three months later: Monday, 8th February 1847

From 'The Sydney Morning Herald':

Our cricket correspondent, Mr Richard Hill, reports on yesterday's match held in North Shore between Mr Mosman's team and the Parramatta District Cricket Club.

It has been my privilege to enjoy a good many, well-fought contests between bat and ball in locations about Sydney in recent years, but, today, I have a special responsibility to inform my readers of the extraordinary events I witnessed yesterday in North Shore.

The teams were those from Mosman and Parramatta District, the latter being, without doubt, the most formidable batting side in all of Australia. Mosman were first to bat and scored 120 runs; this was a respectable score against most teams, but no one with a good knowledge of Australian cricket could think it sufficient, knowing the strength and power of the batsmen from Parramatta.

What happened next was the stuff of legend! Mosman now have a bowler the like of which I have never seen before. He is a tall, well-built man with tousled black hair, who goes by the name of Adam Edwinson. He is, I understand, a blacksmith in Neutral Bay. All I can say is that I should not like to be the iron under his hammer! He charged in, yes, charged in, with the fury of a wild animal, and, with a round arm action, he flung the ball at a speed, and with an accuracy, I would not have thought possible had I not seen it with my own eyes. Soon the stumps were laid waste, and the bails were flying prodigious distances in all directions. But the batsmen who suffered the fate of being clean bowled were the favoured ones! For one unfortunate, the ball reared up from the pitch striking him below the elbow, with the result that he was compelled to retire hurt with a fractured arm[22].

The wretched men from Parramatta scraped together 17 runs from the bowler at the other end, but scored nothing off this Adam

Edwinson who carried all before him, giving Mr Mosman's team a victory by a margin of 103 runs. To conclude this memorable event, our new hero left the field, riding in triumph upon the shoulders of his team-mates, and holding the ball high above his head!

What a man! What an Australian!'

Chapter Seven: 2016

2016 – Dramatis Personae

Bill Edmundson, Civil Servant
Caro, his wife

Freddy Edmundson, Farmer
Sally, his wife
Isabella, their daughter
Adam, Isabella's Australian boyfriend

Professor Suleiman 'Sully' Mousavi, Tehran University
Minah, his first wife
Jane, his second wife
Minah, his daughter

Professor Sir Karl Popper, Philosopher

John, an old school friend of Bill's, resident in Falaise
La Comtesse de Pimodan, a Parisian friend of John's

Sir Charles, Warden of All Souls College, Oxford

2016

Professor Suleiman 'Sully' Mousavi of Tehran University was 55 years old, when his uncle, the Ayatollah Khomeini, came to power in 1979. The well-connected professor of politics, who could have been a professional pianist, was accustomed to living in the utmost danger. In 1965 he and his young pregnant wife, Minah, had been imprisoned and tortured by the Shah's secret police, the SAVAK, in the fearsome Evin Prison – or 'Evin University' as the inmates liked to call it, in a mark of respect to the many academics who were taken there.

Sully survived, but for Minah the experience induced an early labour and the loss of their baby. Soon afterwards she died, still in captivity. In due course, Sully was released, and he went back to work at the university. His wife would have hated it, had he allowed her death to crush him. Rather, to honour her memory, he felt an intense obligation to instil into his students an understanding of the importance of democracy.

But to do this was not a simple matter. Were he to go about this task in a normal way, he would be imprisoned again, and, in prison, he needed no reminding that his lectures would be wasted on rats and cockroaches. On his office wall at the university, there hung a picture of the British historian, Lord Acton. This was a man whose opinion he valued. As he studied the large beard and penetrating eyes, the idea came to him that he should teach the history of England.

SAVAK informers infested the university, and their reports on anti-Shah activity resulted in dawn raids and sudden disappearances, but Sully's circuitous device enabled him to slip through their net. He did not call for democracy in Iran; instead, he lectured on John Wycliffe and the Lollards in the 14th century, and how, although they failed to create a more equal society, their ideas did not die with them. He did not suggest that Iranians should have more of a say in the making of the laws under which they lived; instead, he told his students about what the Levellers fought for during the English Civil War. Likewise, he did not suggest that, without any electoral means of removing those in power, it was inevitable that the government of Iran, should be corrupted; instead, he explained how the British Chartist movement galvanised millions of working people to fight for universal suffrage. To mention Iran was unnecessary; indeed, to do so would have been an insult to the intelligence of his students, who understood perfectly what he was up to. The Shah's security men were sure that his teaching was treasonable, but the professor was too cunning for them.

When the Ayatollah returned from Paris in February 1979, everyone, but Sully himself, assumed that his circumstances would improve. The professor knew his uncle better. In April, General Pakravan, who, as Head of SAVAK in 1963, had befriended the Ayatollah and saved his life, was arrested, tried and executed all on the same day. Under the new regime, even the semblance of due process was abandoned, and its uncompromising leader sent out the message that no one was safe. Sully decided to leave while he still could.

***

Despite knowing so much about its history, the professor had never been to Britain, but he was soon given asylum. From the moment he arrived, the person he most wanted to meet was the philosopher, Sir Karl Popper[1]. His work 'The Open Society and its Enemies' had been a lifelong inspiration. For Sully, then, an invitation to stay at Sir Karl's home in south London, was an honour that could only have been equalled by a summons to Buckingham Palace.

The Austrian philosopher and the Iranian Professor sat long into the night. At first, they talked about music – Sully played a little Bach on his host's Bechstein piano – but, soon, they were drawn, irresistibly, into discussing the problem of how to change a totalitarian state into a democracy.

***

Sir Karl mused: "We all underestimate the arc of history. Just think: Jesus taught that all men are equal, but when the Emperor Constantine made his empire Christian 300 years later, what did he do? He passed a law which allowed masters to beat their slaves to death! In fact, for the first thousand years of Christianity, devout followers of Jesus regarded slavery as part of the natural order of things. And yet, there is an arc. We have made some progress. Today we think of Hitler as a monster; at the time of Alexander the Great or Julius Caesar, he would only have been criticised for his lack of valour or his bad military decisions. We have to be patient, or we go mad."

The great philosopher was warming to his theme. "When I was writing my books, and you were giving your lectures, we imagined the power of our argument making a difference. But, you know, Sully, our wise words are like shooting peas at an ocean-going liner.

"Here in England, it has taken them 900 years to establish the principle that the electorate should be able to remove those in power. What's more, it didn't come about because they were trying to do it. The English like to imagine they have been engaged in a valiant struggle for democracy all this time. It's not really true. The reality is that there has been a power struggle between Anglo-Saxon England and Norman England. Democracy was a useful weapon which the down-trodden Anglo-Saxons found lying around; they picked it up, and discovered it worked rather well as a way of wresting back control from the upper class Norman English.

"It is often the case that the best things happen by chance rather than design. Take the law of 'Habeas Corpus', the protection against arbitrary arrest, possibly the single most powerful protection against oppression yet devised by man. But why did Henry II actually introduce it in the 12th century? To protect the freedom of individual? To further human rights? Good God, no. He just wanted to increase the monarch's central power over local magnates. And yet that law, which, at its inception, was mostly devoid of high-minded purpose, became a foundation stone of British freedom. So very typical of this oddest of countries!"

Sully recalled reading that Konrad Adenauer, the Chancellor of West Germany in the 1950s, made the observation that 'the British have a genius for democracy'. "Is there no truth in that?", asked Sully.

Sir Karl smiled. "But how can you be a genius when you don't know what you're doing or where you're going? The British way is a kind of blind evolution. These islands are to politics what the Galapagos Islands are to biology. Protected by the sea rather than a standing army, the conditions existed for a chaotic, but, I admit, brilliant experiment. This is what I mean by typically English: no plan, no philosophy. They don't know what they want, but they do know what they don't want. It is like Michelangelo's sculpting. If you have the means to get rid of the bad, something good will eventually emerge. But it takes time.

"The most common misconception about democracy is that it's about voting for a good government. Utter nonsense. It is about – to use that most excellent English expression – 'getting rid of the bastards'. If you can do that, you have democracy; if you can't, you haven't. There's nothing else to say. Now, I do accept, that the British, almost uniquely, seem to understand this. So, perhaps, they are touched by genius."

"In other words," said Sully, "it all turns on 'removability'."

"Yes. That is it. That is why every tyrant devotes all his time and energy to making it impossible for his rivals to get rid of him. Holding on to power is an addictive drug which no man or woman, of course, can resist. The British have grasped this; Plato, for all his unmatched intelligence, did not. As you know he believed we could only create an ideal state by having ideal rulers – his Philosopher Kings[2]. Plato, poor chap, did not have the benefit of talking it through with Lord Acton[3]."

Sully was delighted. "I had a picture of Lord Acton on the wall of my office in Tehran. I would have private conversations with him from time to time, and when my students asked me who it was, I could tell them about him. The police thought he was my grandfather."

"Ah, very good! You see, Sully, we are of one mind. Lord Acton is also my hero! I have long thought that when he wrote to Bishop Mandell Creighton to say that 'all power tends to corrupt, and absolute power corrupts absolutely', he gave us the single most important observation about politics that has ever been made. Acton was an earnest Catholic, and this great 'dictum' derives from that vital Christian insight that we human beings are too weak to prevail in any combat against our rampaging appetites and passions. Plato was wrong because he imagined his Philosopher Kings could be made incorruptible; he forgot that 'the best' are also human. And when human beings believe themselves to be superior, they forget to think it possible that they might be mistaken. Their decisions are then at least as bad as their more tentative inferiors, and, quite often, much worse. Plato did not understand that the frailty of human nature has no exceptions, and is without remedy. Politically, the only way to keep this problem in check, is a genuine fear of removal.

"So, what do the politicians do?" Sir Karl could not help laughing. "They wriggle around seeking out ever more subtle ways to insulate themselves from the electorate. They devise systems like proportional representation, which appear to be fair but mean, in practice, that your position on the party list is always more important than what the voters think. The latest clever wheeze is multi-nationalism. In these organisations, the wily politicians pretend to a credulous world that their only interest is the brotherhood of man, whilst constructing a process for getting rid of them which is so convoluted that it can never actually endanger their position. Thus, they hide away, highly paid, powerful, and all but unknown to the rest of humanity. And what follows? Bad government.

"Oh dear, Sully," he said, shaking his head. "We have our work cut out."

***

Sir Karl was in his late 70s and preferred not to drive. This made it easy for him to insist that Sully should borrow his car for a couple of weeks to explore his new homeland. Thus, it was that Sully came to visit Bridgnorth in Shropshire where the great 19th-century historian, Lord Acton, had lived.

The professor booked a room at The Swan Inn on the High Street, and arrived there on a hot, mid-July, Monday evening. Apart from a cheerful young woman behind the bar, it was empty. He took his pint of Banks's Bitter, and went to the back of the pub where there was an old upright piano. He could not resist the temptation to play a little. It was out of tune – and would not have been much better had it been in tune – but, still, it was a piano.

The young woman came nearer to listen. She put her elbows on the bar, rested her head in her hands, and watched this musical stranger.

"Can you play any songs, love?" she asked in her distinctive West Midlands accent.

"Certainly, madam! Why not? What would you like? But I must warn you: my voice is not good."

"Oh, no, you do the playing, and I'll do the singing. Do you know 'Danny Boy'?"

"Ah, do I know 'Danny Boy'? How many times have I heard that on the BBC World Service? It is part of the 'UK Theme', which was composed by Fritz Spiegel."

"Well, I don't know about all that, love," said the woman, "but, go on, play it."

And he did. She lifted the lid of the bar, and came over to the side of the piano, and sang, standing just behind him. She had a naturally sweet voice, and sang perfectly in tune.

> Oh, Danny boy, the pipes, the pipes are calling
> From glen to glen, and down the mountain side.
> The summer's gone, and all the roses falling,
> It's you, it's you must go and I must bide.
> But come ye back when summer's in the meadow,
> Or when the valley's hushed and white with snow,
> It's I'll be there in sunshine or in shadow,—
> Oh, Danny boy, oh Danny boy, I love you so!

As she finished the final line of this first verse, she noticed that the way he played seemed to match, instinctively, the way she sang. She gave the second 'Oh Danny boy' a kind of swell. And so did he. And then, with those last four words: she separated them out ever so slightly, and slowed them down, so as to emphasise the strength of the love. And so did he. It was as if the same person was both singing and playing the song. She saw a tear fall down Sully's cheek.

Here he was, truly, in England. Safe. The green and pleasant land had made him welcome. Not in a loud, showing-off sort of way, but quietly, modestly, without any fuss, and with an old and lovely Irish song. What's more, he had never heard anyone, anywhere, sing anything with more passion. An absurd thought flickered in his mind that, when she sang the words 'I love you so', they were directed at him.

The woman rested her right hand on his left shoulder, and said softly:

"Come on. Let's do the second verse."

Had there been more than two verses, they would have done those as well. In September 1979 Professor Suleiman Mousavi (55) of Tehran was married to Jane Evans (36) of Astley Abbotts in a country church outside Bridgnorth. Sir Karl Popper was his best man. Their daughter, Minah, was born a year later.

***

2016 had been *the* most extraordinary year for Bill Edmundson, and he did not know what to do about Christmas. The children would be going to Caro – she had made sure of that – and he didn't want to stay at Kingsgate by himself. Freddy and Sal would feel they had to invite him to The Old Forge and, although relations were mended now, he did not want to impose himself on them.

Then he had an idea. Why not invite himself to stay with John? John, an old school chum, lived on his own in Falaise in Normandy, and was always pestering him to come over. In any event, Bill had recently discovered something very puzzling, and he didn't know what to do about it. His old friend was, he now realised, the one person whose advice he would value.

John, small, talkative, with a shock of red curly hair, and penetrating light blue eyes, had a large private income. In general, he preferred his own company, but, when he was with others, he was warm-hearted and generous. At school when other boys were being foul, John stood apart. Now he thought about it, Bill couldn't remember John ever being unkind the way all the other boys, including himself, had been. He was a thoughtful, kindly person anyway, but the great contradiction, which informed everything about his life, had made him more so.

His difficulty was that he disapproved of homosexuality, but was gay. And then, although he was gay, he adored women, and, in particular, French women, especially the way they dressed. His oldest and closest friend in France was 'La Comtesse'. Everything was 'comme il faut' about La Comtesse: the clothes, of course, but also the upper-class accent, the apartment near the Étoile, and the rich Comte, who, from time to time, was required to go down to the chateau on the Loire, to supervise this and that, and see the farm manager. On these occasions, she would summon John. She always did her best to seduce him – there was something about his beautifully cut Savile Row tweed suit which she found irresistible – but always failed.

Only one other person knew about these innocent trysts, and that was Bill. He and Bill did not see each other often, but it was the kind of old friendship that needed little maintenance.

John was delighted to have Bill for Christmas. For Bill, it was a relief: he needed to talk, and John was a good listener. 2016 had been *the* most extraordinary year.

***

Over cheese on Christmas Eve, Bill began with the story of the Warden's dinner at All Souls[4] last February. It was the obvious place to start since the calamities – if that is the right word for them – dated from that occasion. But, as he did so, he realised that he needed to delve a little further into his past.

John leaned back in his throne-like chair with an outsize wine glass, full of excellent claret. "Bill, we have tonight, tomorrow, and all of Boxing Day. So don't stint. I insist you reveal all! Here try some of this Pont-l'Évêque. If that isn't perfection, I don't what is."

"Do you remember I was quite a decent pianist at school?"

"'What a thing to say, Bill! Of course, I do. For God's sake, you played the Emperor Concerto with the school orchestra in our last term. You were going to read music at Christ Church, and then changed course or something. We lost touch, what with me being at Peterhouse."

"I gave it up."

"What do you mean? What do you mean you 'gave it up'?"

"I gave up the piano completely. I haven't played it since that last term at school. Well, not until this year."

"Good God! I had no idea. That's dreadful."

"I couldn't talk about it at the time. It was so humiliating. During the week following the concert there was a review by one of the music masters in the school magazine. It went like this:

'Listening to William Edmundson playing Beethoven's Emperor concerto in New Hall on Sunday evening, one was reminded of Dr Johnson's observation regarding a woman who gave a sermon: "Sir, a woman's preaching is like a dog's walking on his hind legs. It is not done well; but you are surprised to find it done at all!"'

"Yes, I do vaguely remember something. But that man was a total prick."

Bill fell silent, sipped some claret, and spread the soft Pont-l'Évêque onto a biscuit. After a while, he continued: "Yes, I can see that now. But I couldn't then. I knew that the reviewer – what was his name? Greenwood? – and Mr Gill, my piano teacher, were competing for the post of Head of Music, but I was too young and innocent to put two and two together. I realise now that the purpose of the review was to demean poor old Gill, and had nothing to do with me; I was just collateral damage. Back then I was a spotty, insecure 17-year-old. I assumed the entire school had the same opinion as the reviewer, but that everyone else was too polite to express it. It was so painful. I decided there and then that I was never going to expose myself to such a humiliation again. I had given up the piano once before; that was during my first term when Mummy died – she had been my teacher until then – but this time I gave it up for good."

"Oh, my dear William, you do realise we all thought you were brilliant. We were in awe of you. Absolutely everyone. We were so proud to be at a school where someone could play like that."

"It was incredibly stupid. God, how I regret it. But, yes, thanks."

"OK, but what I want to know is: what has this to do with the dinner at All Souls last February, and, indeed, with your subsequent dramatic fall from grace?"

"Oddly enough: everything."

***

"The Warden had invited us, and about a dozen others, to 'An Evening with Henry Purcell' in the dining hall. At the candle-lit dinner we had – what was it? – rabbit stewed in wine with nutmeg and lemon, and calves-head larded with bacon and lemon-peel. Anyway, you know the sort of thing. The guest list was straight out of Who's Who. A couple of ambassadors, a shadow cabinet minister, the editor of The Guardian, a QC, their wives and husbands, and, with a little nod towards 'inclusivity', the two musicians, a lutanist and a contralto.

"Most of them had 'handles'. Although I'd done my five years as a Permanent Secretary, I was having to wait until the Queen's official birthday in June for my knighthood, which meant that poor old Caro still had to bear the indignity of a place setting card, with the words 'Mrs Edmundson' on it. But, even so, she had been placed on the Warden's right: I couldn't make head or tail of that at the time.

"It was a Saturday evening. In fact, it was the same day that Cameron announced the date of the EU referendum, so when we gathered for drinks, the room was buzzing with new and brilliant angles on that. All very Oxford.

"Purcell was rather relegated to the background; the slightly scruffy lutanist played galliards, and the decidedly unscruffy contralto – she had a lovely embroidered, black velvet jacket – sang songs. They were just providing a bit of atmosphere. Until we heard those descending notes."

"Ah, yes, I think I can guess what's coming next!", interjected John. "If I recall correctly, it's called 'a chromatic fourth' or 'passus duriusculus'."

"Very impressive! You recall perfectly. Anyway, the conversations petered out, and, by the first 'Remember me', everyone was silent, and had turned to the two musicians. Of course, Dido's 'Lament' is always a bit special, but this was very special. At the end we all clapped, and I was one of several in embarrassing need of a handkerchief: we laughed about being caught out. And, God be praised, it changed the subject of conversation from politics to music.

"I assumed Charles was responsible for the place settings; it's not the sort of thing he would delegate. He knew about me and music. Anyway, I found myself with the contralto on my left, and the Ambassador – or is it Ambassadress? – to Kazakhstan on my right."

"And did you pay the diplomat the attention due to her?", asked John, reaching for the bottle to top me up.

"No."

"I thought not. Go on; I am all ears."

"I am not usually so incautious, but I had been very moved by her singing, and, as we sat down, I asked the contralto if she had lost someone very dear to her recently. Immediately I apologised for my impertinence, but she said 'I suppose it was impossible to hide'. I then learned that her 'Baba' had died last year, and that 'Baba' was Iranian for 'Daddy'. She did, indeed, miss him. Terribly. The place setting card in front of her said 'Minah Mousavi'."

***

Minah told Bill about how her father, the Iranian professor, fleeing from the Ayatollah, met, fell in love with, and married a Bridgnorth barmaid. How despite (or was it because of?) all the differences – he was 55 and she was 36, he was Muslim and she was Christian, he was Iranian and she was English, and, of course, he was a professor and she was a barmaid – they adored one another. Minah was so proud of her family. Her father, with some help from Karl Popper, secured a job teaching history at a prep school in Worcestershire, and they lived in a little estate cottage nearby. In the evening, he would sit down at the piano and play, and she and her mother would sing.

"What I miss most is being accompanied by him. We did all sorts: 'An die music' … 'A Nightingale sang in Berkeley Square' … 'My old man said Follow the Van'." She laughed, "That was a favourite of his."

Bill couldn't help responding: "And don't dilly dally on the way."

"Oh, how he loved England! He would get Mum and me to put braces on, and march up and down the living room 'Doing the Lambeth Walk'. He was convinced that no dictator could survive in a country that had so many silly songs. And then there was 'Erbarme Dich'. Baba was very strict about 'Erbarme Dich'. He only allowed it on Good Fridays, because, as he liked to say, only half-jokingly, without that restriction, we would do nothing else. We weren't religious or anything, but Baba said it was impossible, even for a Muslim like him, to hear the Matthew Passion, and not believe."

Minah had followed in her father's footsteps, first reading PPE at Oxford, and then going to the Royal Academy to study singing. She had since done a DPhil in politics – researching how academics in totalitarian regimes can be influential without being imprisoned – and now she was a lecturer in modern politics at the university. She was not married.

***

John was listening intently. "I bet Caro at the other end of the table was keeping an eye on your conversation with the beautiful contralto."

"You are not wrong. I will come to that. And you are right that Minah and I were getting on well, although, in truth, that was blotted out by something else."

"What?"

"Listening to her I became consumed with self-hatred. I couldn't but compare myself with this Iranian professor." As he talked, while eating cheese and drinking wine, Bill had been sitting back in his chair, but now he leant forward with his elbows on the table, shaking his fists.

"He had been tortured; he had lost his wife and baby to those same torturers; he had lived under constant fear of re-arrest and more torture; he had had to leave his homeland; he had come to the UK with nothing. Here was a man with every possible disadvantage, who ended up playing the piano in a cottage in rural England, with his wife and daughter marching up and down their living room 'doing the Lambeth Walk'."

Bill got up, and began to walk up and down the dining room, waving his long arms.

"And me? I had had every imaginable advantage; I had had a rich, peaceful, pampered, and privileged life. I had never had to be brave. I had never been afraid, as he had been afraid. But what good had all this comfort done me? I too could have married a singer and played the piano. What fun we would have had!"

He went back to his chair, sat down, filled his glass, and sighed a deep sigh.

"You see, John, I was suddenly St Paul on the Road to Damascus. I was asking myself what was the point of the big house, or the status, or the money, or the success, or, for goodness sake, the blasted knighthood? What was the point of it all if there was no fun? What was the point of anything if there was no fun?"

John followed every word, but said nothing.

"The thing is hearing about this Iranian professor had made me absolutely miserable. I thought how sterile my life was compared to his. But also that it needn't have been. It was all my doing. I thought about how I'd given up my music for no good reason, how I'd married someone for … I don't know … because I needed some anchorage … but it wasn't love, and now, day in, day out, I had to 'deliver' HS2 – bloody HS2. So that, in a nutshell, is what was on my mind."

"Big nutshell," said John.

"It gets bigger. When the first course had all but finished, Caro, to my horror, took it upon herself to address the table. Clearly, they had fallen back onto the subject of the referendum at her end, and, in an embarrassingly loud voice, she asked everyone: 'Does anyone actually know anybody who is going to vote Leave?'

"Coming from her, it could not have been a more crass question. She knew that both my brother, Freddy, and his wife, Sal, were UKIP supporters, and that their daughter, Isabella, who now had the vote, was probably inclined that way too. But she had drunk too much, and wanted to show off her 'Remain' credentials to this like-minded and illustrious gathering.

"At first, no one answered. But then the QC, whose mouth was full, raised a forefinger to indicate that he wished to speak. We waited. Wiping his lips with his linen napkin, and still finishing off the rabbit, he said:

'Indeed, I do. Or, rather, I should say, my acquaintance was *intending* to vote Leave. It was just this last week that I had the pleasure of defending a charming young gentleman on a charge of having abused his 5-year-old niece. Unfortunately, my defence that he was in Scunthorpe, rather than Grimsby, did not persuade the members of the jury, and therefore he will be spending the coming 23rd of June in a high security prison at Her Majesty's pleasure, rather than protecting us from the invading hordes, by means of voting to leave the European Union.'

"The well-fed lawyer paused. 'But how,' he continued, 'I hear you ask, could I possibly know about his voting intentions? And the answer is because he told me so himself. More than once. And, as a confirmation, there was a helpful tattoo upon his forehead, displaying the word England.'

"He paused again. 'Now, I do understand that proponents of the Leave argument will contend that they are not all motivated by base instincts. That is true. However, I ask the question: do we tolerate someone spitting into a jug of water because, after doing so, there will still be more water in it than spit? We do not. Do we remain willing to drink water from that jug? We do not. The cause is contaminated. Irredeemably contaminated! We decide, quite rightly, to reject it.'

"'The QC sank back into his chair, before concluding with a sonorous 'I rest my case.' The table had been listening attentively. However, the fastidious Warden was concerned to be judicious and even-handed. He wondered whether the eminent QC did not also encounter similar 'clients', with the words 'European Union' upon their foreheads. The QC was able to re-assure him. 'In my experience, Sir Charles, they are fewer and further between.'"

Bill broke off and was silent for a long time. John allowed him to be.

"I knew it was a faux pas, but, by then, I was feeling so out of sorts that I couldn't stop myself from saying that, 'actually', I knew several people who I expected to vote 'Leave'. The table turned, as one, to look at me with a sort of detached curiosity. Caro did not like it. 'Oh, darling,' she said from the far end of the table, 'you're not counting your Farmer Giles brother, are you?'"

***

John got up and went to the sideboard to fetch another bottle of claret. As he opened it, he mused: "I don't think I care for that. I seem to remember your brother as rather a decent sort." He then laughed to himself: "Well, of course, he's a decent sort; I've known him for centuries."

Bill was accustomed to John saying odd things now and again, and continued. "I didn't know what to say. An All Souls candle-lit dining hall was not the ideal location for a blazing domestic row, especially with Caro and me at either end of the long oak refectory table. I had to let it go. Fortunately, the husband of the Kazakhstan ambassador, who was clearly well-trained in dealing with awkward social situations, brought up a problem he'd been having with his asparagus bed, and the moment passed. Then, as the conversation resumed, Minah whispered to me: 'Actually, you now know someone else who is going to vote Leave.'

"I was astonished. Surely, as the daughter of a Muslim refugee, she would hate the little Englanders who supported Leave. But she wouldn't talk. She explained that to be a Leaver in Oxford was social suicide."

John laughed out loud. "It's exactly the same here! The French don't give a damn, but the English ex-pats will cut you dead if they find out you're a Leaver."

"But, John, surely, you're not in favour of Brexit?"

"Oh, yes I am."

"But why?"

"Ah, ha. The smaller the question, the bigger the answer. I shall have to think."

Having done so for a minute or two, he said: "You know the Rupert Brooke poem, 'The Old Vicarage, Grantchester'. Brooke was thinking wistfully of England, whilst living in pre-First World War Berlin. I'm thinking of those lines:

> 'Here tulips bloom as they are told;
> Unkempt about those hedges blows
> An English unofficial rose;'

"You see if you deprive a continental of his symmetry and straight lines, he becomes ill at ease and nervous, whereas we feel invigorated. It's just how it is. Like gravity. De Gaulle understood us better than we understand ourselves: we don't belong in an organisation that believes in straight lines.

"The continental must have everything in its place, clipped, neat and tidy. It's all about imposing control on the disorderly natural world. And it's impressive. Versailles, Het Loo in Holland: amazing gardens. But can an Englishman love such a place? Impossible.

"For us, a garden must spill over. When the campanula and phlox settle themselves on a flagstone path, we don't reach for the secateurs. Oh, Bill, how we English love the abundance, the superfluity, the disorder, imperfection and fuzziness of an English garden. Nature is not our enemy; we don't try to keep it down and in its place. That's not our way.

"No, we are different. But, of course, the glory of Europe is in its variety. Why can't they see this? Why do they turn their back on the very thing that makes Europe great? It's not just that you can't make a Greek into a German; more, it's that Europe is so diminished by the attempt.

"The thrill is all in 'la difference'. You will say I'm being frivolous, but once I turned up for lunch with La Comtesse, wearing a suit I had bought in Paris, instead of my usual ostentatiously English Huntsman tweed. On opening the door of the apartment, her face fell like a stone. She said everything was 'complètement gâté'. She had been so looking forward to flirting with an Englishman, that when I turned up looking like a Frenchman, it spoilt everything – complètement!

"I rest my case – to quote your ghastly QC. But, enough of all this Brexit bollocks! Let's get back to the dinner at All Souls: it was not going well."

***

"No, it was not. I think it was at that moment I knew I had to end the marriage. I had never thought about it before – at least not consciously – but there I was, suddenly aware that it was both the right thing to do, and the only thing I could do. She was demanding that I choose between her and my brother. That was intolerable. I was already upset, but this tipped me over entirely. I know Freddy and I have been at daggers drawn most of our lives. As is happens, he and I had had a stinker of a row about Brexit just that afternoon, but she was pretending he didn't even exist. That got right under my skin. I might have thought he was really stupid about Brexit, but as you say, he's totally decent. I envy the relationship he has with Sal too. As for Isabella, she's a cracker. Oh, before I forget, I must tell you this story."

Bill, who had become somewhat morose as he told John about the Oxford dinner, suddenly became animated.

"It was about fifteen months ago, in September, just before she went to Cirencester. There was building work at the farm, and they needed their stables for storage, so I agreed she could keep her cob horse, Dash, up at the house for a couple of weeks in one of our empty stables.

"One evening – I could see everything from my study window – Isabella was mucking out, and had tied Dash by his reins to a hook outside in the yard. Caro, who was passing by, accused Isabella of taking advantage of our generosity by putting the animal outside the stable, rather than inside. It was bizarre. Isabella looked at her open-mouthed, said nothing, went back into the stable, and carried on with her work. But Caro untied the reins, and started trying to lead Dash into the stable. The horse was much too strong and backed away. Caro pulled harder, but the harder she pulled, the harder Dash backed away. Isabella came running out in a fury, shouting: "Stop it, you'll hurt his mouth. Stop it! You fucking bitch!".

"Caro came storming into my study demanding that I 'do something'. Soon I was the butt of her anger for failing to be a 'man'. I rang Freddy and, trying to be jovial, said: 'Houston, we have a problem.' A little later Sal came back up the drive with Isabella. She rang the front door bell. I went, but Caro was there before me, trembling with rage. Sal explained that Isabella was very sorry, and had come to apologise for being so rude. She stood back to let her daughter come forward, and be suitably remorseful.

"But when Isabella stepped up, she adopted an innocent girly voice, and said to Caro, 'I'm so sorry I called you a fucking bitch, you fucking bitch'. Sal's eyes widened, and she put her hands up over her mouth; I retreated back into my study in case Caro caught me laughing as well."

John was stroking his chin thoughtfully. "There was no way back, was there? You don't like her. From what little knowledge I have of these things, a marriage can survive a lack of love, but it can't survive a lack of liking. What a to-do! But look, we'll be up all night, and we must be in time for the Christmas Day service in the cathedral in Caen."

***

After the service, Bill was intrigued to see the tombstone of his famous namesake. 'Hic sepultus est invictissimus Guillelmus Conquestor, Normanniæ Dux, et Angliæ Rex' – 'Here was buried the invincible William the Conqueror, Duke of Normandy and King of England'.

John was his guide. "It was an unfortunate funeral. William was a huge man and the grave was too small. They had to fold the body and, in doing so, it split open and a vile liquid poured out; it is said there was 'an unbearable smell of putrefaction'. Later his body was exhumed and, like John Wycliffe in England, his bones were scattered. There is only an enormous thigh bone left in there now."

The Michelin starred restaurant where John had booked a table for Christmas Day lunch, was a ten-minute walk away.

Once they were seated, John was eager for the next instalment. "To recap: we are in the middle of a candle-lit dinner at All Souls, the exemplary life of a musical professor from Tehran has put you in a bad mood, you have fallen in love with his beautiful daughter, a QC is regaling the distinguished company with a story about child abuse, your wife has been publicly contemptuous of your family, your bad temper is even worse, and you have decided to divorce her. Pretty normal fare for an Oxford high table."

"You are quite right: I had fallen for Minah, and Caro had taken note. We stayed in the Warden's Lodgings and, as we were going to bed, she kindly pointed out that there's no fool like an old fool. That was probably the kindest of her remarks that night. But you see the big drama of the evening had come with the final course – the posset."

They placed their food order with the waiter and agreed with the sommelier that he should choose a suitable wine for each course.

Bill resumed. "The Editor of The Guardian was sitting opposite me, and wanted to know if I was happy with HS2. I told him it was going wonderfully well. At a stroke, I said, it would solve the problem of the North/South divide, and the 20 minutes of travel time that a few business people would save on their journey between Birmingham and Euston would bring untold prosperity to a grateful nation.

"The cynical editor narrowed his eyes and looked at me: 'In other words, you think it's a grotesque waste of money.'

"Being a civil servant, I paused before diving in. It was an odd sensation. Although I knew that I was speaking, it felt as if there was someone else speaking through me. Has that ever happened to you?"

"Bill, I know just what you mean. But, go on, what did you say?"

"I told him that the entire department regarded it as a grotesque waste of money. We had filing cabinets stuffed full of cost/benefit analyses, options appraisals, sensitivity analyses, risk analyses, you name it, I'd read the whole bleeding lot of them, and they all came to the same conclusion: it was a dud; it didn't stack up; it was a sensationally expensive dud.

"I told him how we were required to say that the extra capacity would reduce utilisation of the West Coast mainline into Euston when that line, of all the lines into London, already had the lowest utilisation. I told him that we had to say that time spent on trains was time wasted, so that it could be claimed that passengers will be more productive if their journeys are shorter, even though all the surveys showed that train journeys are regarded by such passengers as their most productive time. I told him we had to say that the new line was necessary if we were to compete with our continental neighbours, whilst knowing that the sheer physical size of France and Spain, compared to Britain, made the economic rationale totally different. It was all nonsense.

"As for the cost: the current £55 billion is double what was put to Parliament, and less than half the expected outcome. There were dozens of ways of making far more important improvements to our transport system at a fraction of the cost. In every possible way, it was a delinquent project, designed to line the pockets of the big construction companies, and a national scandal of the first order.

"As I got going, I realised that the rest of the table had fallen silent. To hear a Permanent Secretary speak so indiscreetly about his Department was too good to miss."

John clapped his hands. "How wonderful! I wish I'd been there! But who leaked it to The Sunday Times? Do you have any idea?"

"That night, after the dinner, Caro, was convinced that it would get out, and that I could say goodbye to the knighthood. She was not happy." Bill broke off to laugh. "And fair enough: she was dead right. The expected letter from the Palace never did arrive. On the Monday after the story appeared in The Sunday Times, I had an email from Sir Jeremy, suggesting that I 'might like to pop in for a chat'."

"Who's 'Sir Jeremy'?"

"Sir Jeremy Heywood. He's the Cabinet Secretary and, to all intents and purposes, my boss. He told me later that he was expecting it to be a 'difficult' meeting – in other words, he had been told to sack me! Poor chap, he was worried sick that speaking my mind in a private conversation hardly constituted 'gross negligence', and that the whole thing would end up in a tribunal with all the publicity and expense. But I was far out in front of him: we discussed the wording of my letter of resignation, we agreed a rather generous golden handshake, and we went to his club for an excellent lunch, which he paid for."

"Ha! So civilised!" said John.

"But, John, back to the dinner. Let me give you a little test. Can I ask you to imagine you are Hercule Poirot? There is 'une question la plus importante', and it is this: 'Who leaked the story to The Sunday Times?'.

"Do *you* know?"

"I do."

***

Back in Falaise that evening, the two old friends were in the drawing room, each armed with a whisky in heavy cut-glass tumblers. John was considering the suspects.

"So, the obvious one must be the Editor of the Guardian. He would be pretty seriously anti-HS2, along with the environmental lobby and so on. But why give the story to a rival newspaper? I don't understand that."

"It could be," suggested Bill, "that he did it as a concerned citizen rather than as a newspaper editor, and calculated that no one would suspect him of being the source precisely because it was not in The Guardian."

"Not sure that newspaper editors are ever off-duty in that way. Doesn't feel right to me. What about your lovely Minah?"

"She's not *my* lovely Minah. Anyway 'cui bono'. I suppose some money must have changed hands, but I don't think she's the type to do something like that for a few hundred quid."

"OK. And can we eliminate the ambassadors?"

"We can."

"And their husbands and wives?"

"Indeed."

"So, what have we left?" mulled John. "There's the Labour Shadow Minister: but he's a friend of Philip Manolis, isn't he? He must be an HS2 fanatic, so it won't be him. What about the QC? The money wouldn't have been enough, but he might have wanted an excuse to tell The Sunday Times editor that he'd been dining at All Souls."

"Well, I'm pretty sure he didn't like me. I thought he was insufferably pompous, and, although I, personally, couldn't see any benefit in us leaving the EU, I was repelled by his lawyerly device to associate anyone sceptical about the EU with child abusers and 'base instincts'. I'm sure he noticed. But going to the newspapers, so as to ruin my career? Not really. And, as you say, certainly, not nearly enough money for a QC."

John sipped away at his whisky. "Ah, I know! How about this? It was the mysterious, 'slightly scruffy' lutanist! He is in fact 'Swampy'; you know from the Newbury bypass. He has gone under cover, and taken up the lute so as to infiltrate the higher echelons of English society."

Bill nodded. "In fact, he was already fully infiltrated. When I thanked him for the music before we sat down, I noticed on the place setting card that his name was 'ffaulk', with a double 'f'."

"And you asked him if he was related to the marquess?"

"I did, and his reply was – Bill imitated the lutanist's drawling, upper class manner of speech – 'We shared the same parents.' No, it wasn't him, but good try."

"So that, it would seem, leaves us with Caro and Sir Charles, does it not?" John put his glass down, and leant back with his hands behind his head. He was looking at the ceiling, and trying to work something out.

"Go on," said Bill cautiously.

"How can I put this? You said earlier that you were surprised that Caro was sitting on Sir Charles's right, even though there were more important guests to fill that spot."

"That is correct."

"But you also said you 'couldn't make head or tail of it *at the time*'. If my memory serves me right."

"It does."

"Which, Bill, rather implies that you *could* make sense of it at some later date."

"If you say so, John."

"I do say so, Bill. You see I find myself joining up some dots. I seem to recall that, when Sir Charles was the Permanent Secretary, his wife went off with a 'personal trainer', whatever that is, leaving him disconsolate and a bit useless."

"Indeed, that is so."

"So, to get rid of him, they had to find him an Oxbridge college. Balliol and Peterhouse were not available, and to be Dean of Christ Church you have to be ordained, so they slotted him into All Souls."

"You're doing well, John."

"Now, being Warden of All Souls is both a prestigious and, in as much as no one – 'be ye never so high' – refuses an invitation to dine at All Souls, it is also a powerful position."

"Very true."

"So, we all know that a position of power and prestige is a potent aphrodisiac for a man, and that, in addition, it makes the man attractive to the woman. Especially to the kind of woman who would prefer to be called 'Lady' rather than 'Mrs'." John took up the glass again and had longish sip. "How am I doing?"

"Not bad."

"So, let me see. If they were already having an affair and Caro was planning to leave you, then it would be Caro, who leaked the story so that she could say to the world that you are an unstable, difficult man."

Bill remained silent.

"On the other hand," John continued, "if they were not already having an affair at the time of the dinner party, but Sir Charles was, so to speak, wooing her, then it would be to his advantage to leak the story, ensuring that you would have to step down without a knighthood, thereby making him the one, who could give Caro the title of 'Lady'. Am I right or am I right?"

By now, Bill was laughing heartily. "You are right in one respect, John, but wrong in 'la plus importante' respect."

"So, they *were* having an affair, but it wasn't one of them who went to The Sunday Times. I'm flummoxed. Who on earth was it?"

"I'll tell you in the morning."

On Boxing Day, they drove over to Bayeux to see the tapestry and have lunch in a bistro. On the way, Bill explained.

"That evening at All Souls had turned me upside down. I had to do something. I decided to clear the decks. So, the next week, having made an appointment to see the solicitor about getting a divorce, I wrote up what I had said in the dining hall, and sent it anonymously to The Sunday Times. They love that sort of thing.

"What gave me the idea was Caro saying on the Saturday night that it would 'get out', and that I could say 'goodbye' to a knighthood. I lay awake thinking, when it suddenly dawned on me that it 'getting out' was exactly what I wanted. Firstly, it would make a big impact, although, almost certainly, not change government policy. Secondly, they couldn't really sack me for what I had said in private, so they would have to pay me handsomely to leave, and I wouldn't lose any of my employment rights. Thirdly, Caro could go off with Charles. And then, fourthly, I could retire to Kingsgate, and start playing the piano again which is all I ever really wanted to do.

"Very soon the deputy editor was on the line at the Department to check the story. Of course, I was outraged. It was 'an egregious invasion of my privacy', and 'intolerable that they should even consider publishing what had been said in a private conversation at a private occasion'. He replied very coolly, thanking me for confirming that the account they had in their possession was indeed true. My little ruse had worked a treat."

"Do any of the others know that it was you?"

"Good heavens, no."

"But then they will all come under suspicion, however much they deny it," said John shaking his head.

"Dear John, I was not completely unaware of that! I had a serious apprenticeship at Goldman's, followed by all the rigorous training of a senior Civil Service job, so, what with one thing and another, I have become an ocean-going, calculating shit.

"Think about it. For a start, half the news value of the story was that there was some invidious skulduggery at play. Also, by the end of that evening, I had gone from being a little perplexed about Caro and Sir Charles to being all but certain something was afoot. She'd only met him – as far as I knew – two or three times before at Whitehall drinks parties, but they were laughing at each other's jokes like old friends.

John was much amused: "So this was your subtle revenge!"

Bill thought for a moment. "I don't know about 'subtle', but, you see John, it wasn't really about Caro and Charles. In my Damascene moment I had come to see everyone sitting round that table, apart from the musicians, in such a different light. Would any of them have married a barmaid from Bridgnorth? Would I have? Did any of them – did I? – love England and Britain as Minah's father did? Did we love our country with that kind of simple, wholehearted, unembarrassed, patriotic love? No. They – we – were a class apart, and I found myself hating it. A new aristocracy. An aristocracy of the 'educated', just as separate from the common people as any Dukes or Earls of Norman heritage had ever been, and, if anything, even more satisfied by there being such a separation. Exactly the same, only so very much more smug, so very proud of their superiority!"

"It's curious, isn't it," interjected John, "that humility has ceased to be a virtue. I suppose it's something to do with the demise of Christianity."

"In any event, putting it all together," Bill continued, "I thought it might be a bit of fun to put the cat among the pigeons; if no one knew who had done the leaking, then everyone would suspect everyone, whilst I the perpetrator could play the role of innocent victim."

John laughed: "And there was me thinking 'Poor old Bill! How badly he has been treated!'"

***

Over lunch in the bistro, the 'tapestry' provoked many topics of conversation.

What might the history of England have been like had that arrow missed Harold's eye? Would we have been permanently at war with France if there were no Norman lands to defend? Would we have been permanently at war with ourselves? Would it not have been a very different England? More cohesive? Less class-ridden? Happier?

John had read somewhere that scientists, examining old bones, had discovered that the diet of Anglo-Saxon thanes was identical to that of peasants[5]. What a contrast to the divisions that erupted after the conquest, divisions that continue to dog us today! And how ironic that the greatest work of art to have been inspired by the Norman Conquest of England should have been an example of Opus Anglicanum, entirely the work of Anglo-Saxon broderers!

"So, what next, Bill? What are you going to do with your new found freedom?"

"My formal departure from the Department coincided with Caro clearing all her things out of Kingsgate. As part of the settlement, she kept the house in Notting Hill Gate whilst I, obviously, kept Kingsgate. There was a bit of a leaving party for me at Horseferry Road at lunchtime, and then I rushed back to Staffordshire, in time to take delivery of a new Fazioli piano. Suddenly I was alone again with my music. I played until dawn."

It was with the arrival of the tarte tatin that Bill decided it was time to put the question he most wanted to ask. He had been bracing himself for this moment since the beginning of his stay. He took a piece of white card out of his wallet, and handed it across the table to John.

John looked at it, and turned it over. "Well, well, well," he said.

"I discovered it not long ago in the left-hand pocket of my smoking jacket."

"Yes, yes, obviously. I was thinking it must be something like that."

The Lollard Oak 2016

"She put it there when I eventually spoke to the ambassadress on my right." Bill watched John's inscrutable face. "What do you think?"

"Have you done anything about it?"

"No."

"Why not? She says 'Remember Me!' with an exclamation mark. She could have put a question mark. And that, presumably, is her mobile number."

"I don't know what to do. I'm 55 and she's 36. And then there's Em and Toby to consider."

"Remind me: how old are they?"

"Twenty two and twenty. Em's with Deloitte in London, and Toby is still at Durham."

"And you want my advice."

"Yes."

"OK," said John, "but before I give you my advice, let me ask you something. Imagine that our roles were reversed. Imagine that you were now looking at a place setting card that I had given you. One that was slipped into my pocket secretly, by someone I liked a lot, and who, very obviously, liked me a lot, and which said 'Remember Me', using the 'imperative' rather than the 'interrogative', and which was followed by a telephone number. What, Bill, would be your advice to me? In any event, how old did you say her father and her mother were when they met? 55 and 36? Does that sound familiar?"

Bill did not answer.

John went on, "I've always had this sense that co-incidences are God's way of speaking to us."

***

Eight months' later, on the August Bank Holiday of 2017, Bill Edmundson was walking up through the stubble of Falcon, where great round bales of straw lay strewn like fallen pillars from a lost civilisation. He could see on the bench at the top the unmistakable

The Lollard Oak   2016

figure of his brother with a can of beer. It had been another sweltering day. Sal was sure Freddy must have gone up there to have one last look at The Lollard Oak.

Minah, despite feeling sick again, had been with Sal down at the Old Forge learning how to make cheese, while Bill had been working all day on his book about the history of the Edmundson family going back to Anglo-Saxon times.

"You look like you could do with a beer, Bro," said Freddy as Bill approached. By the bench there was a hole in the ground with a waterproof lid, and, in the hole, were half a dozen cans of Banks's Bitter. Sal had thought it would be a fitting way to mark the spot of both their first kiss and their extraordinary find.

Bill looked down the hill towards Well Meadow, where the great oak tree, always known as The Lollard Oak, stood in all its ancient magnificence. He breathed in, deeply, and then out.

"So, this time tomorrow it'll be down."

The two brothers sat there without saying anything; there was nothing to say.

Eventually, Bill broke the silence. "According to my calculations it must have been planted towards the end of the 14th century, round about the time of the Peasants' Revolt in 1381. Over 600 years ago. I've tried to find out the origin of the name, but, even though there's evidence it was referred to as 'The Lollard's Oak' as far back as 1549, I can't find any information on who the mysterious Lollard was."

Bill was through his first can as if he had been shifting bales all day. Freddy gave him a second, and Bill continued to ruminate: "Philip Manolis promised me he could have the line routed north of Tamworth. That wasn't worth anything."

Freddy looked up. "You kept that under your hat when you were trying to buy the land."

"I'm sorry; it was not my finest hour. I swear I was offering you a lot more than the market price, but I do feel ashamed of that episode. I really do."

"Actually, it was good for me. It was probably the first time in my life that I had stood up to you properly. I was so scared I'd done something crashingly stupid in turning your offer down, but then, what with the buried treasure, I felt, how do you say, 'vindicated?'. It gave me self-confidence. Anyway, the British Museum said that Well-Meadow would be protected, and that wasn't worth anything either."

Below them, near the tree, a quiet army of yellow diggers and bulldozers was encamped. In the past week the rich Staffordshire loam had been churned up as part of the 'enabling work'. The sharpness of the pain was blunted only a little by the sharing of it.

Freddy continued: "I came up here in the middle of your and Minah's wedding reception. That old school chum of yours, the little chap with red hair and blue eyes, who lives in France, asked me to take him. What was his name?"

"John. Yes, I saw the two of you slink off."

"That's right, John. Odd fellow. Is he gay?"

Bill pushed his lips out, as if to help himself think. "Well, obviously. But, you know, at school, although the rest of us could be pretty vile to each other, John never did, or said, anything unkind. Not once. There was something other worldly about him with that flaming red hair. He stood apart. It was as if he was always old beyond his years."

"I'm afraid I think he's genuinely old now. He was so out of breath coming up here. We walked slowly, but he kept having to stop. I don't think he's well at all, but he was desperate to see the 'famous' Lollard Oak. Between breaths he gave me a history lesson about the Lollards and how important they were."

Bill laughed. "He got a First in Medieval History at Cambridge."

"I'd never heard of them. To me, 'Lollard' was just the name of a tree. I'll tell you what was odd though. First, he looked down there as if the tree was sacred or something, and then he started to recite that prayer, you know the one they have at Evensong, with 'lettest thou thy servant' ..."

Bill intervened. "Lord, now lettest thou thy servant depart in peace, according to thy word. For mine eyes have seen thy salvation, which thou hast prepared before the face of all people. To be a light to lighten the Gentiles and to be the glory of thy people Israel."

"That's the one. But then he turned to me and said he had known us all for centuries. I mean, I know he's your friend and that, but it was a bit weird."

"Actually, it reminds me of something he said last Christmas about knowing you 'for centuries'. It was only in passing, but I'm sure he said it." Bill went quiet for a moment. "Of course, it was John who pressed me to contact Minah. And, come to think of it, it was during those conversations with him that I remembered our intemperate argument over the Referendum, and came to feel the most terrible regret about it."

"Oh, I was just as bad as you!", said Freddy. "But, come on, Bill, you're talking about him as if he is our guardian angel."

"Perhaps he is."

***

Tomorrow, the silence would be broken by the deep, heavy rumble of diesel engines and the shrieking of chainsaws.

Bill was ruminating again. "I've spent today writing about one of our ancestors who fought at the Battle of Naseby. He was wounded very badly with a slash right across his face that never healed. I can't help feeling this trainline is not unlike that."

"It's a good way of putting it; an open wound that won't heal, slashed right across our country."

They sat with their beers looking out to the west where, beyond The Lollard Oak, the red sun hung over the spires of Lichfield Cathedral in the far distance.

After a while Freddy continued, "By the way, since we're being nice to each other, can I just say how much we love Minah? Sal says she's like a sister. It must be one hell of a relief for you that Toby and Em have taken to her so much."

"It is," said Bill. "Thanks for that. And what's Isabella going to do now she's left Cirencester? I met the Australian boyfriend at the Old Forge. I thought he was rather charming."

"We don't say a word, but we're keeping our fingers crossed. He's a bit of an intellectual, doing a doctorate at Oxford about 'Spiritual Journeys in English Poetry'; things like Coleridge's Ancient Mariner. But he's also got a cricket Blue. He opened the bowling for Oxford at Lord's. And then there's his Dad, who turns out to be stinking rich. Owns land on North Shore in Sydney. But Adam's a properly decent bloke. He and Isabella have been in the old barn all day fixing the baler; I peered in and watched them. I'll apply for him to have a visa when he finishes at Oxford next year."

Freddy got out a second beer for himself, and opened it up. "Speaking of which: dare I ask what you think about Brexit now, or would we end up having another 'intemperate' argument?"

"What I think is that we should all stop fussing, and get on with it."

"So, you don't think there should be another referendum?"

"Absolutely not. It wouldn't settle anything."

"But I thought that's what all you Remainers wanted."

"I didn't vote Remain."

"You what?"

"I didn't vote Remain." He paused. "I spoilt my ballot paper."

Freddy put his can down on the ground and looked at his older brother. "Did you really?"

"Yes."

Freddy started to laugh. He couldn't stop. "I don't believe this. You couldn't make this up!"

"Why? What?", said Bill.

It took Freddy a little time to regain control of himself sufficient to speak. "So did I!"

The Lollard Oak   2016

Each of them had made the same calculation. Neither wanted yet more division in the family. They both wanted to be able to say to the other that fraternal affection was more important to them than being in, or not in, the EU; more important, in fact, than anything.

Bill put his can down too, and they hugged. It was not something they had done before.

**

The next day, when Minah took the call on the landline, the sound of a chainsaw biting into ancient oak was just audible through the Drawing Room's open French windows. She held her hand over the mouthpiece.

"Bill, it's La Comtesse de Pimodan. She's calling from Paris."

The telephone conversation was not long. Minah could just hear an agitated French voice, and, more than once, the words 'une crise cardiaque'. Bill was monosyllabic. He finished the call by saying very quietly, "Thank you for letting me know."

He pressed the 'End Call' button with a finger that was shaking, put the phone down, covered his face with his hands, and wept.

The Lollard Oak

About this book

If, when you are next in Florence, you walk from the Piazza della Signoria to the Piazza Santa Croce, you will not see anything especially remarkable. However, if you check your tourist map, you will notice how the streets and buildings in this area form an oval. What you are looking at is the last trace of an enormous amphitheatre. You might even be able to imagine that, where you are now standing as a 21st century tourist, there used to be 20,000 Romans baying for Christian blood. Today, the amphitheatre has gone, completely. But the shape of it remains.

The Norman Conquest of England has a similarity with that Florentine stadium. In both cases something from long ago has left its shape behind. But there is also a difference. For, whilst the shape we can detect in a map of Florence is merely intriguing, the shape of English society left behind by the calamitous years following the Battle of Hastings continues to be an important factor in the lives of English men and women a thousand years on.

To understand this, we must first remind ourselves of the enormity of that event. Before the Norman Conquest in 1066, Anglo-Saxon England was one of the wealthiest countries in Europe, and at the forefront of its civilisation. The quality of its literature, illuminated manuscripts, embroidery, metal working, and system of government was not exceeded anywhere. Although it was a rough, early medieval society, ruled by the over-powerful Godwinson family, it was cohesive. There were no castles inland because there was no need of them, there was a common language, the land was widely distributed among about 5,000 thanes, and the diet of those thanes was, according to recent research, similar to that of the peasantry.

Within twenty years of Hastings, Anglo-Saxon England had been destroyed. Fewer than 200 Norman barons took the land of the 5,000 thanes – most whom were killed or exiled. The defeated Anglo-Saxons were forced to build the castles by which they were subdued.

All positions of wealth and power were taken by the conquerors, and French replaced English as the language of law and government for the next 350 years. The Normans imposed their will with exceptional violence. The worst of this was in a campaign known as 'The Harrowing of the North', which laid waste much of northern England. Tens of thousands starved to death, and all the plough oxen were slaughtered so as to prevent any recovery. Across Europe there was horror at what the Normans had done to Anglo-Saxon England.

The effect on English society has been profound and long lasting. The Conquest created a class division which, whilst it has softened and continues to diminish, has not gone away. Indeed, a report from the London School of Economics has shown that, even in 2011, nearly 950 years after the Conquest, Norman names were over-represented among the graduates of Oxford and Cambridge by 28%.

But it is the cultural, rather than the genetic, inheritance which has had the greater and more poisonous impact. Habits of mind, formed in the 11th century, have been passed down through the generations. On one side, the snobbery and use of a separate language, which characterised Norman rule, have survived, infecting all English people who do well, and spreading far beyond the descendants of the original Norman barons. On the other side, Anglo-Saxon resentment and loathing lingers on. Thus it was that G.B. Shaw, an Irishman, could observe that "It is impossible for an Englishman to open his mouth without making some other Englishman hate or despise him".

Today, for example, a new aristocracy has come to the fore, which is London-centric, media-savvy, better-off, better educated, and, above all, 'progressive'. And yet, they too cannot resist regarding their more disadvantaged fellow countrymen and women, with a traditional 'Norman', upper class hauteur and contempt. In all this we can discern the contours – the shape – of an ancient landscape.

In these stories the two Edmundson brothers, William and Alfred, represent the Norman and Anglo-Saxon aspects of the English social order. They are symbolic of the outward divisions of

English society, but they also represent an inner division which is often felt by the English as individuals. In one sense, this continuity, from generation to generation, can be interpreted as a depiction of England still stuck in the 11th century. However, just as a colourful orchid can pop up out of dark and rotting vegetation, so, in human affairs, good things are generated from, and, indeed, need, for that generation, bad things. The Norman Conquest was very much a 'bad thing', both at the time and in its after-effects, but it also seems to have acted as a catalyst for the emergence of something very great and very good.

This book, therefore, charts a progress which runs something like this. The Anglo-Saxon English never forgot the injustice and the wrong; they never stopped being angry about a 'foreign' land-owning class which enclosed common land, and impoverished the poor. They always wanted their country back. This folk memory was a constant irritation, provoking them into fighting, not just for decades, but for centuries, to be rid of their 'Norman yoke' – as, during the Civil War, nearly 600 years after the Conquest, King Charles I's rule was referred to. To pursue their struggle, the Anglo-Saxons developed and brought into service an extraordinarily effective weapon. Today we call it 'parliamentary democracy', with, as its crucial, defining quality, the ability 'to get rid of the bastards'. Their motivation for striving for so long, and with such bloody-mindedness, to establish this form of government was not primarily idealistic, or even idealistic at all. Rather, they were driven by a hatred of being bossed about by a ruling class descended from their Norman conquerors; 'democracy' was nothing more than a helpful tool, which they chanced upon, for wresting back power. And so it was that, without intention or foresight, 'government of the people, for the people, by people' came into being, with all the consequential prosperity, freedom, and diminution of misery which is derived from this arrangement of human affairs.

Notes

Chapter 1: 2009

[1] In 2009, Terry Herbert, a member of Bloxwich Research and Metal Detecting Club, discovered a hoard of Anglo-Saxon gold and silver metalwork on farmland near Lichfield in Staffordshire. The 4,600 items have been described as "possibly the finest collection of early medieval artefacts ever discovered". Terry Herbert and Fred Johnson, the owner of the land on which the hoard was discovered, shared equally the £3.285 million that was paid for the collection.

Chapter 2: 1085

[1] Edward the Confessor became King of England in 1042. He had lived most of his life in Normandy, and a significant number of Normans came with him to England. It is, therefore, likely that some of the children of these Normans will have married into the Anglo-Saxon nobility.

[2] The 'Witan' (or, more correctly, 'Witenagemot') was an Anglo-Saxon assembly of noblemen and bishops. It met when called by the king for advice, and was responsible for choosing the monarch after a king had died.

[3] Walter de Lacy came from the hamlet of Lassy in Normandy – population 344 in 2008. He served in the household of William FitzOsbern who was made Earl of Hereford after the Conquest. He fought at Hastings and was rewarded with about 250,000 acres of land, mostly in Shropshire and Herefordshire.

[4] A 'hide' was primarily a unit of land-value rather than of land-area, but it was roughly equivalent to 120 modern acres or 50 hectares.

[5] Halley's Comet appeared in late April 1066.

The Lollard Oak							Notes

[6] The 'fyrd' was the local militia in Anglo-Saxon England, organised and commanded by a thane.

[7] The Battle of Fulford was fought on 20th September 1066 near York. In pursuing his claim to the English throne, King Harald Hardrada of Norway, together with Tostig, Harold Godwinson's disaffected brother, had landed forces and marched on York. The Earls Edwin and Morcar, supporters of Harold Godwinson, brought an army to resist this invasion but were defeated.

[8] The Battle of Stamford Bridge was fought on 25th September 1066 about 5 miles east of York. Harold Godwinson had marched his army from London in four days and defeated the army of Harald Hardrada and Tostig, both of whom, as well as the majority of their army, were killed.

[9] Cnut the Great invaded England in 1016 and reigned until 1035. Within a year of his coming, his power was secure. This enabled him to send the majority of his soldiers back to Denmark and leave the government of England in the hands of a number of trusted Anglo-Saxon thanes. He then married Emma, the widow of Aethelred, the previous Anglo-Saxon King, and made their son his heir. Thus, whilst there had been changes at the top, the life of England was not, for the most part, greatly disrupted. It is likely that, in the immediate aftermath of Hastings, most of the Anglo-Saxon nobility and bishops, in trying to calculate what might happen next, would have cast their minds back to 1016. They would have supposed that Duke William would follow in Cnut's footsteps. It was a mistake.

[10] Wallingford was the furthest point east where it was possible to ford the River Thames.

[11] The 'Lindisfarne Gospels' is one of the first and greatest masterpieces of medieval European book-painting. An illuminated manuscript gospel-book, produced around the years 715 – 720 AD at Lindisfarne, off the coast of Northumberland, it is now held in The British Library in London. It is 'not an example of isolated

genius', but one of many very fine gospel-books produced in the same time-period and geographic area.

[12]The V&A museum describes Opus Anglicanum as 'highly-prized and luxurious embroideries made in England of silk and gold and silver thread, teeming with elaborate imagery ... sumptuous handmade embroideries, celebrating exquisite craftsmanship'. This remarkable needlework was first developed in Anglo-Saxon England, and reached its zenith in the 12th to 14th centuries, when it was in great demand across Europe as a luxury product, often used for diplomatic gifts.

Chapter 3: 1381

[1] There is a tradition, unsupported by evidence, that the weather on St. Swithun's Day determines the weather for the subsequent forty days.

[2] Ludlow Castle was originally built by Walter de Lacy, who came to England soon after the Conquest. He and his descendants were responsible for the security of much of the border with Wales. For the purposes of this story, I have departed a little from historic reality. Ludlow Castle was the main seat of this branch of the de Lacy family throughout the 12th century and well into the 13th century. The male line then died out and the castle was inherited in the female line, coming, by this means, into the Mortimer family in the 14th century.

Walter de Lacy, when he died, owned 163 'manors', mostly in Herefordshire and Shropshire. This amounts to about 250,000 acres. His 'lordship', however, was of Weobley. Weobley did have a castle, but it was very small compared to Ludlow or Hereford, and it is strange that such a rich and powerful man did not have a grander title. It was only in the 14th century, when Joan de Geneville, the great-granddaughter of Gilbert de Lacy, married Roger Mortimer,

The Lollard Oak   Notes

that they became the Earl and Countess of March. They were the direct ancestors of King Edward IV (r. 1461 -1470).

Ludlow Castle is, therefore, a de Lacy building and, despite its great size and strategic importance, for its first 250 years it was the home of the Lord of Weobley.

[3] The Battle of Crécy took place on 26 August 1346 in northern France between a French army commanded by King Philip VI and an English army led by King Edward III. It resulted in an overwhelming victory for the English.

[4] A squab is a pigeon not yet old enough to fly. Its breast meat, which is tender, moist and rich, is a delicacy.

[5] Gilbert is a French name, and so the 't' is silent

[6] The Black Death, which killed nearly half the population in 1348-9, returned in 1361-2, but this time it was mostly children who died. It was therefore known as 'La Mortalité des Enfants'.

[7] The Statute of Pleading (1362) required, for the first time since the Conquest, laws to be drawn up in the English language. However, it was not until the reign of Henry V (1413 to 1422), that English became the official language of government. It is, therefore, likely that, although everyone could speak English, the ruling class would have retained the use of French.

[8] On the reverse side of the reredos in Hereford Cathedral are boards listing the names of every Bishop and Dean from 676 to the present day. Until 1060, they all had Anglo-Saxon names, and from 1066 to 1404 – a period of nearly 350 years – there was not a single bishop with an Anglo-Saxon name, even though 95% of the population was Anglo-Saxon. The Deans, likewise, were of exclusively Norman stock until 1380, when John Harold became Dean.

[9] The re-building of St. Lawrence's, Ludlow, 'in the perpendicular style', began in 1433 and was completed in 1471.

The Lollard Oak   Notes

[10] The first English Archery Law was passed in 1252. The 'Assize of Arms' ensured that all Englishmen were ordered, by law, that every man between the age of 15 to 60 years old should equip himself with a bow and arrows. King Edward III took this further in the 'Archery Law' of 1363 which made the practice of archery on Sundays and holidays obligatory. It 'forbade, on pain of death, all sport that took up time better spent on war training especially archery practice'. King Henry V proclaimed that an archer would be absolved of murder, if he killed a man during archery practice. In 1542 another Act established the minimum target distance for anyone over the age of 24 years as 220 yards. (Source: www.lordsandladies.org)

[11] I apologise to those readers who, very reasonably, raise an eyebrow at the anachronism I have perpetrated by including a prayer from the funeral service of 'The Book of Common Prayer' (first published in 1549) in a ceremony that is supposed to have occurred in 1381. Of course, much of the Prayer Book was adapted from existing rites and liturgies, so it is not impossible that very similar words might, in fact, have been used in the 14th century. However, I have not been able to find any actual source to support this desperate excuse.

[12] 'Revelations of Divine Love' by Julian of Norwich

Chapter 4: 1549

[1] Macbeth (Act 1, Scene 4) was written eleven years later in 1606 by William Shakespeare.

[2] 'Friar Lawrence' is a character in 'Romeo and Juliet' by William Shakespeare.

[3] John Bayly was the last Prior of Wenlock Priory, the remains of which can be visited in the Shropshire town of Much Wenlock, famous now as the home of the first modern Olympic Games.

[4] Romeo and Juliet, Act 2, Scene 3 by William Shakespeare

The Lollard Oak Notes

[5] The question as to what happens to the bread and wine during the Christian Eucharist service remains, to this day, one of the defining theological issue of the Christian faith. The Catholic Church continues to hold to the doctrine of 'transubstantiation' – meaning that, as Alfred says, the bread and wine become the actual body and blood of Christ. According to Diarmaid MacCulloch's biography of Thomas Cranmer, the only clear thing about Cranmer's beliefs on this issue is that they weren't stationary. In addition to the extreme Catholic position, that a miracle occurs, and the extreme Protestant position, namely, that the ceremony is purely symbolic, there is also a typically Anglican compromise – or Via Media – whereby, although the bread and wine remain as bread and wine, there is a 'spiritual', or 'real', 'presence'. Cranmer hovered over all three positions, although in his final moments, as the flames leapt up around him, he did reject the Catholic doctrine.

[6] Mark 3, 29: '… whoever blasphemes against the Holy Spirit can never have forgiveness, but is guilty of an eternal sin.'

[7] The leaves, twigs and bark of the yew tree are all toxic to horses and the lethal dose can be extremely small. The plant's toxic alkaloids are extremely fast acting and horses have been found dead with the leaves of the tree still in their mouths. The horse dies from cardiac arrest. Prior to this muscle trembling, a lack of co-ordination, breathing difficulties, a slow heart rate and convulsions may be seen. There is no treatment. (Source: Horse and Hound)

[8] On Whitsunday, 9th June, 1549 Thomas Cranmer, Archbishop of Canterbury, introduced the new 'Book of Common Prayer' as the official liturgy of the Church of England.

[9] '… he did not enclose a single acre …'. This sentence is the only mention of the issue that was, alongside the religious disputes, most exercising the English people during the 16th Century. The enclosure of common land by wealthy landlords, so that they could make more money from wool, had the effect of depriving the lower classes of

their livelihood. It was shameful that it was done, and it was shameful that successive governments allowed it to be done. It led to many violent rebellions, including that of the Kett brothers, backed by over 10,000 people in Norfolk, but the rebellions, unlike the theft of land by enclosure, were suppressed mercilessly. The subject has been brought to life in the historical novel, Tombland, by C.J. Sansom.

Chapter 5: 1667

[1] Most of the information in this story that concerns Sir Christopher Wren has been taken from Professor Lisa Jardine's biography, entitled 'On a Grander Scale'.

[2] Even today, over 300 years after his death, it is not widely known that Robert Hooke is one of the most important figures in the history of science. Rather than detain the reader at this point I have included more information about this brilliant man in Appendix E.

[3] Susan Holder (née Wren) was six years older than her brother, Christopher. He lived with Susan and her husband, William, for more than five formative years, and according to John Aubrey, regarded the Holders' parsonage at Bletchingdon as his 'home, and retiring-place'. Aubrey also provides this account of Susan:

> 'Amongst many other gifts she has a strange sagacity as to curing of wounds, which she does not do so much by precedents and recipe books, as by her own excogitancy, considering the causes, effects, and circumstances. His Majesty King Charles II had hurt his hand, which he entrusted his Chirurgians to make well; but they ordered him so that they made it much worse, so that it swole, and pained him up to his shoulder; and pained him so extremely that he could not sleep, and began to be feverish. Then one told the King what a rare she-surgeon he had in his house; she was presently sent for at eleven o'clock at night. She presently

made ready a poultice, and applied it, and gave his Majesty sudden ease, and he slept well; next day she dressed him, and in a short time perfectly cured him, to the great grief of all the Surgeons, who envy and hate her.'

[4] The Great Plague of 1665 was the last major outbreak of bubonic plague in England. It began in February 1665, and, by July, 100,000 people - one fifth of London's population - were dead.

[5] The Great Fire of London swept through London in early September 1666. It made 70,000 of the central London's population of 80,000 homeless, and destroyed the old gothic cathedral of St Paul's together with 87 other churches.

[6] In June 1667 the Dutch navy, under the command of Willem Joseph van Ghent and Admiral Michiel de Ruyter, sailed deep into English waters and burnt or captured a majority of England's largest warships. It was one of the worst defeats in British military history.

[7] 'The three sieges [of Lichfield Cathedral] left a once grand place of worship a completely wrecked shell. The ruined cathedral remained as a sorry reminder of the destruction of the civil wars ... Perhaps moved by the staunch defence put up by the Cathedral's defenders and the damage it had sustained on his father's behalf during the war, Charles II ordered extensive repairs to be undertaken. The damaged spire and roof were repaired and Sir Christopher Wren was called on to provide his skills to bring the Cathedral back to its former glory. A stained-glass window [shows] Wren directing stonemasons ... repairing the building.' Source: Oliver Clark, Visiting Lichfield: Cathedral's Civil War scars – Past In The Present

[8] Any similarity between the de Bourgh family in this story and characters who appear in 'Pride and Prejudice' by Jane Austen is entirely intentional.

[9] The Battle of Naseby was fought on 14 June 1645 during the British Civil Wars. Sir Thomas Fairfax, Captain-General of Parliament's New Model Army, led his troops to victory over King Charles I. Charles escaped, but the loss of equipment and men at this battle made his ultimate defeat unavoidable.

[10] The 'war' refers to the English Civil Wars which occurred between 1642 and 1660 and involved not only England but also Scotland, Wales and Ireland. On the one side was Parliament seeking to wrest power from the monarch, Charles I; on the other side the Royalists were seeking to preserve the king's position. It resulted in the beheading of Charles I in 1949, followed by a republican government under Oliver Cromwell until 1660 when Charles II was restored to the throne.

[11] Prince Rupert of the Rhine was the son of Elizabeth, eldest daughter of King James I, and, thereby, nephew of Charles I. Aged 23, he was appointed commander of the Royalist cavalry during the English Civil War, becoming the archetypal 'Cavalier' of the war and ultimately the senior Royalist general. He surrendered after the fall of Bristol and was banished from England.

[12] The civil war divided friends and families. One example is that of Edmund and Ralph Verney. Edmund fought for the king, but Ralph was for Parliament. Edmund wrote to Ralph:

> 'I beseech you consider that majesty is sacred; God sayeth, 'Touch not mine anointed.' Although I would willingly lose my right hand that you had gone the other way, yet I will never consent that this dispute shall make a quarrel between us ... I pray God grant a sudden and firm peace, that we may safely meet in person as well as affection. Though I am tooth and nail for the King's cause, and shall endure so to the death, whatever his fortune be; yet sweet brother, let not this my opinion – for it is guided by my conscience – nor any other report which you can hear of me cause a diffidence of

my true love to you.' Source: 'Civil War, The Wars of the Three Kingdoms 1638-1660', p.179, Trevor Royle, (Abacus 2004)

[12] 'Manners Makyth Man' is the motto of Winchester College in Hampshire.

[13] Robert Lockyer (1625–1649) was the leader of the 'Bishopsgate Mutiny'. It lasted only a few days, concerned just 15 men, involved no violence, and, overall, amounted to very little. The mutineers supported Leveller ideas and a soldier's right to petition parliament, but the protest was as much about arrears of pay as political ideology. Robert Lockyer's trial and execution were summary, unjust, and an egregiously disproportionate response to an infringement of regimental discipline. The only satisfactory explanation for this execution by firing squad, which took place outside St Paul's Cathedral, is that Cromwell and Fairfax were alarmed by the political ideas of equality and democracy which were being advocated by the Leveller movement. Thousands of Levellers, wearing green ribbons, turned out for Lockyer's funeral in London.

The Levellers represented a widespread political movement during the English Civil War committed to extending the vote, equality before the law, and religious tolerance. The hallmark of Leveller thought was its emphasis on equal natural rights. The term derived from those who opposed the enclosure of common land by 'levelling' the hedges.

[14] £30,000 in 1646 is equivalent to approximately £3 million today.

[15] Just before dawn on 21st March 1644, Prince Rupert arrived outside Newark, to relieve its Royalist garrison, which was being besieged by the parliamentary army. He had with him a 'force of cavalrymen numbering little more than 500' who 'charged headlong into their opponents ... and caused tremendous confusion'. There was then a counter-attack during which 'a parliamentary trooper managed to grab him, only to have his hand sliced off by a Royalist officer ...'

Source: 'Civil War, The Wars of the Three Kingdoms 1638-1660', Ch. 8, p. 286, Trevor Royle, (Abacus 2004)

[16] In 1644 Charles I moved the Royal Court to Oxford.

[17] The burning of the homes of Parliamentary supporters was a much hated, but reciprocated, tactic. Colonel Russell, the governor of Lichfield under siege in April 1643, sent the following message to his royalist attackers:

> 'I have heard there is a man who goes by the name of Rupert, who has burnt near four score houses at Birmingham, an act not becoming a gentleman, a Christian, or Englishman, much less a Prince, and that that man has not in all the King's dominion so much as a thatched house; and if this be the same man, I do not intend to deliver the King's places of strength unto him, let him pretend what authority he pleases for the having thereof.' Source: Willis-Bund, John Williams (1905). The Civil War in Worcestershire, 1642-1646: And the Scotch Invasion of *1651. Birmingham: The Midland Educational Company.*

[18] "… the unique professional partnership between Wren and the indefatigable Hooke (who apparently barely ever slept) made them a force to be reckoned with …" Source: 'On a Grander Scale' by Lisa Jardine, p. 257.

[19] In 1671, Hooke announced to the Royal Society that he had solved the problem of the optimal shape of an arch, and in 1675 published an encrypted solution as a Latin anagram in an appendix to his *Description of Helioscopes*, where he wrote that he had found "a true mathematical and mechanical form of all manner of Arches for Building". He did not publish the solution of this anagram in his lifetime, but in 1705 his executor provided it as *Ut pendet continuum flexile, sic stabit contiguum rigidum inversum*, meaning "As hangs a flexible cable so, inverted, stand the touching pieces of an arch." Source: zonedome.com

The Lollard Oak   Notes

[20] Christopher Wren, senior, Sir Christopher Wren's father, was an Anglican priest. He had the 'living' of the parish of East Knoyle in Dorset, where his famous son was born, and then, on his brother's elevation to a bishopric, he became Dean of Windsor and Register of the Order of the Garter, the most senior order of knighthood in the English honours system. He moved with the king to Oxford in 1644.

[21] The structure of the ceiling of the Sheldonian Theatre in Oxford, designed by Christopher Wren, was for many years the largest unsupported ceiling in the world. It uses a complex lattice system with beams of short length joined together in such a way that they are self-supporting and do not sag. The design was most probably inspired by the work of John Wallis, the Savilian Professor of Geometry and Astronomy at Oxford who, it is believed, taught Wren.

[22] Lisa Jardine writes that: 'At the beginning of one of his unpublished architectural treatises Wren described vividly the role he believed architecture should play in 'establishing a Nation' and 'holding together a People … through infinite changes':

> 'Architecture has its political Use; publick Building being the ornament of a Country; it establishes a Nation, draws People and Commerce; makes People love their native Country, which Passion is the Original of all great Actions in a Commonwealth. The emulation of the Cities of Greece was the true cause of their Greatness. The obstinate valour of the Jews, occasioned by the Love of their Temple, was a Cement that held together that People, for many Ages, through infinite Changes. … Architecture aims at Eternity.' Source: Page 476 of 'On a Grander Scale'.

The art historian, Kenneth Clark, expressed a similar sentiment in his book 'Civilisation'. At one point he says that 'buildings tell the truth about a society', and, at another, that whilst 'painting and literature depend largely on unpredictable individuals, architecture is a communal art.'

[23] The words recorded here – both those of Sarah Edmundson and Christopher Wren – are taken, with only small grammatical amendments, directly either from contemporary sources quoted by Christopher Hill, or, in the case of Gerard Winstanley, from his published writings. Hill, Christopher. 'The World Turned Upside Down'. 1972; Penguin, 2019. 116

[24] Ibid. 22

[25] Ibid. 124

[26] Winstanley, Gerard. 'The Law of Freedom in a Platform'. 1652

[27] This was the final sentence of a letter sent in 1650 by Oliver Cromwell to the General Assembly of the Church of Scotland before the Battle of Dunbar. It was quoted by Professor Jacob Bronowski (father of Lisa Jardine) in his BBC television series 'The Ascent of Man' as he walked into a pond at Auschwitz, and picked up mud from the bottom that contained the remains of Jews murdered there, possibly including his own relatives.

[28] Although a young Wren represented this 'device' to the Elector Palatine as his own, it was in fact invented by William Petty.

[29] It is variously claimed that the inverse square law of gravity came, originally, from Hooke or from Newton or from many other scientists of the 17th century. The only thing which is beyond dispute is that Newton was the first person to put it into a mathematically coherent form. We do know that Hooke wrote to Newton outlining the formula but whether this was new to Newton, or not, we cannot know. If it was not new, it is odd that Newton did not produce any evidence of this effect to lay to rest the subsequent dispute between the two men. If it was new, then there is a good case to be made that the law of gravity is more Hooke's than Newton's.

The Lollard Oak   Notes

Chapter 6: 1839

[1] Sir Robert Peel was Prime Minister from 1834 to 1845 and from 1841 to 1846. His biographer, Norman Gash, summarised his life and character in the following terms:

> 'Peel was endowed with great intelligence and integrity, and an immense capacity for hard work. A proud, stubborn, and quick-tempered man he had a passion for creative achievement; and the latter part of his life was dominated by his deep concern for the social condition of the country. Though his great debating and administrative talents secured him an outstanding position in Parliament, his abnormal sensitivity and coldness of manner debarred him from popularity among his political followers, except for the small circle of his intimate friends. As an administrator he was one of the greatest public servants in British history; in politics he was a principal architect of the modern conservative tradition. By insisting on changes unpalatable to many of his party, he helped to preserve the flexibility of the parliamentary system and the survival of aristocratic influence.'

[2] Tamburlaine Act 2, Scene 5 by Christopher Marlowe

Menaphon:
Your Majestie shall shortly have your wish,
And ride in triumph through Persepolis.
Tamburlaine:
And ride in triumph through Persepolis?
Is it not brave to be a King, Techelles?
Usumcasane and Theridamas,
Is it not passing brave to be a King,
And ride in triumph through Persepolis?

[3] 'The House' is a nickname for Christ Church, Oxford.

[4] In 1837 some radical MPs and the London Working Men's Association drew up a Charter demanding:

1. Universal adult male suffrage
2. A secret ballot
3. Parliamentary constituencies of equal size
4. The abolition of property qualifications for MPs
5. Payment of MPs
6. Annual parliaments – later modified to triannual.

Its final draft was agreed in May 1838. 'During the course of 1838, enormous rallies and huge meetings were held in the great towns and cities across the nation.' (Victorious Century p.182). 'In February 1839 … a petition advocating the Six Points, to which were appended an estimated one million signatures, was presented to parliament; but in July the Commons peremptorily rejected it by 234 votes to 46. (VC, p.182) It was re-submitted in 1848 with over 3 million signatures.

[5] Although this quote is most commonly associated with President Lincoln's 'Gettysburg Address', it originated earlier.

[6] This description of Peel is attributed to Lord Ashley, later The Earl of Shaftesbury, social reformer.

[7] The notion that intuitive intelligence is more reliable than rational thought is supported by modern scientific research. See Professor Jane Raymond's research at Birmingham University: Trust your gut: Most people can spot a fake bank note in under a second (telegraph.co.uk). In conversation with a Professor of Psychology at Oxford University a few years ago, I suggested that intelligence could be defined as 'the ability to tell a shyster at a hundred yards'. He replied saying that: "That's pretty accurate. The only thing I would add is the ability of the shyster to deceive you."

[8] 'Monster rallies' was the term used by O'Connell

[9] In 1832 Parliament passed The Reform Act which abolished most of the 'rotten boroughs' and extended the franchise but not by much.

[10] 'Ar Hyd y Nos' translates into English as 'All through the night'.

[11] Taken from a witness statement at the trial.

[12] In August 1819, 60,000 people gathered peacefully in St Peter's Square, Manchester to demonstrate in favour of parliamentary reform. The speakers were arrested and the crowd was dispersed by the cavalry with sabres drawn. It is thought that 15 people were killed and 600 injured.

[13] This section replicates the actual judgement of Lord Chief Justice Tindal with a few necessary amendments for the purpose of this story. See The Chartist Trials in Monmouthshire The Chartist Trials in Monmouthshire (mongenes.org.uk).

A verbatim account of the trial which runs to 778 pages is available from the website mentioned above. It includes all the witness statements, cross-examinations, and speeches of the prosecuting and defence counsels, as well as the judge's summing-up and the Sentence which is reproduced here as part of this story.

To the 21st century mind, there is much to object to about the trial and sentencing which followed the Newport Uprising. However, on reading these pages it is difficult not to accept that the Lord Chief Justice was speaking honestly when he said that, during the trial, there had been a 'most anxious and careful investigation of the case', and that the accused could 'have no just ground of complaint that [their] case has not met with the most full consideration.' This was not a 'kangaroo court', and credit is due to the British judiciary that due process was applied meticulously.

[14] King Lear, Act IV, Scene 7 by William Shakespeare

[15] See the Trial of John Frost, p.616. See The Chartist Trials in Monmouthshire (The Chartist Trials in Monmouthshire (mongenes.org.uk)

[16] It is believed that Queen Victoria hated the death penalty and used her influence to have it commuted to transportation wherever possible. See Feature: "Working upon the royal sympathy: researching the myth and reality of Victoria's royal mercy" - The Arts Institute (plymouth.ac.uk)

[17] 'Bliss was it in that dawn to be alive ...' from 'The French Revolution as It Appeared to Enthusiasts at Its Commencement' by William Wordsworth.

[18] Archibald Mosman (1799 – 1863).

[19] Until 1830 convicts in New South Wales received grants of land of 30 acres on completion of their sentence.

[20] The concept of 'mateship' is so important to Australian culture that it was included in the original draft of the preamble to the country's constitution.

[21] Today Neutral Bay is wealthy inner suburb of Sydney, abutting the Prime Minister's residence and a few minutes ferry ride from the Opera House on the south side of the harbour. Today thirty acres of land in this area, with development permission, would be worth (very roughly) AU$300 million (or £150 million).

[22] During the first Ashes Test Match at Brisbane in November 2013, the Australian captain, Michael Clarke, greeted the arrival at the crease of the England tail-ender, Jimmy Anderson, with the words: "Get ready for a broken fuckin' arm." The Australian authorities explained that the fine of 20% of his match fee was in response to his use of an obscene word, rather than the sentiment itself.

The Lollard Oak   Notes

Chapter 7: 2016

[1] Regarded by many as the greatest philosopher of the 20th century, Karl Popper was born in Vienna into a Jewish family that had converted to Christianity. In the 1930s he moved to England. His work covers a wide range of philosophical subjects. During World War Two he wrote 'The Open Society and its Enemies' in which he attacks the political philosophy of Plato, Hegel and Marx.

[2] In Book 5 of 'The Republic', Plato, an implacable opponent of democracy, proposed that the ideal state should be ruled by a Philosopher King or 'Guardian'. This would be a person of high intelligence and excellent character, who would have undergone special training for the position in his first 35 years. After 15 years of working in lesser roles, he would, then, at the age of 50, become the ruler. It is not an idea that goes down well in the Anglo-Saxon world, except, perhaps, among senior civil servants. In continental Europe, however, it continues to exert traction. In France, for example, the graduates of the École National d'Administration, have dominated government and business for many generations.

[3] John, Lord Acton was a 19th century English historian and Liberal politician. He was a close advisor to William Gladstone, and in Gladstone's final term as Prime Minister, when Gladstone was not well, Acton became the de facto occupant of the position. He was Regius Professor of History at Cambridge and, at his home, Aldenham Park, near Bridgnorth in Shropshire, he had a library consisting of 60,000 books – supposedly the largest private library in the world. Gladstone helped Acton financially by arranging for his library to be bought for the nation. After Acton's death most of the books were taken to the Fitzwilliam Museum in Cambridge where they form 'The Acton Library'. He wrote in the margins of his books and many letters, but little else. Despite this, some of his insights, most particularly his famous dictum regarding the corrupting effect of power, have been very influential.

The Lollard Oak   Notes

The Encyclopædia Britannica says this:

> 'Lord Acton has left too little completed original work to rank among the great historians; his very learning seems to have stood in his way; he knew too much and his literary conscience was too acute for him to write easily, and his copiousness of information overloads his literary style. But he was one of the most deeply learned men of his time, and he will certainly be remembered for his influence on others.'

[4] All Souls College, Oxford, is a wealthy, graduate college of Oxford University. The All Souls exam, which is only open to those with a First Class degree, has been described as 'the most difficult exam in the world'; the general paper might include questions such as 'Are there any unanswerable questions?' and 'If Margaret Thatcher and Nelson Mandela had died on the same day, whose death should the BBC have reported as its top story?'. In most years only two candidates, from the dozens who take the exam, are elected as 'Fellows'.

[5] Food and Power in Early Medieval England: a lack of (isotopic) enrichment in Anglo-Saxon England. Cambridge University study finds Anglo-Saxon kings were mostly vegetarian - BBC News

Bibliography

Austen, Jane, *Pride and Prejudice* (1813, 1817 and Collins, 1952)

Barker, Juliet, *England, Arise – The People, The King & The Great Revolt of 1381* (Abacus 2014)

Bates, David, *William the Conqueror* (Yale, 2016)

Jim Bennett, Michael Cooper, Michael Hunter and Lisa Jardine, *London's Leonardo – The Life and Work of Robert Hooke* (Oxford, 2003)

Claire Breay and Joanna Story, *Anglo-Saxon Kingdoms – Art, Word, War* (The British Library, 2018)

Chibnall, Marjorie, *The Debate on the Norman Conquest* (Manchester, 1999)

Clark, Kenneth, *Civilisation* (Penguin, 1982)

Disraeli, Benjamin, *Sybil or The Two Nations* (AP Books, 1845)

Eliot, George, *Adam Bede* (William Blackwood & Sons, 1859 and The Folio Society, London, 1999)

Fleming, Robin, *Kings & Lords in Conquest England* (Cambridge, 1991)

Gribbin, John, *Science – A History 1543 – 2001* (Allen Lane, The Penguin Press, 2002)

Hannan, Daniel, *How We Invented Freedom & Why It Matters* (Head of Zeus Ltd, 2013)

Hill, Christopher, *The World Turned Upside Down* (Penguin, 1972)

Hindley, Geoffrey, *A Brief History of the Anglo-Saxons* (Robinson, 2006)

Holland, Tom, *Dominion* (Little, Brown, 2019)

Horspool, David, *Alfred the Great* (Amberley Publishing, 2014)

Inwood, Stephen, *The Man who Knew too much* (Pan Books, 2003)

Jardine, Lisa, *On a Grander Scale* (Harper Collins, 2002)

Jones, Dan, *Summer of Blood – The Peasants' Revolt of 1381* (William Collins, 2014)

Julian of Norwich, transl. by Clifton Wolters, *Revelations of Divine Love* (Penguin Books, 1966)

Paul Kent and Allan Chapman, *Robert Hooke and the English Renaissance* (Gracewing, 2005)

MacCulloch, Diarmaid, *Thomas Cranmer – A Life* (Yale, 1996)

Plato, transl. by Desmond Lee, *The Republic* (Penguin Books, 1955)

Popper, K.R., *The Open Society and its Enemies Vols 1 & 2* (Routledge & Kegan Paul Ltd, 1945)

Popper, K.R., ed. David Miller, *Popper Selections* (Princeton University Press, 1985)

Rex, Peter, *1066 – A New History of the Norman Conquest* (Amberley, 2011)

Royle, Trevor, *Civil War – The Wars of the Three Kingdoms 1638 – 1660* (Abacus, 2004)

Reid, Robert, *The Peterloo Massacre* (Windmill 2018)

Royle, Edward, *Chartism* (Routledge 1980)

Sansom, C.J., *Tombland* (Pan Books, 2018)

Scott, Walter, *Ivanhoe* (Thomas Nelson & Sons Ltd, 1819)

Shelley, Percy Bysshe, *A Philosophical View of Reform* (Forgotten Books, 2012)

Shrubsole, Guy, *Who owns England* (William Collins, 2019)

Siedentop, Larry, *Inventing the Individual* (Penguin Books, 2015)

Stone, Lawrence, *The Causes of the English Revolution 1529-1642* (Routledge, 2017)

The Church of England, *The Book of Common Prayer* (Cambridge, 1662)

William Wordsworth and Samuel Taylor Coleridge, *Lyrical Ballads* (1798 and 1802)

Williams, Ann, *The English and the Norman Conquest* (Boydell, 1995)

Winstanley, Gerrard, *The Law of Freedom in a Platform* (Benediction Classics, Oxford, 2009)

Appendix A

William the Conqueror and the 'Domesday' survey

The scene envisaged in Chapter 2: 1085, involving a dramatic encounter between King William and Father William at Gloucester on Christmas Eve is wholly fictional, but not, I believe, wholly fanciful. That this should be so warrants some explanation, which I shall try to provide here.

There is uncertainty among historians of 11th century England regarding the purpose of the 'Domesday' survey. Although Domesday Book is a document of great interest to historians, it is less clear what benefit King William and his successors derived from it.

To understand why William commissioned this survey, it is helpful to understand his character, and, for that, we must start with his childhood.

After his father's death in 1035, William, then aged seven, was constantly threatened. The most dramatic of these threats was when his steward, Osbern, was murdered in William's bedchamber while the little boy slept nearby. These circumstances meant that he was fearful and suspicious to the point of paranoia. Ultimately, he believed that his survival depended on the ruled being more frightened of him than he was of them. This factor justified, in his mind, almost unlimited violence in pursuit of his own security.

If one focusses exclusively on what King William did, he appears to be a monster, but the evidence in David Bates' 'William the Conqueror' points to a more complex character. He had an uncontrollable temper, but he was both aware, and ashamed, of it. He could be savage with rebellious subjects, but he could also forgive, as in the cases of Eadric the Wild, and Edgar the Aetheling. William of Malmesbury (one of the more reliable historical sources) says that he 'lived as religious a life as was possible for a layman'. His most egregious villainy in England was 'the harrowing of the north'; yet, even this had a strong raison d'état, namely to discourage raids from Denmark, Norway and Scotland; the violence may have been extreme, but it was probably carefully calculated.

In considering William's motivation for commissioning the Domesday survey, the place to start is the widely accepted view that he wished to increase central control, and clamp down on what we now call 'tax evasion'. The Anglo-Saxon Chronicle's view was that:

'The king and the principal men greatly loved, and overgreatly, greed in gold and silver, and did not care how sinfully it was got …'

However, it would seem that something else was going on. The historian, Sally Harvey, has suggested that the survey can be seen as 'an act of atonement'. Bates puts flesh on the possibility of a non-monetary motivation when he writes about the 'scale of exemptions or reductions' that came into existence in 1086; he points out that the effect of these was to reduce the tax revenue dramatically compared with what had been collected a hundred years earlier by Aethelred and Cnut.

But, most of all, we should take note of Bates' observation that:

'It is arguably one of the great ironies of the subject that it is Domesday Book which enables us to explore the charges made against its creator. It is, for example, central to any analysis of the destructive campaigns of 1066 and 1069-70 ['the harrowing of the north'].'

William was a very intelligent man. Is it not likely that he himself anticipated this 'irony'? Is it not possible that what appears to us to be an unintended consequence of this survey was, in fact, a deliberate act on the part of King William? There is good reason to take these questions seriously.

In 1085 William was in his late 50s and, therefore, for the time, a comparatively old man. Two years earlier his wife and Queen, Matilda, had died. Matilda was no ordinary person. She was directly descended from both Charlemagne and Alfred the Great, and was a strong and capable woman. She had to defy both her father's will and a Papal ban in marrying William in 1051. She ruled Normandy successfully during William's many absences, and ruled England for two years immediately before her death. Her death at the age of 52 in 1083 was a massive blow for William. He had always been faithful to her, and, as an expression of his grief, he gave up hunting, his favourite pastime.

We know from three separate sources, Orderic Vitalis, William of Malmesbury and Eadmer, which, elsewhere, did not hold back in their condemnation of William, that William made 'a good end'. Orderic also has 'William express regret for the terrible bloodshed', saying, near the end of his life, that his 'kingdom' [was] 'won with so many sins [and] evil deeds'.

All of this, in addition to his rigid adherence to church attendance, suggests that, when he commissioned the 'Domesday' survey at Christmas 1085 in Gloucester, he was thinking very seriously about his own death. It is reasonable to suppose that William had been examining himself and did not like what he found. He was preparing to meet his maker, and was profoundly apprehensive about the unavoidable encounter. He wanted, not just to repent, but to repent in a way that would make amends. In short, he wanted to give something back to the Anglo-Saxons, from whom he had taken so much.

The curious feature about this survey is that it included within its scope a retrospective survey of land ownership in 1066. Why? The traditional interpretation for this has to do with simplifying the legal administration of the transfer of property, such that Norman Baron X could quickly and easily establish his legal claim to an estate because he was a 'successor' who had 'inherited' from an 'antecessor' Anglo-Saxon Thane Y. Thus, knowing what land Y owned in 1066 would clarify X's ownership in 1086.

Professor Robin Fleming's detailed analysis of land transfers in 11th century England in her book 'Kings & Lords in Conquest England' does not support this interpretation. She says:

'If one actually performs the dreary but necessary task of going through Domesday Book and identifying antecessors and successors and totting up the value of their lands, one finds that from Domesday Book's four or five thousand secular landholders [in 1066], little more than one hundred significant antecessors can be identified. Thus, inheritance by Normans from well-defined and well-to-do antecessors accounts for a minority of secular land transference – just over 10 per cent in all. This suggests that many post-Conquest fees [land held on condition of feudal service] were the result of studied disregard for the Saxon past.'[1]

A little further on, she states:

'... where the evidence is most complete, we witness the breakdown of Saxon patterns of lordship on a grand scale ...'[2]

Thus, gathering this information about land ownership in 1066 provided no benefit either to King William or his Norman barons. Not only did it have no bearing on tax receipts in 1086, but also it would have increased the workload of the survey spectacularly, since the land owned by less than two hundred Normans in 1086 had been previously owned by four or five thousand thanes in 1066.

---

[1] Fleming, *Kings & Lords in Conquest England,* 112
[2] Ibid., 114

What this additional information in Domesday Book does provide, however, is clarity as to what happened in the twenty years after the Battle of Hastings. The existence of Domesday Book has carried into the far distant future – the book itself is now kept in the National Archives at Kew – hard data of, as Professor Fleming puts it, 'The almost complete transference [from Anglo-Saxon to Norman ownership] of all these lands, men and beasts in less than twenty years'[3].

The question is: did King William realise that this survey would provide future generations with such a clear understanding that his 'kingdom was won with so many sins and evil deeds'? Obviously, the question cannot be answered definitively, but it is at least possible to suppose that he did.

Given all of this, we can imagine that something along the following lines occurred. During 1085, he was a lonely man, and he spent much time in prayer and contemplation. As he began to reach out towards the eternal world that his revered, loved and much missed wife now inhabited, he started to regret his earthly and temporal triumphs. He fell into a depression. His despair drove him to a calculation. He could not right the wrongs of the Conquest, but he could help the English do so. He realised that the most effective way of helping them would be to provide hard, documentary evidence of the greatest and most long-lasting wrong – the loss of their land. That evidence would remain in the consciousness of the English long into the future, and it would be like the irritating piece of grit in an oyster. It would provoke them into action, give them an enduring motive to struggle to win back their country, and sustain them in that endeavour over the centuries to come.

---

[3] Ibid., 108

Appendix B

The Peasants' Revolt of 1381

For those acquainted with the history of England, the title of Chapter 2, '1381', can mean only one thing: 'The Peasants' Revolt'.

It seems that the naming of this upheaval was as political as the events themselves. By referring to it as 'The Peasants' Revolt', its significance is reduced. Peasants did, indeed, revolt, but so did, even more so, freemen, and even gentry. At the outset specific changes to the law were demanded, and the rebels sought out documents that made the imposition of unfair taxes possible, and burnt them. All these things indicate a high degree of literacy and organisational capability. That it came close to success was not something the authorities wanted to be known, and explains the ferocity with which anyone even tangentially involved was dealt with afterwards. It was not just a peasants' revolt.

The immediate trigger for this 'Great Rebellion' was the imposition of a third poll tax within four years to finance hopeless foreign military adventures. These taxes caused genuine hardship, and produced no benefit.

Lying behind these taxes, as sources of unrest, were innumerable other wrongs. There were the labour laws, introduced in 1351, following the Black Death, which controlled what labourers could earn. There were the exorbitant rents charged by many landlords with, often, the church and monasteries the worst offenders. Egregious restrictions existed as to who could work for whom. And there were a host of local monopolies and privileges that curtailed the ordinary freedom to trade. The rebels had their pikes pointing at all these wrongs.

However, it would appear that something more profound was afoot than mere violent objection to rank injustice. 1381 marks the first moment in English history, perhaps world history, when there had been widespread, intelligent and reasoned rejection of the authority of church and state. Although the scholar and theologian, John Wycliffe, did not support the Great Rebellion, it was his teaching that animated it. Here is not the place to try to summarise the life and work of this hitherto Master of Balliol College, Oxford, but there are two points which deserve mention.

Firstly, Wycliffe argued that the only real spiritual authority we have is contained within the Bible. Therefore, it is, ultimately, to the Bible, not priests, that all Christians must go to learn about their faith. For this reason, he was responsible for the translation of the Latin Vulgate into contemporary English. (150 years later, William Tyndale followed up on this exercise and was burnt at the stake for his efforts.)

Secondly, Wycliffe did not believe in transubstantiation – the Catholic doctrine that, when, during the Eucharist service, the priest blesses the bread and the wine, a miracle occurs which changes this food and drink into, literally, the flesh and blood of Jesus.

In both cases, Wycliffe's stance diminishes the importance and authority of the priesthood. He is asserting the idea, in a profound way, that among us human beings, in the eyes of God, there is neither high nor low, neither master nor slave, neither first nor last.

Today this idea is routine. We do not quibble with the second paragraph of the United States Declaration of Independence, which states that: 'We hold these truths to be self-evident, that all men are created equal …'. But we forget too easily that, down the long river of human history that has gone before us, and even in many societies today, it is an alien concept. We may indeed hold it now as 'self-evident', but this is only true because others have made it so.

In 1381 it was a dangerous idea. Dangerous to the social and political order of the time, and, therefore, dangerous to hold. It animated the events of 1381, and it was articulated most famously in the couplet of John Ball, the Lollard preacher, who was hanged, drawn and quartered on Monday, 15th July, 1381, St. Swithun's Day:

> 'When Adam delved, and Eve span
> Who was then the gentleman?'

A month earlier, on 14th June, an agreement had been reached between the rebels and the young King Richard at Mile End, to the east of London. It was copied by thirty clerks for distribution throughout the country, and sealed with the Great Seal of the King. It was an agreement that, had it been implemented, would have given the English more freedom under law than was ever achieved 400 years later by the French Revolution. The reasons it was not implemented is a matter for the historians, but John, the Lollard featured in this story, was certainly right in saying that the mass drunkenness, which followed this extraordinary meeting at Mile End, was a decisive factor.

Appendix C

The Lollards

Lollardy was a Christian movement which sprang up in England during the 14th century. The Lollards were followers of John Wycliffe who, as Master of Balliol College, Oxford, criticised many of the practices of the Roman Catholic church, in the same way that Martin Luther did 130 years later.

For the Lollards the only true religious authority was the Bible. To this end John Wycliffe published the first English translation of the Bible in 1384. At a time when French was still, over 300 years after the Conquest, the language of the court, law, and government, this empowering of the English-speaking people was a challenge both to the church, and to the entire political and social order.

In 1381, the Lollard priest, John Ball, was a key figure in the 'Peasants' Revolt'. It is recorded that at the beginning of this uprising, he spoke to a crowd of 200,000 at Blackheath, saying:

> "… things cannot go right in England and never will, until there are no more villeins and gentlefolk, but we are all one and the same. In what way are those whom we call 'lords' greater masters than ourselves? If we all spring from a single father and mother, Adam and Eve, how can they claim that they are 'lords' more than us … Therefore, the time is come, appointed to us by God, in which ye may cast off the yoke of bondage, and recover liberty."

Within a short time, this enormous revolt was put down. Wycliffe was expelled from his Oxford college, and Ball was among the 1,500 rebels to be executed. After Wycliffe's death, the Pope ordered that his body be exhumed and his bones scattered.

Lollardy died out, but the movement's legacy, which consisted of a widespread sympathy for its teachings and a great appetite for equality, lived on. It is what made England's break from Papal authority possible 150 years later. It is what drove the country to Civil War in opposition to absolute monarchy in the 17th century. And, having crossed the Atlantic, it is what drove the Founding Fathers, in the opening words to their Declaration of Independence, to make the distinctly Lollard assertion that 'all men are created equal'.

Appendix D

The Book of Common Prayer

At the heart of Chapter 4: 1549 is the idea that something miraculous happened during the late 16th century in England. The English found a voice. It did not come out of a void, but it did come in a rush. Within two generations England had produced a large clutch of some of the greatest writers ever to have written in English, or, indeed, in any language. By comparison, there was little before. Whence came this flood? One explanation, I suggest, is the introduction in June 1549 of Cranmer's 'Book of Common Prayer'.

Imagine growing up in a small Midlands town, where you attend the local grammar school on weekdays, and the local parish church on Sundays. Every day you read, hear and speak prayers and collects composed with a perfect command of the cadences of the English language, expressing your deepest thoughts and strongest feelings with unrivalled power and beauty. How could such soil not be productive?

This was the cultural soil in which Shakespeare, Marlowe, Donne and the many other extraordinary writers of the time grew up. I cannot compete with George Eliot in my appreciation of the richness of this phenomenon, and so I will not try. Instead, I offer up the following passage from Chapter 18 of her novel 'Adam Bede':

> 'But Adam's thoughts of Hetty did not deafen him to the service; they rather blended with all the other deep feelings for which the church service was a channel to him this afternoon, as a certain consciousness of our entire past and our imagined future blends itself with all our moments of keen sensibility. And to Adam the church service was the best channel he could have found for his mingled regret, yearning, and resignation; its interchange of beseeching cries for help,

with outbursts of faith and praise – its recurrent responses and the familiar rhythm of its collects, seemed to speak for him as no other form of worship could have done; as, to those early Christians who had worshipped from their childhood upward in catacombs, the torchlight and shadows must have seemed nearer the divine presence than the heathenish daylight of the streets. The secret of our emotions never lies in the bare object, but in its subtle relations to our own past: no wonder the secret escapes the unsympathising observer, who might as well put on his spectacles to discern odours.'

Appendix E

Robert Hooke

The story told in Chapter 5 of 'The Lollard Oak' is only a pebble thrown into the lake of ignorance regarding Hooke, but it is, I hope, better than nothing. My interest in this man stems, to a large extent, from Sunday morning conversations in Christ Church Cathedral with Dr. Allan Chapman of Wadham College, Oxford. John Gribbin, a Cambridge astrophysicist, is another historian of science, who has sought to rectify this lack of renown:

'The three people who between them established both the scientific method itself and the pre-eminence of British science at the end of seventeenth century were Robert Hooke, Edmond Halley and Isaac Newton. It is some measure of the towering achievements of the other two that Halley clearly ranks third out of the trio in terms of his direct contribution to science; but in spite of the Newton bandwagon that has now been rolling for 300 years (and was given its initial push by Newton himself after Hooke had died), it is impossible for the unbiased historian to say whether Newton or Hooke made the more significant contribution. Newton was a loner who worked in isolation and established the single, profound truth that the Universe works on mathematical principles; Hooke was a gregarious and wide-ranging scientist who came up with a dazzling variety of new ideas, but also did more than anyone to turn the Royal Society from a gentleman's gossip shop into the archetypal scientific society. His misfortune was to incur the enmity of Newton, and to die before Newton, giving his old enemy a chance to rewrite history – which he did so effectively that Hooke has only really been rehabilitated in the past few decades.' Source: 'Science A History 1543 to 2001' (Allen Lane, 2002, chapter 5, p.149)

To the best of my knowledge the first person to recognise, articulate and publicise this lacuna in the history of science was Edward Andrade, F.R.S., Quain Professor of Physics at University College, London. This is how he opened the 1949 Royal Society Wilkins Lecture:

'Science in England in the latter part of the seventeenth century is overshadowed by the mighty name of Newton, who has justly received the praises of all the great natural philosophers who came after him. In that springtime of science there were, however, in England a number of other men of genius ... Of these Robert Hooke has good claims to be considered the greatest. Probably the most inventive man who ever lived, and one of the ablest experimenters, he had a most acute mind and made astonishingly correct conjectures, based on reason, in all branches of physics. Physics, however, was far from being his only field: he is the founder of scientific meteorology; as an astronomer he has observations of great significance to his credit; he did fundamental work on combustion and respiration; he was one of the founders of modern geology. He has, moreover, a particular claim to the attention and respect of our Society, for from 1662 to 1677 he held the office of Curator and from 1677 to 1682 he was one of our Secretaries. He was always indefatigable in his services to the Society, and for a period he produced new experiments or discoveries at practically every meeting ... yet ... his name does not seem to be honoured as it should be among men of science in general.'

Two of Hooke's contributions to science are easily overlooked. Firstly, there is what he did for the world's oldest and most prestigious scientific society; Professor Andrade makes this comment:

> '... without his experimental demonstrations, which over long periods took place weekly, the Royal Society would have died, as did the Accademia del Cimento, or declined into scientific insignificance, as did the Academie des Sciences on the death of Colbert in 1683. To turn the pages of Birch's History of the Royal Society, which is a ... detailed record, of the meetings, week by week, from 1660 to 1687, is to convince oneself that Hooke's experiments and theoretical ideas, and the discussions which they provoked, were the main agent that held the Society together.'

Secondly, Hooke did more than possibly any other individual to make empirical experimentation and scepticism – the idea that one might be mistaken – the building blocks of scientific investigation. This is how, awkwardly, he described the process we now call the scientific method:

> 'For I neither conclude from one single Experiment, nor are the Experiments I make use of, all made upon one Subject: Nor wrest I any Experiment to make it quadrare [square] with any pre-conceiv'd Notion. But on the contrary, I endeavour to be conversant in all kind of Experiments, and all and every one of those Trials, I make the standards (as I may say) or Touchstones by which I try my former Notions.'

This mode of thinking – that we should approach science with an open and sceptical mind – has travelled well beyond the realms of science to have a most profound impact on our civilisation. It takes the biblical insight that humankind is frail and prone to error, and gives us, not only scientific discovery, but also a civilisation based on freedom of expression and political plurality.

Appendix E: Robert Hooke

No portrait of Hooke survives. There is an unsubstantiated theory that, after Hooke's death, Newton had the Royal Society's painting destroyed. We therefore have to rely on contemporaneous descriptions, which are probably accurate, but not flattering. Richard Waller, Secretary of the Royal Society from 1687 to 1709, tells us that 'as to his person he was but despicable' and that '… he went stooping and very fast having but a light body to carry and a great deal of spirits and activity, especially in his youth. He was also meanly ugly, very pale and lean. His eyes grey and full, with a sharp ingenious look whilst younger; his nose but thin, of moderate height and length; his mouth meanly wide and upper lip thin; his chin sharp and forehead large … He wore his own hair of a dark brown colour, very long and hanging neglected over his face, uncut and lank.'

Acknowledgements

For my generation and beyond, it was difficult to be at Abberley Hall School in Worcestershire, without developing a love for history. This was because of Mr Birt. When I met Mr Birt, now David, again a few years ago, I put it to him that the 950 years since the Battle of Hastings should be viewed as a single historical period, and that, in some important ways, we are still living in the shadow of the Norman Conquest. There followed a correspondence in which he encouraged me to write about this, and gave me suggestions for doing so. 'The Lollard Oak' is the outcome. The flow of ideas did not abate as I made progress, and I cannot thank him adequately for his help and interest.

When I asked Lois Letts if she could look at my first chapter, I was warned by her husband that she is merciless. It was not always comfortable to hear her detailed feedback, but it was always fun, and never without exceptional value. I am immensely grateful to her.

If there is an insufficiency of commas in this text, it is not the fault of Jamie Stewart, who has done his best – which is very good – to correct my wayward grammar and punctuation. My daughter, Ruth, in a most elegant reversal of roles, has taken me in hand, and forced me to believe in what I have been doing. Matthew Faulk subjected me to an icy shower in a brave, and, I hope, not completely unsuccessful attempt to turn me into a more professional writer. Nick Thomas has similarly noticed infelicities that had passed me by.

Angus Donald and I revel in not agreeing with each other, but, when he suggested that the title of my book should be 'The Lollard Oak', I knew that, on this particular occasion, he was right. He has since made any number of intelligent and greatly appreciated comments and suggestions. Klaus de Rijk is another whose opinions I have to rectify on my visits to The Netherlands, but, without those combative, and well-lubricated, lunches in The Hague, I would never have benefitted from reading Larry Siedentop's 'Inventing the

Individual', which shows, with brilliance and learning, what very long periods of time are required for human history to work itself out.

I have been reluctant to allow anyone to read this effort of mine before its publication, but my target audience is the clever and lively mind, and so, when, on separate occasions, Ann Vowles and Liz Wilde pressed me to let them see it, I relented. I am very glad I did.

A dinner party found me lucky enough to be sitting next to Lou Mair. With an incautious friendliness, typical of the antipodes, she offered to help me with the design and publication process; I knew then – and know now, but even more so – that I would have been lost without her expertise.

Finally, writing is an anti-social occupation, and I could not have done anything without the patience and forbearance of the least anti-social person I know, namely, my dear wife, Claudia. She has wisely stayed out of it, except when it came to the cover and the blurb, when her intervention was crucial.

To all of you, I give my heartfelt thanks.

Anthony Thompson
Hereford 2023

About the Author

Anthony Thompson was educated at Winchester College, London University, and London Business School. In addition to writing, he has occupied his life as a comprehensive school teacher, a grocer, a salesman, a management consultant, and a software entrepreneur. He lives in Hereford, is a Church of England Reader, and is currently working on a novel about Jo Elgar and his brother, Edward.

Printed in Great Britain
by Amazon